THE
Rules
OF
Seeing

Joe Heap was born in 1986 and grew up in Bradford, the son
of two teachers. In 2004, he won the Foyle Young Poets award,
and he is a published poet. He studied for a BA in English
Literature at Stirling University and a Masters in Creative
Writing at Glasgow University.

Joe lives in London with his long-suffering girlfriend, short-
suffering baby, and much-aggrieved cat. *The Rules of Seeing* is
his first novel.

🐦 @Joe_Heap_
📘 /joeheap.author
📷 Joe_Heap_

THE

Rules

OF

Seeing

JOE HEAP

HarperCollins*Publishers*

HarperCollins*Publishers* Ltd
1 London Bridge Street
London SE1 9GF

www.harpercollins.co.uk

First published by HarperCollins*Publishers* 2018
This edition published 2019
1

A catalogue record for this book
is available from the British Library

ISBN: 9780008293192

Printed and bound in Great Britain by
CPI Group (UK) Ltd, Croydon CR0 4YY

MIX
Paper from
responsible sources
FSC™ C007454

To Alice,
And to Sam,
Who was being written
While this was being written.

Suppose a man born blind, and now adult, and taught by his touch to distinguish between a cube and a sphere [be] made to see.

[Could he] by his sight, before he touched them . . . now distinguish and tell which was the globe, which the cube?

William Molyneux in a letter to John Locke.

1

Shapes

One

January

KATE IS HOLDING A white square with both hands. A piece of paper. She will remember this later, in the hospital. She will try to remember if she could see anything through the folded paper – handwriting, perhaps, or printed words, or a restaurant bill. But these details will not come back. The square will remain a perfect blank, a square cut from the fabric of her memory.

Details that will return:

1) His breath.

2) His aftershave, petrol-smelling.

3) His body, which despite her six-foot-one frame seems to tower over her.

There is a long moment where neither of them moves, and the only sound she is aware of is her own heartbeat, whooshing in her ears.

'Give it to me.'

'Why? Why are you so angry?'

'Give it to me.' This is all he will say, over and over, as though he's broken.

'Tony, you're scaring me.' She says it with a laugh, because it is silly that she should be scared by him.

'Give it to me.' He advances another step. Kate forces herself not to step back, to stand her ground.

They have fought before, are even proud of their fighting. Marriages are supposed to be passionate. Her husband has a temper, but better that than someone who doesn't give a damn, right? Their fights are loud. Sometimes she cries. Sometimes they throw things. But this is different – it is the silence, the way he won't say anything, the way the air in the room seems to be running out.

'Give it to me.'

'No. What is it?' That is all she wanted to know, from the moment she saw the white square. One moment they were chatting in the kitchen. Kate had already been out of bed for an hour, chopping carrots and celery for a stew and listening to the morning radio. Most of the news was about New Year's celebrations the night before. They had stayed up long enough to see the fireworks.

Tony had come in, showered and dressed for work, and they had talked. Everything normal, normal, normal, until the moment he reached into his wallet to take out a note to pay for the groceries.

Tony's wallet is black leather, with PROPERTY OF THE METROPOLITAN POLICE in faded silver letters. There is a badge with 'police' written in Braille. The square of white paper had fallen out of the wallet's inner compartment, onto the kitchen tiles.

In the hospital, she will remember the white square like a hole in the floor. Like a hole that might open up, a hole she might fall through, into endless white sky. But she does not feel this yet.

She bent down to pick it up. She was going to hand it to him, but then she noticed the tension in his body, and before she could say anything—

'Give it to me.'

'Why? What have you got to hide?' She smiled, holding the folded piece of paper to her chest playfully. But he wasn't smiling.

'Give it to me.'

'What is it?' Still playful – still expecting this to be a game, wondering if this is a surprise for her. A printout for airline tickets maybe, or the receipt for a present. Maybe he has bought something to go in the new flat that she has been renovating for them both. Mundane objects, mundane desires. Remembering them later, she will feel disgusted with herself.

The air in the room is choked with his aftershave; she can't breathe. She used to like the aftershave, but now it's as though she's locked in a garage with the car running

and running

and running.

Both her thumbs are on the piece of paper, her arms tucked close to her body. She will not let him have it. Kate needs to know what's written on the paper. She will stand her ground.

When he lunges forward, trying to grab the paper out of her hands, she steps back as a reflex. She has forgotten the crate of wine bottles that she placed on the floor by the sink. Kate stumbles back, already falling, the white square clutched over her heart.

She lands, the back of her head slamming into the floor. There is a moment of bright pain, like a lightbulb blowing, then darkness.

✷

'This place is great – they have a sandwich named after me!'

It is late morning, and the Soho lunch crowd is starting to form. Nova is swinging her brother's hand back and forth like a pendulum. The air smells richly of coffee and toasting bread.

'You're joking, right?' Alex looks at her.

'Nope. Check the board.'

He looks up. On the order board, below *Chicken Club* and above *Hawaiian Special*, is *The Safinova Surprise*.

Alex laughs, shaking his head. 'What did you do to deserve a sandwich named after you?'

She breaks her hand away, mock-offended.

'Excuse you, but what haven't I done? I think I'm very deserving of sandwich fame.'

Alex raises an eyebrow, though she can't see this. 'Seriously, what did you do?'

'Check out the ingredients.'

Alex gazes up at the board.

'"*The Safinova Surprise* – pepperoni, pickles and peach slices."' His brow furrows. 'Did you . . . invent that sandwich?'

'I had a hunch that foods starting with the same letter naturally belonged together – that you sighted people used words of the same letter because they were similar. So, I came in here and ordered one. Hallelujah – a sandwich was born.'

'But, peach slices?'

'Don't knock it till you've tried it.'

'I don't think that's going to happen.'

'It's not for the faint of heart. Maybe one day you'll be ready.'

'Do many people buy your sandwich?'

'Just her.' They've gotten close enough to the counter for their conversation to be overheard and Mike Zephirelli – broad and black-bearded like a cartoon pirate – calls over to them.

'Mike! Looking good!' She waves her folded white stick at him and he explodes with laughter. This joke, in all its variations – *Looking good. Good to see you. Have you been working out?* – never grows old. Alex rolls his eyes, another thing his sister can't see.

'How you doing, Nova? You want the usual?'

'Yes, please.' She turns to Alex, grinning. 'Extra peach slices, please.'

'And for you, sir?'

'Oh, um . . . an egg and cress roll.'

Zephirelli chuckles. 'She's never convinced any of her girl-friends to get the sandwich, either.' With that, he swings away to start making their food.

'You bring dates here?'

'Sure. Wouldn't you want to sleep with someone who had a sandwich named after them? Come on – find a table; my feet are killing me.'

Alex finds a table and Mike brings the coffee.

'So, what did you want to talk about?' Nova asks. 'Not that

I mind – it's good to eat somewhere other than the Scotland Yard canteen.'

'Tell me about it – hospital food is as bad as its reputation.'

Nova smiles but says nothing – she is waiting.

'So, I wanted to tell you about something. Something I read in a journal . . . an operation.'

She frowns, still smiling. 'What kind of operation, doctor? Are you trying to get me lobotomized?'

He ignores the joke. 'An operation that could cure you. I mean . . . restore your sight.'

He knows that 'restore' is the wrong word – you can't restore something that was never there. This is the moment that their sandwiches arrive, and Nova stays silent. When she speaks again, her voice is quiet.

'What are you talking about?'

'Eighty percent, maybe more.'

'Chance of seeing something?'

'Chance of seeing *everything*.'

Her brother's voice, so familiar to Nova, is made exotic by excitement.

'That's . . . a bold claim.'

'Yes' – she can hear him smiling – 'but true.'

She sits back, kicking her Doc Martens under her chair. The quick echoes of their words tell her that they are in a corner booth. He is trying to judge her reaction. When she speaks, she feels like an actor, her responses pre-prepared.

'Most people think of blindness as darkness.'

'I know. But you can see black and white, and red in good light . . . '

'No, that's not what I mean.' Her hands form shapes in

front of her, which Alex guesses are supposed to convey hesitation, or thought. 'People think of blindness as binary, as an on-or-off switch. Either you can see or you're blind, right?'

'I . . . guess so.'

'But it's a spectrum. Even if you can see, you can only see a tiny portion of all the light that's really there. Did you know that? I've always found that comforting, in a stupid way. It's cool.'

Alex says nothing. He's looking at his sister, in her biker jacket and *I Want to Believe* T-shirt, wondering how she can still infuriate him this much, after all these years. Her ridiculous sandwich is sitting in front of her, with a toothpick Union Jack flag claiming it for Britain, oozing sweetness onto the plate.

'Just think about it for a second. You feel the heat of the sun, like I do, but you can't see the infrared light glowing off my skin. And you can't see radio waves, even though you know that when you turn the radio on, you'll hear the breakfast news. And it's all made of the same stuff – you just call the bit you can see "light". But it's *all* light. Fizzing around our heads. Even at night when you can't see your hand in front of your face, there's light shining all around.'

She's grinning like she can see it – all the extra light. Alex looks around the café, at the chrome counter and the vinyl seating, as though searching for backup. He grunts, smoothing his eyebrows with thumb and forefinger.

'Stop being . . .'

'What?'

'A smartarse.'

Nova smirks. 'I have a point though, right?'

'This is medicine, not science-fiction, Jillian.'

She huffs. 'Nobody calls me *Jillian* but you.'

'Would you rather I called you *The Safinova Surprise* – pepperoni, pickles and peach slices?'

'Now who's the smartarse?'

'Look, I'm not saying this would even work, but it's a straightforward choice. Either you can stay blind, or maybe you can be cured. This isn't a mind game, or a riddle; it's about being able to read a map or look at your outfit in a mirror. What's so complicated?'

She shakes her head, dark hair tumbling over her face.

'What could be more complicated? How do you learn to see? Because all that extra light, those X-rays and cosmic rays and radio waves – they're all *really there*, Alex. This big field of pure light is rippling all around you, right now, and you can't see it.'

Alex says nothing. He's watching her face, her body, reading silently in a language she doesn't know. Nova goes on.

'So, say I'm an alien, and . . . and I've got big ol' bug eyes! I can see all those extra colours, so your puny human vision seems pathetic to me. I could "cure" you with my ray gun because, to me, you seem to need curing – and you would see *all* the light. Night would be like day, shining with colours you've never seen before . . . ' She pauses for effect. 'What would you see? Would you understand it all? Would it scare you, Alex?'

He sighs, grasping her meaning reluctantly.

'You were always good with words.' He is quiet for a minute. 'I can't tell you what it would be like for you to see, any more than I can tell you what music would sound like to a man who'd been deaf from birth. I can find you case studies, first-person accounts. But I'm a doctor, not a poet. You need to ask a philosopher. Or an imam.'

Nova pouts. 'You know I don't do that.'

Neither of their parents is religious. The source of Alex's faith has always puzzled Nova. He'd tried Buddhism, then Christianity, and had settled on Islam as though he'd been shopping around for the best deal. It interested her for a while, mostly for the words.

'I know, but the question you're asking isn't medical. What was the line from the Qur'an you used to recite to me?'

She knows the one he means. 'No vision comprehends Him, but He comprehends all vision.'

He smiles at the memory, but she doesn't see this. 'Yes. Maybe your "extra light" is like that. Like God.'

It's her turn to sigh. 'You know what I think, doctor.'

'Yes, I do.' His tone hardens to something smooth and professional. She tries to win him back.

'In your case studies, how do people react? Are they happy?'

He doesn't say anything for a minute, and when he does, Nova knows he isn't telling the whole truth.

'They find it difficult, but they recover. Anyway, it's your decision to make. If you want, I can refer you to someone who knows more about the procedure.'

'Okay, but one thing.'

'Yes?'

She leans closer to the table, grabs her sandwich, and takes a huge bite. Through stuffed cheeks, she says, 'If you tell our sweet, Pakistani mother about this "cure", I will destroy you.'

✳

Kate wakes on the sofa. There is a blanket over her. The lights in the flat are off, and the sky she can see through the front window is dull. How long has she slept? She doesn't remember. The sun is setting so it must be about four. There is no sign or sound of Tony.

She remembers the fall, and the argument that preceded it. Lastly, she remembers the piece of paper, a white square.

Experimentally, she turns her head, but the sinews in her neck are like high-tension wires. Her head aches, predictably, but there is a spot at the back of her skull where she can feel nothing at all. She reaches back and touches it, just to make sure her head is still there. She looks at her fingers, but there is no blood.

Slowly, feeling the strain of supporting her head, she sits up. She's queasy, but she doesn't feel like she's going to pass out again. Kate is certain now – Tony put her on the sofa and left the flat. Why did he do that? She was unconscious. He should have taken her to the hospital. A wave of sluggish anger rises, then subsides. She's too sick to be angry.

Kate goes to the kitchen, swallows painkillers with a glass of milk to line her stomach, and puts the radio on, half listening from the table.

After a while, as though on a whim, she gets up and walks through to the study. She doesn't know why. She reaches into the space behind the bureau and pulls out a black art folder. It is scuffed and dusty, and a peeling sticker on one corner reads, 'Katerina Tomassi, 7F 8F 9F'. She unzips the folder and opens it with a sound like dead leaves.

She hasn't looked at the folder since they moved to the flat, hasn't looked inside it in even longer. Now Kate can see the colours of her old paintings – watercolours, acrylics and pencils. She can see a tree, and a still life of fruit and acorns. She does not touch any of the paintings, as though they might stain her, or as though she might stain them. When was the last time she painted? It must have been . . .

Kate zips up the folder again, replaces it behind the bureau, and returns to the living room. On the sofa by the window, she listens to the traffic outside, while the contents of her head shift and rearrange.

Two

February

'UNATTENDED LUGGAGE MAY BE destroyed . . .'

Nova stands on the platform, waiting for the train doors to open. The February wind bleeds heat through the denim of her jeans. She dislikes Paddington. She dislikes all the big London termini. The Tube she can manage, and the smaller stations. But King's Cross and St Pancras, Euston and Paddington – they're all too big, too loud and echoing, with too many people in a rush to be somewhere else. With Paddington, at least, she remembers the way to the ticket office from previous journeys, where she can ask for help in getting to the platform. Now she just hopes there won't be an alteration.

Sometimes, Nova wishes she still had a guide dog. It would help with big journeys like this, with so many connections. But, day to day, she can find her way with her white stick and doesn't have to clean up after a golden retriever. She knows dozens of journeys around London, from her flat in Brixton and back. She had a guide dog as a teenager, but Bruno always felt like more hassle than he was worth.

The train doors unlock with a beep-beep-beep, and Nova starts forward cautiously. Suddenly, there is a hand on her arm.

'Do you want a hand?' A female voice; elderly. It's almost always a woman. Men are afraid to touch her for fear of causing offence. Then there are the men who use it as an excuse to grope her, but that's another story.

'Yes, please. What carriage is this?'

'Oh, uh, it's coach B.'

'Ah, lucky me!'

The woman guides her forward, but gives no information about what's coming up until—

'Big step now!'

Nova steps forward uncertainly, until her boot connects with the footplate. She climbs into the carriage and waits for the old lady to catch up. Lately, Nova has become very aware of her reliance on acts of kindness like this. Mostly, she can get by, but the average day contains several offers of help, a few of which she accepts. This is how it has always been. She accepts that this kindness is part of human nature. If she could see, would everyone leave her alone? The thought saddens her.

'What seat are you, love?'

'Thirty-two. I think it's a window seat. Not that I need it!' Nova quips. The old lady clears her throat uncomfortably, clasps her elbow and guides her through the carriage until she is at her seat. Somebody is sitting there already, but is persuaded to move by the old lady.

Nova slides carefully into the space by the redundant window seat, clasping her rucksack in her lap. If she puts it in the luggage rack she might never find it again, and wouldn't know if someone tried to steal it.

It's a month since her first conversation with Alex. She has seen experts in human eyesight, neuroscience, and psychology. She's spoken to her parents. When she wakes in the morning, exotic words and phrases like *rhodopsin, pupillary light reflex* and *occipital lobe* repeat in her head like a tune she can't stop humming.

The train pulls out of the station, and Nova listens carefully to the announcements before putting her headphones on. She listens to the playlists on her phone until she finds the one she's looking for – '80s disco tunes that she hasn't listened to since university.

That's where she's going – back to Oxford. She hasn't been since graduation. She's stayed in touch with people, but it seems like another world now. After ten years of ferrying herself between work and home, Oxford is a distant galaxy.

✳

Nova gets a taxi from the station. She can still remember how to get the bus, but she doesn't need the hassle today. The taxi deposits her a minute's walk from her old college, and Nova stops someone to help orient herself. The first person is a tourist, so she tries again and finds a student.

'Am I near the Modern Languages building?'

'Yeah, you're just around the corner, on Bristol Street. Want me to take you?'

'No, thanks; I've got my bearings now.'

She edges down the street, swinging her stick ahead of her in narrow arcs, tapping at the wall until she finds the turning into a wide courtyard.

When people talk about Oxford, they talk about the soft, golden stone of the buildings or the jewel-green of the lawns. They talk about dreaming spires piercing the sky. But Nova's memories are all of the sound of Oxford. The gentle hum of a city where so many people cycle. The murmur of the quads. The threnody of bells from colleges and chapels.

Oxford, to Nova, is like a well-worn quilt, soft and blanketing. Its sonic signature is all the more striking for leaving London behind. The contrast is as clear as the first time she stepped from an air-conditioned plane onto the airport concourse in Pakistan as a child. The climate here is different.

Nova stands and listens for a moment, then moves toward the steps of the Modern Languages building. Her stick taps in front of her, to the left as she is stepping forward with her right foot, to the right when she is stepping with her left. The motion is as automatic as walking itself, though sighted friends have told Nova how difficult it is. They veer off course when they try it. They say it is nerve-wracking, which makes Nova wonder if she got over the fear, or just got used to it. She can feel everything the stick is telling her – the gentle undulations of the path, the border between the path and the lawn, the varying textures of the stones.

Getting lost is always a possibility. *Just a chance to meet new people!* she'll deadpan, though it's truly frustrating. She wants to ask sighted people what it's like to know where everything is, when you're standing still. What it's like to know that the path is curving to the right, and there are trees over there, and a lake on the horizon. Do they see these things constantly, like an instrument playing an unbroken note, or do they come in bursts? Is it difficult, seeing all that stuff?

She knows that sighted people can be distracted by things they see, like a man crashing his car because of a flashy bill-board. Is it difficult, seeing and carrying on a conversation, or walking? She guesses it must be like walking with the stick – you get used to doing both.

Nova comes to the steps of the Modern Languages building, and her feet remember the height of each stone, so that the climb is quick and easy. She feels for the door and grabs the handle just as someone starts to open it. She starts to topple forward, then catches herself.

'Oh, sorry! Saw you coming and thought I'd be helpful.' The girl's voice is panicked.

'Not to worry!'

This is something else Nova does not understand – how someone can see through a window or a glass door. No matter how often people use words like *transparent* and *opaque*, the idea feels impossible, like trying to sing two notes at the same time. Seeing through solid objects is as strange as passing your hand through them. Like walking through walls.

Another familiar thing now – the smell of the corridors. Nova supposes it is something to do with the plastic floors, or the kind of cleaning product they use. But the smell, so long forgotten, is instantly recalled. It's a clean smell, though not a homely one. It reminds her of long hours spent in the library and computer labs.

She knows her way very well now. She could move without her stick, except there might be objects in the hall for her to trip over. But she walks quickly, turning corners and counting down doors until she finds it, Room 204. She runs her hands over the door until she comes to a small sign, written in Braille:

Sanitation Supplies and Hamburger Storage Area.

Nova smiles; the dumb joke must be superglued to the door. She knocks gently and listens for the shuffle of feet within, the hand searching for the handle. The door opens.

'Yes?'

The voice is familiar, though perhaps a little thinner, in person – a voice no longer entirely in its prime.

'It's me, John.'

'Jillian Safinova! Stay there so I can get a good look at you.'

She stands still while the professor puts his arms on her shoulders. This is their joke – John is as blind as she is. More blind, even (Blinder? Is that a word?) – he has no light, no pastel colours, as she does.

'A little shorter than last time I saw you.'

'It's true – I've been shrinking. Saves on renting a big flat in London.'

'Come on, come in, make yourself comfortable.'

He retreats from the door and she steps into 204. The smell in here is quite different, but every bit as familiar. Nova can break it down into three main components:

1) bergamot from countless mugs of Earl Grey tea;

2) the books that line all of one wall;

3) the leather armchair that sits in one corner.

John closes the door after her, and Nova finds the chair in which she has always sat. Everything is always in the same place in 204, just like things are always in the same place in her own home. There is never a fear of bumping into an unexpected obstacle. She hears John cross the room and settle himself into his own chair.

'Can I get you anything? A drink? I've still got the cookie jar.'

'No, thank you. It's good to be here – it hasn't changed.'

'Really? I suppose you're right. How are you?'

'I'm okay,' Nova starts, then stops. She is not entirely okay, and they both know she wouldn't be here if she were. They've always stayed in touch, through emails and calls, but actual visits are challenging. They haven't sat in the same room for years. John chuckles, softly.

'Do you want to tell me about it?'

Nova takes a deep breath, as though she's about to cross a crowded room, and starts to talk. She explains the procedure, the chance of success (good), and the chance of full rehabilitation afterwards (not so good). She describes the details – how it would be done and how long it would take, but does not mention her fears. She doesn't pose riddles or thought experiments. She just wants to hear his reaction.

When she is done, Nova pauses, not prompting him.

'Well . . . fuck me.' John says, simply.

'Yeah.' Nova grins, waiting for more.

'So, I'm making an educated guess here,' he says, slowly. 'You're worried about what it would mean to see. You're worried about not understanding it. And you want to ask me what I would do.'

Nova laughs at how quickly he has understood. 'Yep, that's about right.'

'I see.' John pauses for a long moment, thinking. 'Of course, we're not entirely the same, you and I.'

'No, I know.'

Nova has been blind from birth – other than the soft, gauzy light, she has never seen anything. John is sixty now, but was sighted until his early thirties, when an infection burned his vision away, leaving no consoling haze.

He pop-pop-pops his lips, a habit of his when thinking.

'I wouldn't do it,' he says, suddenly.

Nova feels like the air has been knocked out of her. 'What? Just like that?' She says.

'You wanted more?' She can hear his smile.

'Well, maybe a bit. Some context, maybe?'

'Mmm . . . mm-hm,' he murmurs. Nova has spent so much time in this office, listening to John Katzner thinking. He was her tutor, very briefly. He specializes in literary translation, but her degree was interpretation. The difference is important, to those who care. John is careful with language, in a way that Nova isn't. She uses language freely, like someone running downhill, carried by her momentum. John uses language like someone picking their way over a minefield. He clears his throat and begins to translate his thoughts.

'After I went blind, I still saw things all the time. Did I ever tell you that?'

'No.'

'At first I saw them only when I was dreaming. In my dreams, I would see as well as I used to, when my eyes were working. My house, my office, the campsite we went to when I was six . . . Then, I started to see things during the day as well.'

'What sort of things?'

'Oh, all sorts of things. Trees, traffic, pages of blurred text, hovering in front of me. Nothing so awful, though it was a sad reminder of what I used to have. A distraction, too – as if it wasn't difficult enough to get used to being blind!'

He laughs, then sighs.

'Anyway, these hallucinations carried on for a long time. I got used to them. I even appreciated them – they were a memento of a place I used to live. Sometimes in the morning or evening, I would see a white semicircle hovering in front of me, shimmering. I think it was my memory of a sunrise, or sunset . . .'

He falls silent. After half a minute has passed, Nova prompts him.

'So?'

'So, after a little longer, these visions started to get fainter. I was starting to forget what it was like to see. I stopped seeing in my dreams all the time. I was sad that my keepsakes might not always be with me, but I wasn't too sad. I was getting used to being blind, by this time.'

He clears his throat, and Nova feels bad for bringing this up. John has always helped with her problems, but he's never talked about himself like this.

'One day I woke up and . . . how can I put it? It was as though my last memories were going up in flames.'

His voice is shaking, very slightly.

'I saw things that made no sense – endless grey bodies, walking up endless grey staircases, flashes of colour as I fell down infinite drops, grotesque faces that screamed then melted back into the grey. I was crossing over a threshold, you see – though my eyes hadn't worked for many months, I remembered what it was like to be able to see. Now, that was crumbling away, and I was stepping into another world. A nightmare world. I didn't know if I would ever escape it. For two weeks, I couldn't leave the house. For two weeks, the visions never stopped. Then, after two weeks, they grew fainter and fainter, and stopped altogether. And I felt peaceful . . . '

He sighs a long, shaky breath.

'So, that's why I wouldn't do it, Nova. Not because it wouldn't be good to see again. But because I don't think I could make myself walk through that door again. I don't think I could voluntarily step over that threshold. Becoming blind was a kind of rebirth, for me.'

After this, they talk about other things. What they have been doing with their lives. How students are getting more inventive at plagiarism (John). How criminals are getting more inventive at lying (Nova). How restaurants *still* don't have Braille menus. Finally, Nova asks her phone the time, and discovers it is time to be going.

'You must come back soon.' Perhaps Nova is imagining it, but he sounds more wistful than usual.

'I will, when I have a chance. You should visit London sometime. I can show you the sights!'

He chuckles at the bad joke. 'Are you happy down there, Nova?'

'I suppose. Not unhappy.'

'Well, if you ever get sick of talking to murderers and rapists, give me a call. They owe me a favour around here, and if you ever wanted a job . . . '

He trails off. Nova is too surprised to say anything meaningful, and just says, 'Thank you.'

'Well, just bear it in mind, eh? Talk soon.'

She's about to leave, when she thinks of one last question.

'John – do you remember anything? From when you could see?'

Again, the pop-pop-popping as he thinks.

'Perhaps . . . ' He sounds uncertain. 'Sometimes I think I can remember what that sunset looked like . . . a semi-circle . . . a curve and a line . . . but the colours are all gone.'

Nova pats him on the shoulder. 'Talk soon, John.'

She finds her way out of Room 204, out of the faculty building, out onto the lawns. The sun is starting to set. It's raining, lightly, and she doesn't have an umbrella, but Nova doesn't notice much. She has more questions than when she arrived. She trudges off to find another taxi rank.

✳

It's the weekend, and Kate is alone. She has done nothing with the day – just sat and watched TV, hardly focussing on the moving pictures. Her head hurts, and she's groggy, as though she never really woke up.

She stands up carefully and walks to the window. At the new flat there is a Juliet balcony where she will be able to sit and watch the sun rise and set. Here, the view is over standing waves of slate roofs, prickling with aerials and chimney pots. This sunset seems especially colourful – a pollution sheen of bronze and pink, bands of silver and bruise-purple. Everything fading into the navy blue of the city night. It's never truly dark here.

When Tony finally came home from work yesterday, he'd

acted as though nothing had happened, coming up behind her in the kitchen and kissing her neck.

'How're you doing?'

She hadn't turned to face him. 'Well, my head hurts . . . '

'Yeah, that was some tumble you took!'

Kate looked at him for the first time, and he was smiling, kindly, a totally different person from her memory of the man who had loomed over her in the kitchen. He was carrying a bag of shopping, and she could see the brand of raisin cookies she likes. Doubt crept in.

'What was that argument about? The piece of paper?'

'Argument? I didn't think we were arguing.' He put the shopping down and took her by the shoulders, looking into her eyes as though concerned for her sanity. 'I was just joking around, not letting you open that piece of paper. Then you stepped back and . . . ' He trailed off into silence, shrugging.

His face was open and smiling – Kate couldn't believe the version of events in her own head anymore. Had she misinterpreted the whole thing? She didn't flinch when he pulled her into a hug.

Now Kate stands and watches the semi-circle of sun as it dips below the houses, watching the colours lose their lustre. She feels that this moment is important, but doesn't know why. The feeling has haunted her all day – the sense that she has stepped out of her own life and into a story. She put on music earlier, and felt as though it were the soundtrack to the movie of her life. She keeps thinking of the folder full of her paintings, but does not get it out again. Perhaps she is going crazy.

It seems strange that one day she will know the answer to

this question – whether her interpretation is right or wrong – but won't be able to come back and tell the version of her who is now standing at the window. She won't be able to rewind.

When the sun has truly set, she allows herself to sit down on the sofa. The flat is dark and quiet, and Kate is waiting.

Three

THE CAFÉ IS NOISY and Nova can tell it is dimly lit. The pastel haze that she sees in bright light has faded to nothing. She can smell cheap candles and bitter coffee.

She's sitting at a table somewhere near the door, with a cup of green tea. If she weren't waiting for someone she might put her headphones in and listen to an audiobook or music. She knows that sighted people will often sit in cafés, doing nothing more than gazing out of the window. They enjoy it. They call it 'watching the world go by'. But Nova must wait, in the dark, listening to the clamour of conversations around her, unable to pick out any words.

Nova is not jealous of sighted people. Not acutely. She used to be; as a teenager, she thought constantly about how everything would be better if she weren't blind. All her problems would be solved. But over time she came to realize that this wasn't true. Sighted people were not intrinsically happier than blind people. They had their own things to be unhappy about.

She is thinking about this when a pair of hands lands on her shoulders, making her jump.

'Ha-ha!' A voice cries, triumphantly.

'Fuck! Rebecca, you know I hate it when you do that!'

'I know.' The hands withdraw, there is a wet kiss on her cheek, and Nova hears Rebecca sliding into the chair across from her. 'That's why I do it.'

Nova sighs, smiling in spite of herself. 'You're late.'

'I know, I know, I'm sorry. I had to wrap up some science-y stuff.'

'You're a *theoretical* physicist, Becca. Nothing was going to explode if you left early.'

'You don't know that.'

'No? What are you working on then?'

Rebecca clears her throat. 'Semi-classical Virasoro symmetry of the quantum gravity S-matrix.'

'Ah, of course,' Nova deadpans, feeling unexpectedly awkward.

Rebecca reaches out and touches her cheek. A shiver runs down Nova's back before she moves out of reach.

One of the questions that Nova is asked most often is how she knows she's gay, when she's blind. Sighted people tell her that a lot of attraction is based on looks, and Nova shrugs. She doesn't understand this, any more than she understands why a slice of apple pie looks tasty, but she knows what it smells like and how it tastes. She has early memories of feeling different in the company of girls – she liked the soft tone of their voices, their perfume, the way they were gentle in their play. But anything more than that is a mystery – it's just the way she is. Rebecca has soft hands, and a soft voice – low alto, smoky with cigarettes.

'How are you?' Rebecca asks.

'I'm okay. Tired.'

'You don't look tired.'

'How do I look?'

'Pretty. Pretty as a picture!' Rebecca sing-songs. Nova hears her pick up the cup of tea and slurp.

'You're in a good mood . . . ' Nova leaves the sentence hanging.

'What are you implying?' Rebecca asks. Her tone is still jokey, but she knows exactly what Nova is implying. Still, Nova needs a sofa for the night, so she can't afford to piss Rebecca off too much.

'Nothing. I'm just tired.'

'Sure . . . So, what brings you back to these parts? You were pretty vague on the phone.'

'Just catching up with old friends.'

'I'm an "old friend" now, am I?'

'I wasn't talking about you. I went to see John Katzner earlier.'

'Oh, really?' Now Rebecca's tone sours. Though they have never met, she and John do not like each other. It was John who told Nova to break things off with Rebecca.

'Look, Becca, I have news. There's an operation . . . I might be able to see. To not be blind any more.'

There is silence from the other side of the table for a long time, and Nova starts to wonder if Rebecca has simply walked away. This is something that sighted people do from time to time, forgetting that she can't know they've left. It is something Rebecca has done frequently, just to fuck with her.

'Becca?'

'Wow. That's really something.' She sounds more earnest than Nova can ever remember. 'So, when are you going to do it?'

'Well, that's the thing – I don't know *if* I'm going to do it.'

'Why not?'

Nova thinks about how to explain it to her. She thinks about giving the same spiel she gave to Alex, about the radio waves and the ultraviolet, all the fizzing light that goes unseen. Instead, she dips her head and says, into her chest, 'Because I'm scared.'

Rebecca doesn't say anything for a long time.

'Do you remember that time you asked me what I imagined, when I was doing physics?'

Nova tries to remember. 'Maybe . . . '

'We were in the laundrette, eating ice pops and waiting for our clothes to be dry.'

'Oh yeah, I remember that.' Nova hasn't thought about that day for years. She's amazed that the memory has existed inside her all this time, that it hasn't withered away.

'You asked how I pictured something that was a particle and a wave at the same time. Or how I pictured four dimensions, or eleven dimensions, or whatever bollocks I was talking about at the time.'

Nova is strangely touched that Rebecca has remembered her words, carried them around with her all this time. She didn't make an effort to forget her – it was like something her body had done for her, like fighting a virus. Her immune system had rejected Rebecca.

'And I said that I pictured this or that – sometimes lots of ping-pong balls, or a slinky toy . . . '

'Okay?' Nova questions, not sure where this is going.

'But the point is – none of those things that I'm picturing in my head are real. I can never know what those things look like, even though I think about them all day. Those are just pictures that help me think about the problem I'm trying to solve. And I bet every single person in my department has different pictures. But if you gave me the opportunity to see those things for *real* . . .'

She trails off.

'What?' Nova asks. 'What if you had that opportunity?'

'Then I would take it,' Rebecca says, and Nova can hear her shrug. 'And I bet it would be really scary. I bet it would drive me a bit crazy. But it would be worth it. It would be worth it to understand all that extra stuff.'

Her hands reach out and take Nova's. Her hands are big and cool, and Nova doesn't pull away. They sit in silence for a long minute.

'Wow, Becca, that was like, a real thing.'

'Meaning what?'

'Meaning it was very sincere, for you.'

Rebecca chuckles, and squeezes her hands. 'I can be sincere! I'm a very sincere person these days.'

There's a heat in Nova's chest that is taking her by surprise. Rebecca's perfume smells like coconut.

'These days?'

Rebecca is silent for a moment. 'I've missed you.'

Now Nova does pull her hands away. 'I thought you were being sincere?'

'Don't be mean. I have – I've really missed you. My super-nova.'

Nova softens, smiles at the old nickname.

'I've missed you too.'

'So, do you want to get a drink? Other than tea, I mean?'

'I don't know if that's such a good idea . . .'

Nova leaves it unspoken. They both know what she means.

'I'm different these days.' Rebecca leans closer, so Nova can hear her. 'I'm not like that any more. Just one drink. For old time's sake?'

✳

The next morning, Nova wakes on Rebecca's sofa. It's Friday, and she needs to get back to London for her early shift tomorrow. She regrets staying, a little, but at least she's on the sofa. She remembers kissing Rebecca and winces. Still, her head is clear and she didn't do anything really stupid.

She opens her eyes wide,

wide,

wide,

letting in all the light that can be let in. It isn't much. She's lying on the sofa facing the front windows, through which the morning sun is streaming – she can feel the warmth on her face. But the most that Nova sees is a grey haze, like a misty morning.

This is the most she has ever known, so it should seem ordinary. But for the first time in years, Nova peers intently into the gloom, willing it to reveal the shapes of things on the other side. She wills the mist to dispel. If she could just have a glimpse – a sneak peek – she could make her decision.

The warmth of the sun fades, and Nova hears the patter of

rain on the window. She knows the shape of rain from a book she had when she was a child – it had a shape made from silky fabric, curved around and pointed at one end. After a long time of feeling the shape, running her fingers over the soft fabric, she had asked her brother what the shape was.

'That's a drop . . . a drip. Like rain. Or when you cry.'

Nova still does not understand how tears and rain look alike. She closes her eyes again, shifts until she is comfortable, and sleeps a little longer with the blanket pulled over her face.

✳

There is a harpsichord playing as Kate eats her breakfast, from the kitchen stereo that Tony got her for Christmas. Handel's *Messiah*. Kate likes classical music. Tony doesn't care much about music, but doesn't mind stuff without words. She's eating marmalade on toast, with a coffee recently magicked out of a golden plastic pod.

Her head is throbbing, both the spiky harpsichord and the acidity of the Seville marmalade prodding at the ache like needles. She skips a few tracks to something with just strings and dilutes each bite of toast with a swig of milky coffee. Tony appears, smelling of two-in-one shampoo and shower gel, fastening his tie. Not a real tie, of course – the sort that pulls off if you grab it, like a gecko's tail.

'Anything going on?' Tony asks, spotting that Kate is reading the news on her phone. He pecks her on the cheek and sits next to her.

'Just the usual.' She puts the phone down for a moment and squeezes his knee.

'Are you wearing that to work?' He points to her outfit, a navy-blue T-shirt with tiny cactuses printed over it and a pair of jeans. She hasn't worn the T-shirt for months.

'Oh, I spilled something on my blouse. You don't like?'

'No, it's just, maybe . . . not for work.'

'Okay, I'll change into something else. I think my cream blouse is clean.'

Tony is checking his own phone now. 'Mm. What are you doing today?'

'Job over in Borough. The office I told you about.'

He nods, though she's not sure he's remembered. Why should he?

'What are you doing?' she asks him – an old joke, since the answer is always the same.

'Catching criminals. Saving the world.'

Kate nods sagely at the stock answer. Sometimes Tony comes home with cuts and bruises. He's had black eyes and a fractured radius in his left arm. Often, he won't say anything, but Kate will notice him limping or catch him wince when she hugs him.

She's met some of his friends on the force and gets the impression that Tony has a reputation for doing crazy things – chasing people down single-handed, jumping into the line of fire – but they clam up when she asks for details. It worries her, but Kate always knew Tony was a thrill-seeker – skydiving and bungee jumping at university seeming like placeholders in his life for something genuinely scary.

The pain in her head turns up a notch, and she decides she needs to take something. She gets up and rummages in the cupboard over the tea and coffee area, where there are various boxes of pills, jars of vitamins and bags of loose-leaf tea.

'Feeling off?'

'Just a headache.'

Tony doesn't respond. She's been having headaches since the day she hit her head. She should probably go to the doctor, she thinks, but he'd only give her paracetamol, and she can't take time off work. She finds a box of pills and pushes a couple through the foil.

'What time are you home?' Tony asks. 'We could rent a movie.'

'Sorry, hun, I'm seeing the electrician at the new flat after work. I'll probably be back late.'

They've owned the new flat for a couple of months now, but it was a wreck when they got it, the only sort they could afford. Kate wanted something she could make her own. She has stripped it back to almost nothing, knocked down an unnecessary wall, and raised all the floors with sound insulation. It's still an empty space, but once the electrics are done, she will make a start on decorating.

'Okay.' Tony nods, drinking his tea. 'How much longer do you think until we can move in?'

Kate swallows the pills with her coffee and turns, resting against the worktop. 'I don't know. A couple of months? Depends how much time I spend there.'

Tony nods slowly, and Kate senses where the conversation is going.

'That's a long time . . . ' he says.

'Well, we're comfortable here, aren't we? There's no rush.'

'That's not what I meant.' Tony sighs.

No, Kate thinks – I know what you meant. The subject of children keeps coming up recently. She doesn't want to argue about it now, with her head throbbing.

'Look, I'm happy to start trying as soon as we get into the new place.'

Tony puts his head down as though examining his shoes. 'I don't see why you need to wait.'

'Because I'm renovating the flat. Because I have work to do!'

Tony looks up and his eyes narrow. 'There's always *work* to do.' He spits out the word 'work' as though she's mentioned the name of a lover.

'Just . . . can we talk about this later? I don't see what the hurry is.'

Tony stands, pulls on his jacket, takes one last look at her and leaves the room without saying anything. Kate hears him moving around in the hallway, gathering his things. She hears the front door open, winces as it slams shut.

She hunches over the sink and cradles her head in her hands, willing the pills to find their target. She watches water from the tap going drip . . . drip . . . drip . . .

She knows already that the next time she sees Tony, she will agree to try.

Kate has always wanted kids. She repeats this fact to herself through the day, standing in the shower or sitting on the bus, as though trying to convince herself of its truth. As though it is a prayer. These are just nerves, she tells herself. She has a good life, a good job, and soon she will have a good home – the risk of upending everything is what makes her pause. Once she has made the decision, the nerves will vanish, and she will feel excitement.

Pretending hasn't occurred to her yet, but the possibility is there. It will be easy to justify to herself – just for a while, until she has finished renovating the flat.

The pills are not difficult to hide.

He'll never know.

Four
April

'SIT UP PLEASE, MISS. It's time.'

Suppose a man is born blind, Nova thinks, remembering Locke's 'Essay Concerning Human Understanding'. *Suppose he learns, through touch, to recognize two objects – a sphere and a cone. Now suppose, years later, that the man is cured of his blindness, by science, or a miracle. Would the man then be able to tell the sphere and the cone apart, just by looking at them?*

Alex would call this a mind game, a riddle. But mind games are all she has, as Nova prepares to find out the truth behind the story.

Stories meant everything to her. When she was young, she would learn Dr Seuss and Edward Lear, first by listening to her father, then by lines of Braille in a ring binder too heavy for her to move. Later, when Alex became religious, she read the Qur'an out of curiosity. She read the sura that says 'He makes you in the wombs of your mothers in stages, one after another, in three veils of darkness', and thought – when I was born, one of those veils remained. People imagined blindness as darkness, but for Nova, the world was a mysterious shadow-play behind that veil.

Her pillows are rearranged. Several people enter the room unannounced, plastic shoes squeaking on the plastic floor.

'Close the blinds.'

As she grew, Nova learned other things, like Shakespeare, when he has Romeo say – 'he that is strucken blind cannot forget the precious treasure of his eyesight lost'. She hadn't been 'strucken', but she felt a loss. Nova imagined that words were her compensation, learning languages by tape, memorising poetry. She was not Romeo, but the world of romance was not closed off to her. More than one young man had explained her beauty to her, as though confirming what she could not confirm. Not that Nova was interested in young men.

'Are you ready?' a female voice asks.

'Lady, do I *look* ready?' Nova quips. The doctors laugh. Out of a sense of occasion, or because of her silent audience, Nova searches for something more to say – a quotation to introduce the magic act she is about to perform. But she finds herself dried up. Her mouth is dry; her tongue feels too big. How can she be ready when her mouth is so dry?

'Okay, here we go.'

Fingers tug at the bandages around her head, unknotting and unwinding. The cotton pads fall away. From darkness, she becomes aware of soft light, still familiar. Her eyes are shut.

'Try . . . ' the doctor begins, but she is already trying. Pain rushes in, as though her eyes are fresh wounds.

'We've dimmed the light. Can you see anything?'

Everything is blurred. There is light like Nova has never known before – insistent light, pushing into her eyes. As she watches, the brightness curdles. She concentrates, balancing on the edge of this new threshold, trying not to fall forwards or back. There are no shapes yet, only clots of light.

'I can see light . . . much brighter . . . I'm not sure yet.'

'There's no rush. We'll wait.'

Nova keeps watching the blobs of light as they become more defined, their colours separating out. Then something changes, like someone opening a door into a room where music is playing. One second there is only muffled noise. Then, suddenly, there is *detail*.

'I can see you . . . I think.'

The thing in front of her seems vast, terrifying. She turns away – her heart is pounding.

The world is a dangerous place when you can't see what's moving around you, the tracks and arcs of objects passing by, but she has never felt fear like this. This isn't a fear for self-preservation; it's like holy terror. The image in front of her seems to press physically onto her eyeballs.

'Is . . . is that your face?'

'Yes,' she chuckles. 'I'm sorry that it had to be your first.'

Nova's audience murmur their laughter – she is funny! she is cute! she is an inspirational video! Nova turns back to face the doctor. Instinctively, she reaches out to touch the thing in front of her. She doesn't even try to flirt – she feels sick. The thing feels like a face. But the image is so unfamiliar, she can't match the two.

A raiding party has landed in her skull. The disciplined divisions of her sensory stimuli – officer ranks of sound, touch and smell, and the deck-swabs of balance, temperature and so on – are being forced back by this pirate band. At the back of her brain, where the optic nerves terminate, a steady stream of invaders is flooding the posts where touch and hearing have long stood sentry. These raiders aren't afraid to hack through synapses, burn neuronal bridges, in pursuit of their prize.

Nova looks again. Her own hand, which she is seeing for the first time, blends into the mixture of shapes and colours that swim and blur. *This* seems to be a nose, but when she lets it go, it drifts from its rightful place. The eyes, burning like terrible stars, move in irregular orbits around each other. Eyes watching eyes; circles watching circles. She searches for new words – flaming, flaring, blazing . . . There is a flash of white things, clustered.

'It'll take some getting used to,' the doctor says, 'but for now, congratulations.'

※

'I asked for brushed steel. It *says* brushed steel in the plans.'

'It is brushed . . . lightly brushed.'

'Lightly? At a microscopic level? Because my optometrist tells me I'm 20/20, and that beam looks kinda *smooth* to me.'

The foreman sighs.

'Look, Ms Tomassi, this is just the way it is. Sometimes there's variability between what we order and what arrives, and you have to improvise.'

'Improvise? I'm an architect, not Charlie Parker. I did the creative part already, and it's *here*.' Kate stabs the papers so hard the foreman winces. 'So don't talk to me about "variability". They pay me to design their ideal office, and they pay you to build my design. You should have sent this shit back as soon as it arrived.'

'Well, it's unpacked now.'

Kate rubs her 20/20 eyes with thumb and forefinger. Her head is throbbing.

She feels like she's going to e-x-p-l-o-d-e.

'All right. We'll use them for the hall. Sand them, paint them black to match, nobody'll know the difference.'

'Thanks.'

'But from now on, check the order before it's unpacked, or I'm sending it back on your account.'

The foreman says nothing. Kate looks over his plans, gathering her thoughts. The office is across the road from Borough Market, a consultancy firm with aspirations of cool. She prefers the office on the page to the one taking shape. The ratios are perfect on paper, but translating them into real objects is imperfect. It's like the film of a favourite book – it might be good, but it's never the same as what is in your head. Not that she has the time to read books.

'How's the corner office coming on?'

'Half done. The frame looks great.'

She has designed an exposed wooden frame for the room, with window panes that make it look like a river boat, or an old train carriage. They're going to love it.

'Let's take a look.'

She picks up her phone and shop-bought macchiato, leaving her hard hat on the table, and follows the foreman to the other half of the office. Pine beams are being divided by a circular saw, aluminium panels riveted, and, over in the corner, an arc welder is connecting two girders. She glances at the dazzling blue fire.

'What do you think?' The foreman points. It's just the frame, without any of the panels or windows, like a three-dimensional drawing.

'Looks good. Is it sturdy?'

'See for yourself.'

She steps into the doorway and gives the beam a hard slap.

The frame, in fact, is not sturdy. The upper section is loosely pinned together by a carpenter who will return later to finish it off. The lintel, released by the impact, swings down without warning. At the last moment, Kate dives out of the way. The lintel hits the floor, the sound echoing through the room.

'Shit! Kate . . .' the foreman breathes.

'That was too close,' is all she can say.

She feels the tingle in her hands and feet, the pulse fluttering in her throat. She gets to her feet and starts to walk away from the frame. She wants to say something to the foreman, to curse at him, but the words won't come out.

She feels the room tilt

once,

and

twice,

and

threeeeeee times.

She stumbles forwards.

'You okay?' the foreman asks, more amused than concerned.

Kate doesn't respond – she can see a shape forming in front of her. It's a circle. The circle shimmers, and it reminds her of a childhood memory. In bed at night, when it was dark, she would close her eyes and press the heels of her hands into her eyes, until a mysterious light built up, stars sparkling to life in the darkness, and a shimmering circle would appear before her. It was a sort of secret magic.

The circle is there now, without her summoning it.

She smiles at the appearance of this old friend before falling to the floor and blacking out.

✦

Kate wakes but does not wake. She is no longer asleep, but this does not seem like waking either. Her brain is bubbling like a boiling pan. Memories roll fatly to the surface and break.

BUBBLEPOPPINGTINSELBREATHINGPOLAR BEARANDITWOULDBESOSIMPLETOSTAYINBED ALLDAY

Kate can taste marshmallow cocoa – the sort her father made on cold winter Sundays, before church. The warm drink sloshes around in her mouth, and she can feel the half-melted mini marshmallows, until it all fades away and she catches a glimpse of where she is.

PULSARS!FLARING!!INDEEPSPACE!THELAWN OFGRASSBEHINDHERHOUSE!AND!!COLALOLLI-POPS!!GONEFUZZYUNDERTHECOUCH!

Kate is lying on her back on a gurney. There are people around her, but she can't see any of their faces. All the people are wearing clothes of a single colour – blue and green and crimson – and this makes Kate want to laugh. She is moving down the corridor, but then another memory blister bursts, and she is gone.

Kate is standing in the middle of the road, waist deep in

snow. Usually, she wouldn't be allowed to stand in the road outside their house, and wouldn't want to anyway – it is always busy with traffic. She has never seen snow like this before, and more miraculous than the snow itself is the way it has upended the usual rules. There are no cars, no noise, and today there will be no school.

PILLPOPPINGPERFECTPRANKSTERPRISTINE PRALINEPROPANEPROPELLERPRANK

A house party, last year of university. Kate feels the subwoofer rumble of the bass in her chest. Cheap disco lights stain the room red-blue-green in endless repetition. She sips the 'party punch', which is equal parts tropical squash, peach schnapps and vodka. She's here with friends – her flatmates – eager to get shitfaced now their dissertations are turned in. Kate has a final bit of coursework to complete and has vowed to have only one drink.

She's sitting in the corner of the room, watching the windows weep while everyone else gets off with one another. Brian comes over and starts chatting to her. Kate has known Brian – or known of him – since first year. He has a reputation for not owning a towel, or shower gel. She feels sort of sorry for him, but her sympathy only goes so far. In the humidity of the room, Brian is a lot to take.

She must have backed up into the corner, trying to politely reply to his line of conversation – about how shit the music is – which Brian only takes as an invitation to draw closer. She tries to get out of the conversation several times, tries to catch the attention of each of her friends. Everything has failed when a hand rests lightly on her shoulder.

'Oh, hey! I should get you that drink I promised you.'

Kate looks up into the face above her, noticing that this person is a stranger. But, if she hesitates, it's only a moment.

'Oh, yeah. Sorry, Brian – I'll catch you in a bit, yeah?'

The mystery man offers his hand, pulls Kate up to standing, and silently they walk out of the house, through the kitchen, Tony grabbing a couple of beers from an ice bucket on the way out.

The night air washes over her, a total-body feeling something like love.

'You want this?' Tony offers her the bottle, smiling. She nods, and he opens both beers with a tool on his keyring.

'How did you know, in there?'

'How did I know that the cute girl pressed into the corner, trying to breathe through her mouth, wanted some fresh air?'

Kate laughs, hoping he can't see her blush in the dark. 'He's not so bad, Brian . . . '

Tony says nothing, a smile twitching at the corner of his mouth.

They stand and watch the night sky, sipping beer, while the house heaves and sweats behind them, and the delicious cold dries them out and makes their skin taut.

WAKE UP WAKE UP WAKE UP WAKE UP WAKE UP WAKE UUUUUUUP

Kate is in a new room, and the gurney has stopped moving. The colour-coded people are moving around her, but she still can't see their faces. She tries to hold on to this place, this room, but it's difficult when nobody is talking to her. If she could just have a conversation . . . but Kate sinks down, as though under the waters of a lurid bubble bath, choked by rainbows and glitter.

JELLY AND ICE QUEEN BEE BONNET

She is sitting at her dormroom window, holding a crayon and looking out over the grounds. In front of their building is a winding path, with patchy grass either side, and two trees, one beech on their side of the path and one sycamore on the other.

Kate has drawn the view from her window many times, in pencil and charcoal, with pastels and watercolours, but every time it looks a little different. This is because she is not very good at drawing, she thinks, and smiles. But the act of drawing is relaxing. Unlike her architectural drawings, on paper or on a computer, there are no wrong answers with a painting. She doesn't have to worry about getting the dimensions wrong, or having the fire doors in the right place. In a week's time she will be moving out of dorms, going home until she can find a job in London.

Today she is drawing with the box of kids' crayons her flatmates got her as an affectionately jokey goodbye. Kate likes the crayons. The waxy smell reminds her of childhood in a nonspecific way, the same as poster paint and spaghetti hoops. She puts down one crayon (Dandelion) and is reaching for another (Granny Smith Apple) when her phone starts to buzz in her pocket. Kate takes it out and looks at the caller.

Mum and Dad Home

Later, Kate will think that she knew, from the moment she saw the caller, that something was wrong. But that's not quite right. She answers the phone, and it's at the moment of hearing her mother's voice that she feels her stomach twist.

She doesn't say much for a minute. A minute is all it takes. When the call is done she checks the call log on her phone. One minute and nine seconds.

That was all it took to erase her father.

She sits frozen for a minute more, looking at the phone in her hand, at the view out of her window, at the half-finished drawing. How stupid, it suddenly seems, to have drawn this view over and over. When was the last time she spoke to her father? She used to call every week, but recently she has been too busy.

She thinks of her father, suddenly unwell on the bus, feeling the pain radiate through his shoulder and down his arm. She thinks of how long it has been since he heard his daughter's voice. There is no grief – not yet. All Kate feels is a furious hatred of herself. She wants to feel pain, to do something truly awful to herself.

Kate dials another number on the phone, listens to the dialling tone and it's only when she hears the voice on the other end that her tears start to fall. Her voice sounds far away.

'Hi, Tony, it's me . . . Kate . . . would you . . . would you come to my dorm? Please?'

HE LOVES ME HE LOVES ME NOT HE LOVES ME HE LOVES ME NOT HE . . .

There is no memory this time, but Kate has gone somewhere deep within herself. Everything is going wrong, mixing together and bubbling over and melting out of shape . . . she can no longer separate sounds from smells, tastes from words, faces from days of the week. Everything is jumbled up, and Kate doesn't know how she's ever going to sort this mess out.

The circle shimmers in front of her.

Outside – in the world beyond Kate's skull – a plastic mask is placed over her mouth, and she breathes the thin gas seeping from it. The bubbling world inside her brain fades by degrees, then is gone.

Kate ceases to be.

Five

May

NOVA SITS ON A plastic chair in the alcove where they keep the communal phone. The ward is quiet at this time of night, and Nova misses the noise. She doesn't want to be overheard. They have taken away her mobile phone, to stop her from using the accessibility features, on the premise that total immersion is the key to learning a new language. For the first time, 'total immersion' seems to Nova like a synonym for drowning.

There are a lot of rules to learn. They're like rules of grammar, and Nova is listing them all in her head. Maybe one day she'll be able to write them down.

RULE OF SEEING NO.1
If object A occludes object B,
object A is <u>closer</u> than object B.

This rule is simple enough, but tricky to put into practice. Everything is two-dimensional to Nova – streetlights through the window look like bright stains on the glass, clouds in the sky look as close as the polystyrene ceiling tiles in the ward. Nova remembers a quote from Jorge Luis Borges – going blind at fifty-five, he described losing his sight as a process by which 'everything near becomes distant'. Learning to see is like the opposite of that – everything that was once spaced out is now tightly compressed around her. The sky pushes down; walls vacuum-pack her.

RULE OF SEEING NO.2
Objects look smaller
as their distance increases.

Again, this rule is easy to understand, but judging how big something *should* be is difficult. She cannot tell the difference between the colourful gumballs in the bowl by the nurse's station and the squishy yoga balls they get the patients to sit on for rehab. Often, she will reach out to grab an object, only to be told it's on the other side of the room.

The hospital doesn't have a ward solely for people learning to see. Nova is in the Stroke Rehabilitation Unit. A lot of the exercises are the same, they tell her. She feels bad for thinking it, but the sounds of the other patients – slurring their names and shuffling around – make her skin crawl.

RULE OF SEEING NO.17a
There is no consistency between which
objects are transparent, translucent, opaque
or reflective. For example, a lightbulb can be

transparent <u>or</u> translucent. Water can be
transparent <u>or</u> opaque, depending on the
conditions.

RULE OF SEEING NO.17b
**Objects can display more than one of these
properties at once. For example, soap bubbles
can be transparent *and* reflective, *at the same
time*.**

Nova has four phone numbers written on a scrap of paper,
but deciphering these marks could take ages, and she's only
got ten minutes. Why does she feel like she's being punished?
The first number is her parents' landline, but she can't face
their questions right now. They haven't seen her yet – they
wanted to be there, when the bandages came off, but she told
them to wait until she was out of hospital. In case it didn't
work, she had said. The second number is Alex's mobile, but
he's changed it recently and she doesn't know it off by heart.
She will see him soon anyway. The last two numbers are John's
and Rebecca's.

Though she has forgotten many things about Rebecca, Nova
can still remember her phone number clearly. She's surprised
the number hasn't changed – Rebecca loses things faster than
she can acquire them. Credit cards and umbrellas, scarves and
sunglasses all get left on public transport or in bars. Books
and films lent to her go missing and never resurface. Rebecca
seems naturally resistant to these things, shedding them like
oil off a non-stick pan. Nova can't understand how something
as insubstantial as a number has clung on.

She dials, and thinks of hanging up when the line clicks.

'Yeah?' Rebecca says. There is noise in the background, a crowded room.

'Becca? It's Nova.'

'Who? Hang on – I'll go outside.'

There is a lot of rustling, garbled voices, and the line gets quieter.

'Yello?'

'It's Nova.'

'Hey, babe. What's this number?'

'I'm calling from the hospital.'

'Oh, hey, yeah! Shit!'

'You forgot.' Nova accuses.

'Not forgot! I just didn't think you'd still be in there.'

'Well, I'm in rehab.'

'Right, right . . . I sent you a get-well card! You'll see it when you get home.'

Nova doesn't say anything to this. She will believe it when the card is in her hand.

'Are you at a bar?'

'Nah, just a faculty thing – party for the new grads. I'll probably head home now.'

'Don't let me keep you from the fun.'

'I'm walking home now. Talk to me.'

Nova founders. She had not thought about what she wanted to say, assuming that – given an opening – all the frustration would come pouring out of her.

'I don't know what to say . . . ' she admits. She can hear Rebecca's footsteps down the line, and her breath on the receiver, and these things are strangely reassuring. Reassuring of what? Reassuring that there is a world beyond this facility. Instead of expanding Nova's world, as everyone promised, learning to see has contracted everything. Always comfortable in snug spaces, Nova feels claustrophobic.

'Well, why don't you tell me how it's going? Can you . . . can you *see*?'

The last word is highlighted with incredulity, as though Rebecca can't imagine a version of Nova who is not blind.

'I don't . . . it's like . . . The operation was a success,' she ends, limply.

'It was a success? So, you can see?'

Nova takes a breath and tries to put the experience into words. 'Well, my eyes are working . . . My brain is receiving information. Lots of information.' She's worried that she's going to cry – her miraculous eyes are starting to water.

'But?' Rebecca asks, waiting for Nova to go on. Nova feels a swell of affection for her ex. This is the Becca that she remembers from the early days – the one who listened more than she talked. Maybe she wasn't lying when she said she had changed for the better.

'But I'm still blind.'

'You're . . . what? That doesn't make any sense.'

'I know. I don't understand any of it. Half the time I feel more blind than I did before. It's so confusing, I can't even move around like I used to! I can't remember the shape of a room, or where I put my glass of water. I tried to sneak out of here, just to go to a shop and buy some crisps, but I got completely disoriented . . . I was stranded . . . and all I wanted was a packet of . . . of *crisps*!'

Nova is crying now, gently, the ends of her words turning up in a petulant accent. The sound of footsteps has stopped on the other end of the line and for a moment she is worried they've been disconnected.

'Becca?'

'I'm still here, babe. I'm just sitting on someone's garden wall.'

'Oh yeah?' Nova sob-laughs. 'Describe it to me.'

'Well, for one thing there's this creepy-ass garden gnome looking at me from the flower bed. Um . . . there are rose bushes, I think. You know I'm not good with flowers. There are tulips; I know those.'

'Me too.' Nova smiles. There are daffodils blooming across London. Alex has pointed some out to Nova on a walk. She was surprised by the colours – rubber-duck yellow and lipstick red. She imagined flowers being softer somehow, ghostly, like the hazy light she used to know. Tulips look like they were injection-moulded in a factory.

'It's raining a bit, but not much.'

'You should go somewhere dry.'

'Nah, it's okay. I'll dry out when I get home. How are you doing?'

'A bit better for talking. Tell me about the party?'

'Just the back room of a pub, warm beer and a dozen physics geniuses arguing about quantum entanglement. Boring. You saved me, actually.'

'Hm. No cute girls?'

'Oh, well, now you mention it, there was this redhead in skinny jeans . . .' Rebecca begins.

'All right, all right!'

Rebecca chuckles. 'I'm joking anyway – they're mostly male and stale. And nobody half as pretty as you.'

Nova smiles and takes a deep breath. 'Who knows – if I work out this seeing business, maybe I'll finally understand what it is about someone's hair colour that makes you like them so much.'

'That's the spirit. Not that I want you chasing all the redheads on campus.'

There is silence for a moment. 'I should probably get off now – they only give you ten minutes on this thing.'

'Wow, it's like I'm getting a call from prison. Kinda hot.'

'Easy, tiger.'

Another pause. Nova stares at a sign on the wall – a white cross on a green background. She knows this can mean 'hospital' or 'first aid', and it's one of the shapes she knows the best. Rebecca speaks again, her voice low and gentle.

'Well, I'm always here if you need to talk. Or not talk. Whatever.'

'Thanks.'

'You're going to be okay, Nova. If anyone can do it, I know you can.'

'I'll try.'

'All right . . . You want to talk to the gnome?'

After a few more minutes of chat, Nova says goodnight and hangs up. It's only at this point that she becomes aware of someone nearby, lurking in the shadows.

'Hello?'

The unseen person clears their throat.

'You wanna buy crisps?' They slur a little – this is a patient, not a doctor. 'I know where you can get some.'

'I'm listening.'

✴

Kate isn't sure what time it is. There are no windows. She's standing in a corridor. A hospital corridor. This hospital seems to be quiet, but maybe she's just in a quiet ward. What kind of ward would she be in, anyway? She doesn't know. She doesn't remember what's wrong with her.

Of course, this could be a dream – Kate has had a lot of strange dreams over the last couple of weeks, and a lot of them involved hospitals. Kate feels as though she could walk and walk, through endless corridors of flecked-blue plastic floors and magnolia walls, and never find what she is looking for. What *is* she looking for?

Anyway, Kate is pretty sure she's awake. It's just that her brain hasn't quite knitted back together yet. Nothing seems real. She walks on down the corridor, feeling cool air around her ankles. She looks down and remembers she's in a gown, with slippers on her feet. Her right hand is closed tight around something hard. She opens the hand in front of her and sees a shiny gold coin.

Ah yes, she remembers now. She asked if she could buy a chocolate bar. There was money in the drawer of her bedside table and Kate guessed it must belong to her. They had told her where she could find a vending machine. She doesn't remember who 'they' are. Perhaps 'they' had asked if she wanted them to show her the way, but Kate refused. She doesn't need looking after.

She walks a little further, pushing through a fire door, then taking a right turn where there is no other option. Is she lost? She pushes through another fire door and sees what she is looking for – a row of vending machines.

Standing in front of the glowing machines is another woman, also wearing a gown. This tiny woman is hammering the plexiglass of the machine with her fists, yelling with each blow.

'Give . . . me . . . my . . . crisps . . . you . . . BASTARD!'

Kate is not sure if this person has noticed her entrance and, though she is worried that they might be violently unhinged, thinks it only polite to announce herself. She clears her throat, and the other woman turns briefly in her direction. Kate sees light brown skin and a messy halo of dark hair. The woman is wearing sunglasses – mirrored aviator shades. It is not especially bright in the corridor, and Kate isn't sure if the woman has seen her. She turns back to the machine and starts to beat her fists against it once more.

Kate walks up to the machines, determined that this isn't going to stop her getting her chocolate bar. It's the only thing she remembers wanting, and she's not even sure she can find her way back to the ward. She looks at the three machines. The left one sells drinks. The right one sells healthy snacks – porridge pots, apples and bananas. Kate's nose wrinkles in distaste. She has a childlike need for refined sugar. Only the middle machine – the one currently getting the crap kicked out of it – is stocked with crisps, jelly sweets and chocolate.

She watches as the woman in the hospital gown and aviator shades swings back from the machine and shoulders it hard.

There is silence and stillness for a moment, then the tiny woman whispers:

'Ow . . . fuck.'

Kate can see the problem – a packet of prawn cocktail crisps has slumped out from the dispenser without falling, wedged between the coil and the glass. She clears her throat again. The woman in the aviator shades spins around.

'Yes?' she demands.

Kate sees herself reflected double in the mirror shades and swallows.

'Uh, I was just going to say, maybe I could help?'

The woman smiles for a second.

'You wanna help me smash this piece of crap vending machine that stole my money?

'Uh, no . . . ' Kate says, hurriedly. 'I was just thinking, I'm going to get a chocolate bar, and maybe I could knock your crisps out.'

Behind the aviators, the woman seems to frown.

'Knock them out?'

'Yeah, like, if I get the chocolate bar above, it might fall and knock your crisps out?' The woman is still frowning. 'You know, because they're jammed?'

'They are? I thought it had just swallowed my money.'

'No, they're right there.'

'I don't really use vending machines . . . but I like this plan!'

The tiny woman moves aside, grinning. Kate steps forward and puts her coin in the slot. The chocolate bar that she really wants is just one up from the crisps, but she's worried that if she chooses this one, it won't gather enough momentum to knock them free. So she keys in A7, three rows above, for dark chocolate and coconut. Not her first choice, but still good.

The coil starts to turn.

Kate holds her breath.

The chocolate bar falls, glances off the bag of crisps and lands with a clunk at the bottom of the machine. For a second, Kate thinks her plan hasn't worked, then the crisps shift sideways, hesitate for a second and fall.

'Yes!' Kate smiles at this tiny victory.

'Did it work?' the woman asks. She can't seem to see anything through the shades. Kate wants to tell her to take them off, but doesn't want her to go back to shouting and punching things. She crouches down and grabs their snacks from the dispenser tray.

'Here you go.'

The woman takes the crisps and grins up at Kate.

'Thanks, I really—'

'Hey, you!'

They are cut off by the shout, which comes from the other end of the corridor. Kate looks up and sees a man in a navy-blue uniform – a security guard.

'You in the glasses!'

'I assume you mean me?' the tiny woman replies, as the security guard advances on her.

'Yes, you, who else is wearing sunglasses here? I've been watching you on the CCTV.'

'Took you a while to get here.'

'You can't just start laying into hospital property like that.'

'Well, the thing is . . . '

Kate is beating a hasty retreat out of the corridor, and doesn't hear the woman's excuse. The fire door closes behind her, and as she hurries back the way she came, Kate could swear she hears the security guard laughing at something the woman has said. Then there is nothing.

Kate clutches the chocolate bar to her chest, winding her way back through the maze of corridors. Somehow, she finds the ward, and from there a nurse shows her back to her bed. By the time she has settled down to eat her snack, Kate has completely forgotten about Nova.

✳

'Cheese, ham or egg?'

'The ham, and a coffee.'

'Okey-dokey.'

The woman places the sandwich, a paper cup of coffee, and some napkins on Kate's over-bed table and moves on. She stares at the new objects, fixing on them like scenery out of a window. If she closes her eyes the room will start to heave. The doctors have given her an anti-sickness shot, but it doesn't stop her from feeling like she's on a boat. She could try to sleep again, but they keep waking her up to do more checks.

It's the morning after she went to the vending machines, but Kate doesn't remember any of that. In the hours of sleep since then, her brain has put itself back together, and her dreamlike trance has been replaced with nauseous clarity.

'Hello, Ms Tomassi.'

A new doctor appears, reading the notes made by the previous three. The ward is making Kate feel like she's in a recurring dream. The new doctor runs the same tests, checking her pupils, her reflexes, her heart rate and blood pressure. She asks Kate to confirm her date of birth and telephone number for the sixth time, which she does while staring at the white-on-green cross on the wall behind her head. *First aid*, Kate thinks. *I am in need of aid.*

Finally, it is done.

She has been in hospital for two weeks. Though she has been awake for much of it, she has no memories of her stay prior to this morning. Her last memory is eating toast with marmalade. But if she reaches up to the back of her head, under her hair is a shaved patch. She keeps running her fingers over the stubble when the nurses aren't looking. There is a patch of gauze where they removed the shunt that was draining her brain. If she touches the puckered stitching there is pain, but otherwise she wouldn't know that someone had opened her head up to take a look inside.

'Well, Kate, I think you're making really good progress. Your reflexes are all normal.'

'So, I'll make a full recovery?'

The doctor readjusts her expression.

'You had a subdural hematoma – a bleed in the matter between your skull and your brain. We operated on you to relieve the pressure, and your scans show no damage to the affected area. But you should be on guard for anything unusual.'

'Okay . . .' Kate nods slowly, trying to take everything in.

'We don't see any need for rehabilitation. I'm prescribing you painkillers and anti-emetics. We'll be keeping you under observation for a little longer, but if nothing changes, you'll be discharged tomorrow. Is there someone who can take you home then? Will you need a taxi?'

'I need to find out what shift my husband's on. He's around here somewhere . . .'

Kate isn't sure if this is true – she saw Tony a while ago, but she doesn't remember him saying goodbye.

The doctor frowns a little, Kate notices, then nods.

'I'll send someone to find him for you.' She walks off.

Kate sips the coffee and regards her ham sandwich. No – still too soon.

'*How's it going in there, Brain?*' she asks.

'*Not bad . . . we've been worse.*'

'*Okay. Let me know when I'm good to eat this sandwich, yeah?*'

'*Don't hold your breath.*'

She sips some coffee and looks around the ward. There was a scuffle with a man who may have been drunk about half an hour ago, but otherwise her stay has been uneventful. There are a dozen messages on her phone from the plasterer currently working in the new flat, but she can't think about him yet.

She lies in the hospital bed, feeling the world rushing in, rushing out, nothing quite right. She closes her eyes, trying to relax, but the sickness won't let up. After a couple of minutes, she hears two people approaching. One of them is Tony, chatting animatedly to the nurse who has found him.

'So, I kicked down the door, and there he is, this scary drug lord, eating a Pop-Tart on the toilet.'

The nurse laughs at the anecdote. 'Oh, my God!'

Kate opens her eyes.

'Tony?'

He is the way she remembers him: a pressed, short-sleeved shirt, work trousers, hair smoothed over. He looks very calm, smiling. The nurse stops laughing, presses one hand to Tony's shoulder as though pushing him away and smiles politely at Kate.

'I'll give you two some privacy.'

A long moment passes while the nurse walks off and neither of them says anything.

'How are you?' he asks.

'I've been better.'

Kate becomes aware of another body behind Tony, moving as though stepping out of his shadow. It is another doctor.

'Hello, Ms Tomassi. Before we discharge you, I'd just like to ask a few questions about the accident you had back in January. For our records.'

Kate frowns, knowing Tony must have already explained this to the doctors, knowing that she had already explained it herself.

'I fell, in the kitchen . . .'

The doctor's eyes dart between her and Tony. Tony doesn't take his eyes off Kate's face.

'Yes, I just wondered about the nature of your fall. We just want to understand what caused your bleed. Could you explain how it happened?'

'I tripped over a box of wine bottles, on the floor. I fell backwards.'

'You fell backwards?'

Kate's stomach churns; she wonders where he is going with this.

'You were walking backwards, and tripped?'

Tony's eyes are on her, the same way they were on her when she was holding the square of white paper. What had happened to the square of white paper?

'Yes, I was stepping back . . .' This is the moment that she could say something. This is the moment that she could say she was stepping back from Tony. But what is there to say? He did not push her, did not hit her, could not have intended for her to fall. They weren't even arguing. Not really. She shakes her head, feeling the muscles in her neck protest.

'Yes, I was just stepping back, out of the way of Tony, as he was chopping vegetables. I forgot that I'd put the wine on the floor. Stupid, really.' She smiles.

'Not a mistake you'll make again soon, I'm sure.' The doctor smiles. He talks for a minute more about medications and exactly what Kate should do if she feels unwell or lethargic. Then he leaves, and she is alone with Tony. He steps closer to the bed but says nothing.

They have been married for two years, and Kate has never known him like this. Tony is quiet, yes – this is what she says to friends. He can be uncommunicative, but who wants a chatterbox? They understand each other. That's enough, isn't it? But this silence is something different. This is a silence that he is inflicting on her.

Kate could ask him now, again, about the piece of paper. But, somehow, she knows that things have not changed. If they had, he would have told her what the paper was already. He would feel sorry that she was hurt, that she was in hospital, that he had caused this by not telling her. Kate has always felt safe, with Tony. At home. But it wasn't a passive kind of safety. She always felt that, if anyone tried to hurt her, Tony would hurt them in return. Now it feels as though he is guarding Kate from herself. She waits, hoping he will say something.

'Do you want anything?'

'No, I think I have everything I need.'

'Okay . . .' He looks down at his shoes, breathes in deeply, breathes out again.

'I should probably be going. My shift starts in half an hour.'

'Yeah, you should go.'

'See you tomorrow.' He bends over her and places a kiss on her forehead. She is glad that her arms are under the sheets, so he cannot see how she clenches her fists.

Six

June

'YOU SHOULD TAKE THE glasses off.'
'Not yet.'

The bus is crowded, sticky in the heat, and Nova can't wait for the automatic voice to call her stop. She's wearing the clothes she went to the hospital in, back when the weather was cold. She has her eyes closed, dark glasses on. Alex sits by her, arm looped through hers. Occasionally, she will open her eyes, but the world is rushing by like water, and she gets the tumbling feeling of being swept away.

RULE OF SEEING NO.36
**Buses, cars etc. – because glass is both
see-through <u>and</u> reflective, the inside of
these glass boxes, particularly when in
motion, is a constant, swimming mixture of
images. It is best, where possible, to get
close to the window. Otherwise, travel with
eyes closed.**

Anyway, it's pointless — she can understand things when they stand still, but as soon as they start to move she can't keep track. Leaving the rehab ward, she feels like a foreigner, with only a handful of phrases at her disposal: 'Hello'; 'Thank you'; 'Where is the bank?' Those were enough, when she was just holidaying in this foreign place, but now she must do her job, have relationships, have a whole life — all in a language that she barely knows.

So, she screws her eyes shut and tries to forget for a little longer. She never thought it would feel strange to ignore her new sense — to close her eyes — since she had lived thirty-two years with her eyes closed.

'You'll never get used to it . . .' Alex nags.

'Just give me some time, okay?'

Her training in rehab consisted of seemingly unrelated activities. She sat at a computer, pressing the button when a certain shape appeared on the screen. She stared down lengths of string with coloured beads on them, trying to line them up. She wore glasses with strange, thick lenses. She balanced on a wobbling platform, trying to keep her eyes focussed on a black dot on the wall in front of her. More than once she vomited from the effort. She was told that her therapy was revolutionary, a combination of techniques to develop different parts of her visual brain. It felt to her like orchestrated torture.

Of the problems Alex warned she might suffer, Nova seemed to have them all. Objects had halos, auras and colourful tracks like comet tails. Colours changed as she looked at them. Everything seemed to move around, to grow and shrink in waves. Even the air would become textured, grainy. Her mind struggled to contain this volume of light. By the end of each day in rehab, Nova was exhausted, hardly able to talk. Sometimes she fell asleep in the middle of a lesson.

When things started to improve, nurses taught her shapes and colours using flashcards. These were the things that came first – squares and triangles and circles, blues and reds and yellows. They were like the first syllables of a child – oo, aa, eeee.

Even in isolation these were difficult, but her progress was subject to an exponential increase in difficulty. A plain square was easier than a yellow square. A red triangle above the yellow square was four times harder again. Then adding the squares, circles and crossed lines required to make the picture look like a 'house' only multiplied the difficulty. Finally, tears of frustration would break the image into fragments.

Slowly, Nova came to recognize faces, and their geography became more fixed, if not less alien. Faces scare her, because they seem like any other objects – lamps or tables or toilets – yet imbued with life. She can't tell what they are thinking. Voices are clear. She can hear truth or lies in a voice. But human faces to Nova are no different to insect faces – alive, but grotesque and inscrutable. (She doesn't even want to *look* at pornography.) She saw her own face in a mirror, but it was no different from the rest. It certainly didn't feel like *her* face. 'Prosopagnosia, or face-blindness,' the doctor said, as though that helped.

In addition to faces, she still can't understand depth. Everything is on one plane, like a screen a few centimetres in front of her face. If people walk away from her, they seem to be shrinking. 'Stereo-blindness,' the doctor said. Nova is amazed by the variety of blindnesses that have nothing to do with her eyes. Some of these may also be healed, but there is no guarantee. She learned the colours orange and purple (though she often confused both with brown), and learned to tell the time on a clock.

Alex visited once a day. When he got over her lack of joy at seeing his face, he helped Nova practise. Though she had no sense of depth, they practiced hand-eye co-ordination, Alex moving a ball on a stool around the practice room. Because it kept moving, Nova couldn't just memorize where the ball was – she had to use her eyes. At first her hand couldn't follow the bright red dot she was seeing, and she would always knock the ball off the stool. After a fortnight, she could grasp the ball about half the time. A week later, she could grab it every time.

Outside the practice room, Nova still knocked over glasses of orange juice and put her hand in the soup instead of grasping the spoon, but grabbing the red ball was her first small victory – a sense that, by increments, she might actually get better.

'Nearly home,' Alex says, his voice still keen with an excitement Nova can't feel. He wants to be the older brother, to help her out of her shell. She wants to tell him that, after thirty-two years, the shell is part of her.

Nova grew up speaking English and Urdu, learned French at school, then Italian and Arabic at university. She got freelance jobs as an interpreter, then a full-time job working for the police. It brought her satisfaction, but there was nothing difficult about learning those languages. Seeing for the first time required the same rote learning – the repetition of faces, cutlery, shoes, with all their conjugations. But the patterns were hard to find, and she couldn't predict them.

'What do you think this is?' a nurse had asked, holding up a card. There are rows of circles which could be buttons, or teeth.

'A telephone? A smile?'

The object was corn on the cob.

Now her time is up. Her 'rehabilitation' is not over – this is like being let out on parole for good behaviour. She's allowed to go back to work, if she feels able. Nova wants to try. Maybe, as with other languages, immersion is the best way to learn.

They get off the bus and walk the short way to Nova's flat. She tries not to look at the sky.

RULE OF SEEING NO.45
Clouds look surprisingly solid. Do not worry – planes/birds will not crash into them.

She can tell Alex wants to come in, but she's too anxious.

'Can I do this on my own?'

'Oh . . . ' She can hear his disappointment. 'Sure. I'll see you soon?'

'Yeah . . . be *seeing* you too, doofus,' she tries to appease him.

'Okay.'

He hugs her and leaves. Inside the door, Nova stops, waiting for the ebb and flow of her fear to settle. She takes off her dark glasses, to see the place where she lives. The room is like others she has seen, its geography bound by certain rules and containing objects that, with a little thought, she can ascribe to a category. She cross-references these objects with her memory, like trying to match a map to a landscape. Is this way north? Are the mountains over there? Is that her armchair?

Whether the room is attractive or not, she doesn't know, but it seems more cluttered than the room in her memory – objects piled around the edge of tracks that wind through the space. She hasn't had a guide dog since she was seventeen, but she wishes she were coming home to one now. Dogs are good companions, and they don't ask questions.

The living room is dark, so she finds the switch. The light won't come on – perhaps the bulb is broken. She walks into the kitchen, to the sink. There is a window in front of the sink where she sometimes stands, feeling the sun while she does the dishes. Now she can see outside, though with no depth perception, the window is like a screen.

Her flat backs onto wasteland. She'd heard residents complain about the litter, the broken concrete. The sun is bright, and she can see the litter – blotches of colour poking through a dazzle of silver weeds. Dominating the space is a tree, its roots tangling through the concrete.

The tree is as tall as the buildings surrounding it. Nova has never realized that trees are so big. She looks at its leaves. Each of them is a familiar shape, and it takes her a moment to remember what the shape is. Almost like a teardrop, but with an indentation at the fat end. It's called a heart.

There are thousands of these hearts, stretching for dominance on a hierarchy of branches and sub-branches, rippling together until a breeze disrupts the pattern, shivering it apart, and they become a million separate hearts again. The tree isn't a single thing. It isn't a single word, or thought. It isn't 'tree'. It's a shimmering cloud, forming and dissolving in front of her, over and over, and the more she looks, the more she is dissolving with it, all the parts of her scattering in the wind.

Nova turns away from the window.

✳

Kate orders a pizza on the taxi ride home from the hospital. She felt strangely flat, while in the hospital – unable to enjoy the normal things. The pizza was the one thing she could find to look forward to.

The flat is quiet, of course. Her time in the hospital seems unreal, but she expected to return home and find the life that she left behind. Now she's not so sure. Whose home is this? It seems to be hers – the quilted blanket her mother gave her when she left home is thrown over the sofa. The food in the kitchen cupboards is stuff that she likes. Her running shoes are sprawled in the hall where she kicked them off.

Most convincingly, there are pictures of her family in frames on the wall. One of the pictures is friends from university, faces daubed in Day-Glo paint, all crushed together to get in the frame, grinning like gorgeous idiots. Mark and Sally and Jenna and Andy . . . When was the last time she spoke to any of them? Kate can't remember. They just seemed to fade out of her life. Another of the frames is heart-shaped, and she's standing next to a man. After a moment, she remembers that the man in the picture is Tony.

But the more she searches, the more she feels like this flat is an imposter. It's a clever recreation. A film set. If she pushes hard enough, the walls will come toppling down.

She stands in the kitchen, and replays the memory of falling.

She brings her hands up to her heart as though holding something there. But the square of white paper is nowhere. She looks at the tiles where her head surely made contact. The hard surface that did the damage. But there is nothing there – no mark, no crack.

She waits.

Twenty minutes pass, and Kate is feeling none the wiser when the buzzer announces her pizza. Bored with silence, she puts the radio on for the news. The doctor told her not to drink, but she deserves a beer. She is down to the last slice when her phone rings.

'Kate?'

'You rang my number, Vi.'

She laughs like this is a new joke. Vi – Violetta to her mother – is her oldest friend. Their parents emigrated at the same time and found houses a few streets apart. They grew up together, eating dinner in each other's kitchens.

'You want to see a film tonight?'

'I only just got home from the hospital.'

'You all right?'

Kate rolls her shoulders, trying to smooth the tension out. 'I'm okay.'

There is a pause.

'Well?'

Kate sighs, not wanting to go out, but not wanting to make her excuses to Vi.

'Okay, sure.'

Seven

'COULD YOU GET HIM to repeat that?'

In Urdu, Nova asks the man to repeat his name.

'Hassan Rana,' he sighs. The interviewing officer takes a quick note, checks a glance from his colleague stood by the door, and they get down to the interview proper. The room is cold, and under the fluorescent lighting the prisoner looks blue, corpse-like.

RULE OF SEEING NO.61
An object may be viewed under various conditions. It may be illuminated by sunlight, a fire or a harsh electric lamp. In each of these examples, the colour of the object will vary.

Sighted people don't notice this. They have learned 'colour consistency'. To them, an apple always looks red, day or night, under the sun or by candlelight. To Nova, the pale blue of

Hassan Rana's face is unnerving. He looks unhuman – a god or a demon. Her heart is beating so hard she thinks someone is bound to notice.

Nova has been working for the police for ten years, full-time for seven. In her own voice she has related the words of arsonists, murderers and rapists. Of course she never knows, when she is interpreting for them, whether they are guilty or not. Many of them she never hears from again, unless she is assigned to their trial. She never has a problem with the interviews, other than initial nervousness that their aggression might be directed at her instead of the officer. But most of them are on their best behaviour.

This isn't the first interview she has done since the operation. She does a lot of them from home, over the phone. But the more important or complicated interviews are done in person, and this is the first time she has been into the station. She came in with her dark glasses but without her white stick.

Now the walls of the room are washing in and out, and the patches of colour that make up the man in front of her swim over each other like oil on water. She could have kept her dark glasses on, but everybody at the station knows about her operation and seems to think she has already recovered. Nova accepted their congratulations and left the glasses off, even though her new sight is more hindrance than help.

The officers took turns to be 'seen' by her for the first time, finding her reactions to their faces hilarious, as though she was revealing some truth about their appearance that others were too polite to articulate – big nose, receding hairline, ruddy cheeks. Nova wanted to tell them that what she saw was anything but accurate, and changed from minute to minute, but she hardly had the words to describe what she was seeing, even to herself.

'What were you doing in the Sunny Morning corner shop, Brixton, at 10.36 p.m. yesterday, Mr Rana?' the officer asks, facing him.

The prisoner doesn't look at him, but at Nova. The question is unhurried. In the brief, Nova was told that there were five witnesses and good CCTV footage showing him holding up the store, then beating the owner around the head with a baseball bat. This interview is a formality.

She translates the question, making an effort to look Mr Rana in the eye, which Alex told her is important. He is handcuffed, wearing a white T-shirt stained brown with dried blood (his own), and is bandaged around the head. The raid was stopped by a shopper, who clubbed him with a jar of dill pickles as he emptied the till.

When Nova finishes the question, the man keeps staring.

'Would you like me to repeat the question?' she asks.

'No,' he replies in Urdu. Hassan Rana doesn't say anything for a long moment, breathing loudly through his nose, which was recently broken. Finally, he asks, 'Why are you looking at me like that?'

Nova flicks a look at the officer, but is unable to read his expression. She starts to panic, unsure what to say. For a moment, she looks down at the floor. The plastic tiles are a shape she remembers – a hexagon. So many of them, fitting together perfectly. The shape of cells in a beehive. Nova can hear a buzzing, and wonders if it's only in her head. She looks back at Hassan, forcing herself to focus.

'I'm sorry . . . I used to be blind.' The words come out before she can realize how badly judged they are.

'What's he saying?' the officer asks, irritated.

'Sorry. He's asking where I'm from.' She plays for time, aware that for the first time in ten years, she has lied in a recorded interview. 'Give me a minute,' she says, aware that she isn't supposed to lead proceedings.

'All right.' The officer shrugs.

Nova turns back to Hassan, who seems to be smiling, though she can't be sure. There are things similar to a smile. The buzzing is louder.

'You used to be blind? What is this, a police trick?'

'No, it's true . . . I've done this job for years, but I had an operation.'

'Wow,' he drawls, 'a real miracle. So tell me – what do I look like to you?'

Nova isn't sure what kind of answer he wants. He looks awful – small, cold and grey. Before she could see, people seemed bigger, somehow. Sometimes now, when she looks at the people around her, they seem to be shrinking away to nothing. She doesn't know what to say, but she knows that if another Urdu speaker listens to the recording, she's already in trouble.

'You look like you could use some help,' she says.

He sneers.

'I'm fine. I'll be looked after now. I'll be seen by doctors, given meals . . . put somewhere *safe*.' He growls the last word.

Nova makes a guess.

'You didn't do this for yourself, did you?'

He looks at her for a long moment.

'My children. Two girls. And my wife. If I can't get a job . . .' He tails off.

'That's no excuse for beating someone senseless.'

He shifts, and though Nova can't read body language, she doubts he is adopting a friendlier pose. Panic is pumping through her, rattling her half-made vision like a hurricane. The sound of bees is near-deafening. When Hassan speaks again, his words buzz.

'You know what the Qur'an says about blindnezzz? Huh?'

'I . . . I'm not Muslim.'

'I can see that.' Nova says nothing. He recites to her: "It is not the eyes that grow blind, but it *izzzz* the heart."'

Hassan Rana laughs. Her eyes are stinging. Why does this bother her so much? She wants to brush the bees away from her face. She remembers the line, remembers the first time she read it in Braille. On the lips of this criminal, this father, it becomes an accusation – Nova can see, but can't understand. Her eyes are cured, but she is still blind.

Addressing the officer now: 'I'm sorry, I . . . can't go on with this interview. He already confessed.'

Without waiting for the officer's response, she leaves.

✳

Nova doesn't exactly run from Scotland Yard. In her whole life, she has done very little running. Running means bumping into things, and it isn't something that naturally occurs to her, even under duress. Nevertheless, she hurries from the station, eyes tracing the path her feet are to take, ignoring a call of her name from behind. In her rush to be free of the building, her dark glasses are left behind – they are in her locker with an avocado salad and a can of pink lemonade.

None of that is important now, because she only wants to be away from the man and the way he made her feel. She wants to escape, as though moving quickly enough might stop the memory from forming. All she has to do is get the bus home, get back to her flat, and she will be fine. She can phone the station on her journey, tell them that she had to leave because she's unwell, something to do with the operation. They will understand. In ten years, she has been sick twice – once with food poisoning, once when she was knocked over by a cyclist and broke her collarbone.

She has made the journey countless times. But she doesn't have her stick now, and without the glasses she doesn't feel she can ask for help. Her story seems ridiculous every time she says it out loud.

She sets off, as quickly as she can, not wanting to be caught. The pavement in front of her is easy enough to follow at first, a band of pale yellow bordered by dark tarmac on one side and a red-brick wall on the other. But by the end of the street the path breaks up – there are pale patches, strips of tarmac, dark squares of drain cover.

Nova hesitates, like a gymnast balancing on a beam. It's too much – she can't tell what is solid and what is space. She can hear and feel the street rushing around her. One wrong move and she might be washed away. This walk has never been difficult before.

She tries to tune out what she is seeing, to think about how she has moved and how far she has walked, and where that would put her in her mental map. Before, the map was clear, but now all this foggy light has rushed into her head. She looks around again, trying to find something that might give her bearings. Huge forms tower around her, prickling with straight lines and dark squares. The buildings seem to get closer the longer Nova looks at them, looming like gigantic waves – waves made of glass and stone and metal, heaving gelatinously, ready at any moment to crash down on her head.

Her heart is beating too fast, propelled by the same awesome fear she felt back when she first saw the doctor's face. She screws her eyes shut and breathes slowly, trying to pull her heartbeat into sync with the rise and fall. She tries to forget what is waiting for her behind the closed door of her eyelids.

'Excuse me, excuse me, 'scuse me, 'scuse?' The voice is cracked, and very close to her shoulder. 'Spare a quid, love?'

Nova opens her eyes and looks at the beggar. She can't tell if it's a man or a woman. Their face is dark with grime, and the body next to her is an even brighter patchwork than the city – neon green, pink and yellow. There is a terrible smell, but that is behind the vision. Eyes burn in that dark face, terrible eyes. An eager hand grabs her sleeve and tugs Nova as though trying to bring her closer to the vision.

'I'm sorry, I . . .' Nova stumbles away, terror tightening around her like a second skin. The buildings are crashing down.

'Come on, love, don't be tight . . . hey, you all right?'

Nova crumples to the floor. She can't breathe. She doesn't know what is happening. She has never felt like this before. Without an explanation, she assumes that the beggar must have grabbed hold of her, and is squeezing the air out of her chest. She tries to call for help, but has no air. She tries to struggle, but her body has gone numb.

85

Nova blacks out, thinking of swimming up, back to where the air is.

✳

The cinema is five minutes' walk away, the same one they always go to, unchanged since they were kids. The colourful carpets are stained with a million spilled soft drinks, the plaster of the faux art deco lobby is crumbling, and the whole place has an ingrained smell of stale popcorn. Basically perfect.

There are only two screens, one showing a gaudy kids movie that has been out for a month, the other an action blockbuster. Vi and Kate haven't shared many interests since they were five – Vi likes *Vogue* magazine, country and western music and menacingly spicy curries. Kate hates fashion, listens to classical, and has a sensitive stomach. But they have always liked action movies, can list their favourites and rank the heroes. The movies are dumb, but that's part of the fun.

'What, no bandages?' Vi teases, striding up to Kate. 'I thought you'd come in here wheeling a drip.' Vi hugs her, which is something of an honour. 'I missed you. Don't do that again, yeah?'

'How is he?' Kate changes the subject, pointing to Vi's pregnant belly as they break away. Vi shrugs.

'Keeps kicking me in the bladder, so I guess he must be happy.'

'Men.'

'I know, right? His dad had long legs. Well, I *think* that was his dad.' Vi smirks.

'Time will tell, I guess.'

The Rules of Seeing

They each get a small box of sweet popcorn and walk into the darkened auditorium. They chat through the adverts about Kate's stay in hospital and Vi's latest checkup. Kate doesn't say anything about the argument with Tony. Vi doesn't like Tony, and it's not a conversation Kate wants to be having now.

She doesn't look at the screen until the film starts. Like some of the best, it goes straight into the action. They are in the middle of a gunfight in a half-finished tower block. Bullets ricochet off bare concrete, bodies duck in and out of sight, the game of cat and mouse rising through the building.

The view cuts to a helicopter on the roof of the building. The bad guys are trying to escape. It is the first scene, so they probably will, but Kate is still enjoying herself.

Up to this point, nobody has been hurt – bullets zip past ears, everything kept at a distance by the guns. As the chase rises another level through the tower block, one of the henchmen stays behind, hiding around a corner. When the hero rounds the corner, the henchman leaps out, pointing a gun to his head. The hero fends this off, hitting the gun right out of his hand, then punching him in the face. The henchman falls back, his head slamming into the concrete.

Kate feels her lungs contract. A wave of anxiety washes through her, radiating from her core, shivering out to her fingertips and toes, settling in her belly like acid. She tries to breathe evenly. How the image on the screen has connected with her memory, she does not know. But the two films, inside and out, played in sync, two heads slamming into the floor at the same moment.

She's not sure what is happening, only that something bad is going to happen to her, any minute now. She feels doomed.

An invisible straightjacket is tightening around her, pulling her arms in close and cramping her lungs.

The action continues on-screen, but Kate isn't looking any more. She glances sideways at Vi, who is munching popcorn and grinning at the action. She closes her eyes and thinks of returning home. She wants to be somewhere safe, but she doesn't want her friend to know that something is wrong.

If Vi notices, Kate will pretend that she fell asleep.

Eight

THE WAITING ROOM HAS eight plastic chairs. Four are taken. There are magazines on the table, but Kate has no desire to read about carp fishing or celebrity weddings. She looks at the other people who are waiting to see the neurologist.

Opposite is a woman in her fifties, clutching tightly to her handbag but otherwise normal. Two seats down from her is a young man who rocks back and forth – not in a rapid, catatonic way, but like someone on a boat. He keeps his eyes fixed on a picture on the wall, a quit-smoking poster, but otherwise seems untroubled.

The last is an old man, sat as far from the rest as possible, pressed into the corner near the door. His head is bandaged, and a dull brown patch has seeped through the dressings near the temple. His body is still, but his eyes flick about the room. Kate suspects that the man is tranquilized in some way, and that his eyes are the only parts of him still able to move.

As for Kate, what does *she* look like? She hopes that she

looks normal, but is finding it hard not to stare at the other patients. As she looks at the woman with her bag, an ill-defined dread settles on her like a shroud. She looks down at the magazines and decides that she does want to know about carp fishing after all.

Kate flicks through the year-old magazine, looking at pictures of smiling men in rubber waders. She reads a recipe for 'boilies', a kind of bait, which extolls the virtues of pineapple chunks for luring wary carp. She is almost enjoying the diversion of the magazine when she turns the page over to the centrefold. A man is holding up a tremendous fish, its scales tinselling the light, suspended by its mouth from the fishing line. The picture makes her feel sick.

Kate decides to copy the young man, deciding to fix her attention on the carpet, though. The carpet is fine – the carpet cannot feel the feet that press down on it daily, cannot feel the points of high heels or the cold mud of workmen's boots. Since the film yesterday, Kate hasn't shaken off the invisible straightjacket, making her breath shallow, her shoulders bent inward. She barely slept, and now her eyes are heavy. The carpet is fine but dull.

Her eyes are starting to droop when the door to the waiting room opens.

Kate looks up and sees a young woman being ushered into the room by a nurse. The woman has her eyes tightly closed, and it seems that she's being guided. She wears a battered leather jacket and cherry-red boots, and is about a foot shorter than Kate. She has light brown skin and a halo of dark hair, and for a moment, Kate feels as though she's about to remember a detail from a dream she had. The woman will have to sit next to someone in the waiting room, but nobody looks keen.

'Just wait in here,' the nurse says, as soon as the woman is inside the room, 'the doctor will find you.'

The door closes behind her, and the woman stands there, abandoned. Kate is about to offer her help when the woman opens her eyes.

Years before, Kate had watched a programme about glaciers in the Arctic. The top ice was white, like you expect, but then the old, deep ice had turned blue over time. Something about air bubbles being forced out until it was just pure, frozen water. That is the colour of the woman's eyes – dazzling and pure.

It's just a flash, as she scans the room, trying to get some essential piece of information. When she finds what she's looking for, she closes her eyes again, walking slowly over to the seat next to Kate, and sits down. Kate watches her for a moment out of the corner of her eye. She is very still, her eyes still closed. She is beautiful, Kate decides. Her skin is tinged pink at the cheeks. Her wavy, dark hair was tied up in a bun, but has mostly escaped. She is small and perfect like Kate is tall and ungainly.

Kate looks at the wall, where there is a defibrillator. The symbol on the box is a green heart with a white thunderbolt passing through it.

After a minute, the woman inclines her head towards Kate.

'Sorry, but do you have the time?'

Kate guesses the woman can hear the ticking of the giant clock on the wall in front of her, but has decided she doesn't want to look. Her accent is northern, Yorkshire perhaps.

'Sure. It's half-three.'

'Ah. Thanks.' The woman flashes her a grin. They sit a moment more in silence, and the woman breaths a trembling sigh.

'Are you okay?' Kate asks, immediately regretting the question.

'Peachy keen.' The woman smiles again, then pauses. 'Well, no, not really.'

Kate tries to think of something kind or consoling or just *not stupid* to say when the consultant peers out of his office and calls her name.

'Sorry, I'd better go.'

✵

Kate sits on a low wall outside St Mary's, smoking a cigarette. Behind her, the hospital towers in its shining glory. It feels almost indecent, to Kate, for the building to look so grand when such awful things are happening inside.

After the film, Kate had left Vi to walk home. When she got home, she found a pack of cigarettes and a plastic lighter in her jacket pocket. Kate doesn't smoke, but Vi had sensed she might want one. The thought of her friend's clumsy affection makes Kate want to cry, but she holds it back. That's what she feels like all the time now – always on the verge of laughing or crying, always about to embarrass herself in some way.

She has to hold it in.

She has to act normal.

Now, after the first cigarette, Kate feels a little better, more distant from her own thoughts and feelings. She considers walking, but is lightheaded from the nicotine and decides to sit a moment more. She's about to get up when someone sits down next to her.

It's the woman from the waiting room, the girl with the blue eyes. But she's wearing dark glasses now. Something stirs in Kate's memory – a face, lit by a fluorescent glow, dark glasses, an angry man – but does not surface. A nurse has ushered the woman this far, as though she really is blind. But Kate is sure she had looked around the waiting room, and chose where to sit.

'Just wait here, love, the taxis pull up right in front.'

'Thanks.'

The nurse leaves, and Kate debates with herself for a second. Her stupid question in the waiting room makes her pause. But she is drawn to the woman, not with the quick-snap of magnets attracting, but with the invisible current of a planet being lured into orbit a new sun. She watches the girl as she sits on the wall, arms hugged around her middle, bent slightly forward. It's a subtle posture, something Kate wouldn't usually notice. Looking at the girl, who doesn't seem to perceive her at all, Kate feels herself bend forward, hunching her body against the world. Watching her unseen, Kate feels protective, not predatory.

'Hi.'

'Oh, hi! I didn't know you were there.' She turns in Kate's direction.

'Sorry. We were in the waiting room together.'

'Oh sure! My name's Nova.' She puts out her hand, smiling radiantly, and Kate shakes it. 'Jillian Safinova, actually, but everyone calls me Nova.' Her hand is small and warm, like a child's.

'I'm Kate. Uh, would you like a cigarette? I don't usually smoke . . .'

'Me neither.' Nova rolls her head around as though deciding. 'But I think I'd like a death stick right now.'

Kate shakes a couple of cigarettes from the pack and pauses awkwardly for a moment, wondering if she should hand it to the girl, or place it in her mouth. Nova resolves her dilemma by pouting, and Kate carefully places the cigarette between her lips.

The strange intimacy gives her butterflies. Nova is pretty – Kate wants to take a picture so she can remember her better. She takes the neon-plastic lighter and cups the flame while Nova draws on it. They sit and smoke in silence for a minute.

RULE OF SEEING NO.68
Smoke looks alive – twisting and
puffing itself up like a grey snake.
Don't be scared.

'So . . .' Nova drawls in her soft, Yorkshire accent. 'What's driven a sweet girl like you to take up this sinful habit?'

Kate laughs, feeling awkward.

'I gave you a cigarette – you owe me.'

'Oh really?' Nova grins devilishly.

'I mean, uh, you go first.'

'All right, then.' Another drag on the cigarette. 'Get this – I used to be blind.'

'Oh.'

'Yeah. Since I was born. And then, a few weeks ago, I was

cured.' She drawls the word as though it's ironic, but Kate doesn't understand why.

'And that's not good?'

'No . . .' Nova holds the cigarette up and considers its thin, rectangular silhouette against the sky. 'Well, it's complicated.'

'I can imagine.'

'No offence, but I doubt you can. It's a *royal* pain in the arse. I can see, but not clearly yet.' She pauses, and Kate wonders if she's looking out at the passing cars, from behind her dark glasses. She wonders what they would look like to her.

'Anyway, mystery lady – your turn!'

'Oh, nothing that interesting. I hit my head and had a bleed on the brain. I'm just here for a checkup and to . . .' She trails off, feeling that she has said more than she intended to.

'To what?'

'To get some medication . . . I've just been very anxious, since the operation.' She clears her throat.

Nova doesn't reply, but reaches and pulls her dark glasses down to the bridge of her nose. Her eyes open, glittering blue in the sunlight. She considers for a moment, and Kate wonders what she's seeing. Placing the cigarette between her lips, Nova reaches forward carefully and strokes Kate's cheek with the back of her hand, just once.

Kate feels Nova's touch, and a shiver passes through her. She's relieved that the other woman probably can't see her blushing. When did she start *blushing*, anyway?

It is over in a moment. Nova closes her eyes and pushes the dark glasses back up. They smoke in companionable silence for a minute. Kate watches as the strange woman takes a final drag.

'This is done, right?' She holds up what is left of the cigarette.

'Yeah.'

Nova stubs it out on the wall and sighs.

'Thanks again.' She pauses. 'Look, I don't know if you're busy, but do you want to get a drink?'

Kate doesn't pause before saying yes.

Nine

THEY HAVE TO WALK to find a pub, and Nova takes Kate's arm. The hospital has furnished her with a pair of dark glasses, but there were no white sticks to spare, and Nova said she could manage without.

'Wow, you're tall!' she blurted out, when the two of them stood.

'Yeah.'

'Sorry, I just can't tell, sitting down.' Nova waves up at Kate as though she's on a balcony high above. 'Hellooooo there!'

Kate laughs, disarmed. They walk on as the sun starts to set – the air is warm. When they come to the place, Nova looks up and is momentarily dazzled.

'What is that?' She points.

'That? It's the sign for the pub. It's lit up.'

'Oh.'

'Because this place is called the North Star,' Kate explains. 'A star . . .'

Nova looks up, her mind crystallising around the shape –

97

A

star

with five

points, burning against the blackened brick, clearer

and brighter than anything that she has

seen before this moment,

a point that seems to sizzle

with   white

hot   fire.

She doesn't believe in omens, but she's prepared to pretend that this is auspicious. Inside, the North Star is cool and dim and a little musty. Nova, reassured by the lack of bright light, takes her glasses off, while Kate fetches her a pint of bitter and a white wine for herself.

'Cheers.' They clink glasses and sip. The pub dog – a fat Labrador – does an orbit of their table before disappearing behind the bar like a shaggy comet. Kate looks at her companion, taking in her well-worn NASA T-shirt, the tiny heart tattooed between the thumb and index finger of her left hand, the way her cheeks dimple when she smiles.

'So, Kate, what do you do?'

'Architect.'

'That sounds like fun. It's all about triangles, right?'

'Huh?'

'Something I heard . . . a triangle is the strongest shape,

right? You can make all sorts of things out of triangles. Triangles are badass.'

Kate laughs. 'Yeah, I guess you're right.'

'So, have you designed many buildings?'

'Only one – I'm very proud of it, but it seems nobody else felt the same.'

'You should show me it sometime. Not that my opinion is worth very much. All buildings bigger than a house look . . . precarious.'

Kate laughs. 'Well, I just do interiors now. Actually, I'm renovating a flat to move into . . .' She almost says, 'with my husband', then stops without knowing why. 'So, what about you?'

'Interpreter, for the police.'

'That explains the interrogation.' Kate pauses to judge whether her joke has offended, but Nova's bullet-proof grin gives nothing away. 'What languages?'

'Arabic, French, Italian and Urdu,' Nova reels off. 'And before this palaver' – she points to her eyes – 'I was learning Russian. *Konechno*.'

'My parents are from Italy, but my Italian sucks.'

'You should practise! Everything sounds good in Italian.' She raises an eyebrow suggestively. Her blue, blue eyes open for a moment, and Kate has to stop herself from staring.

'I tried once, but I'm better at maths than words. I like shapes – you don't have to explain a triangle to someone.'

'You do to me! But I know what a triangle looks like now. And a circle, and a square. The others I can figure out with a bit of thinking.' She sounds proud.

'Humour me – you've learned, what, five languages? Why is learning to see so difficult?'

Nova turns the pint glass around in her hands, thinking.

'Because . . . it's like trying to learn all five languages at the same time. Because it's like all of these conversations are going on simultaneously – colour and depth, shape and texture, light and dark – and I'm trying to translate them all at once.'

'That sounds like something that would drive a person to drink.'

'*Mais oui.*' Nova drains her beer. 'Like, right now, with my eyes closed, I'm finding it easy to listen to what you're saying. But if I were looking at your face at the same time, I would see your lips moving, head nodding, eyelashes flicking. It would be distracting.'

RULE OF SEEING NO.78
Watching someone while they talk is like hearing an echo – the image lags behind the words. Sighted people do not experience this.

'Wow . . .' Kate is lost for words.

'But, hey, I think it'll get easier.' Nova chuckles – a habit of hers when she feels she's made someone uncomfortable. 'I'm coming up with these rules in my head, to help me remember it all. *The Rules of Seeing.*'

Nova hasn't mentioned the rules to anyone before, and she's not sure why she does now. Kate is silent for a moment, thinking.

'That reminds me of a book my dad bought me when I was a kid. We were on holiday in Venice, and he got me this Italian book on drawing called *Impara a Vedere.*'

The Rules of Seeing

'*Learn to See?*'

'It's from a Da Vinci quote. It was on the inside cover . . .' Kate closes her eyes and tries to remember. '*Impara a vedere. Renditi conto che ogni cosa è connessa con tutte le altre.*'

Nova thinks for a moment, then interprets – 'Learn to see. Realize that everything is connected to everything else.'

Kate smiles. 'Everything is connected – I always liked that. The trouble was, my Italian was always rubbish, so I never got much out of the book except for the pictures.'

'You draw?'

'Yeah. Well, I used to. I liked to paint, but I gave it up. I guess I draw enough things for work.'

'Drawing is crazy. I don't know how you can take all of this' – Nova gestures vaguely around the room – 'and put it all on a flat piece of paper. It seems like a magic trick. You shouldn't give it up.'

Kate feels heat in her chest and ignores the comment. 'I'm sure you'll be able to, with practise.'

'Hm, you never know. I should just practise the seeing bit first.'

'How do you practise?'

'Well, they gave me these cards . . .'

Nova reaches into her bag, pulls out three playing-card-sized packs, and lays them on the table. On the packs are the words SHAPES, OBJECTS and BODIES, with the same written below in Braille.

'What are they?'

Nova opens the first pack – SHAPES – and hands the cards to Kate. On one side, there is a picture of a simple shape: a square, a triangle, a spiral. On the reverse of each card is the name of the shape, along with the name in Braille.

'They're pretty cool, actually, like a kid's dictionary.' Nova's good cheer sounds forced.

Kate opens the other packs. OBJECTS is a mixture of manmade items and natural forms: kettle and oak leaf, toothbrush and mushroom. BODIES is full of human body parts: hands, eyes, lips, plus a selection of the more common animals: cat, pigeon, squirrel.

'Want me to tell your fortune?' Nova shuffles the cards.

'Sure, I guess.'

Nova picks a card at random from each of the decks, places them face-up on the table and peers down.

'Is that a triangle?'

'Yeah.'

'Ha – there you go, Miss Architect!' She looks a moment longer, while Kate watches her face. 'I can't figure out the other two.'

'That one's a baguette and the other's a knife.'

'Oooooh!' Nova intones, putting her hands to her temples as though a vision is appearing. 'You're going to give up your job as an architect. Then you'll rent a garret in the Latin Quarter of Paris, retrain as a sous chef in a sexy new bistro, and shack up with the nubile dish washer.'

'Sounds like me.' Kate laughs.

'You want another drink, to toast your career change? My round.'

'Sure.'

Nova navigates to the bar and orders two more drinks, and two whiskies, abandoning any pretence that she's drinking other than to get drunk. Okay, maybe there's *one* other reason. She was sure that flirting was easier before, but at least she doesn't have to ask Kate where the toilets are. She recognizes the pictograph for the ladies' loos, though can't see how it looks anything like an actual lady. She carries the drinks back on a tray. Kate accepts the whisky, laughing, and knocks it back with a wince.

'So, you were blind from birth?'

Nova chases her whisky with a sip of beer and nods solemnly. 'Yep, that was me. I could see colours, a little bit. Just this big, fuzzy world, like the inside of a duvet.'

'You make it sound nice.'

'It *was* nice.' Nova nods, and Kate can hear the tightness in her voice. 'I didn't have much to complain about. Though meeting girls was a pain in the ass.'

Kate registers 'meeting girls', but says nothing. Another moment where she could mention Tony. It passes.

'So, does it help, the drinking?' Kate changes the subject.

Nova sips her beer thoughtfully.

'This is a preliminary experiment. If successful, I might begin a full-scale observational study. How about you?'

'Hm . . .' Kate looks around the room. 'I've a sneaky suspicion it's making things worse. She leans forward to rest on the table, breathing in Nova's musky perfume, and her head swims.

'If not beer, maybe cigarettes are the way to go.'

'Or hard drugs.'

'Aw, cheer up, sparky! At least that knock on the head didn't kill you. Then you wouldn't be here, enjoying a drink with another attractive fuck-up like me.'

Nova tries with all her energy to perceive if her flirting has worked. This would definitely be a good thing to get better at.

Kate sips her drink and – Nova thinks – smiles.

'Very true.'

✳

They leave when office workers start to fill the pub, but this means travelling at rush hour. They say goodbye and Kate puts her hand out to shake, but Nova has other ideas, pulling her into a hug. Her face buries into Kate's breastbone, then Nova pushes up on tiptoes and plants a kiss on her jawline. Kate mumbles goodbye and the two go in opposite directions.

✳

Nova somehow finds standing space on the Tube, pressed on all sides by other commuters. She's desperate for a pee. Opening her eyes, she can see all the people in the carriage, their tight-packed heads like hairs lining a gut. The train moves slowly, in laboured peristalsis, until finally they arrive at her stop, the last on the line.

The streets of Brixton smell bad, the run-off from the fish stalls and cast-off vegetables in the bins heating and fermenting in the summer heat. Nova feels woozy from booze and the Underground, rebreathed air. At the hospital, they'd told her she'd had a panic attack and given her Valium. The neurologist told her to avoid crowded spaces and try to integrate her new sense bit by bit. She wanted to tell him that there was no 'bit by bit', but it didn't seem worthwhile. It's not like there are any alternatives.

She walks past one of the fish stalls, slowing to take in the display. There are row upon row of silvery-bright lozenges (presumably fish), cancerous nodules that she knows are crabs, and red-mesh bags of blackish lumps that she guesses are mussels. They are resting on a shimmering bed of nothingness – Nova can't see the crushed ice, only the way it bends and buckles the light like heat haze.

She turns the corner to her road and sees a shop sign, in high, yellow letters. She has learnt the shapes of the Roman alphabet, but is slow to recognize them. As she walks, the words become clear: SUNNY MORNING. It's the shop that Hassan Rana tried, unsuccessfully, to burgle. Nova thinks of him, back in his cold cell, with the blue light staining him corpse-like. Her breathing speeds up, and for a moment she thinks of the arms of the phantom beggar squeezing the air from her chest.

Inside her flat, Nova triple locks the door, draws the curtains, and swallows a Valium with some cold water. She sits on the sofa and waits for the tension to melt out of her. It duly does, on order and on time, leaving her calm and liquid, pooling comfortably into the hollows of her sofa. She puts her head down, the pull of sleep lapping over her. Before she sleeps, the last thing she thinks about is Kate.

Nova can't recall anything about how the other woman looked – she is still completely face-blind, but for most people she might remember their hair colour or if they had a prominent mole. She remembers precisely Kate's voice, which carries all the attributes that sighted people read into an 'honest face'. Her voice is not deep, but seems anchored inside her somewhere, gentle without being quiet. Nova feels safe with a voice like that.

The *absolute* last thing she thinks, which causes her to bob back up for a second into wakefulness, is that they have arranged to meet again.

'My phone is dead.' Kate had said and, for a moment, Nova assumed she was making an excuse. 'But I've got a pen, if you know your number?'

'Yeah, I do.'

Kate had taken a beermat and scribbled it down.

'I'll send you a message.'

Nova smiles at the memory, then sleeps.

✳

The flat is quiet when Kate gets home. The whisky and wine are sloshing around in her, but she hasn't minded until now. Suddenly she is scared without knowing why. She is scared of being found out, but by whom? And for what? The flat feels empty. She starts to walk down the hallway when Tony calls out.

'You're back?'

Kate freezes, heart hammering. 'Yes, it's me.'

Kate is sure that she can't be this afraid of the man she married two years ago. She steadies herself with one hand on the passage wall. She looks at the pictures in frames on the wall – holidays in Greece; her own feet sticking over the edge of a boat; standing with a group of friends at a wedding, their own wedding; cutting the cake; standing under a lichgate as paper confetti rained down on them.

Kate thinks of all the people who were there that day – family, friends, colleagues. She remembers all the eyes watching her at the altar, feeling ungainly in her dress – too tall, too broad, too *much* to be a bride. She thinks of all those happy faces, all those kind words. She thinks of the earnest words she spoke.

Her mind moves without her permission these days. It seems like an animal, pacing inside her skull, wanting to get out. If she could just find a way to open the cage, maybe she could get some peace. She takes a deep breath.

I don't want to think about this now.

She walks down the corridor, pushing open the door to the living room and kitchen. Tony is at the dining table, reading papers with a coffee in front of him.

'Still working?'

'Nothing important, just keeping on top of things.' He starts to gather the pieces of paper, but leaves them there in a pile on the table, not hiding anything. Maybe it's the whisky, but Kate feels an urge to reach out and take the paper and read whatever's written on it, just to show she can.

'You've been gone ages.'

'Yes. The hospital took a while . . .' She thinks about lying to him, but she knows he will pick up the alcohol on her breath.

'And then I went to the pub.'

'The pub? Is it that bad?' He laughs.

'No, no . . . I just needed to relax.'

'Did you go with Vi?'

'No.' She searches for something to do with her hands, with her eyes, knowing that she's not good at lying, and especially not to him. But he seems not to notice. Things seem more normal, though Tony hasn't gotten up from his chair to hug her. Still, Kate feels calmer, as though she could slip back into her old life. She walks over to the table and sits down.

'What did the doctor say?'

'Nothing. Just that I'm still recovering.'

Tony nods once, then stares at her as though trying to figure something out.

Anxiety bubbles up in her, and Kate gets up again. She goes and puts the kettle on to boil, takes out a peppermint tea bag. She needs to sober up.

'Did you say you went to the pub on your own? You were gone a long time.'

His hand is on her arm, making her jump. He holds her bicep between thumb and forefinger. It doesn't hurt, but the gesture feels strange, like something you'd do to a skittish animal. Kate turns to face him. 'No, actually. I went with somebody I met at the hospital.'

'A man?' Tony's eyebrow is raised, and there is still the hint of a smile on his lips, but Kate feels she is in dangerous territory. He lets go of her arm. Tony is protective of her around other men, but also likes to make a joke out of the idea that she could be seeing anyone but him.

'No, a woman. She's seeing the same doctor as me. We both had a hard day.'

Tony nods once, his interest visibly fading. She hates how he can tell when she's telling the truth. She hates that he was worried about her going to the pub with another man, but the other woman doesn't interest him. She's angry that Nova doesn't interest him.

Nova is everything that Kate isn't – confident, clever with words, graceful. The whisky is catching up with her. She feels grotesque, lurching around the kitchen. She wants to shrink down, down, down, until nobody notices her any more.

She makes the peppermint tea and carries it through to the bedroom. She sits on the edge of the bed for a while, too tired to move. Slowly she gets ready for bed, undressing, putting on a comfortable cotton nightdress that Tony doesn't like, brushing her teeth and getting into bed.

Kate reaches for her alarm, then remembers tomorrow is the weekend. Then she remembers that, in any case, she's signed off work for another week. She thinks about going back to the kitchen, to tell Tony that she's going to bed. But there's no sound from the kitchen, and she isn't in the mood to talk. Life has become a bad dream, and if she goes to sleep, maybe she can wake up from it.

She hovers by the bed for a second, then goes to the bottom drawer of her bedside table. Under old photographs and loose paperwork is a hardcover book, *Impara a Vedere by Giovanni Mezzasalma.*

The familiar pictures on the cover – Vitruvian Man, an unfurling flower, the golden ratio superimposed over a seashell – are faded with age. She wonders if, in the lines of Italian that she cannot read, Nova might find the rules of seeing she's looking for.

Kate opens the cover. There, above the Da Vinci quotation, a message scrawled in English – *To Katerina, Happy 9th Birthday! Keep practising until you learn to see. Love, Dad xxx*

She blinks a few times, then flicks through the book until a picture falls out. The drawing, done in pencil, is quite good – a sketch of some Venetian apartments on a canal, with mooring masts sticking up out of the water. The colours, crudely daubed over the sketch in watercolour, are obviously not by the same person who drew the picture. Kate remembers asking her father for a sketch that she could colour in with her new paint set, watching him work, head against his shoulder, his flannel shirt soft against her cheek.

She puts everything away, gets into bed, turns off the light, pulls the duvet over her and lies in the dark, feeling the empty space next to her.

✳

Saturday dawns. Tony is on shift, Kate is left to mooch around the house. Outside, the June sun barely struggles through a thick cloud layer. Kate turns all the lights on, puts the radio up loud, but still feels as though the house is a diving bell, and the grey air is pressing in on all sides. She doesn't want to be alone, but doesn't want to be with anyone either.

At lunchtime, for twenty minutes, she sits at the kitchen table with a piece of paper in front of her. She has a pencil in her hand, poised over the paper as though waiting to record something that is about to happen. But nothing happens.

She goes to the hall and finds the jacket she wore the day before. From the inside pocket, she pulls out the beermat with Nova's number scribbled in biro and stares at it for a long time. Then she goes through the pockets of her coat, pulling out used tissues and old receipts and takes all of them to the kitchen. The bins are squeezed into the cupboard under the kitchen sink. Kate opens the cupboard and throws the scraps of paper, including the beermat, into the recycling.

Ten

November

'OKAY. YOU KNOW THE drill – I just want you to pick up the balls and put them into the bins that match their colour.'

Nova looks around the room and sighs. There are four coloured bins, and many coloured balls, littering the floor, chairs and tables. It has been seven months since her operation. Seven whole months. Summer has faded into memory and the air outside has a bite.

'Come on, Jillian, I know you can do this.'

Nova doesn't correct the use of her first name. She's too tired. She's always tired, these days. She doesn't make jokes. She doesn't flirt. She feels like a zombie.

Dutifully, Nova makes her way around the room, picking up balls, one in each hand, examining them for colour and placing them in the correct bin. She is getting better at picking the balls up. She still has no depth perception, but the objects themselves stay in the right places, and don't swim around.

The first two balls are red and yellow, and, having remembered these two colours, she sticks to red and yellow for the next few, trying to keep things simple.

'Change it up, Jillian.' The nurse says.

Nova grits her teeth and carefully picks up two more. They are different colours, that much she can see. After some thought, she remembers blue and green, but can't remember which way around they go. Blue and green are like foreign words that sound similar but mean very different things. Blue is the ocean, and ice, and the sky (though how ice and the sky can be the same colour, she doesn't know. How can you even see the sky? Isn't the sky just *nothing*?). Green is the colour of trees, grass and mint-chocolate ice cream.

She places one of the balls in a bin, not really knowing if she's right.

'Nope, try again.'

Nova sighs audibly, clenching her fists. She hates this, too – how she is grouchy all the time. She used to pride herself on being a cheery person. Fun to be around. She has one more month of going to the hospital on weekends. She's exhausted, but she has to make the most of this time.

She picks the ball out of the bin and prepares to try again.

The last thirty or so of Nova's Rules of Seeing consist of definitions of objects. For instance:

RULE OF SEEING NO.92a
A tree is an object, but it contains <u>other</u> objects, such as leaves.

RULE OF SEEING NO.92b
A leaf is an object, even on the tree, because it holds the certainty of one day being separate.

But then she saw a picture of Venus Williams holding a tennis racket and wondered: why is Venus-Williams-holding-a-tennis-racket not an object, despite them being connected, like a tree with its leaves? Of course, she knows how a hand picks up a tennis racket or puts it down. She has done it herself, when Alex played in school. She would strum the strings as though she were playing her dad's guitar. The real thing was locked up because she kept strumming too hard and breaking strings.

But this does not help when learning to see one thing as separate from another – two bodies interacting in the realm of Newtonian physics. What she can *feel* does not translate to what she can *see*. People holding coffee mugs look as though they have a strange, extra appendage for containing fluid. A woman wearing a feathery hat seems to have plumage. When objects separate, it looks to her like a cell undergoing mitosis. When they come together, they form a seamless whole. She can't understand the illusion, any more than she can understand how she sees a three-dimensional world as flat.

Still, she keeps trying, hoping that logic will fix the problem.

RULE OF SEEING NO.105

Objects are separate when they are not firmly attached, such as apples in a bowl, or a T-shirt on a body.

And, confident in this definition, she goes on:

RULE OF SEEING NO.106
An object is whole when it is continuous, without borders. For example: the sea, Mount Everest, a human body.

But doubt creeps in – what about when the sea goes out, leaving part of it behind on the land? When does Everest turn into another bit of the Himalayas? When does the water she drinks become a part of 'Nova'? When does the water stop being part of her? When she pisses it out? The whole thing is absurd. So she scratches it all out (metaphorically speaking, because this is all still in her head), and goes back to:

RULE OF SEEING NO.92

There are no such things as objects. Things come together and fly apart. Every solid thing is made of tiny pieces. Attaching a label to any of these things is a matter of convention.

It's the book that does it. She's sitting by one of the windows in the stroke rehab ward, and it's sunny outside, she can tell, but there is a blind drawn over the window to make the light soft. Alex will be here to pick her up soon, and she's keeping her eyes shut until then. She's found a Braille book in the tiny ward library, an abridged *Wuthering Heights*. She's read it before, but she's happy to have found it again. She just wants something to take her mind off training.

Except she can't seem to focus on the words. Her finger runs smoothly over the shapes of the Braille at first, but then she finds she can't remember what she just read. She goes back and starts again. After a couple of lines she is lost and starts over. She is concentrating hard this time, so it is not a lack of focus that stops her after a couple of words.

Was that word 'desolation' or 'isolation'? Or something else? She traces over the word again, and instead of becoming clearer, it seems to melt away, as though her finger is wiping the dots clean off the page.

Nova is not a superstitious person. She does not have lucky numbers, pieces of clothing or charms that she carries with her. She does not have unlucky days of the year or certain events that spell doom. She believes in reason. And yet she is beginning to think of her vision as something separate from her, something separate and sentient.

Malevolent.

Her vision is a clever parasite, eating away at every part of her – her ability to go out on her own, her ability to follow a conversation, and now her ability to read.

When Alex arrives, she doesn't notice him standing near her.

'Jillian? Jilly Bean?'

Her eyes are open, she's looking at a picture of ocean waves on the wall, and she's crying so calmly that Alex assumes she is not upset at all, but experiencing some kind of rapture, a private vision.

✦

'Right. Okay.'

Kate speaks small words to herself, no more than reassuring sounds. She's standing in the downstairs hallway of
their building, with a canvas bag slung over her shoulder.
Fiddling with the strap on her umbrella, trying to tie it
neatly together, she waits for the right moment to step onto
the street.

She can do this. Just yesterday she went all the way to
the chemist to pick up a prescription. It wasn't easy, but
she fixed her eyes on the pavement and it was okay. Today
feels different. Every time she thinks of pushing through
the door there is the sound of high heels tapping by, or
someone talking into their phone, or a burst of schoolboy
laughter, and she stops. The patch of stubble on the back
of her head has grown long, but the fear is still there. She's
sweating.

'Right . . . *right*.'

She takes a deep breath, shoves the umbrella in her coat
pocket, opens the door and steps out.

There is a blare of a sound as a passing ambulance switches
its siren on. Kate jumps, pulling her arms into her sides, but
the ambulance is already gone. She's shaking, but she refuses
to go back inside now. She clears her throat and sets off down
the street. It's just a few things for dinner, something to make
for Tony. She tried to do an online shop, but there were no
delivery slots.

Kate keeps her eyes down, studying the paving slabs, but
the path between the buildings and the road is narrow, and
she needs to look up occasionally to avoid people.

She checks her left arm. It's covered by a black cardigan,

but she wants to make sure the bruises aren't visible in the light.

They're nothing, really.

Tony apologized straight away.

She used to be clear on this – if Tony ever hit her, ever hurt her, she would leave. She always said this matter-of-factly to herself. It had been hypothetical, but she had no doubts.

But why would she leave, over something so small? He'd had a drink – it was nothing, not even a hit – he'd shoved her out of the way in frustration. Just a stupid moment.

Nothing to end a marriage over.

The first person she sees is an old man, stooped with age, in a worn-out waxed coat. Kate imagines her back bending, the spaces between vertebrae compressing, bones grinding together. She passes the man and he peers at her through bushy brows. He says nothing, but Kate feels that he's judging her.

The next people she sees are a mother and toddler. The mother is slightly behind, pushing an empty pram, laden with shopping. The toddler (mostly eclipsed by her puffy pink jacket) is running ahead, and comes within a metre of Kate before she trips and falls forward, scraping her hands on the wet pavement. Kate stops dead in shock. It takes a moment of silence for the toddler to react, then she bursts into tears and Kate feels like she is about to cry herself. She's so shocked that it takes her a moment to hear the mother's sarcastic, 'Just stand there, don't mind us.'

Too late, Kate bends down to help the screaming child, but the mother has caught up, and shoos her away. Kate walks on, but now she feels shaky.

She has hardly walked any distance, only about a third of the way to the shop, but every step feels like she's stretching a cord linking her to the flat. The elastic is getting tighter and tighter, so that even standing still requires effort. Is she becoming agoraphobic? Her doctor warned her that the Valium she's taking could cause agoraphobia, and to be careful of taking it too often. But what counts as too often?

She works from home now, only has to go into the office to meet new clients or make presentations, which is rare. Tony had encouraged her to press for it. 'Why do you need to go in, anyway?' She had been grateful for the encouragement, and the new arrangement had seemed a blessing, to begin with. Now she wonders if she has made a mistake.

She struggles on a little further, until the pavement widens and she comes to the first of the shops. Breathless, she looks up, as though scaling a mountain.

The street is full of people, young and old, big and small, and Kate feels her attention drawn to each of them. She feels their feet shuffling along, feels the smoke of a grubby roll-up enter her lungs, the hand of someone else's boyfriend groping her arse. She feels a dozen second-hand things, and all of them make her feel dirty.

She stumbles forward a few more paces, focusing back on the ground, then halts. But this is a bad place to stop – sitting in the nearest doorway is a body, wrapped in blankets and a soiled fleece.

'Spare some change?'

Kate cannot ignore the man, yet she must. His voice is gentle, but she can smell him from where she's standing.

'Spare some change, love?'

Without looking, Kate rummages in her pocket and finds some change. Her breath is growing short. She turns, closing her eyes, and drops the money onto the man's blanket.

'Thanks. You all right?'

Kate straightens up, head swimming. 'Yes, fine . . . I'm fine.'

She starts to walk, quickly, and it's not for half a minute that she realizes that she's walking back in the direction of the flat, borne along by the tension in the invisible cord.

✦

Kate is lying on the couch when Tony comes home. The lights in the flat are off and she doesn't have the radio or television on.

'Hello? Kate?'

'I'm on the sofa.'

Tony walks through and turns the lights on.

'Ow, hey!' Kate puts a hand up to her eyes. 'You could have warned me.'

He frowns. 'What are you doing in the dark anyway? Got a migraine?'

Kate sits up and runs a hand through her hair. She does, in fact, have a headache, but wants to be honest. She wants to tell Tony about what happened on the street. After months of trying to cope with her anxiety in silence, she wants his sympathy. And, mirroring his sympathy, she might feel some sympathy towards herself.

'I tried to go out, but there were so many people on the street . . .' she begins, but Tony's expression doesn't soften, and she wavers.

'Have you not cooked?'

'I couldn't get to the shop for ingredients.'

'You *couldn't* . . .' he begins with a sneer.

Kate curses herself for being stupid. Why is she bothering him with her stupid feelings? It's like hearing about someone else's dream.

'I'm sorry. It was difficult . . .'

Tony stands for a second, then, as though she hadn't spoken, asks, 'So what are we going to eat?'

'We can get a takeaway?' She smiles a little.

'I can't afford to be buying takeaways all the time.'

'I'll get it – my treat.'

Tony grunts and walks out. Kate listens to him getting changed in the bedroom. On other days, she would have gone to him. Things might have been fixed with a kiss. But today she feels like she can't break through the wall between them. The wall that she put there.

Kate remembers how things used to be, before her fall, and thinks about how they are now. She has the weird sensation of not being a separate person. There are still good times, but she can only be happy if Tony is happy, only have fun if he is having fun. And she wonders – is this new? Or have we always been like this? When 'we' were in a bad mood, was it just that *he* was in a bad mood? All this time, has she been nothing but a mirror?

But no – it's obvious what has changed. Kate knows, in that moment, that the only way to make things better is to pretend. She will make changes to her life, she will do the things she needs to do to get by, and she will hide her feelings from her husband.

They are sitting on the sofa, waiting for the food to arrive, and Tony has turned the television on. He scrolls through channels, wordlessly, while Kate reads on her phone. He flicks to the news – a report about a war-torn nation – and her eyes avoid the screen like magnets repelling.

'What do you want to watch?'

She puts the phone down and looks at him.

'I dunno; I was enjoying reading . . .'

'You don't want to watch with me?'

'No, I just mean, you could stick on something that I don't need to concentrate on. Like a panel show. I dunno.'

He sighs. 'Look, if you don't want to watch anything . . .'

Kate almost tells the truth, then thinks of her new resolution.

'Forget it, I don't need to read. I just want to spend some time with you. What do you want to watch?'

'A film, maybe?'

'Sure.' Kate feels a knot tighten in her belly as he scrolls through the movies they can rent. She hears herself agree to a film, but cannot remember the title a moment later. It's an action film.

'I'll just pop to the loo.'

Kate goes through to the bathroom, opens the cabinet, hooks her fingernails under the white hardboard back, and lifts it a crack. There is a space between the cabinet and the wall, with several foil cards of medication stuffed inside. Kate ignores the green rectangle of contraceptive pills that she's still taking and fishes out a card of Valium.

She swallows three with water from the tap. A single pill makes her woozy, and she knows that three will be no fun.

But she needs something to take the edge off. Something to help her fake it. Either she fakes being a normal human being or everything she has worked for and accomplished in life will slowly crumble. The fightback starts here.

By the time she comes out of the bathroom the food has arrived, so they sit with their trays to eat on the sofa as the movie starts. From the beginning, there are explosions, gunfire, punches being thrown. Except it doesn't feel like they're watching a movie – it feels like Tony has opened a window into a war zone, and at any moment a bullet might fly through that window and strike Kate.

She tries not to look at the screen, and the food helps – she can focus on tearing a chapatti, or fishing a piece of chicken out of her korma. But she is aware of Tony looking at her. She refuses to look at him, but she knows he's watching her. Every so often she will look up at the screen when she thinks she might be safe. But the action is unpredictable – one moment she looks up and a body lunges out of the shadows.

As the drugs kick in, she starts to feel sick and stops eating. She stares at the food, but it makes her feel worse. She tries to look up at the wall just past the television, but she can see too much of what is going on. Tony's gaze keeps turning on her every so often, and she tries to concentrate. A henchman is shot in the leg, and Kate can't help but flinch this time. How did she ever enjoy this kind of violence?

'You're not going to finish your curry?' Tony asks.

'I'm not as hungry as I thought.'

Tony makes a noise, and for the first time that night she

may actually have pleased him. He doesn't like it when she overeats. Kate always tells herself that this is part of how he cares for her – that he's looking out for her. But now she's just irritated. Angry, all of a sudden. Angry that she's being made to watch this stupid film. Angry that everything she says is doubted – that her husband thinks she's crazy.

Ignoring the churning in her stomach, Kate picks up her fork and starts eating again.

Tony says nothing, but she can tell that he's watching her. A mortar shell explodes. Kate shovels a mouthful of chicken and rice into her mouth and barely chews before swallowing. Tony scratches his nose. An enemy fighter is knifed in the chest. Kate reaches for a poppadum, which breaks into shrapnel in her fingers. Tony makes no noise. Another enemy, standing on a ledge, is killed by a single shot to the head, his brains springing from his head like a party popper.

Kate stops, feeling that she is teetering on a precipice. She puts her tray down quickly, runs to the bathroom and vomits into the toilet. She flushes once, then vomits again, a mixture of rice, chicken and half-dissolved pills. She is trembling, slick with sweat.

Propping herself on the sink, she turns on the tap and watches the water spiral. This is what water does when it falls – it spirals. Those spirals have carved out valleys and caves and Kate thinks of these natural forms, losing herself in the ever-falling water.

She's been there for about five minutes when she hears a noise from the bathroom door. Thinking that Tony has finally come to check up on her, Kate turns her head. But the door is still shut. She turns the water off, just in time to hear footsteps in the hallway, and the sound of the front door opening, closing, and being locked.

'Tony?'

No response. Smoothing out her blouse, Kate unlocks the bathroom door and turns the handle. The handle turns, but the door doesn't open. Thinking that it is jammed, Kate kicks the door lightly, near the floor. It doesn't budge. Holding the handle, Kate swings herself back and slams her shoulder into the door.

Dull pain, and the door hasn't moved an inch. She's starting to panic, and the ache in her shoulder isn't helping.

'Tony? Are you out there? Open the door.'

No reply. Has he really gone out? There must be something up against the door. Did he put it there?

Kate rattles the door, but it's not opening. There is no window in the bathroom, just an extractor vent to stop it steaming up. She starts to pace over the tiles, back and forth in the tiny space. Something like fear is stopping her breathing – she can't draw a full breath, can't feel the satisfaction of her lungs stretching out.

Back and forth, back and forth . . .

If she keeps pacing she can ignore the pressure on her chest.

✳

Much later, Kate wakes with a crick in her neck. Why does her neck hurt? She is lying on the bathroom floor. The cold of the slate tiles has bled into her. Standing, she goes to the bathroom door and grips the handle.

The door opens smoothly.

Kate emerges from the bathroom. Everything in the hall is as it was. The television is off and the plates have been cleared into the kitchen. The bedroom door is closed – later, Tony will tell her that he went to bed early. He will tell her that the bathroom door must have jammed.

She goes to the kitchen, where the under-cabinet lighting illuminates the room like a shop that's been shut for the night. She runs a glass of water and sits at the kitchen table, thinking about nothing. Her mind is blank, as though she vomited everything up.

When reality bleeds back, Kate stands and scrapes the plates into the bin. She loads and runs the dishwasher, then washes out the foil containers in the sink. When she comes to put them in the recycling bin, it's already full, so she fetches a plastic bag from the cupboard and empties the tins and wine bottles into it.

Something catches her eye, in the shadowy space behind where the recycling bin sits. There is no back to this cupboard – the pipes from the sink and the dishwasher are exposed, and there's a gap at the back where things sometimes get lost. Kate takes out the bins and fishes in the cobwebbed space behind them. She pulls out the thing that caught her eye – a used tissue. Then, because she's already put her hand in there, she feels around for anything else.

She finds a crisp packet, the foil top from a milk bottle and . . .

A dark square. Kate's breath catches. She takes the square from the cupboard. Not a white square, but a dark one.

It's a beermat.

A beermat with a number written on it. It must have fallen behind the recycling bin when she threw it in. Five months ago.

Kate holds it for a moment, as though she's found a loaded gun, then carefully places it on the kitchen table. She finishes putting the recycling away, wipes down all the surfaces with antibacterial spray, washes her water glass and puts it on the rack. Then she sits down at the table again, types the number from the beermat into her phone, and starts to write a message.

Hi, Nova, this is Kate. We met at the hospital. I'm really sorry I've been ignoring you . . . things have been crazy. I was wondering if you'd like to go out some time? x

She hits Send, then sits in the twilight of the kitchen, staring at the bright screen. After five minutes, she puts her phone away and goes to brush her teeth. It's the middle of the night – no way she's getting a reply now. Just as she's about to push the bedroom door open, she feels the phone buzz gently against her leg like an animal rubbing against her. She jumps.

Hey there, invisible woman. Didn't think I'd hear from you again.

Kate is already typing as she walks back to the kitchen.

I know, I'm so sorry. I'm an idiot. Let me make it up to you?

She watches, holding her breath, until she sees that Nova is typing a message. Does she type? Kate doesn't know. Maybe she dictates. Or maybe she can type now that her vision has improved. A flurry of messages come through.

You're not an idiot.

Want to take me to the zoo?

I want to see a giraffe, because I'm pretty sure they're a cruel hoax aimed at blind people.

The Rules of Seeing

Kate is already laughing, and the knot in her stomach loosens as she types back.

Shit, you've called our bluff.

I knew it!!!

Eleven

December

'HAVE YOU BEEN TO a zoo before?'
'Once, when I was very young. Some charity
arranged for us blind kids to come and handle the animals. I
held a corn snake – it was cool, like a bar of soap, but then
it moved . . .'

Nova is dressed in a shirt with the sleeves rolled up, grey
waistcoat and matching trousers, with a faux-military coat with
gold brocade that makes her look like a pirate. Kate is wearing
a blouse with a tweed skirt. It's a work outfit, one that Tony
approves of. She feels dowdy, and wonders if Nova can tell.

'I never thought I'd come back here. It's not much fun when
you can't see the animals . . .'

Nova laughs, but Kate isn't sure what to say. She's wondering
why she got in touch with her again – it just seemed like a
good idea at the time. But what seemed natural in the dark
of her kitchen seems stupid in the bright sunlight of London
Zoo. It's early on a weekday, and the schools haven't broken
up for the Christmas holidays yet, so it isn't busy. Nova works

shifts and Kate has flexible hours, so a quiet day in London is one of the perks.

Kate feels the invisible cord linking her to home. It is always there, but for now it is yielding, compliant, docile. Now that she is with Nova, she hardly notices it.

Nova is wearing regular sunglasses, not the ones they gave her in the hospital. In the light, Kate can see her eyes behind the yellow-tinted glass, like another part of the zoo, something that has to be kept in the shade. She'd stood on tiptoes to hug Kate and peck her on the cheek.

'Prendiamo un caffè, bella signorina?'

'Sorry?'

'Ah, so you weren't joking about not speaking Italian.' She laughed. 'Do you mind if we get some breakfast? I'm afraid I slept in.'

They sit in the first café they find in the zoo, Nova hanging onto Kate's arm. They find a table and Kate fetches two breakfast rolls and two coffees.

'I forgot to ask if you take milk?'

'Black as night for me.' Nova says. 'Well, not the London night, you know? I was quite excited to see stars, but so far I haven't managed more than an incoming passenger jet. I did see the moon though – that was *awesome*.'

She puts her hand on Kate's arm for emphasis, and Kate feels a rush of warmth at the brief contact. Nova talks with her hands, and Kate wonders if she always did that, or if she recently learned.

'Oh yeah?'

'Yeah, though I thought it was a streetlamp at first. I had to ask someone. But then I just started crying, because there it was – the most distant thing I've ever seen, four hundred thousand kilometres away, and I can *see* it. And I'm just *sobbing* in front of this stranger!'

Nova is laughing, but Kate feels awkward and changes the subject.

'I have my coffee with gallons of milk and four sugars. Very un-Italian.' Kate sips her drink. Nova slurps hers exaggeratedly.

'Ahh, liquid love! I've been so dopey since I started taking the Valium they gave me.'

'That's what they gave me.'

'Worryingly moreish, aren't they?'

'Yeah. It's not like they do much anyway – when I go out I want to take one, but when I take one I don't want to go out.'

'What about now? No pre-date nerves?' Nova raises an eyebrow. For a second, Kate is too taken aback to say anything, then decides the younger woman is joking. She's not sure what game she's playing – why she hasn't told Nova about Tony. She's wearing her wedding ring, but isn't sure whether the interpreter can see it, or whether she understands the significance.

'I'm clean, other than cigarettes, of which I smoked two on the way here.'

'Naughty – you'll get a habit!' Nova bites into her breakfast roll – a white bap with a fried egg and brown sauce. 'So,' she mumbles with a full mouth, 'how's it going? The anxiety?'

Kate sighs – a mixture of frustration and relief to be talking about it. Somehow, she can say these things to Nova. 'It's okay. I work from home a lot . . . the radio keeps me company. I've never listened to the Shipping Forecast before in my life.'

'Ah, the Shipping Forecast! I practically live by the World Service schedule.'

'Really?'

'Sure – I don't always sleep so well. I put the radio on and listen until I drift off.'

Kate watches as Nova opens and closes her eyes. She seems determined to use her sight more, but keeps her eyes closed half the time, as though resting.

'How's it going? Fluent in seeing yet?'

Nova smiles, surprised that Kate has remembered her turn of phrase after half a year.

'Nope, not even close. It's been the best part of a year since my operation, and sometimes I feel no better than when they took the bandages off. I'm still using these' – She fishes one of the packs of flashcards from her coat – 'so I don't forget what a bloody hexagon looks like.'

'Well, you seem better, to me.'

Nova shrugs noncommittally. 'Yesterday, I spent a long time staring at a thing in my kitchen. I was convinced it was an animal that had found its way in to eat the contents of my cupboards.'

'What was it?'

'A pineapple.'

✳

They finish breakfast, Nova takes Kate's arm again, and they start to walk around the zoo. Kate watches the clouds on Nova's lips as she talks into the winter air.

'Thanks for being my chaperone.'

'Thank you for coming. People must think we're a couple,' Kate replies, immediately regretting her words. Why did she say that?

Nova flashes her a grin. 'Then people must be jealous of my cute girlfriend.'

Kate's heart leaps like a salmon jumping a waterfall.

Just ahead of them, a little girl lets go of the helium balloon she's holding – a silver heart with HAPPY BIRTHDAY in pink letters – and lets out a cry as it sails up into the air.

RULE OF SEEING NO.142
When seeing a balloon disappearing up into the sky, it is easy to feel that the balloon is stationary, and it is you who are falling. Try not to panic.

Nova squeezes Kate's arm, who searches for something to say.

'Where did you grow up?' she asks, as they study an enclosure of damp sticks and leaves that may or may not contain capuchin monkeys.

'Oop North,' Nova replies in an exaggerated accent.

'I can tell that.'

'Yeah, I'm not exactly hiding it. I grew up in Bradford. My parents are teachers there.'

'You didn't want to stay?'

Nova just shrugs.

'I dunno. There wasn't much for me to do there. Why did you want to be an architect?'

Kate, glad for the change of subject, starts to talk about the trip to Venice when she was nine, to meet her mother's relatives. They wander as she remembers.

'And I just thought – I didn't even know buildings could look like that! So colourful and pretty. It sounds dumb, but I just thought that people over here would love buildings like that, if someone would just build them.'

'Was that when your dad bought you the drawing book?'

'Uh, yeah, I suppose it was . . .' Kate says, startled that Nova has remembered this detail. 'Anyway, my mum always said that being an artist wasn't a proper job, but I still loved drawing, so when I saw those buildings, I felt like I'd discovered a secret niche I could fit into, that nobody else had fitted into before. Like nobody from England had ever visited Italy!' She laughs at the memory. 'You probably think that's dumb.'

Nova cocks her head. 'You call yourself dumb a lot, you know. And, no, I don't think that's dumb, but I don't really understand. Buildings are just buildings. You live in them. Or buy baked beans in them. Or go swimming in them.' She's grinning shyly. 'I didn't really think that buildings looked like anything. Just shapes . . . spaces.'

Kate smiles. 'Shapes and spaces – that's a very popular way of looking at architecture these days.'

'But you don't see it that way?'

'No . . . It's like music that's all drums and bass. There's a shape there. But it's missing something that brings it to life. For me. Anyway, I'm boring you.'

'No, you're not. You should relax; you don't have to entertain me.'

Kate is not sure whether this statement makes her feel better or worse.

'Anyway, you should go to Venice.'

'Oh yeah?' Nova looks at her, eyebrow quirking up.

'Yeah, you know, if you're looking for things to see. You should see Venice.' Kate can feel herself blushing.

Nova smiles.

'I'll bear that in mind.'

✳

The first outdoor enclosure they come to is the penguins, who are very active. They swim, dive off rocks and waddle from one place to another. Nova raises her sunglasses, transfixed, and Kate watches her eyes trace one, then another, as they move through the water.

'What can you see?'

'Well, are they all the same thing?'

'The same animal? Yes, they're all . . .' Kate reads the sign, 'Humboldt penguins.'

'But they look so different when they're in the water!'

'Yeah – I guess they're not best suited to walking. Here, come look at this.'

Kate leads her down a short ramp next to the pool, at the end of which is a concave glass window showing the pool underwater. As they watch, a penguin dives, corkscrewing down through the water, bubbles of air rolling off him in silvery threads.

'It's beautiful!' Nova exclaims.

Kate watches the other woman out of the corner of her eye, wanting to be the person to show *everything* to her.

Next is the butterfly house, a humid room full of tropical plants. As soon as they push through the protective plastic curtains at the entrance, butterflies flicker around them. Nova squints at the room.

'Can you see them?' Kate asks

'Not really. They move too fast against the leaves, but I can see their colours. That one's blue!'

She points to a huge, swooping butterfly, which a display tells Kate is a blue morpho. Its wings are an electric, iridescent blue. A man next to them turns and frowns as though Nova is stupid, but she doesn't notice. Kate scowls back and he turns away. They walk slowly, as zebra longwings and owl moths glide and flutter around them. A Madagascan comet moth – banana yellow and big as a hand – rests briefly on Nova's forehead, its long tails tickling her nose, before flying away again, leaving her in fits of giggles.

When the butterflies disappear behind foliage, they really disappear for Nova. When they reappear, they seem to materialize out of thin air.

RULE OF SEEING NO.147
Like a baby, you will have no idea of how an object persists in time. This seems stupid. Of course you know that a butterfly does not disappear just because you are not looking at it, but that does not mean you're not surprised – perplexed, even – when it reappears in front of you.

The aquarium is Nova's favourite. It's dim in there, but not dark, so she can see more easily. The tanks are lit from above, often casting the fish in a bright spotlight.

The Rules of Seeing

'Are these *all* fish, dude?'

'Yes.'

Nova shakes her head, dubious. 'But there are so many different colours, so many shapes! They look nothing alike!'

'Well, they all have fins, and tails . . .'

'That one doesn't!'

She points to something eel-like, which tapers like a spear at the back.

'Point taken. They all look like fish to me, for what it's worth.'

'But that's what I mean. It's like a verb conjugation table – all the words mean pretty much the same thing, but they sound completely different!'

They eventually visit the giraffes, but it takes some time for Nova to see them as complete animals. She cranes her neck up and down, scanning the details over and over. The creatures in front of her look so distorted, she must ignore the intuition that she is seeing them wrong. One of them crosses the yard towards them, spindly legs moving with grace, and pokes its blue-grey tongue into a pot of vegetables suspended above from a pole. Slowly, Nova breaks into a grin.

'That is just *wild*.'

✵

They take a break in the café, eating baguettes and drinking fruit juice, saying very little to one another. Kate can tell Nova is getting tired – she has closed her eyes behind her glasses the whole time they're eating. As for Kate, she feels lighter than any time she can remember.

They leave the café and smoke a cigarette each as they walk down a wide avenue. Kate is on the lookout for a warden who might give them a telling-off. There are more people in the zoo now, but Kate finds it easier to ignore them when there are so many animals to focus on. They see flamingos, otters and a potbellied pig. Each one has something new to offer, and though Nova is tiring, Kate always wants to show her just one more. Finally, she can tell Nova has had enough. 'Do you want to stop?'

'Yeah, I feel like I need a lie-down. What haven't we seen?' Kate scans the map.

'Not much . . . Oh, but we haven't seen the tiger yet!'

Nova laughs. 'Come on then, last one.'

They walk to the tiger enclosure, which is a long walkway with windows on either side, looking out onto greenery. There is a small pond, and some artificial rocks to climb on. It looks quite nice.

'Tigers are basically big cats, right?' Nova asks, looking at a picture of the tiger on a sign in front of the glass.

'Yeah, pretty much.'

'I think I understand them more because we used to have a cat when I was little. I think if I can touch something first, I can understand what it looks like.'

'But you can't just ask to touch a kangaroo, or a rhino.'

'Right! Full points. You'll have to tell me if you see him,' Nova says, peering through one of the windows. 'It's quite crowded in there.'

They walk down half the curving walkway, until Kate can see a group of people ahead, gathered in front of one of the windows. They join the group and find space to see. The tiger is as big as the one in Nova's imagination, paws bigger than her hands, padding the floor.

'Can you see him, Nova?'

'Yes . . . he's moving quite a bit.' Nova drops her voice into the breathy tones of a wildlife documentary. 'Prowling his domain . . .' She's tracking the cloud of orange and white and black as it moves back and forth.

In fact, back and forth is all the tiger is doing, weaving in a figure of eight, up and down the small stretch of rock. A chill enters Kate's stomach.

'What's he doing?' Nova asks innocently.

Kate tries to answer, but her lungs feel tight, like she can't breathe properly.

'Mummy, why is he doing that?' a small girl near them asks.

'I don't know, dear. Come on, let's go get an ice cream.'

'Yay!'

Kate is unable to take her eyes away from the tiger, the movement of eight hundred pounds of fluid muscle, as it walks the same path over and over again. Her legs ache, her arm aches, and she starts to feel a tremendous weight bearing down on her.

'Kate? Hun?'

Nova's voice is muffled, as though behind glass. Behind the glass of an enclosure. Kate paces, turns, paces, turns, rubbing her face against the same patch of rock each time as she goes. Her limbs feel like they are bound, but the only way to stop those bindings from getting any tighter is to keep pacing. She can't remember a time when she wasn't pacing. Tonight, she'll sleep on the cold bathroom tiles.

The panic attack has her in its grip before she knows what's happening.

'Kate, what's wrong?'

Nova shakes Kate's shoulder, pulling her attention away from the trapped animal. She looks at Nova for a moment, vision swimming, then faints.

Twelve

KATE WAKES BUT DOESN'T open her eyes. She knows where she is though; she doesn't need to see for that. The smell of disinfectant, the squeak of shoes on the plastic floor – she's in hospital. Again. It takes her longer to remember *why* she is in hospital, but when she does, she opens her eyes quickly.

Nova is sitting next to the bed, apparently reading a science magazine, though she seems to be looking at the pictures of stars and galaxies. They are in a private room, and the blinds are drawn, staining the light a soft blue. Kate shifts, feeling pain in her neck. Nova looks up at her and smiles.

'Hey, there, sleepy Jean.' She puts the magazine down and reaches over to stroke Kate's hair back from her forehead. The contact makes her shiver.

'Hey.'

'How are you feeling?'

'I'm feeling . . . like I should . . . stop falling on my head.'

'I think that might be a good plan.' Nova laughs, then her

face falls. 'I'm sorry, Kate – I should have known something was wrong. I should have got you away from there.'

'Don't be silly – you weren't to know.'

'That poor tiger.' She shakes her head (a new skill) but she's looking intently at Kate's face, as though trying to work something out. 'Oh, I forgot – the doctor told me to fetch him when you wake up.'

'Can it wait a minute? This is nice.' Kate says, then wonders why she said it – is she sedated? She should be careful about what she says around Nova. The other woman just smiles.

'Yeah, okay.'

Nova strokes her hair some more, and Kate feels like she's going to drift back to sleep. Nova clears her throat.

'Um, they called your husband . . .'

Kate's eyes snap open; she doesn't feel sleepy any more.

'They called . . .?'

'Your husband. Tony? You have one of those Medic Alert cards in your purse.'

Kate remembers – she'd been given it after her first admission, and filled it in with Tony's details. She scans Nova's face, but she's not sure what the other woman is feeling. She's stopped stroking her hair.

'Nova, I'm sorry if I . . .'

'Oh, hey, it's okay! You just never mentioned him is all.' Maybe Kate is imagining it, but she sounds disappointed.

'I thought you might have seen my ring.'

'Nah.' Nova points to her eyes. 'But it's totally fine. I'll just cancel that candlelit dinner I had planned.'

Nova grins, but Kate is too shocked to say anything. The

confirmation that – yes – the other woman *was* interested in her, makes her blush crimson. For the time being, she attributes her sense of devastation to embarrassment.

'Well, I better get you that doctor.'

The doctor arrives and runs through the battery of tests for concussion that Kate knows too well. She's advised to rest until Tony comes to pick her up. Nova disappears while all this is happening. When the doctor is gone, she returns, pushing a wheelchair in front of her.

'Where did you get that from?'

Nova smiles mischievously. 'Better not make you an accomplice to my crime.'

'O-kay.'

'How are you doing?'

'Not bad. My dignity is bruised.'

Nova smiles. 'Dignity is overrated. When you're blind, you get used to bumping into things. Usually on a date or in a job interview, in my experience. Wanna go for a joyride?' She wiggles the chair.

'The doctor said I should rest . . .'

'And rest you shall, with your very own chauffeur!'

Kate is laughing, and she can't say no when she has strung Nova along like an idiot. She eases herself out of the bed and into the chair.

'Buckle up, cowgirl – I know the way to a café. They have pots of *jelly*.'

'Do you have a licence to operate this vehicle?'

'I don't want to alarm you, miss, but I used to be blind.'

The wheelchair veers out of the room, making Kate squeal, as Nova speeds her down the corridor.

✳

'This is delicious.'

Nova is at the dining-room table, kicking her legs back and forth like a child, and Kate can't quite believe that she's here. It's like she's brought something perfect into her imperfect life.

Not for the first time, she's scared – scared that she will spoil Nova in some way. Perhaps Kate is scared that Nova's blindness was a protective barrier, that her optimism came from not being able to see how awful the world is. That's stupid, Kate knows, but still, she doesn't want Nova to change.

In a few days it will be Christmas. It's been a week since the incident at the zoo, and they haven't seen each other since. Nova made her excuses and disappeared from the hospital before Tony arrived and it had taken time for him to agree to Nova coming around for dinner.

'She's just some woman that you met at the hospital?'

'Yes, but we're friends.'

'You can have her round, but I'm not doing the cooking, okay? I have a busy day.'

'Fine, all right.'

Working from home, Kate has spent the day cooking in between replying to emails. She can catch up tomorrow. Cooking is good – it takes her mind off things. She pulled out the recipe book her mum gave her when she went to university, into which had been folded dozens of her own recipes, copied on the corner-shop photocopier. Kate made her mum's vegetable soup, her mum's lasagne and her mum's apple turnover cake. Finding she had extra time, she also made bread sticks and a jug of sangria. Nova seems to love everything Kate puts in front of her.

'It all looks so good! So different!' She grins maniacally, laughing at her own, private joke.

'Different?' Tony asks.

'Well, it's all food, right? But look, this is so . . . red? And this is so . . . white? Yellow?'

'About right.' Kate smiles, looking at the pasta Nova is pointing to.

'Amazing.' Nova smiles back, shaking her head.

RULE OF SEEING NO.151
Food does not <u>look</u> appetising, the way it <u>smells</u>. Sometimes it looks like plastic, or like dog poo. Sighted people do not like it if you point this out.

Nova had some trouble getting into the flat, negotiating her way over the patterned carpet in the hallway, which Kate's landlord had refused to replace.

'Sorry, it just looks like it's lumpy. Or full of holes. I feel like I'm going to fall through it!' She held tight onto Kate's hand, and Kate had tried not to think about how good that felt.

'Don't worry, I won't let you fall.'

They had made it to the dinner table, where Tony was waiting. He stood to greet her.

'I don't think we've been introduced, but I know your face.'

'I wish I could say the same.' Nova saluted. 'But, yeah, I've been working at the Met for seven years, so you've probably seen me around. I'm an interpreter.'

'Even though you were blind?'

'It's easy enough, so long as I can hear what people are saying.'

'And you're . . . better now?' Tony asked. Kate winced.

'I'm different now. I'm not really used to it yet.' Nova smiled reassuringly. 'Now, what's this about free food?'

❋

They are happily eating, and Kate is starting to feel okay. Nova and Tony have been chatting about the police, sharing stories about the craziest confessions they've ever heard and Tony is laughing – actually laughing – at Nova's jokes.

'And I was like, *Shit*, what is the French word for dildo?'

Nova is wiping tears from her eyes. Kate remembers what things used to be like.

'It's *godemiché*, by the way.' Nova turns to Kate and winks.

Tony raises his eyebrow, but says nothing. Nova just flashes her grin and takes another bite of lasagne. 'You're such a good cook, Kate! I can't believe you made all of this yourself.'

'Me neither,' Tony says under his breath.

'Well, I never usually have the time!' Kate says, trying to brush it off. Nova is frowning, and Kate wonders if she knows that they can see her expressions. Maybe she just doesn't care.

Sensing that Kate is looking at her, Nova smiles, going back to the delicate task of spearing pasta onto her fork. The dinner goes on, though there is less laughter than before, and Kate decides not to bring Nova home again. She will invite Nova around to the new flat instead – still mostly empty, a life waiting to begin.

✴

Dinner is over, and Nova is getting ready to leave. Kate has gone back to the kitchen to wrap up some of the apple cake for her to take home. Tony hovers while Nova pulls on her boots and jacket.

'Thanks so much for everything – it was so nice of you and Kate to have me round.'

She smiles up at him while lacing her boot. Tony doesn't say anything, and Nova can't read his expression. She stands, and suddenly he seems to have taken a step closer to her. He seems as though he's about to say something when Kate reappears.

'Here we go!' She hands over a chunk of cake wrapped in tin foil.

'You're too kind.'

'No, thank you for coming. We should do this again soon.'

'That would be nice.' Nova smiles. 'Though not too soon – I'm going on holiday.'

'Oh, where to?'

'I took your advice, actually – my friend is taking me to Venice for a month. We're going to be over there for New Year.'

Kate isn't sure why the word 'friend' bothers her so much. 'That's great; you'll have to send me a postcard.' Her words feel forced.

'Oh, that reminds me.' Nova reaches into her pocket and takes out an envelope and a parcel, which she hands to Kate.

'What is it?'

'Nothing, really, it's stupid. Oh, and sorry for my handwriting – I did it to practise.'

Kate puts the unopened present on a pile of letters on the sideboard. They part with an awkward hug, and when Kate turns back from the door, Tony has already disappeared.

✳

It's dark in the High Energy Physics building, so Nova is totally reliant on Rebecca's hand, dragging her forward through the shadows. Just as the Modern Languages building of Nova's college has its own smell, so do the corridors of the HEP department. But these smells are less easy for Nova to define – not BO and cheap disinfectant. There is something exotic about these smells. The smells of alien worlds and interstellar space. Unearthly.

Tomorrow they fly to Venice, but tonight Rebecca says she has something special to show her. Finally, she finds the door she's looking for and lets go of Nova's wrist.

'Here we are! The cave of wonders!'

She rummages in her jeans pocket, pulling out several crumpled receipts, a hair scrunchie and a small key, which she proceeds to put in the lock.

'Are we supposed to be in here?'

Rebecca pauses in the act of opening the door. 'My friend Dave gave me the key . . .'

'So that's a no?'

'That's a no. Do you want to turn back?'

Nova pauses for a moment, thinking about her answer. Finally, she shrugs.

'It's not like I can be expelled.'

'That's the spirit.'

Rebecca throws the door open and gestures for her to step through. Nova walks into the laboratory. The lights are off in here, but there's some light from the windows looking out onto a desolate, sodium-lit quad of concrete slabs, weeds and crisp packets.

'Can we turn a light on?'

Rebecca steps into the laboratory and closes the door behind her.

'Check you out, Miss "Can We Turn a Light On?" – to think of all the times I stayed in your flat when all your light-bulbs had blown.'

'Well, can we? It's dark.'

'Yes – but what we're going to do requires the cover of darkness.'

'I do not like the sound of that.'

Rebecca doesn't reply, just takes Nova's hand and leads her through the maze of workbenches. Nova can see the forms of objects on the benches like shadows in a mist. One table is covered with scientific glassware – boiling vessels and cooling towers, three-globed Kipp's apparatus and spiralling condenser coils, joined by valves and rubber piping. Nova cannot see the invisible-man glassware, only the way the light bends around it. Another table is a spaghetti dish of colourful, tangled wires.

Finally, Rebecca brings her to a table on which squats something shiny, sprouting pipes and wires. If Nova had watched more thriller movies, she might think that the thing on the table looked like a bomb.

'Here we go!' Rebecca pulls up a lab stool for Nova. 'Just sit there while I work.'

'While you work? On this thing? I thought you were a *theoretical* physicist.'

'Yeah, so?'

'So, that thing doesn't look very theoretical.'

She can't see Rebecca's face in the half-light, but she can hear the smile in her voice.

'Don't worry – I may be a bumbling theoretician, but I can do some stuff for myself. This is just a toy that they keep here to impress the undergrads.'

'And that's what we're doing, is it? Impressing the under-grads? Or one undergrad in particular?'

'Oh, shut up and let me concentrate.'

Rebecca flips a switch and a rumbling hum starts from the machinery. An involuntary shudder runs down Nova's spine, like when the hairdresser gets too close with the clippers.

'Oh, I forgot – here.' Rebecca hands her something made from clear plastic that Nova can't understand without touch.

'Goggles?'

'Yeah, put them on.'

'Why do I need to?' The shudder returns as the hum goes up a tone.

'Calm down. I'm just pumping the air out of the chamber, so there's a *veeery* small chance of implosion. We wouldn't want to hurt your lovely eyes, when you've only just learned to use them, would we?'

Nova doesn't respond, just fumbles the goggles onto her face and grits her teeth.

'What is this thing?'

'This, my lovely little supernova, is a Farnsworth-Hirsch nuclear fusor.'

'Nuclear? You're operating a *nuclear reactor*?'

'A nuclear *fusor* – there's no fissile material in there.' Rebecca turns a red tap on a gas tank, and a low hiss adds to the rumble of the compressor.

'Well, don't *I* feel safe. No plutonium!' Nova folds her arms over her chest, protectively.

'Oh, hush – you're fine.' Rebecca taps a pressure gauge, checks several things that Nova can't see, and nods. 'Okay, I'm going to turn on the power – you just look through this little window, right?'

She points through the glass of a round hatch in the body of the machine, which Nova hadn't noticed before. It is heavily riveted, like the porthole of a rocket ship. There is nothing to see through the glass – the inside of the machine is black. Rebecca flips a switch, then turns a dial very slowly, watching the gauges.

'What am I supposed to . . .' Nova starts, then trails off. She can see something inside the machine. It's only faint at first, but the shape is there – three rings, arranged to form a globe, like an unusual lightbulb filament. But it's not the filament that's glowing. Held loosely inside the rings is a faint, purplish glow.

'Is it working yet?' Rebecca peers her head around to look through the porthole. 'Ah, there we go! Warming up.'

'What . . . what is it? What's it doing?' Nova feels transfixed by the glow, which grows in intensity as Rebecca turns up the voltage.

'Well, first I got rid of all the unwanted atmosphere in the chamber,' Rebecca says, talking like a stage magician, 'then I introduced a thin stream of deuterium atoms, which in the near-vacuum can move very very very quickly. Then I turned on the power, trapping them in the middle there and smooooshing them together.'

She grabs Nova with one arm and squeezes her close.

'Okay, but what's that glow?'

'That's what you get when you push atoms together really hard – nuclear fusion.'

Nova watches, entranced, as the purple haze grows in intensity.

'It's beautiful . . . but why are you showing it to me?'

Rebecca goes back to the voltage control and starts to ramp up the power.

'Well, you know that nuclear fusion is the stuff that happens in the heart of stars, right?'

Nova doesn't reply. The light she can see through the porthole is getting brighter and brighter, shedding its purple hue, the plasma shimmering indigo, then faint blue, then pure white. Beams of energy shine from the core like sunlight.

'Well,' Rebecca goes on, turning the dial up through its final few degrees, 'when we talked on the phone, you said you were disappointed that you couldn't see the stars. They were too small. And the guys here, the *practical* physicists, have a name for this thing when it's up to full power.'

'Oh?' Nova's voice feels distant from her body. The glowing point of light takes up her whole world – everything else is darkness. She is floating in space.

'Yeah. They call it a "star in a jar". And I thought, well, if you can't see the stars up there, at least I can show you one down—'

Rebecca never finishes her sentence, because Nova has leapt off the lab stool and propelled herself forward. Her lips find Rebecca's, which turn up in a grin.

'*Oof!* Careful now – I *am* operating a nuclear device.'

'You said it was safe.' Nova's voice is muffled, her face pressed into Rebecca's chest.

'What I said was—' Rebecca is cut off again by Nova's lips, pressing against hers. Her hands, soft and warm, go up and underneath Rebecca's shirt, running fingers down her spine as the miniature sun flickers and burns.

✦

It's only the next day, as she's putting junk mail in the recycling, that Kate remembers Nova's card and present.

The present is crudely wrapped, despite being box-shaped. Kate tears the paper off to discover a paint-by-numbers kit. The picture is of a parrot, like one of the ones they saw in the zoo, sitting on a branch. The example picture is painted vividly in shades of red and yellow and blue, with a background of green leaves. Kate looks at the tiny pots of pre-mixed colour, feeling as though she has been spied on. There is no way Nova could know about the half-dozen times Kate has sat down to sketch something recently, only to find that there's nothing she wants to sketch.

The handwriting in the card looks like a four-year-old's – the letters grow and shrink, and refuse to stay on the line. The message is short, though it must have taken a long time to write.

Kate – thank you for everything! Nova

On the front of the navy-blue card are the words 'Thank You', and a large, golden star. She stares at it for a long time, until the star leaves an afterimage and her eyes are watering.

2

Bodies

Thirteen

January

K ATE IS IN THE bathroom, fishing in the back of the cabinet for her birth-control pills, when a message comes through on her phone. She sees Nova's name, stops what she's doing, and sits on the edge of the bath.

Yo, Kate! Greetings from Venice.

Kate thinks about Nova speaking the words into her phone – she would send the message right after she had dictated it. Kate thinks of her, far away, putting her phone back into her pocket and walking with her girlfriend (as she is sure this 'friend' really is) to a *gelateria*, while Kate is sitting here in her dingy London bathroom.

Things are good here, though I cannot figure Venice out. It is mental – I don't know where the sky ends and the water begins. Two much blue!!!

How are you? Hope it is not pouring it down in London. The whether here is very nice. (Just had to get the obligatory British mention of the weather in there, eh?)

Anyway the coffee and all the food here is amazing. I am

sure I will be spherical by the time I get home. If I ever come home, ha ha!

I have been looking lots at the buildings, like you said I should. Can't pretend to be an expert yet, but they do look more colourful than British buildings – they are pink and blue and green! I don't really understand why someone would paint their house blue – isn't this confusing when the sky is blue and the water is blue? Maybe it is like camouflage. Maybe they want their house to be invisible. Actually, that sounds quite cool.

Anyway, I hope you are okay and the flat conversion is going really well, which I'm sure it is because it is you who is doing it!

Have to go now – Rebecca wants to go to an exhibit about Gally lay oh. Bloody physicists.

Thinking of you!

Novafish ><;>

(Mistakes courtesy of my stoopid phone)

Kate stares at the message for a long time, wondering why it makes her feel so crappy. Nova is off having fun, and she has nothing more exciting on her schedule than talking to an electrician. She doesn't like missing out, that's all it is. She puts her phone in her pocket, extracts the birth-control pills and swallows one with water from the tap. She hides the pills away again, studies herself in the mirror, and walks out of the flat.

✳

The new flat is quiet, and Kate doesn't want to make any noise. She feels as though she's trespassing. The electrician has gone, taking the spare key with him, and will return the next day. She perches on the windowsill and surveys the room. The flat was a wreck when they got it. They had stripped everything back to bare walls and floorboards, then they had pulled down the crumbling plaster and pulled up the sagging floors. Nothing original is left. It has been hard work, and expensive, but worth it, she keeps saying, to have the perfect home. Although the space is bare, the floor dust-strewn, Kate knows that the hard work is done, and what remains can come together quickly.

But she doesn't feel this way. She feels as though the new flat will never be finished, and she will never live here. She feels like the flat is a metaphor for something, but she cannot decide what.

Kate walks through to the room that will be her study. On an easel in the corner is a half-finished paint-by-numbers picture of a vase of flowers. Since she completed the one that Nova gave her for Christmas, Kate has done six more of the kits, all here at the new flat. Tony thinks that the kits are stupid, 'something for old ladies', so when the builders go home she has stayed behind to paint. While she's painting, her mind is quiet.

She stands in the unfinished room, listening to her tiny movements echoing back from the bare walls, until the cold seeps into her and she needs to move.

✹

Nova has her eyes closed. She's sitting on a chair by the window, her arms resting on the window ledge, forehead pressed against the cold glass. She can smell the mould of the wooden casing. She can feel the cold coming off the window, like heat off a fire. She never thought that Italy could be so cold. The cold seeps into her body.

Her strongest impression of Venice so far is the light. It is grey, above and below, and without warning, mist will fill every space. Venice seems to float not on water, but light.

RULE OF SEEING NO.174
If you go outside and everything is murky grey, do not worry. You are not developing cataracts. Fog changes the colour of everything.

Along with the mist is the smell of damp. Nova is sure that this cannot be ubiquitous to the city, but then she has seen so little of the city and so much of the Hotel Ernesto.

The Hotel Ernesto is thin but deep, a sliver of a building from the outside that seems to extend far back, like a rabbit warren. Much of the centre of the hotel is in permanent, windowless twilight.

Rebecca lies on the bed, fully dressed and snoring gently. They went for lunch at a restaurant a few streets back from St Mark's Square, advertised as one of the cheapest in town. That's what Rebecca told her, anyway. Actually, the food was overpriced, but the carafes of red wine were large and cheap.

They had drunk the first one between them, and Nova enjoyed herself. Rebecca became voluble with the wine, told jokes, and gave compliments to the waiters. Nova agreed reluctantly to the second carafe, but Rebecca had drunk most of it anyway. Nova was wearing her dark glasses, to take a break after a busy morning of looking at beautiful things, and couldn't see where the wine was going.

Now she suspects that, at some point, Rebecca quietly finished off the second carafe and signed to the waiter to bring a third. This kind of communication is a mystery to her. People use hand signals, she knows – tapping an empty bottle or holding up a finger – and somehow this gets around any language barrier.

She isn't sure how she got Rebecca back to the room. It wasn't that she couldn't walk, or that she wasn't awake, but that she refused to admit she was lost. Finally, Nova had taken her dark glasses off, found the guidebook in Rebecca's rucksack, and asked at the first café she'd spotted for directions. Following them had tired her out far more than dragging Rebecca along with her.

Now she's tired, but Rebecca is taking up all the bed, and she has no desire to join her. She could go out again, but the exertion of finding her way back to the hotel made her want to curl up and keep her eyes closed for a long time. She could order coffee up to the room for Rebecca and put the TV on. On the first night, they had flicked through the Italian channels, and Nova had translated the cartoons and game shows to a giggling Rebecca.

But she doesn't want Rebecca to wake up. She wants her to sleep all afternoon and into the evening, and wake to an empty room, knowing she has wasted the day. But of course, the room won't be empty – Nova is going nowhere.

She wants to talk to Kate, but that would involve leaving the room. She could dictate another message, but that presents the same problem. Instead, she closes her eyes, rests her head against the cold glass of the window, and waits.

✳

Last night, Kate sat at her architect's desk, opened an unmarked floral-print notebook that her mother had given her for Christmas, and wrote 'NOVA . . .' on the first page.

She wasn't sure what she was supposed to write next. Maybe she had intended to write a letter to her friend. Or a list of pros and cons about the interpreter. Or maybe she wanted to write something else – something not really about Nova at all, but about herself.

Her hand hovered over the page for a long time. But the message, whatever it was, would not come out of her. She felt blocked, stymied, constipated. Something had driven her to come to this room, and sit at this desk, and write this name in this empty notebook. Was she so screwed up that she couldn't understand her own motivation for doing that?

There were no more words, but tears fell onto the expensive paper, making it warp. The page went from a plane to a hilly landscape, and Kate looked down at it, wondering why that image bothered her so much. Finally, she had torn the first page from the notebook and buried it under the other rubbish in the bin, as though it were an awful secret.

What was she doing? Kate was not so blind that she didn't understand that the other woman had a powerful effect on her. But what effect was it, exactly? Was Nova a question or an answer? A beginning or an ending? Was she a friend? Or . . .

The Rules of Seeing

Kate had not finished the thought. She tied the wastepaper basket liner and took it through to the kitchen, put it in the main bin, tied that up, and took it out to the garden for collection.

Crumpled, wrapped in all its layers of plastic and destined for a corner of an anonymous landfill, Kate cannot not forget the word she wrote – four letters, N – O – V – A, like a magic formula that cannot be unmade.

※

Kate is sitting at the kitchen table when Tony comes home, looking over a sheaf of architectural drawings for the wine bar she is designing. Something isn't quite right with the drawings. Symmetries and tessellations that once would have pleased her, stand out. She imagines the people sitting or standing, walking from here to there, chatting each other up or trying to make their friends laugh, kissing or arguing, and the perfect shapes seem to get in the way of the imperfect bodies.

'I'm home,' Tony calls.

Kate does not believe in any sixth sense, but knows in that moment that something is wrong. Usually, she would have made something for dinner, but he sent her a message at lunchtime to say that he would cook tonight. She had smiled at the gesture. He has been coming home late, recently, or disappearing at odd times. This seemed like an apology.

'I'm in the kitchen.'

He appears, shucking off his boots in the doorway, a plain plastic bag in one hand. Kate can see something wrapped in white paper.

'You still working?' He looks down at the plans on the table.

'No, just nitpicking.' Kate gathers up the plans. Tony puts the carrier bag down on the table and takes out the paper parcel, then goes and washes his hands at the sink. Kate stares at the parcel as though it might explode.

'Making something special?'

He dries his hands on a tea towel and takes not one but two knives from the block, one small and sharp, the other wide-bladed and heavy. Practically a cleaver – a knife that Kate never uses.

'Thought I'd try something different today.' Kate can smell his too-strong cologne. It's filling up the kitchen. 'So I went to the market and bought this. Haven't had one in years.' He lays the knives either side of the parcel and starts to unwrap it with care, though his eyes are on her.

Kate gets her first glimpse of what is inside, and it confuses her. For a second, she thinks this must be a joke, because this is not food – Tony has wrapped up a fur stole. Then she realizes. The food is twice-wrapped, once in paper and once in fur. In the centre of the square of paper is a whole, dead rabbit.

Her eyes are wider than she wants them to be, and she fights to regulate her breathing. She cannot look away from the animal between them. It is dead, she tells herself – it is dead and cannot feel pain. But she does not feel that this is true. The rabbit is too whole, too rabbit-shaped. It is perfectly still, but its eyes are open and gleaming. Kate feels her own body, cold and limp, laid on the white paper shroud.

'The butcher asked if I wanted it skinned, but I said I wanted to do it myself.' Tony says, lightly. She looks to his face, which admits no hint of malice. He looks like he's cooking her a nice dinner. An unusual dinner, perhaps, but still. Kate forces herself to smile.

'I didn't know you ever had.'

'Dad taught me how.'

Kate clears her throat, feeling like a bad actor. 'Do you . . . want any help?' She gathers the plans and starts to rise, ready to make her escape.

'No, I've got this. You can keep me company while I cook.' He makes it sound like a suggestion, and Kate knows she could just make an excuse. She could go have a bath, or hoover the bedroom . . .

'Sure.' She sits back down.

Tony takes the smaller of the knives and picks up the rabbit by its back legs. She closes her eyes for a second and forces herself to talk.

'Good day at work?'

'Just the usual. Not too busy.'

She looks again as Tony brings the knife to the rabbit's ankle, slicing around it with a shallow cut. Her breath catches, and for a second Tony stops.

'You okay, love?' The words are friendly but there is no warmth there. For this moment, Kate is sure he is doing it on purpose. She won't give him the satisfaction.

'Fine – I just have a headache.'

'You should take something.'

'Mm.'

She rises from the table and goes to the cupboard where they keep medicines and boxes of tea. She takes her time finding tablets, pours herself a glass of water. All the time she can hear Tony making further cuts. She swallows the tablets, looking out of the tiny kitchen window. She will make her excuses now, go for a bath . . .

'Actually, you could help me with this bit.'

She turns slowly to see Tony holding the rabbit by its hind legs. She expected there to be a lot of blood, but his hands are almost clean.

'I just need you to hold its feet while I get the skin off.'

There is a dull weight in Kate's stomach as she steps towards the table. She feels sick. She struggles to keep her face straight as she leans forward and takes hold of the feet.

'What's up? Not squeamish, are you?'

'No, of course not.' She takes the feet from him, feeling the claws like chips of stone. 'It's only a headache.'

'Just hold tight,' Tony says, then starts to pull on the skin.

Kate tries to look somewhere else, anywhere else, but it is in her peripheral vision, and once she's seen it, it's no good closing her eyes. She can feel the vibration as skin peels from flesh. It sizzles – a sound like meat in the frying pan. She can see pink muscles and the thinnest layer of nicotine-yellow fat.

'I think I'm going to have a shower.'

Kate drops the half-skinned rabbit and walks calmly from the kitchen to the bathroom, shutting and locking the door behind her. She bends over the toilet but is not sick. She sits on the tiles, shivering. Her breaths quiver in and out of her. Is this a panic attack? She expects Tony will knock on the door, to ask if she's okay, but he doesn't.

She needs a distraction, and grabs the toothpaste tube from the sink. She reads the ingredients – hydrated silica, sorbitol, PVM/MA copolymer – as though the words are a spell to stop her thinking. Slowly, her breaths grow longer, and she wipes a slick of cold sweat from her brow. The trick half works, and after another minute she feels well enough to stand.

From the kitchen, she can hear Tony cooking – cutting and frying the meat in oil, and she realizes that she still has to eat the meal. A fresh wave of nausea rises up her throat. She turns the shower on and undresses quickly, desperate to feel something other than the eerie prickle on her skin. She steps into the bathtub and turns up the heat. The water is so hot she has to move around constantly, bringing tears to her eyes. Her skin turns red. She gets used to the heat but the tears keep flowing.

Kate stays there for a long time, until the heat exhausts her. She gets out of the shower, puts on her bathrobe and quietly takes her phone to the bedroom. The flat smells of rabbit stew, and Kate knows she should find it delicious, but it just smells of iron. Of blood. Kate has never considered becoming vegetarian. She has always liked meat. But eating meat never seemed so . . . *cannibalistic*.

On her phone, she opens the message chain with Nova and reads through the conversations. The old words calm her immediately, like a morphine shot. Kate takes several deep breaths – hesitates – and starts to type.

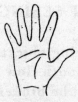

Fourteen

February

'**H**AVE YOU BEEN GETTING out much? Practising?'

Alex's flat is very clean and very modern. Nova has always found it a little uncomfortable – all the armchairs and sofas are too firm, with low backs so she can't slouch. Now, being able to see it and compare it to her own cluttered home, it's like looking at a completely different ecosystem. It's like her flat is a lush, overgrown forest, and Alex's is an arid, beige desert.

What makes up for any discomfort is her brother's ability to make mint tea. Nova waits patiently, answering his questions, while the infusion of mint leaves, tea and sugar steeps in the pot.

'Practising?'

'Practising your seeing.'

'Yeah, sure. Loads.'

More and more, Nova's Rules of Seeing are less like a guide to learning a new skill, and more like an instruction manual for operating a broken brain.

RULE OF SEEING NO.183

**Sometimes moving objects will appear to
'stutter'. The smooth flow of coffee poured
into a mug will be broken into strobing
snapshots, and before you know it there is
coffee all over the table.**

RULE OF SEEING NO.184
**The brain will hang onto objects
after you have stopped looking.
Stare too long at the duck pond
and the pavement will look wavy.
Stare too long at the pavement
and the duckpond will look gritty.**

'But have you been getting out? Or have you just been holed up in your flat?'

'As a matter of fact, I went to the zoo the other day,' Nova lies. It's a couple of months since she and Kate went to the zoo, but she wants to talk about Kate without making it seem like a big thing.

'The zoo? London Zoo?'

'I saw fish, and penguins, and an orange snake, and a kangaroo . . .' Nova reels off the animals that she had seen clearly, though many more had briefly appeared in front of her, as though passing through a break in the foliage. The memory makes her smile. Alex gives the teapot one last swill, places a metal strainer over one of the teacups, and pours.

'I'm impressed. You got around all right on your own?'

'I didn't go on my own.'

'A friend?'

'Someone I met.'

'What, a date?'

'No . . . a girl I met at the hospital.'

Alex laughs.

'A doctor? I've got to tell you, Jilly, we don't make the best husbands. Or wives, rather.'

Nova sighs melodramatically. 'Not a doctor, dumdum. A patient.'

'A patient? In the neurology ward? What was she there for?'

'What business is it of yours? She's a perfectly nice girl. An architect.'

At 'architect', Alex makes a noise of approval, to which Nova makes a corresponding grunt of irritation. 'Still, it's a funny place to find a friend. I hope she's not crazy.'

Nova punches him on the arm.

'Ow! I could have been pouring!'

'I could *see* you weren't. Anyway, I was there as well – are you saying I'm crazy?'

'No comment.' Alex rubs the spot where she caught him. 'I just think it's not the best place to be looking for love.'

'Ugh! Who said anything about love? Just give me the tea.'

Nova sips from the cup, a shiver of warmth passing up her spine. She's annoyed with Alex, but mostly because she has her own concerns. Kate had messaged her the other night, asking if she wanted to meet up. For the first time, she hadn't replied straight away.

Kate is kind and gentle and funny. But since her strange turn in front of the tiger enclosure, and the awkward dinner party, Nova wonders if she's getting too deeply into someone else's problems, when she has enough problems of her own.

'Does this girl have a name?'

'Kate. She's Italian. Well, her parents are.'

Alex sits back a little more, though not to the point of seeming comfortable, and sips his tea. Their mum used to make them this tea, once a day, when they got back from school.

'And you met her in the neurology ward?' he repeats.

'Ugh, like I said: what difference does it make where I met her?'

Alex holds up his hands to placate her. He is slowly getting used to signalling feelings to his sister with his hands or face. He is starting to understand what she can see and what she can understand. Paradoxically, Nova has always talked with her hands, but the gestures were all her own. She seemed to be feeling the shape of the idea in front of her, rather than trying to communicate anything.

'I'm just saying, be careful.'

✯

When Kate gets home from work, there is music on in the kitchen and the sound of the kettle boiling. The radio is on some crappy station, but Kate doesn't care, because the relief of coming back to this warm, noisy bubble is physical – she feels a tingling rush sweep over her as though she's just stepped into a hot bath.

She can hear Tony making something in the kitchen, opening cupboards and chopping, and even this makes her smile. She takes her time getting out of her boots and coat, happy to delay the moment. Running her hands over her eyes, she walks through to the kitchen.

Tony is standing with his back to her, rinsing vegetables in the sink. Kate opens her mouth to say hello, but the word never comes out. She catches sight of it in her peripheral vision, on the table. Later, she will think how, if she had been Nova, she would never have spotted it. Such a small shape in a room full of so many other shapes. But she does see it, and the shape stops her dead – a green rectangle.

Her birth control pills.

She stands, rooted, looking at the out-of-place shape, as all the warmth drains out of her.

He turns. The radio is playing a dance track that keeps repeating the words LOVE and NOW and UNIQUE in revolving combinations, with a robotic, echo-saturated voice.

'Well?' He dries his hands on a tea towel and waits for her to talk. She searches for the right answer, like the first move in a game.

'Where—'

'No,' he cuts her off before she can finish the question. 'You don't get to ask where I found these. You don't get to ask me questions, because I've done nothing *wrong*.'

The final word is a snarl, and Tony takes a step towards her. The words have dried up in her throat.

'Well?' he asks again, and Kate thinks this is what he must be like at work, interrogating suspects. But there are no recordings here, or one-way mirrors where people might be looking into their cell. She is all alone. She tries again

'Those are old—'

As she says the word, Tony steps forward again, brings his arm back and slaps her, hard, on the cheek. Her neck snaps to one side and she gasps.

Kate isn't aware of anything for a moment except the pain and the tears that are breaking her vision into pieces. Then Tony speaks into her ear, close enough to feel his breath.

'Don't *ever* lie to me.'

And he is gone, out of the kitchen and out of the flat.

Kate is shaking. It's not from the pain – she's had worse. She stepped on a nail on a building site once that went right through her foot. She's had two electric shocks. No, it's that Tony hit her.

He hadn't been drinking. It hadn't been a heat-of-the-moment thing. He had waited for her to come home. He had waited patiently to strike her.

But here she is, and she doesn't feel like she's about to leave. She sits there for a long time, feeling the tingle in her cheek. Then she gets up, takes the card of pills and pops them out into the sink, one by one, turns the warm tap on and watches them dissolve.

Fifteen

March

'WHAT IS IT?' NOVA turns the lump of metal and plastic over in her hands. Looking at the object hasn't helped her identify it, but neither has holding it. Kate guesses that nobody has handed her one before. They are standing in Trafalgar Square, and Nova is wearing a giant, fuzzy brown jacket, like one half of a bear costume. Kate has no idea where it came from, but wants to hug and be hugged by Nova in her ridiculous jacket.

'It's a camera. Look, this switches it on . . .' Kate guides her, positioning Nova's fingers. 'And this button takes a picture.' The shutter clicks, and a picture of one of the fountains flashes up on the small screen.

'Kate, this is very kind, but I can't—'

'Oh! I'm so sorry, I thought you'd be able to use it.'

'No, I mean, I can't accept this. It's too generous.'

'Don't be silly – I owe you for saving me at the zoo. Think of it as a late Christmas present.'

'You don't owe me anything.' Nova pauses, then asks, 'Are you okay? You've changed colour.'

Kate doesn't know what she means for a moment, then realizes she must be blushing. She ignores her, trying to hide her nerves. She didn't tell Tony about buying the camera. She bought it with her own money, of course. And it's just a gift – a gift from one friend to another.

'I was thinking about how you said it was frustrating, because nothing holds still, so you can't figure out what it is. But if you can take a picture' – Kate presses the button again to hear the click – 'you can take all the time you need to work it out.'

Nova smiles reluctantly, looking at her face. Kate stays still, trying to be a photo. She stares into Nova's eyes, dazzling blue in the sunlight. Finally, Nova looks down.

'Does this have a strap? Help me put it on.'

Kate takes the camera from her, bending down to hang it around her neck. As she does, Nova leans forward and kisses her.

It's over in a moment, and then Nova is pulling Kate through the square, and Kate hopes that she can't feel the pulse that is racing in her hand.

RULE OF SEEING NO.189
When you go walking, remember that your vision will bob up and down like a boat on the ocean. This is normal.

Kate guides Nova towards the National Gallery, through the crowds, dodging tourists and scattering pigeons. Every so often, Nova pauses to take a picture. Then she carefully turns the camera off and takes Kate's arm again. Kate likes being her guide, though she never knows how much Nova really needs her. She's begun to feel like it's the other way around – like she can only face the world when Nova is there.

They reach the gallery and Kate feels more sheltered. It's quiet in here, and when they're past the entrance hall there are only a few people in each room. Nova can't use her camera, but it doesn't matter – she can just stand and stare at the gigantic canvasses, trying to take in every detail. They move slowly over the Parquet floors, polished smooth like slabs of toffee. They stop in front of Titian's *Bacchus and Ariadne*, looking up at the running, tumbling figures. Nova has gone very quiet.

'What are you seeing?' Kate asks, looking up at Bacchus in mid-leap.

'People . . .' she replies, sounding uncertain.

'Yes.'

'But *weird* people.'

Kate looks again at the picture. She doesn't know anything about it, or the myth it represents. It doesn't look like a happy story – there's a man with snakes writhing around his naked body, a decapitated deer's head on the floor. The chariot is being drawn by two cheetahs. The more she looks, the more uncomfortable she feels.

'What's it called?' Nova asks, and Kate tells her. 'Oh, so that's Bacchus' – Nova points to the figure leaping from the chariot – 'and that's Ariadne. He's seeing her for the first time – love at first sight.'

'How do you know that?'

Nova shrugs. 'I like stories. This one's in Ovid's *Metamorphoses*.

Hang on . . .' Nova screws up her eyes, something she often does when trying to concentrate. '*So that she might shine among the eternal stars, he took the crown from her forehead, and set it in the sky . . .*'

Kate doesn't know what to say. She's feeling something she doesn't understand. Nova senses that she's wanting to move away from the picture, and follows after.

Nova likes Van Gogh's sunflowers. 'It's so . . . *yellow*,' she whispers, then makes a little *humph*, knowing that she hasn't expressed what she means.

'I know what you mean,' Kate says.

They move on. They wander through religious iconography, pictures of people ascending into Heaven or descending into Hell. Nova can't quite fathom these pictures, the people hovering in space, the wings and tails that sprout from otherwise human figures.

In person, Kate can't deny what she feels for the interpreter. Nova isn't an abstract idea, or an answer to a question. Kate is not interested in her because she represents freedom, or another way of living. She doesn't 'see herself' in the younger woman.

She's interested in Nova because she has a crush. A massive, schoolgirl crush on this strange, sexy person.

And she hasn't felt this way for so long. Which wouldn't matter if she didn't feel, suddenly, like she's been faking it for the longest time.

'What're you thinking about, runner bean?'

Nova crashes her inner dialogue, nudging Kate in the ribs. She has unzipped her fuzzy jacket, and today's T-shirt reads, CLUELESS WONDER.

Kate drags her attention back to the picture in front of them – an oil painting of Venice.

'You didn't tell me about your holiday.' She points at the painting, to make the connection clear.

'Oh, is that what this is?' Nova squints at the frame as though looking through a fog. 'It doesn't look anything like that.'

'Well, I guess it's quite an old picture; Venice has probably changed.'

'No, but the light is all wrong . . .' Nova remembers the too-bright colours, the hazy sun shearing off the roofs, the flashes from water and windows.

'Anyway, that's not what I meant. Did you have a nice time?'

'It was fine . . . nice. We had a nice time. The food was good.'

Nova seems to squirm a bit under the question, and Kate thinks she must resent this intrusion into her private life. Still, she asks:

'Did, uh, Rebecca enjoy it?'

Nova turns to her, looks up into the architect's face and frowns. For a moment, Kate forgets to breathe.

'You . . . have dots on your face.'

'I have dots?' Kate puzzles for a moment, then laughs. 'Freckles! I have freckles.'

'Oh. I guess I couldn't see them before,' Nova searches the constellations that have appeared on Kate's face.

'I get more of them in the summer, if I've been out in the sun.'

Nova nods slowly, frowning.

'Come on then, freckle face.'

⁎

They pass several versions of the crucifixion, but none trouble Kate. In Raphael's version, Christ seems to hover serenely on the cross, weightless and painless. His death looks like another act in a colourful pantomime. Then they come to the Crucifixion Altarpiece. The painting is much older. Kate reads the label, noting the date of 1490, searching for something else to focus on, but she can't look away.

Her mother is Roman Catholic. Well, she was, back in Italy. Her parents' faith waned with distance from home. By the time Kate was born, in Finchley, there wasn't enough holy mystery left to spare, and she has never believed in anything much beyond the world she knows.

Christ's arms are thin, pulled taut, and seem to bear the entire weight of his body. His ribs protrude, his whole being made of knuckle and sinew. Then there are the nails – not the dainty bits of metal in the other paintings, like cute accessories, but fat bolts, driven through skin and muscle, forcing the bones of the hand apart to make space, until they crack like chicken ribs. Looking at him, Kate can feel the tension in her shoulders, her upper body pulled into a position more architectural than human. Her weight seems to hang from that inverted triangle. She feels the raw wood at her back. Faint fire burns in her palms.

'Come on,' Nova says, untroubled, 'let's go cruise the gift shop.'

She puts her hand on Kate's back and leads her away from Golgotha.

In the café, they buy slices of carrot cake and strong coffee. These days, Kate feels always in a half-dream, and the shot of caffeine draws her into waking.

'Thank you for today.' Nova puts her hand over Kate's.

'You're welcome. It's nice to get out of the flat.'

'You been staying in a lot?'

'Well, no, just working from home as much as I can . . . but I feel like I should go back to the office.'

'Why?'

Kate shrugs, reluctant to admit. 'Because everyone must think I'm being lazy.'

'No, they don't! You can't think like that.'

Kate takes a shaky breath. 'Anyway, I've got the new flat to work on. I've painted some walls. How about you? Been getting out much?'

'Not since Venice, really. I go into work and come home again. I get stuff delivered, I ask people to come to mine. You got me out of the house.'

'Should I be flattered, or am I dragging you out against your will?'

'Don't flatter yourself that you could drag me anywhere against my will,' Nova riffs. 'But, no, I want to come out. It feels like an event. Like a special occasion.'

'I'm flattered.'

Nova grins, then her expression turns serious. Kate loves this about her – that her moods are so obvious, so open. Nova doesn't hide anything.

'Look, it's none of my business, but . . . is everything all right?'

'What do you mean?' Kate shrugs. 'Everything is weird.'

'Yeah, I know. What I mean is, when I came around . . .'

'The meal?'

'Yeah, the meal.'

'Didn't you enjoy it?' Kate can't keep the hurt out of her voice.

'Yes, of course! But . . . Tony . . .'

It isn't really a question, but she leaves his name hanging a second, trying to make Kate fill in the blank. She seems unhappy, and it isn't all to do with what's going on in her head.

'Tony? He's fine.' Kate's face is hot. How can she know?

'Okay, he's fine.' Nova won't stop looking into her eyes. 'But what about you?'

Kate doesn't reply for a moment, fiddling with a napkin as though trying to fold it into an origami shape. Sometimes Kate wonders where Tony's anger came from, but she already knows. Tony is one of those people who remembers old conversations, childhood moments of humiliation, ex-girlfriends' parting words, and boils them down into a kind of psychic rocket fuel. For as long as she has known him, it was a clean fuel – it burned away, driving his life but leaving nothing behind. This anger hasn't 'come from' anywhere – it was always there. It has just never been turned on *her*.

'I'm fine. We're fine. It's been . . . a difficult few months.' Kate pauses for her friend to say something, but Nova just waits. 'That's all. He's not good at talking. That's why I'm so glad I met you.'

She reaches her hand out and puts it on Nova's, and if her breath speeds up a bit, Kate doesn't seem to notice. They finish their drinks.

'Would you like to come back to mine?' Nova asks, not knowing exactly what she means by the question. Kate pauses, as though it's unclear to her too.

'Maybe sometime soon? I should be getting home.'

Sixteen

'**S**HE'S JUST A FRIEND.'

'*Friend . . .*' Vi rolls the word around her mouth experimentally, like a wine tasting, before spitting it back out again. 'Friend – nope, you're going to have to explain.'

Kate sighs. Vi was not invited around; she's just shown up. After a week of Kate ignoring her calls, she finally staked out the flat and was waiting there when she got back from the museum. She should feel bad – Kate still hasn't been to see Vi's baby, has only spoken to her friend over the phone since the birth. She fetches her a drink while Vi establishes herself on the sofa, flicking through the channels on the television. Kate hasn't watched it for weeks. If Tony's watching something, she goes through to the kitchen and puts the radio on.

'We're friends, okay? I feel like she understands me.'

'And you met her at the hospital?'

'Yes.'

'And she used to be *blind*?'

'Yes.'

'And that's . . . all right?'

Kate groans – Vi is making her nauseous. 'I like her, okay – is that so weird?'

Vi grins, sensing weakness. 'Weird? Not for most people. But for you, Kate, it's pretty fucking odd.' She shrugs, then changes tack. 'God, it's good to have five minutes without a tiny human attached to my boob. Mind if I vape in here?'

Kate shakes her head and Vi starts rummaging through her handbag.

'Jesus, how did this get in here?'

Vi pulls a thin book out of her handbag, called *Baby's First Shapes*. Kate looks at the book, not immediately remembering what it reminds her of.

'What is it?'

'Oh, the health visitor gives you one when they come to check out the baby.'

She hands her the book and Kate flips through the pages. On each is a different black and white picture – three dots, a spiral, a smiling face.

'Apparently, babies like it, 'cos they can only see in black and white or something, but Finn doesn't seem interested.'

Kate is silent for a moment, remembering Nova's packs of cards, then hands the book back.

'Why is it weird that I should make a friend?'

Vi twists her mouth.

'I didn't say that. You've just . . . always kept to yourself.'

'Have I?'

'Yes, you have. Name me *one* friend you've made in the last couple of years?' Kate opens her mouth to respond, but Vi is there before her. 'You can't, right? Because you haven't made any friends since you married Big Man. I'm your best friend, and even I've hardly seen you . . .'

She doesn't say 'since I had a baby', but Kate hears the words.

She isn't wrong, of course. Kate hasn't made any real friends since she got married, and has lost plenty by turning down invitations. She has ignored everything from nights out to weddings. It's not that Tony tells her to turn them down, exactly. He just always seems to have made another plan – seeing a film, visiting a relative, shopping for a new vacuum cleaner – which he has neglected to tell her about until this moment.

Vi bounces up and down on the sofa, a sure sign that she's uncomfortable, and Kate feels herself bobbing in time with her. Surely there is something wrong with her hormones – it's like being friends with a Labrador puppy. Kate is angry now. Vi has always hated Tony, and she's dragging Nova into it just to prove a point.

'So, what are you saying?'

'I'm saying, Katerina Tomassi, that you've suddenly become besties with a girl you met after hitting your head.'

'And what, you think I've gone soft? Crazy?'

For once, Vi doesn't respond straight away, and when she does, Kate can tell the sincerity is making her squirm. She feels it like a tightness in her chest.

'I'm just worried about you. You're acting weird.'

'So what do you think I should do?' Kate sounds angrier than she intended.

'Maybe stop for a bit. Just . . . take some time.'

'Just stop! You sound like my fucking doctor.' Her voice is rising, high and shaky. Her emotions are not hers to control any more – they ebb and flow to a tide table which she knows nothing about.

'Maybe he's right.'

'So fuck off if you think that's all I am – I'm not some kid who can't make her own decisions.'

Vi sits there for a moment, not saying anything. Kate has never shouted at her like this before. They've had a thousand arguments, all of them about nothing. She puts her drink down, gets up from the sofa, and lets herself out of the flat. Kate walks to the door which Vi has calmly closed behind her. Carefully, she turns the latch and puts the bolts on, locking herself in.

✳

She is beautiful, lying on the rocks in the sun.

Her hair is golden, falling over her shoulders and down her back in waves. Her skin is pale, freckled on her arms and chest. She is naked to the waist – no, she is entirely naked. It's just that, at her waist, she changes. She has no pubic hair. The scales are the colour of soap bubbles, shifting greens and purples and blues. Her tail is long, elegant, but heavy looking – real.

It concerns Nova that such a heavy, soft fishtail is resting on those sharp rocks, but the woman seems unconcerned. She looks back serenely, and though Nova still can't read expressions, she feels that there is a question in her gaze. She's about to ask what the woman wants to know when she wakes up.

The sunlight dies, snuffed out in her head. She's in bed, and knows that it's sometime midway through the night.

Though the dream was peaceful, she finds her breath is fast and ragged.

People often ask Nova what blind people dream of. For them, dreams are mostly images. They wake and remember a confusion of pictures, doubting that there is any sound or touch. But of course blind people dream, even if they have been blind from birth.

Nova dreams of spaces she knows, which will rearrange themselves – her living room leading into Scotland Yard's canteen, or her first school's classroom. She dreams of people – their voices and their touch, the shape of them. She would even see colours in her dreams – the shifting pastels that she saw during the day, but no more than that. She didn't know what it meant to 'see' when she was asleep any more than when she was awake.

After the operation, her dreams stayed the same – she saw in the day and was blind at night. It was a relief. Time out. No matter how tiring it was to learn to see all day, at night she could rest. Sleep was easy, when you were that tired. Nova would wake up, refreshed by the warm, dark waters that she'd sunk into.

The image of the mermaid is clear in her memory. The light of the foreign sun has died, but she can remember it. Where did the shape of the mermaid come from? She remembers holding an ornament in the doctor's office, trying to divine its purpose.

'A gift from my daughter,' he'd explained. 'She loves mermaids.'

But the ornament had been dead, its expression painted on. The mermaid in her dream was something she had never seen

– pasted together from faces she knows, swimsuit adverts, fish in Brixton market . . . It seemed alive, in a way that her waking visions of other people still don't.

Unable to sleep, she closes her eyes in the dark and weeps.

✳

'How have you been since our last meeting?'

Nova is back in the doctor's office, looking down at the desk where the mermaid ornament looks back at her.

'Better, I guess.'

'You guess? What improvements?'

Nova likes Dr Schulman. He's matter-of-fact when she needs him to be, amazed when she's describing something she considers strange. She supposes it's all part of his manner, and that none of her symptoms are truly a surprise to him, but it's comforting anyway. Her life has become so alien, she's grateful for any assurance that her reactions to it are correct.

'Faces are a little easier to pick out . . . I can tell when people are smiling most of the time now, even if they don't show their teeth. I'm getting better at making out letters – I read a couple of sentences the other day.'

The words, from a book loaned to her by the library:

It is a truth universally acknowledged, that a single man in possession of a good fortune, must be in want of a wife.

Nova had read *Pride and Prejudice* before, by Braille, and had listened to the audiobook. But somehow the words seemed to mean something different when she read them on the page. The 'universal truth' seemed encoded, its meaning locked up in hieroglyphs.

'That's good – faster progress than I would have expected. Have you been experiencing fewer visual disturbances?'

The illusions that made her first months especially challenging – colourful auras and comet-tails, free-floating objects and dissolving surfaces – have become rarer as time passed, but haven't vanished altogether. Sometimes, if she is tired or hungry, these symptoms will reappear.

RULE OF SEEING NO.207
The developing visual cortex is a gas guzzler – it needs glucose to run. If vision deteriorates, do not worry – you are not losing your sight. Have a sandwich and wait.

Often Nova doesn't know if something is an illusion or not, like the first time she saw the display screens with their colourful adverts in Leicester Square.

'Yes, they've gotten better. But last night . . .'

'Yes?'

She tells him about her dream, the mermaid on the rocks. He smiles – that flash of white is a familiar sign – and makes a noise of more than simulated interest.

'Amazing! I wouldn't have thought your visual imagination was capable of something so complex.'

'Do you think it'll happen often?'

'Seeing in your dreams? Yes, I imagine it will become more common. The more developed your visual cortex becomes – the more information it assimilates – the more it will want to sort through all that information when you're sleeping. Dreams are a part of learning.'

'Ah. Right.' Nova suppresses the urge to cry.

'Are you okay?'

'I'm just . . . I'm really tired.' She presses her lips together and closes her eyes. Doctor Schulman sighs and leans forward.

'Nova, I can't imagine what it's like to be seeing the world through your eyes. It must be very difficult.'

She nods. 'It just doesn't seem to be getting any easier.'

'It will.'

'How long?'

'You know I can't put a number on that. People have different experiences. Partly it depends on how much time is spent performing exercises, developing your new sense.'

'But I can't think. I can barely work. I can't do anything else. Learning to see is a full-time job.'

'Yes . . .' He seems uncertain of what to say. This is simply the way it is.

'What I'm trying to say is, I used to have a life – I had a job, I had friends. I had hobbies. Now I just have this *task*.'

'And you want to go back to the way things were?'

Despite the scepticism in his tone, the words seem full of hope to Nova.

'Could I do that?'

'If by that you mean "can a surgeon perform an operation to make you blind again", then the answer is obviously no.'

'Sure, I get it. Ethics and all that jazz.'

'Right.' He smiles, more subtly this time – no flash of white, but an upward curvature of the pink line that is his mouth. 'Well, yes, I suppose you could just ignore your sight. You could put on dark glasses and let the visual ability that you've developed die away . . .'

'And then the dreams would stop?'

He rubs his eyes and sounds, for the first time, annoyed.

'Was it so bad to dream, Nova? There are a lot of people in the world who would chop off a limb to gain what you have.'

Tears prick her eyes. She keeps them shut.

'I know. I know that. I *do* know that. But . . .'

'But?'

'But I'm scared that I'll lose my mind.'

A long sigh, the sound of anger deflating. 'I'm sorry, Nova. I didn't mean—'

She's shaking her head, angry with herself as much as the doctor. 'That's okay. Just tell me what I need to know.'

'It's only what you already know – you have a choice. You can persevere with learning to see, at a cost to your work life and relationships, or you can close your eyes, go back to being blind, and have the life you had from the day you were born.'

Nova opens her eyes and picks up the mermaid ornament. She turns it over in her hands, feeling a disconnect between the jagged thing under her fingers and the shimmering bubble of compressed light that she can see. How can they be the same thing? How can they *ever* be the same thing? She puts it back down on the desk, with a precision she never had before.

'Thank you.'

Seventeen

Are you busy?
It's okay if you are.
I just need to talk to a normal person.
Or an abnormal person.
You know what I mean.

Kate feels her phone buzz against her thigh, five times in quick succession. She stares at the stacked messages for a long moment, then starts to type.

I'm at the new flat. Want to come round?

She feels butterflies in her stomach, knowing she shouldn't. Nothing is going to happen, after all. She paces twice around the front room, before adding:

It's just me.

There is a pause. Kate watches the screen, her stomach jolting when the '. . .' pops up to show that Nova is writing. Then,

That would be nice.
I'll send you the address.

✦

The new flat is easy enough to find, once Nova has made her way to Acton Town on the Piccadilly. She presses the buzzer and is let into a pleasantly dark hallway, walks up two flights of stairs, and comes to a doorway, where Kate is leaning against the frame.

'I wasn't sure if you were going to come.'

'Do I look unreliable to you?' Nova asks. Even with her inexperience at reading faces, she can tell that Kate looks startled. 'I'm joking!' They hug and Nova plants a kiss on her cheek. Kate smells Nova's now-familiar perfume and feels dizzy.

'Can I come in?'

'Oh, sure! Come see my work-in-progress. There's hardly any furniture. I'm afraid.'

Nova walks past her, stepping carefully to make sure she doesn't bump into any walls. This isn't difficult, because Kate's hallway has light floors and dark walls. The moment she steps in there she feels at home, which is only strengthened as she goes from room to room, a sense of having been here before, a sense that this is a safe place. It's an animal sense, Nova thinks. Kate's flat feels like somewhere safe that she is just returning to after a long time away.

'Let me take your coat.'

'Thanks. I brought wine, and some movies.'

'You brought movies? I don't have a telly here yet.'

'Don't worry, I didn't really want to watch one. My doctor gave me a whole bag of them.' Nova takes off her backpack and pulls out a handful of plastic cases.

'What for?'

'To test me – to practise seeing new things. He thought I'd like them, I guess.'

'That was nice of him.'

'Yeah.' She shrugs. 'I've not watched many movies yet – most of them are too fast to follow. I still get on better if I close my eyes.'

'I don't watch much at the moment. I've started reading books more.'

Kate hangs up Nova's coat and takes her rucksack. Nova slips off her shoes to reveal fuzzy black-and-yellow socks, striped like bumblebees. Her T-shirt says NEVER TRUST AN ATOM – THEY MAKE UP EVERYTHING.

'What are you smiling at?' Nova asks.

'Your T-shirt.'

'Oh yeah. You should know, I make horrible chemistry puns, but only *periodically*.'

It takes a moment for the joke to land, and Nova just stands there, grinning. Kate mock groans. 'Come on, let me give you a tour.'

They go to the kitchen, then the front room. Everything is softly lit, and it is very quiet here. Her flat in Brixton seems porous – sound leaks in from the trains on the viaduct, the car horns on the street, the cafés playing reggae. Somehow, Kate has hermetically sealed her world away from the noise of other people.

'It's super-quiet in here, dude.'

'Oh, architect's hocus-pocus. When I bought this place, I raised the floors and had everything insulated. I designed some home-recording studios at the first agency I worked for, so I know a few tricks.'

'I like it. Mind if I sit?'

'Sure. Want me to break into this wine?'

'Please.'

'Oh, it's not a screw-top . . .'

'Shit, do you have a corkscrew?'

Kate thinks for a moment. 'No, but I do have a screwdriver and a claw hammer.'

'Which helps us how?'

'I'll twist a screw into the cork, then use the hammer to pull it out.'

Nova grins. 'You're a regular Girl Guide.'

'I don't think Girl Guides drink wine.'

'Kids these days.'

Kate goes to find her tools. Nova sits on the sofa, which is charcoal grey. The front room, like the hallway, is dark red. The window is outlined by a white frame. The floor is light cream. These blocks of colour reassure her. Though the flat isn't lived-in yet, she senses that there will be no clutter here. Not like her own flat – so full of patterns and designs that she never knew were there. Patterns are tiring, because she can't stop looking at them.

RULE OF SEEING NO.227
After a while, pattern-seeking becomes a reflex over which you have little control. You will see faces in clouds, clouds in wallpaper, and strange animals dancing in the oil-sheen of a puddle.

Kate is in the kitchen, talking while she twists a screw into the cork, asking polite questions about her day, how her journey was. But Nova can't hear the words. Suddenly she's crying, silent tears streaming down her cheeks. She feels as though she couldn't leave Kate's flat even if she wanted to. Like a planet that has gotten too close to a black hole. But instead of being alarmed, she feels intense relief. The tears flow, and it is only when Kate returns, holding two glasses of wine, that Nova becomes aware again.

'I'm sorry.' Kate says, putting the wine down quickly.

'What f–for?' Nova grins, choking on a sob.

'I don't know. I must have done something.'

'Y-you're like Catholic guilt became a person.' Nova laughs. 'I just . . .'

'What?'

Nova looks into Kate's eyes and Kate looks back. Her look feels like it means something – something important – but Kate isn't sure what. Signs, symbols, codes. Foreign languages. They sit on the sofa in silence for a while.

'What does my face look like to you?' Kate asks.

'Well, it has two eyes, a nose, a mouth . . .'

'No, but what do I *look* like? What kind of person?'

'Do you mean, are you pretty?' Nova laughs – a mischievous chuckle – and Kate is glad that the other woman can't tell how uncomfortable she looks. 'But really, I'm not sure. I can't use faces to read a person.'

'In the movies you always see blind people touching faces to get used to them.'

'Ha, yeah, that really doesn't help me. Don't believe everything Hollywood tells you, toots.'

'Oh,' Kate says, unexpectedly disappointed. 'That's a shame.'

'Well, I can give it a go if you like,' Nova shrugs. 'See what I come up with.'

'Sure.' Kate swallows hard. 'Humour me.'

'Okay, hold on to your butt.'

Nova waggles her fingers like a concert pianist.

She closes her blue eyes, scooches closer on the sofa, then puts her hands out in front of her. Kate leans closer, her breath speeding up until Nova's fingertips touch her cheeks. Nova runs her fingers over her cheeks, very gently, over her cheekbones, her jaw, her mouth, nose, eyebrows – smoothing out to the edge – her brow, temple, ears. Tiny movements gauge every millimetre. Kate presses her eyes shut, suppressing the shivers passing through her.

She imagines her face appearing in Nova's mind like an Ordnance Survey map, with tight rings of lines describing the peak of her nose, the valleys of her eyes and the broad-spaced bars of her forehead. Nova's hands come to rest again under her jaw, and Kate hopes that she can't feel her heartbeat hammering in her throat.

She opens her eyes. She watches Nova, as she explores her face with gentle hands. Her face is so close to hers, and it feels like something of a reflex. She does it before she knows she's doing it. She leans forward, what – one or two inches? A small margin of error.

Her lips touch hers.

If Nova's lips part, it must be in shock.

For a second, maybe two, they kiss. Then they both pull back, propelled by another, opposing force.

Nova's blue eyes are open now, scanning Kate for something that her hands missed. She's confused. Panic swamps Kate.

'I . . . I'm s-sorry . . . I d-don't know . . .'

'Calm down.' Nova smiles. It's a reassuring smile, but not a happy one.

'Oh, God, I'm sorry, I don't know where that came from.'

'Look, I'm not offended. But you're *married*, remember?'

Kate's breath comes quickly, in shuddering bursts. Her skin is burning. How could she be so stupid? Why has she ruined everything? If she hadn't done that, she could have stayed near her, been close to her. Everything could have been okay.

'I'm sorry.' Kate stands up, stumbling over herself, and goes to the window. Nova hesitates for a second, then stands.

'Kate, this doesn't mean—'

'Would you . . . would you go?' Kate doesn't look at her.

'Please, listen—' Nova tries to calm her down, but Kate walks past her, in the direction of her bedroom, and closes the door behind her.

Nova looks around the flat. The urge to stay here is undiminished. She hasn't felt so at home for months. Then, slowly, she finds her coat and rucksack. She waits at the door in case Kate comes bursting out of her room. But there is no sound.

She closes her eyes.

She leaves.

Eighteen

September

SIX MONTHS AFTER SHE left Kate's flat, Nova slips her hand into her coat, grasps the object in her pocket, and rolls its weight against her fingers. The September air is a muggy haze, and she savours the weight of the object, its solidity and coolness.

The night after the kiss, she had dreamt of Kate's face. In the dream, she understood it perfectly, and could answer Kate's question. She knew exactly the kind of person this face belonged to, and she wanted to tell her, but the words wouldn't come out right. The touch and the image became a single thing – the first thing that Nova truly understood as a sighted person.

'You *are* pretty,' she told her, in the dream. 'You're beautiful.'

She did not wake up this time, to cry in the dark. She slept through to morning and woke with no memory of the dream.

In the morning, lying in the darkness, Nova felt as though a decision had been made for her. With Kate, she would have kept trying. Without Kate, there is no point going on. She would give up, starting now.

She would go blind again.

Tears spilled down to Nova's pillow, as though her extraordinary eyes understood the decision that was being made and were already grieving. From now on, they would be imprisoned behind dark glasses, starved of light, shape and colour – those delicious, nauseating candies – until their appetites shrank away to nothing.

But blindness seemed unimportant to her, in that moment. Kate was gone, and would not be coming back. Nova was already living in that outer darkness, beyond light and warmth. All that remained was to get used to it.

Later, as she was getting ready to go out, dark glasses on and white stick under one arm, her hand had closed around something in the pocket of her leather jacket. It took her a while to understand what the object was. It was small and dense. She turned it over and over, feeling the lines of it, the small ring attached to one end. It was a penknife. Somehow, she knew it must belong to Kate. She must have slipped it into the pocket, a surprise for later, before everything went wrong. Nova wonders over its significance, but cannot remember any conversation about penknives. She supposes, if the kiss hadn't happened, that Kate would have explained.

※

It's been months since Kate took her last contraceptive pill. It doesn't matter – there has been no sex. Tony comes home later than whatever late shift he's on. The last couple of weekends he's been away, rock climbing with friends. She expects to start her period soon. She is in bed with Tony and the lights are off, and they have been trying to sleep for five minutes.

She feels his hand on her hip.

Kate feels all the muscles in her stomach tighten, but she tries not to show her fear. She doesn't react when he rolls her onto her back. She tries not to make a noise. This is what she chose.

When it is over, she rolls back onto her side of the bed, while Tony goes to the bathroom. She doesn't make a sound as the tears fall. She doesn't shiver or shake. She just lets the tears flow as Tony gets back into bed and quickly falls asleep. She doesn't move, and after a while, she stops feeling.

✸

'He says he couldn't have stabbed him – he was getting a haircut when it happened.'

Nova listens for a moment more to the unbroken flow of words.

'And he says that three people can vouch for him. People who know him at the hairdresser's.'

The officer asks Nova to ask the suspect for the names of these three people, and Nova does so. The accused man reels off alibis while the officer makes notes. Abruptly, the interview is over. Nova picks up her cane and gets up. She knows the dimensions of all the interview rooms well, but bumps into an out-of-place chair on her way to the door.

'Sorry,' the officer mutters. 'You want me to take you any-where?'

Nova shakes her head – a habit she picked up when she was learning to see. 'Nah, I'm just going to get a coffee. I know the way.'

She makes her way through the corridors of Scotland Yard. There is bustle in the corridors, but people make way for her. It's a couple of months since Nova came back to work, telling colleagues that the operation to restore her sight had been a failure. She'd made up something about her body rejecting the procedure. She said she could still see blotches of light but not much more, and had kept her glasses on at all times. For a group of professional investigators, they'd easily swallowed the lie. Some had offered awkward commiserations, but Nova just smiled and told them that she didn't miss it. They hadn't known what to say to that, and the conversation moved on.

It took her time to return to normal, after her decision to 'become blind' again. It was easy to keep her eyes closed, keep the dark glasses pressed close to her face so that no flashes of light could trick her into peeking. To begin with, that was all she was – not blind, but a person keeping their eyes closed. She was stuck in a limbo between sight and blindness. If she opened her eyes, which she occasionally did at home, she would find her abilities – which seemed so fragile before – annoyingly tenacious.

After a month of keeping the glasses on, Nova could tell something was starting to change. If she looked, her perception of the room took a moment to solidify, and lacked definition. She couldn't reach out and pick up objects, as she had done before. She couldn't use her sight to walk around a cluttered room. Her sight was starting to slip away. After two months passed, the jumble of 'seeing' was becoming more and more confusing – a shifting sea of shapes and colours. After three months, there was nothing left. If she opened her eyes, she saw *something*, but could make no sense of it. All she let in, by opening her eyes, was a messy blur.

She could see, but she was blind.

Nova finds the staff canteen, buys herself a coffee and something in a packet that she's reliably informed is a blueberry muffin. She navigates through the tables, mostly by listening for voices, and asks, 'Anyone sitting here?' to an empty table.

The canteen isn't busy, but there's enough background chatter for Nova to tune out. She sips her coffee, thinking about what she will eat for dinner. One of those pasta meals, perhaps. But she'll be careful not to buy the spaghetti one this time. She's never liked spaghetti – maybe it looks appealing if you can see it, but she doesn't like putting wormy things in her mouth. She could make a joke out of that.

Of course, Kate liked spaghetti . . .

She stops thinking for a second, and pinches hard at skin on her inside wrist. She's like one of those people trying to kick a bad habit. One of those people who picks their nose or chews their nails. She just needs to get out of the habit of thinking about Kate. She's almost cracked it. She almost went a whole day.

An unfamiliar voice calls to her: 'Jillian Safinova?'

'That's me . . .' Nova starts, unsure what direction the voice is coming from in the echoing room. The man comes closer.

'Miss Safinova, you're needed in Interview Room Six, if you can come now.'

She mock sighs.

'All right, buddy. But you're carrying my muffin.'

She's told to wait outside the interview room for the officer and sits on a plastic chair until she hears someone approaching.

'I'm surprised it's taken so long for us to cross paths.'

It takes Nova a moment to place the colourless voice, but her body has already reacted. There's a cold feeling in her stomach, like she drank ice water.

'Tony? Hey – it's been a while.'

'It has . . .' He leaves the sentence hanging. 'You still in touch with Kate?'

Nova tries not to flinch.

'No, I've been a bit caught up with my own stuff recently.'

'I heard your operation didn't work.'

'That's right.' She shifts uncomfortably, wanting the interview to begin, for someone else to be interrogated. Tony pauses, and she wonders if he is looking at her face. She wonders what clues she is giving away.

'I'm so sorry to hear that. Have you been briefed already?'

'No, not yet.' Nova relaxes a little as Tony runs her through the details of the case – a kidnapping, a twenty-three-year-old female in North London, possible trafficking. The man in the cell speaks limited English and Italian is his first language. He's not a suspect, but there's a chance that he's aided the kidnapper unwittingly. The girl may still be in the country and time is of the essence.

Nova nods through all of this, her mind becoming calm as it focusses on the details. She knows how to do this. She knows how it goes. Briefing complete, they enter the room. She sits down first, then Tony, who goes through the usual routine for setting up. The man on the other side of the table makes no noise until Nova introduces herself and explains that she will be his interpreter today, that she is blind. The voice that comes back is older than she expected, and gentle.

'Good morning, miss. It's nice to meet a young lady with such perfect Italian.'

'Not perfect, I'm sure, but I do my best.'

The old man chuckles once. 'Under different circumstances, it would be nice to have a coffee and talk. I never talk to anyone any more.'

'I'm sorry to hear that . . . ' Nova begins.

'What's he saying?' Tony interjects.

'Just small talk, introductions. Shall we get started?'

Tony starts his questioning, and one thing immediately becomes clear to Nova – the old man isn't an acquaintance of the suspect. He's the suspect's father. Why didn't Tony tell her that? She feels wrong-footed.

'Do you know where your son is now, Mr Petrucci?'

'Please, call me Luca. Only the bank calls me Mr Petrucci. Luca means "bringer of light". Someone told me.'

'Has he answered the question?' Tony sounds impatient, but no more so than any interrogating officer.

'No, hang on . . .' She makes the mental switch back to Italian. 'Do you know where your son is, Luca?'

The old man clears his throat, and Nova can hear his discomfort. He's not being evasive – he doesn't want to talk about this. He's embarrassed.

'No, I don't know . . .'

Nova relays the answer back to Tony.

'Ask him when he last saw him.'

Luca's reply is halting. 'I saw him . . . yesterday morning . . . he was eating breakfast. Then he went out.'

Nova goes through the details of this last encounter, establishing time and place, the fragments of their conversation. She can tell that Luca is becoming upset by the policeman's voice and wonders if Tony can detect this, despite the language barrier.

There is a long pause after she has given Tony the answer to his last question. Then,

'Where is the girl?'

Nova pauses, unsure if she is being asked to translate. She's sure that Luca has enough English to understand the questions, but not to answer. She asks him.

'I'm sorry; I don't know what you're talking about.'

Next question: 'Where has your son taken the girl?'

Nova asks the question.

'I'm sorry; I don't know where my son is.'

Tony reminds Luca that it is a crime to lie under police interrogation, and a serious crime to aid a kidnapper. Luca says he understands, but that he is doing neither. The next few questions are variations on the same question, and the answer is always a variation on the same answer.

'I'm sorry; I don't know what I can tell you.'

If Nova feels uncomfortable with the questioning, it's hardly more than usual – most interrogators, in this situation, would try to force an answer. Sometimes it yields results. Sometimes people open up under pressure. The switch can be startling. But the old man isn't changing his answer, and there's only so far you can go. His breath is short and tight. She expects the questions to change tack.

They don't.

'Ask him again,' Tony says. Nova doesn't say anything, but she pauses. In the controlled environment of the interview room, this says all she needs to say.

'I said ask him again.' Tony's voice is low.

Nova asks Luca once more.

'I'm sorry, one more time – where is your son?'

Luca does not sigh or swear, she does not hear him move. But his answer is strained. He is about to cry, this dignified old man.

'I do not know.'

Tony doesn't wait for her to translate before he jumps out of his chair. The explosive movement makes Nova jump. She can't see what he's doing, but she thinks he's leaning over the table.

'Listen to me, *fucker*,' Tony says, quiet but menacing, 'I know you can understand me. Tell me where your piece-of-shit son is. Tell me where he's gone. Tell me what he's doing.'

Luca is silent.

'Tell me!' Tony yells.

Luca cries out, and from his yelps, Nova gathers that Tony has reached over the table and grabbed the old man by the ear. Luca staggers to his feet, his chair scraping back. She can hear him now – he's sobbing.

'Please,' he says in English, 'please . . . I do not know. Not hurt me. Not hurt me, please!'

Nova stands, reaches without sight, grabbing Tony's arm.

'That's enough!'

She can hear the blood surging in her ears. She has never done this before. It's against the rules. She can't stop an interview like this – it's not her place. Distantly, she remembers training on what to do if an officer acted inappropriately, but it is so long ago, and she's never had to put it into practice. She feels Tony lean back, turn to her.

'*You* don't tell me how to do my job.'

She tries to make peace.

'No, I know. I'm sorry. But I don't think he knows anything.'

'What *you* think,' Tony snarls, 'doesn't interest me.'

He shrugs out of her grasp.

'I'll be reporting you for impeding an interview, Miss Safinova,' he says in a smooth voice, then leans closer, so his breath is in her face. 'And if the girl dies because you stopped me doing my job, you'll be hearing from me again.'

With that, he's gone from the interview room, and Nova is left standing there, with nothing but the quiet weeping of the old man.

✴

Later, she sits at home and replays everything in the interview room as though she's replaying a recording. Nova has a good memory for words. Sometimes she wishes she didn't, that at least some of them would slip away.

She wonders about Tony, and about Kate (breaking her resolution over and over), and a new feeling creeps into her old repertoire. Not fear, exactly. Worry.

She wonders if Tony will tell Kate about the interview.

She wonders whether Kate will believe him, if he tells her that the interpreter screwed everything up.

She wonders if she should send Kate a message. Despite

her resolution, Nova hasn't deleted the architect's contact from her phone. But what would she say? There's nothing to say. Nothing that will change what happened.

She sits and – without opening her eyes – remembers the ghost of Kate's face. The last shape she can remember with any clarity.

Nineteen

October

'Do you want tea? Coffee?'
'No thanks – just had one.'
'Just shout if you need me.'

Kate leaves the carpet fitters to their work in the bedroom and goes through to the study, which already has its sandy, oak-veneer floor laid. Her work computer and cork-topped architect's desk are here, with all the file boxes from the old flat. The rest of the flat is half empty, but this room is complete. She likes working here. She often sleeps on the sofa. At the old flat, she started to feel like a prisoner. Here, she can stay inside, and it feels like a choice. Tony doesn't seem to mind – they'll be moving out of the old flat in a couple of weeks anyway.

It has taken such a long time to finish the flat. Kate, usually so efficient, dawdled over booking people in, and endlessly put off the jobs that she planned to do herself. She had insisted on doing as many jobs herself as possible, from cutting the skirting boards to fitting the kitchen cabinets. She said it was to save money, but it's taken so long, she doubts this is true. She isn't sure why. If Tony cared that they were spending so much money on rent and a mortgage at the same time, he didn't say anything. Kate felt complicit in something, though she wasn't sure what.

There's a box in the corner of the study containing her paint-by-number kits. Sometimes she can smell the plastic tang of the paints, seeping through the cardboard. There is a ship at sea, a country lane in autumn, and the parrot. Kate hasn't painted for months. She will throw them all out soon.

She turns on the computer and realizes she's smiling. It takes her by surprise, and she wonders if she's happy. She is busy, she decides, and that is good enough.

Kate browses through emails, then looks at a website selling Babygros and slings made from bamboo (how do they do that?).

She's not pregnant.

Not yet. But she's ready for it now. It's the right time.

After a while, she goes back to her emails, looking over a message from the council. To get a new food bin, she needs to show two kinds of identification. *Ugh*. Everything is online these days, and Kate wonders for a moment if she has anything other than the Council Tax bills. Ah – the mortgage papers. She pads through to the kitchen and makes herself a lemon verbena tea, then goes back to the study to search through their file box for the mortgage documentation. The mortgage folder is empty.

Did she do that?

No – she remembers putting everything away in the right folder. Did Tony go through this for some reason? She searches through the other folders, but doesn't find the papers. She sits, the cold weight of the file box pressing on her lap.

Something is wrong. She searches the study and, finding nothing, bids goodbye to the carpet fitters, who have their own key, and returns to the old flat. There she searches through boxes of files, piles of paper stuck in drawers and sheaves of discarded envelopes.

She does not find the mortgage papers.

✴

Over the next week, she searches for clues. The more she does not find what she is looking for, the more Kate is accumulating something else, one piece at a time, until she can no longer deny that she is carrying the weight of it around with her like an over-stuffed folder.

Suspicion.

It is a long time since she has thought of the square of white paper. Not directly, at least. Memories of that period of her life recur quite naturally, but she has not looked at their radiant centre for a long time, as someone who looks *close* but not quite *at* the sun.

She does not say anything to Tony. She could simply ask him where the folder is, of course, except now she has this suspicion, and it wouldn't be fair to him, in a way, to just ask, because then she would be handing him the initiative. If he had every chance to prove his innocence, how would she ever believe him? She has to discover his innocence herself.

She thinks (though the thought does not make her anxious) that she has left Tony on his own in the old flat so often, while she slept in the new flat. At the time, she had appreciated the time apart.

She does not jump to conclusions.

But she does stop sleeping at the new flat. She comes home before he does and leaves after he leaves. She looks through his work bags, his suit jacket, and the pockets of his trousers.

At first there is nothing. She almost gives up. But by the end of the week, she has accumulated a small collection of everyday objects.

1) A receipt for a café she doesn't recognize –

> 1 CFE – CAPP TALL
> 2 CFE – FLAT WHITE
> 3 KWI FRUIT TART x2
>
> (4 ITEMS)

2) A crumpled napkin that has a red smudge in one corner.

3) A pen from a chain hotel that they have never stayed in.

4) A long strand of straight, auburn hair.

None of these objects is proof. Tony takes people to cafés for work. The smudge on the napkin could be anything – it only looks like lipstick because she's thinking that way. The pen could have come from anywhere – she might have picked it up herself in a meeting without a second thought. The auburn hair, from the back of one of Tony's jackets, could have come from any chair that he sat on that day.

The objects mean nothing, but they are enough to sustain Kate's suspicion. She hates creeping around. She wants to hear his mundane explanations.

Perhaps, she reasons with herself, she needs to find something he is guilty of, to neutralize her own guilt about snooping around (though, like the square of white paper, she tries not to think directly about the source of this shame). Perhaps she believes she can't fuck things up more than she already has.

Of course, the first place she wants to look is his wallet, for the piece of white paper. It has been almost two years, and she knows there is no chance Tony's kept it in there all this time, but she still wants to look. His wallet is almost always in his trouser pocket. If she wants to get it, she will have to wait until he is getting ready for bed, in the bathroom. That's too dangerous for now. Instead, she goes through his drawers in the bedroom.

She finds nothing out of the ordinary. She doesn't know what she expects to find. There are condoms in the bedside table, but they have been there for months. They haven't been using contraception, so it would be more suspicious if the condoms were gone.

His work is the only thing that reassures her, a multipurpose alibi. Perhaps the piece of white paper was evidence – something secret, something she couldn't see, something that he was protecting *her* from, and not himself. But what kind of evidence would be kept in his wallet? What kind of secret would be written on a piece of paper?

She knows that if she wants real answers, she must look at his bank account, but that's easier said than done. They have a shared joint account and a solo account each, but Tony doesn't get paper statements – he does everything online. There's no way she can get his password and details to log into the account.

At one point, Kate would have made up something about the water bill (which is charged to his account) and he would have shown her the account. But now she's not so sure. She doesn't want him to suspect her suspicion.

When they got the mortgage for the new flat, they had to submit twelve months of statements from their personal accounts. Tony had gone to the bank and had them print out the statements. Kate put them all together with the mortgage paperwork and sent them off.

No.

No, that's not how it happened. Tony had sent them off. He had waited until Kate filled out her forms and added her bank statements, then he'd taken the bundle, gone to the bank to get his own statements, had put everything together and sent it off.

Kate hadn't thought anything of it. The mortgage was approved online, and the documents were sent back to them two weeks later. She hadn't even looked at them – Tony had taken the papers and put them somewhere. At the time, she had assumed he was putting them in the file box.

Somewhere in the house, he has hidden those bank statements. She is sure of it. She needs to find them.

It's easier said than done. Kate searches under the bed, in Tony's work papers, through the police training manuals that he keeps on the shelf. The statements aren't in any of them, and she starts to wonder if he threw the file in the bin. But it is supporting documentation for their mortgage – even once it was approved, Tony is far too cautious, too meticulous, to have thrown that out.

✵

She is searching in the old study – the boxroom half empty now, full of furniture they'll be getting rid of – and takes the bottom drawer out of the bureau to make it easier to search through. That's when she sees it – not in the drawer itself, but in the cobwebbed space under the drawer at the bottom of the bureau.

The square of white paper.

She picks the paper up, feeling an odd certainty.

The square isn't folded how she thought it was – not in half, then quarters, but into a tiny envelope. Her hands are shaking as she undoes it.

White powder spills out of the white paper.

There's not much of it – less than a sachet of sugar. She raises a finger and dabs the powder on her tongue. Not sugar – there is a faint vinegary smell, then it's gone. Kate rubs her tongue on the roof of her mouth, feeling the spot where it has gone numb.

She sets the paper square down, dusting her hands off as though she's baking. She looks inside the bureau, finding nothing. Then she turns over the drawer she took out. Taped to the underside is a double-thickness black bag. Carefully, she tears the plastic.

A dozen white squares spill out.

Under them, sealed in zip-lock kitchen bags, are several kilos of the white powder.

✳

By the time Tony comes home from work, Kate is sitting at the kitchen table, with the handful of white squares spread in front of her. She hasn't had a drink. She made herself peppermint tea instead. It's something to hold at least, to stop him seeing how much her hands are shaking. She could have phoned the police. But she hasn't.

'Home at last!' he shouts from the hall. 'Did you see my message? I thought we could have the leftover tomato sauce with some . . .'

He trails off as he comes into the kitchen and sees Kate at the table. His eyes dart between her and the paper squares.

'What are you doing?' he asks. His voice is smooth, flat – a featureless kind of voice, no handholds, unscalable.

'What am *I* doing?' she says, and her voice is so small. How can her voice be so small? She is so tall, so broad, so outsized, yet her voice betrays her. He doesn't say anything for a long time. He turns his back to her, walks over to the window, and looks for a while at whatever is happening on the street below. She glances back down at the paper squares in front of her.

He turns and walks back to the table.

'How dare you—'

'Clear out the drawers in my own home?'

'How dare you spy on me!' He advances, and she stands up from the table, still holding her drink protectively. Before she knows what Tony is doing, his hand darts up, dashing the mug from her hands. The hot water splashes over Kate's shoulder, scalding her, and the mug falls, smashing on the tiles.

'How dare you,' he says again. 'Those sachets are police evidence. Evidence that you've contaminated.'

For a moment, doubt creeps in. Kate quells it. She prepared herself for this.

'The police don't hide evidence in their own homes. In their own wallets.'

Tony does not reply. She can smell the anger rising off him in waves. He doesn't look angry, though – his face is blank. But his body is bunched up, as though he's ready to throw himself at her. The pain from the tea brings tears to her eyes, and her breath comes in hot bursts. She's getting ready to run – to run around him, to run out of the kitchen and the flat, to run somewhere safe. She makes the move and—

Something hits Kate in the face.

Tony.

She staggers back, clutching her cheek.

'See what you made me do?'

The tears are flowing freely now.

'I didn't make you do this,' she says, flatly.

'No? You don't think so?' He laughs once, brightly. 'Do you know how fucking boring it is, living with you?'

'You did this because you're bored?'

Tony says nothing, just smiles thinly, as though to say, *You wouldn't understand.*

'How could . . .?' Kate starts, but never gets to finish the sentence. He hits her in the face again, and this time she feels the skin over her cheekbone burst like a grape. Blood trickles down her cheek. She's trembling all over. She gets ready to make her move, to dash to the other side of him, the one he won't be expecting. She moves and—

He trips her as she ducks past him and Kate goes flying. She's airborne. For a second she's moving, unable to stop. But then she lands, her hands scraping the tiles, her wrists bending back painfully. Her palms are sliced by shards from the broken mug. She instinctively curls into a ball.

There is a moment before he lands on her, a moment before she starts screaming. She tries to scream words – to scream at Tony to stop, or for somebody to help, to form the scream into the shapes of words. But she's too scared. His blows come too fast, and she just screams.

Kate expects she will black out, like she did when she fell and hit her head. But it doesn't happen. She's begging for it to happen, yet terrified, because if she falls asleep now, she doesn't know if she will ever wake up.

How long has it been? Thirty seconds, maybe a minute? Tony hits her on the head, in the ribs, in her lower back, as if he knows exactly which points will hurt the most. If he's aware of how much he's hurting her, he no longer cares. It doesn't feel like him any more. It feels like an animal is on top of her. Like a bull, or a dog, something that is trampling and mauling her at the same time. For the first time in her life, Kate believes she is about to die.

There's a banging noise, fast and insistent. Nothing changes for a moment, then Tony stops hitting Kate. He gets up, kneeling next to her. In that position, it might have looked like she had fallen and hurt herself, and he had knelt to help her. Tony stands, while the banging continues. Kate realizes that someone is at the door. Somebody is hammering at the door.

She tries to make a noise, to get the attention of the person at the door. The sounds that escape her are tiny, but it's enough to anger him again.

He walks back to her, in his steel toecap shoes, and brings his foot down, just once, on her head.

Tony gathers the white squares on the table and walks out of the kitchen. Kate can't move to stop him. She listens as he goes into the spare room and takes the bags of white powder from the bureau. Then he goes through to the bedroom and starts packing a bag. Every few seconds there is another burst of banging from the front door, and muffled shouting.

Kate listens to it all, and can see it clearly in her head. She's still awake but she thinks maybe her neck is broken, because she can't feel the rest of her body. She tries to focus on the sound of banging. She doesn't want it to ever stop. It's the only thing that's keeping him away from her.

She hears Tony walk through to the hallway, then a dull thud that she does not recognize, but will understand later – the sound of Tony hitting himself on the side of his face with the glass paperweight they keep in the hallway as an ornament. Later she will spot the paperweight on the floor and see, against its swirl of oceanic blue, a smear of dried blood.

He opens the door. She hears angry voices. Kate hears him talking calmly, them shouting, but she doesn't know what's being said. Her ears are ringing. She can hear the whoosh-whoosh-whoosh of blood in her ears. She hears the other person speak again, not shouting now. They are doubting themselves. For a moment, Kate thinks it's all over. Then a shout, Tony this time.

'Hey! This is my house.'

'If you've got nothing to hide, why not let me past? Otherwise I'm going to call the police.'

A moment passes.

Kate hears feet running towards her, heavy impacts, and she thinks it must be Tony, coming back to get her.

Soft hands are laid on her.

There is no more shouting, but there are many voices. They wash around the room like underwater things. The flat seems to have filled with people, but Kate can't move, can't roll over to see who's in her house.

It seems rude, not to offer them a drink or somewhere to sit. She feels bad. Finally, a hand is laid on her shoulder.

'Don't worry, love, there's an ambulance on the way. Do you want me to call the police?'

Kate doesn't cry. Or rather, she doesn't sob, or make any noise like crying. Tears fall freely from her eyes. It's more that she has been cracked open.

'No,' she whispers, 'no police. They were already here.'

Twenty

November

S HE DOESN'T THINK OF her, to begin with. There is too much going on. She thinks about hospital appointments and work commitments. Slowly, she ties up each loose end, speaks to the people she needs to speak to, and arranges another round of time off work.

She turns down the offer of a counsellor, repeating her story that she and Tony had both been fighting, that she fell awkwardly, that it wasn't his fault. She doesn't expect anyone to believe this story, but that's not the point. The story is a placeholder for something more inconvenient – that Tony hurt her, and she's going to let him get away with it.

She does not entirely avoid talking to the police. Someone at the hospital referred her case, and Kate repeats the story to the officer who comes to talk to her. He seems supportive, encouraging her to tell her story, but when Tony's name comes up, Kate sees a flash of recognition in his eyes. Does this man know Tony? Are they friends? What story has he been telling people? He notes down her lies and asks no further questions.

She finds out not long after from a friend of Tony's, calling to ask if he can come pick up some things. She has met Phil once before, at the police Christmas drinks a couple of years ago. She thinks about saying no, but curiosity gets the better of her. He arrives at the flat with a couple of empty gym bags and studiously avoids looking at the bruises on her face. Slowly, Kate shuffles through to the bedroom and shows him to Tony's drawers.

'So, is Tony staying with you?'

Phil glances nervously in the direction of her navel, then back to the drawer.

'No . . . He asked me not to tell you, but he's taking some time off work.'

'Time off?'

'Some kind of therapy. To deal with . . .'

'Deal with what?'

Phil sighs, apparently annoyed to have to spell this out. 'To deal with the breakdown of his marriage.'

'*His* marriage?'

'Look, I'm just here to get his clothes, okay? I didn't tell you anything.'

Eventually, Phil leaves, and Kate packs her own bags. It's time to go. She will pay someone to empty the old flat, give notice to the landlord. This is not her home any more.

✳

Everything is done, and Kate has nothing to think about. She doesn't like it. The chores were all that she had to hold onto. Driftwood from the wreckage. Left to herself, with nothing to do, Kate is alone in a wide ocean, and her mind turns to the last time she was happy.

She thinks about going to the zoo and seeing the penguins. She thinks about walking through the National Gallery and seeing the sunflowers. She thinks about seeing Nova.

Kate has no way of contacting her. After the kiss, she made a simple promise to herself – no more fantasy, no more fooling around. She was married to Tony and she was going to make a life with him. A family. Anything or anyone who didn't fit with that, however enjoyable, had to go. Nova was a shape that no longer fitted into the schematics of Kate's future. Beautiful in her own right, but no longer serving the overall design.

She had deleted the interpreter's contact from her phone and put the old beermat in the bin. Now, Kate realizes, she doesn't even know where Nova lives. The one time she invited Kate back, she had turned her down. Somewhere in Brixton, but that's all she knows. Not enough.

At first, she phones the police. She asks them if they can give her a contact for one of their interpreters. Of course they say no. They're not allowed to give out the personal details of any of their employees. Kate says she doesn't need personal details – just a work email will do – but the woman on the other end of the phone is suspicious and ends the call.

She searches online, but finds nothing except a couple of articles from an Oxford student magazine, dated eleven years ago. One is about accessibility ramps, the other about a late-night radio show, *Aural Pleasure with Jillian Safinova*. There aren't even any pictures. After that, she has no ideas for a long time. It seems hopeless. She could go down to Brixton and wait in the crowds by the Tube every day. But that's plain crazy, and Kate doesn't even know that she takes the Tube.

Besides, she's too nervous to stand in crowds any more.

She cries, a gentle flow of tears that never gets worse but never stops, for several hours. (She's frustrated, that's all. After all that has been taken out of her control, she wants this one thing to be fixable.)

She remembers something while thinking about an anecdote Nova told her, about a police raid at a house party she'd been to at university, and how her tutor had broken the tense silence by upending a plate of spaghetti bolognese over his head. She had cried with laughter, telling the story.

That's it. Kate can find a contact for the tutor. She remembers that he is also blind. He's a friend to Nova, a mentor. She searches online, praying that he's still working for the university, until she sees a picture on the Modern Languages Faculty page – eyes shut, face round and hammy-pink, smiling gently as though listening to a favourite song.

Professor John Katzner
MA, MSt, DPhil (Oxon)
Research – Literature and the history of ideas of the
   late 18th-century.
Selected publications . . .

Her breathing speeds up as she reads his biography and recognizes the man she's looking for. She picks up the phone without taking time to compose her thoughts and dials. The phone starts to ring, but nobody picks up right away. Suddenly, Kate realizes that she might only get one chance at this – if she makes the wrong impression, she will have burned her last bridge. She's about to hang up when the hiss from the receiver changes tone.

'Hello?' John Katzner speaks through the noise.

'Oh, uh, hello.'

'Hello? How can I help?' The voice is older than she expected, even a little frail, but forceful in its intonation.

'Yes, sorry. My name is Kate, and I was wondering . . . Well, I was *hoping* you could put me in touch with someone.'

'In touch? With whom?' There is rustling on the other end of the line, and a thump as John sits down.

'I was wondering if you had a contact for one of your alumni. Her name is Nova?' There is silence on the other end, and Kate corrects herself. 'Sorry – I mean Jillian Safinova. Do you have a contact for Jillian Safinova?'

He hasn't hung up. She can hear his breathing. Then,

'You were right first time. She never uses her given name.'

Though he can't see her, Kate nods emphatically.

'Yes, I know! Only her brother calls her Jillian. Or Jill . . .'

She prays that the detail convinces him she's not a crank.

'Did you say your name was Kate?'

She hears the recognition in his voice, realizes her mistake too late.

Shitfuck.

'Uh, yes. We met at an interpreter's conference in London but I lost her card.'

The lie is good, considering she's just thought of it, but too late.

'Kate, I've heard about you. I know how you met.'

233

She feels her heart falling away, and grips hard on the phone. She changes tack.

'Look, John – Nova and I parted on bad terms, and I really just want to apologize to her—'

He cuts her off.

'She doesn't want to talk to you, Kate. That's what she told me. And she doesn't tell me much about her private life, so it must be important to her.'

Kate can feel her voice shaking when she replies:

'Look, John . . . I know you probably think I'm a bad person.'

'I didn't say that.'

'But I'm not asking you to give me her contact. Just let her know . . . let her know that I'm really sorry . . . and that I'm not doing so well . . .'

Her voice breaks. She mustn't cry.

'Are you all right?' His voice is small over the line, and Kate isn't sure if he's concerned for her or concerned by her behaviour. If he thinks she's a stalker. She can't bring herself to reply.

'Look,' he says slowly, 'give me your number. I'll get in touch with her and let her know you called. And if she wants to contact you, she can.'

'Yes! Yes, that would be perfect. Thank you, John, thank—'

'But,' he cuts her off, 'this is the only time I'll do this. If she says no, then I don't want you to try and contact her again, okay?'

Kate swallows with difficulty. 'Yes, of course. Of course. Yes.'

She gives her mobile number and her landline, worrying about how a blind man is noting them down, and hangs up when he does. The flat seems to hiss softly like a telephone line. There will be no callers today. Kate walks to the living room, sits on the sofa and waits.

✳

There is a pigeon on the windowsill. It built a nest there, from ragged bits of cardboard, and laid two moon-white eggs, which now it leaves only for short spells. When night falls, Kate will turn the lights off in the living room and peek around the curtain to look at the bird. It doesn't seem to see her. She will watch the mother pigeon for a long time, until the ache in her legs and back forces her to retreat, turn the lights back on, and sit on the sofa until she catches her breath.

The new flat is very quiet. Of course, Kate made it that way. She raised the floors, lowered the ceilings, built a box within a box, filled cavities with insulation and used every trick to make these rooms quiet, quiet, quiet. This space was supposed to be a secret one for Tony and her. It was supposed to be a place where they could escape from the world, together.

Now she thinks that if they'd escaped here any sooner, nobody would have heard her screaming.

His name is on the mortgage, but she has the only keys. His contribution to the mortgage is still paid into their joint account every month. She did all the work converting the flat, arranging the builders and electricians and carpenters. His keys are cut, but she still has them. So, she is lucky – this is her safe place to be, now that their old home isn't safe.

She should be angry, but the main thing Kate feels is shame. There were so many people in their home. So many people watching as she was taken out on a stretcher. As she left in an ambulance. As she told her made-up story. The shame burns in her chest like acid reflux.

Kate wants to shower, to get clean, but showers are difficult. She has three cracked ribs, a fractured wrist, a punctured eardrum, concussion and a covering of bruises so complete that it might as well be camouflage.

The flat is her armour, like a lobster's shell. Leaving would feel like shedding her carapace, walking pink and raw down the High Street. She's drawn the blinds, locked the door. She's sealed herself away, but has forgotten one way in. The weak spot. As she is sat on the sofa, the phone on the side table starts to ring.

Kate jumps. The phone is a rotary. Its ring is loud – tiny hammer smashing against metal. She grinds her teeth. She picks up the receiver, ready to silence the intruder. It will be the police, or a social worker, or a lawyer, or her work, asking her (if it's all right) when she's going to be back (but no pressure [but really, yes, pressure, because how much can you expect an employer to put up with?]). She nearly puts the receiver straight back down when another possibility registers. Kate doesn't put it to her ear, but brings it a little closer. She can hear a voice, very small.

Nova's voice.

Nova is calling her.

Kate hesitates. She suddenly doesn't want to talk to her, but doesn't want to reject her either. She moves the receiver closer so that she can hear better, but doesn't let it touch her face.

'Nova?' Her voice is croaky, but nothing out of the ordinary. Nothing that would give her away.

'Hey, Kate. I got your message . . .'

She talks without Kate needing to. She has rehearsed what to say.

'I just want you to know, I'm not angry, and you don't have to worry about me.'

It's clear from her voice that Nova has not guessed what happened with Tony. She thought a rumour might have reached her at work. She doesn't know, yet, how isolated Nova has become in the time since they last met.

'Nova . . . I . . .' Kate's voice breaks.

There is a moment of silence on the other end of the line. 'Kate, I'm sorry, I didn't want to upset you. I just . . .'

'You didn't upset me . . . you didn't upset me . . . you *didn't.*' Her voice crumples.

'What's the matter? Kate?'

Kate mumbles something down the phone that she won't remember later. But she must have said Tony's name, because the next time Nova speaks, she doesn't sound uncertain any more.

'Kate, are you staying there? In the new flat? I'm coming now.'

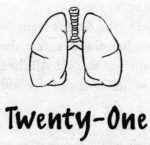

Twenty-One

NOVA MUST HAVE GOT a taxi, because she arrives fifty-one minutes later. It takes Kate a while to get up from the couch, to walk to the hallway, to unlock all the bolts on the door. So, by the time she opens it, Nova is frantic.

'Kate? What's going on? Are you okay?' she asks all at once, but Kate says nothing. She is mute with breathless appreciation of Nova's presence. She is wearing a canary-yellow T-shirt that has

YOU WANNA
PIZZA
ME?

spelled out in the toppings on a slice, which is also winking lasciviously at Kate. Nova is holding a white stick – the significance of which Kate does not grasp – and has a pair of dark glasses pushed back on her head like a hairband.

Nova pauses, trying to see.

Kate wants to hide. She doesn't want Nova to see her like this. She remembers her old idea, that the reason for Nova's goodness was that she was so *pure*. All the bad stuff never had a chance to get into her system, to pollute her, to make her like everyone else.

To make her like Kate.

And now Kate feels bad, because it seems like she's the one who's going to spoil her. Perfect Nova, spoiled by her ugliness. Nova's blue eyes roam over her face, trying to understand, trying to translate the signs written all over Kate's body, the calligraphy of cuts, the punctuation of bruises. Kate doesn't know that Nova is blind again, that all she can see is a pinkish blur, flashbulbs of blonde. But Nova is good at guessing.

'You're . . . hurt?'

'Yes, I'm hurt. But I'm okay.'

Nova is shaking her head. 'No, no, you're not all right . . . I can tell you're not all right.' She steps forward, uncertainly, hands in front of her, not knowing whether she can hold her or not. Kate doesn't move. She's frozen. She doesn't know what she expected from today, only that it couldn't be worse than what has already happened. It hadn't included the possibility of being held by Nova.

Nova puts her arms around her, very gently. She's so small, her face only comes up to Kate's collarbone. Kate winces in pain.

'Sorry! I'm sorry. Are you all right?'

'Yes, it's fine, I just have some, uh, broken ribs, and wrist.'

Nova looks up suddenly, into her eyes, and Kate can see the tears forming. Her jaw is clenched in anger.

'Fuck.' Nova whispers, looking down. 'Come on, let's sit on the sofa.'

Kate closes the door behind them, and they walk together, slowly, to the sofa, Nova cautious in her blindness, Kate hobbling from the pain, each throwing the other off whatever balance they might have had alone. They sit on the sofa, in the same places, the same positions, where Kate had kissed her.

Nova takes her hand and places it on her own. She lets Kate's hand rest on hers, perched like a bird. She senses that Kate can't be held in any way, mustn't be in a position where she cannot run away. She knows that, but knows also that Kate needs to touch someone.

'You don't have to, but if it would help, you can tell me what happened.'

Kate nods. 'It's not a very nice story.'

'I work with the police. I've heard worse, I'm sure.' Then she shakes her head, regretting the words. 'That's not what I meant. I didn't mean to make you feel like what happened wasn't . . .'

'It's okay, I know.'

Kate starts talking. She tells the interpreter everything, though not in the right order. She tells her that Tony hit her. She tells her about the white squares. She tells her that she doubted herself, even with the evidence in front of her. She tells her about what her husband said, what he had done. She tells her about the first square of white paper and how she hit her head, the first time. She tells the truth, for the first time.

When she is done, they are quiet for a long time. Nova doesn't seem to know what to say. Kate thinks maybe she is waiting to see if there is anything else. But no – Nova doesn't know what to say. Usually she listens to people talking about crimes. She never had to say much herself.

'Kate, I'm so sorry.'

'Don't be sorry, it's not your fault.'

'I'm sorry, Kate. I'm so sorry.' Nova is crying, quite gently. She tells Kate about the interview where Tony threatened her, trying to explain her own guilt – that she had sensed something was wrong and did nothing about it. Tony had never reported her, as he had threatened. But if she had just reported him . . .

'It's not your fault, Nova.'

The interpreter says nothing, seems unable to utter anything more than she has said. Kate has done it, she knows. She has ruined Nova. She has shown her ugliness. But she's still glad she's here.

'Nova, out of all the people of the world, all those people whose job it is to help me . . . you're the only person I want to see.'

Nova doesn't say anything in response. Her eyes are wet with tears, her lips pressed together as though holding something in. They sit like that for a long time. Sometimes Nova can hear a car horn outside, or a police siren, faintly, very faintly, but otherwise it's very peaceful, and all she can hear is her breathing. Tension bleeds out of her. She rests her head gently on Kate's shoulder. It doesn't feel awkward. It feels right.

Kate closes her eyes, sleepy. She's on so much pain medication it doesn't take much to doze off. She feels like she's falling asleep in a warm, warm bath. Something smells good, something floral – the bubble bath? What a nice smell.

'So warm,' she mumbles.

'Sorry, I'm like a human radiator. Should have warned you.' Nova's voice wakes Kate enough to know that she's not in the bath.

'S'okay.'

'Are you falling asleep?'

'Sorry, I'm being rude.' She chuckles softly.

'You have a good excuse.' Nova smiles. 'Do you want to go to bed?'

'Mm. Maybe I should. Sorry . . .'

'Don't apologize. Come on, let me help you up.' Nova stands, holds out her hands, and pulls Kate to her feet, holding the hand that doesn't have the wrist fracture.

'Which way is the bedroom?'

'This way.' Kate limps along with her, as Nova holds an arm out to hold onto. There is almost nothing in the bedroom. A bag of her clothes is sitting in the corner of the room, untouched. A duvet, some sheets and other bedding are piled in a corner.

'Sorry – I haven't made the bed.'

'Let me make it for you,' Nova says.

'You can see well enough to make a bed now?' Kate asks innocently. 'That's great.'

'Eh, not so much.' Nova shrugs, not wanting to tell Kate yet about her decision. 'But I've always made the bed by touch, you know?'

'Oh, right, of course. But still, I can't make you do my chores.'

'It's no trouble. You go to the bathroom and get ready, I'll make the bed.'

'Okay.' With difficulty, Kate bends down to get some pyjamas out of the bag and carries them through to the bathroom, where she already has a few things. She brushes her teeth and splashes water on her face, though it stings her black eye. All the time she can hear worrying noises coming from the other room. When she returns, Nova has got the sheet onto the mattress and has fitted the four pillow-cases, but is wrapped, like a confused ghost, in the duvet cover.

'Nova, are you in there?'

'I think so!' She slumps onto the bed, giggling. 'I guess your sheets are different from mine.' Kate starts laughing, hobbling over to help.

'Come on. If you hold still for a second, I think I can get you untangled.' With some rearranging, Kate pulls the sheet off Nova. She emerges, laughing, curly hair askew.

'Sorry, I'm not the world's best chambermaid.'

'Don't worry. We can finish it together.'

Nova holds the corners while Kate shakes the duvet out, feeling the bright ache in her ribs.

'There we go – a bit lumpy, but it'll do.'

'Do you want anything else?' Nova asks. 'Need any balls of yarn untangling?'

'No, I think you've done enough damage. But . . . if you'd like to stay?'

Nova pauses. Kate doesn't actually hold her breath, but rather it feels as though her whole body pauses for a moment. Marrow stops making blood, follicles stop growing hair, and biological time stands still, until Nova says, 'You don't mind?'

'No, you'd be doing me a favour.' Kate says, leaving unsaid

– *I don't want to be alone*. 'I have a spare toothbrush, and you're welcome to borrow a nightie, though I think it'll probably come down to your ankles.'

'That would be nice. I can sleep on the sofa.'

Kate pauses, unsure of herself. 'You can sleep in here, if you want. It's a big bed.'

Nova answers more quickly this time. 'No, you should have the bed.' She runs a hand through her hair. 'If I kicked you in my sleep, I'd never forgive myself.'

Kate smiles and nods, heart thundering secretly. They go about their preparations for bed. Kate finds the spare toothbrush and a nightie. As predicted, it comes down way past Nova's knees, and she makes a show of waddling around like a penguin. Kate makes up a bed on the sofa and fetches a glass of water. When Nova comes to join her in the front room, Kate notices that she's following her voice, using slightly outstretched arms to warn of any obstacle. She wants to ask about it, but doesn't.

'It's so quiet in here, I think I'll sleep well.'

'I hope so. Night.'

Kate walks back to her room, feeling foolish. Why had she asked Nova to sleep in the same bed? It's so obvious that Nova isn't interested in a relationship. Is *she* interested in a relationship? The question is too complicated. Until recently, she hadn't been looking for a relationship with anybody. She doesn't know what to want, or what to feel. She doesn't know what she's allowed to want. They took her wedding ring off at the hospital, but she's still married.

She gets into bed carefully, swinging one leg up, then the other, trying to find a position that's comfortable, realizing there isn't one. She takes a final codeine pill to help her sleep, turns off the light and closes her eyes.

✳

It's not much later when Kate wakes up screaming. The room is dark and quiet. There is no air. She doesn't know where she is, and she thrashes, trying to find something that will identify her surroundings. She feels like she can't breathe and there is a pain in her chest. That's it – she's having a heart attack. She's going to die in bed. She becomes aware of someone else in the room.

'Kate? Are you okay?'

Slowly, Kate remembers where she is, and why she's there, and why Nova is there. But none of this stops the panic that she's feeling, the rising fear. The air is being crushed out of her lungs. She's going to die.

She feels Nova getting closer, sitting on the edge of the bed. She fumbles around in the dark and finds the bedside light and turns it on. Kate is blinded but feels arms around her. Nova holds her while she shakes and her breaths heave in and out.

'It's okay, you had a bad dream. It was just a bad dream.'

'No . . . don't understand . . . can't breathe . . . think . . . heart attack . . .' Kate gasps between tiny sips of breath. It's like her lungs have set in stone.

'No, listen, you're having a panic attack. You're going to be okay. It's not going to kill you.'

'Are you . . . sure?'

'Yes. Now listen to me. I need you to breathe. You're going

to breathe in and out as we count backwards from one hundred, okay? And you're just going to listen to my voice.'

Kate no longer has any breath to answer her with, so she just nods. Nova seems to understand.

'Okay. One hundred . . . ninety-nine . . . ninety-eight . . .'

Kate breathes in and out, though the difference is almost too small to notice. But Nova's voice is something to hold onto, as she drowns on dry land. Every ten breaths, Nova tells Kate to notice something around her – notice her voice, notice the soft bed under her, notice the smell of the new sheets. 'They smell like mountains, don't they? Like mountain forests, full of wildflowers . . . or something.'

By the time they reach sixty, Kate's breathing starts to open up, though she's still gasping. By the time they reach fifty, she's almost calm, though she's covered in sweat and shivering. By the time they count down to one, she just feels tired and ashamed. Nova takes her arms away.

'Are you okay?'

'Yes . . . thank you. If it wasn't for you, I think I would have died.'

'You would've been fine. But I know it doesn't feel that way.'

'It really doesn't.'

Nova puts a hand on her arm, and Kate resists the urge to pull her back into a hug.

'You had a bad dream?'

'Yeah . . . I don't really remember what it was.' Kate shakes her head. 'But *he* was there.'

Nova stays still for a long moment. She's struggling with her own anger. She feels as though she could have stopped this all from happening, though she doesn't know how, exactly.

She is angry with Tony and angry with herself. She follows the advice she gave Kate, noticing her breathing and her hand on Kate's arm.

'Do you want to go back to sleep?'

'Not really. This is lame, but I don't really want to turn the light off.'

Nova blows a raspberry. 'Not lame! Sleep is for boring adults anyway. We should have a midnight feast!'

Kate smiles back, marvelling at Nova's ability to be cheerful in the crummiest situations.

'I don't know if there's much to feast on. I have a few things in the freezer, but the fridge is almost empty.'

'What about the shops?'

'It's . . .' Kate glances at her clock. 'It's one thirty in the morning! Although, now you mention it, there's a 24-hour garage five minutes down the road.'

'Let's go!' Nova scrambles off the bed. 'If you feel up to it?'

'Well, I really don't want to be in this bedroom any more.'

'Yessss! Come on.'

It takes them a little while, but they put their coats on over their nightwear, pull socks and shoes on, shuffling out of the flat like rebellious teenagers. Nova loops her arm through Kate's and lets herself be guided. It takes Kate a long while to walk down the stairs, but somehow, with Nova there, she doesn't mind. They disturb the downstairs cat, curled up on one of the steps, the ginger-and-white tom rubs up against Kate's ankles.

At the front door, Kate hesitates.

'You okay?'

'Sure. I just haven't left the house in . . . a while.'

Nova nods but says nothing. She just waits until Kate is ready to step forward, through the door.

The air outside on the street is cold and scrapes her face, but it's nice to feel something fresh. She fills her lungs with air. They walk down the deserted street in the direction of the 24-hour garage, puffing silver clouds of breath-steam. Every minute or so a car goes past, but there are no people to be seen. Everything is quiet. The promised five-minute walk is more like ten owing to Kate's lack of speed, but when they get there the forecourt is bright with fluorescent lights, the petrol machines humming gently in the night.

They go up to the window. There's a boy behind it, barely a teenager, who is somehow trusted to guard this outpost of civilisation through the night. Through an intercom, he asks what they want.

'Can he hear me?' Nova asks Kate.

'Yes, I can hear you; it's an intercom,' the boy replies tetchily. Kate wonders how long he's been awake.

'Well, we want some snacks!' Nova says, laughing. The boy frowns, looking at Kate's beaten-up face, and Nova, grinning and giggling behind dark glasses, clearly high on *something*.

'What kind of snacks?' He sighs into the microphone. 'We've got crisps, muffins, tubs of ice cream . . .'

'That all sounds good!' Nova reaches into her coat pocket, pulling out her purse and extracting a couple of notes. She passes these through the letterbox to the boy.

'Just fill up a bag with all those things, whatever we can get for that much.'

The boy's eyes widen at the amount of money he's being asked to spend on their behalf. 'Are you sure?'

'Absolutely. Now chop-chop! We're very hungry.'

Nova can't see what's happening inside the glowing box of the petrol station, but Kate watches as the boy goes around, filling a basket with things from every shelf, crisps and sweets and buns and fizzy drinks. Finally, when he's passed everything back through the window to them, they make their way back down the road, laden with bags of food, laughing and listening to their laughter echo back from the houses around them.

Kate stops them both.

'What's up, kid?' Nova asks.

'I'm just looking at the moon.'

A yellow moon hangs at the end of the street, like a fat peach a couple of days off being ripe. Nova opens her eyes behind her glasses, but doesn't see. There is a fuzz of light but nothing clear.

'Can you see it?' Kate asks. She remembers how much Nova loved astronomy, her worn-out NASA T-shirt, and her excitement that one day her sight would be good enough for her to see stars.

Nova frowns, shrugging. 'I kinda gave it up.'

'Gave what up?'

'Um, seeing stuff.' For the first time her shoulders slump, and Nova looks small and childlike.

'You gave it up? Like cigarettes? Or refined sugar?' Kate tries to make a joke, but a note of hurt creeps in.

'Yeah,' Nova deadpans, 'just like giving up cigarettes – seeing was bad for my health. So I quit.'

Nova had thought that choosing to be blind again would

feel natural. Not just natural, but *easy* – it would feel like slipping back into an old habit. Though it has been months, and she is truly blind again, she cannot say that any of this feels natural. The change that came upon her in the hospital is not so easily ignored. Now she fits in neither world, just as when she was learning to see. Her life is lived in limbo.

Kate is silent for a long moment, still looking at the moon.

'Okay. But if you ever change your mind . . .'

'If I change my mind, what . . .?'

'I'll help.'

Nova's face screws up for a split second, then resolves into a smile. 'You'll be my rehab nurse? Physio and cold showers?'

Kate elbows her a little.

'You're incorrigible.'

'Do people really use that word? *Incorrigible.*'

'It would just be nice . . . to look at the moon together sometime.'

Nova moves her head from side to side as though looking for something, and for a moment Kate thinks (though it's stupid) that she's about to run away. Like, just pelt it down the street in the middle of the night. But the moment passes.

'Come on,' Nova says, grinning, 'or the ice cream will go melty!'

Twenty-Two

December

NOVA WAKES FIRST. KATE'S face is pressed into her shoulder and she can feel her breath. She wishes she had her camera to take a picture, but maybe that would be weird. Then again, what isn't weird about this situation?

One of Kate's arms is thrown over her torso.

Nova remembers the night before – how they stayed up and told each other stories and stupid jokes in Kate's bed. Just like the first night she stayed, when they'd eaten junk food from the petrol station until they'd crashed. She'd known she was falling asleep, but Kate hadn't told her to go to the sofa, and Nova didn't want to.

They've slept in the same bed every night for the last month.

Every night, they've stayed on their sides of the bed.

Every night, Nova has kept her hands to herself.

Except sometimes, when she wakes, Kate has moved in the night so that she's curled up against Nova's side, or is pressing her face into Nova's shoulder, or has a leg thrown over Nova's hip, and she makes little noises in her sleep like she's whimpering . . .

In short, Nova is going crazy.

She wants to reach out and touch. She wants to stay in bed, with Kate so close, but she's scared of being caught awake. Caught *looking*, because that's something she does these days. An old habit she's fallen back into. She had slid back down on the game of snakes and ladders to a much earlier square, but not right back to the start.

She can recognize Kate's face again.

She takes a deep breath, smelling Kate's shampoo – like warm honey – then slides herself out from under the duvet.

Kate wakes, but doesn't remember how close they were a few moments ago. She's fascinated by Nova's gracefulness. She moves slowly, consciously, putting her socks and hoodie on. Kate keeps her eyes half closed, so Nova doesn't realize she's being watched. A guilty pleasure, but Kate doesn't stop.

Like everything in these fragile days, Kate knows it can't last, but doesn't want to be the one to end it. Someday, Nova is going to have to go back to her life. She's already helped Kate more than enough. Her body is healing and the panic attacks come less often. Nova has her own problems. Kate is being selfish.

Nova doesn't move as though she's blind, but not exactly as though she can see. She moves through a shifting landscape, mindful of everything around her. Kate wants to see the world the way she sees it, to understand. Finally, Nova leaves the room, and Kate drifts back to sleep.

Nova wakes her, setting a tray down on the bedside table.

'Hey, there, angel face.'

'Mmph . . . M'rning.'

Every morning, Nova has made her coffee in a cafetière that Kate had never even taken out of the box. Kate had made cups of instant for the builders, bought fresh for herself from a tiny shop on the corner with one stool and a raffia camel in the window. She had forgotten the existence of coffee grounds in the sparsely populated kitchen, but somehow Nova found them.

Some days Nova goes into work. But most days she can take calls in the study, or she's off shift and will stay in the flat with Kate. They will talk, or listen to the radio, or Nova will watch Kate daub colour onto her latest paint-by-number kit. Every morning, and every night, she is there in Kate's bed. They never talk about why she stays. Never talk about how they're basically living together. Kate would get her a key, for when Nova does go out, if she weren't here all the time to let her in.

Today there is a plate of buttered toast to go with the coffee, and a collection of tiny jars that Kate pinched from the last hotel she stayed in. They sit up in bed, spreading jam (Kate) and honey (Nova). A third jar is wholegrain mustard, but Kate doesn't point this out. They eat and drink in silence. Nova feels a familiar tension. Each of them is waiting for the other to make the next move.

RULE OF SEEING NO.248
Body language isn't a single language at all, but an infinite number of dialects. One person's hunched posture is not equal to another's. A frown is not always a frown. Sometimes, it is enough to know that *something* is being communicated.

'What are you doing today?' Nova asks, at last.

'Nothing. Hiding away. What about you?'

Nova shrugs, then tries to remember if she always shrugged, or if it's something she learned from watching other people. 'Nothing. Off shift for a couple of days.'

Her statement is an implied question. Kate treads carefully. She can't handle Nova leaving right now.

'We could watch one of your movies, if you like?'

Nova smiles. 'That sounds good.'

They go and find the bag of movies the doctor gave Nova, and start to sort through them. Nova looks carefully at each of the covers, finding the title, reading each of the letters by placing her thumbs either side of it, blocking out anything unnecessary, before moving onto the next one.

She's been practising, with Kate's help, and the films are part of it. Though she's not back to where she was, some of her progress returned, as though a withered version of it had persisted in her head. From her flat she brought the packs of cards – SHAPES, BODIES and OBJECTS, and sometimes Kate will take them out and try to read her fortune.

'*The Wizard of* On?' Nova asks, frowning at a film.

'*Oz* – that's a Z.'

'Ugh, I'm so bad at this.'

'I think you read a lot quicker than if I were learning Braille.'

'I don't think I can read this one . . .'

She hands it to Kate, who looks at the sweeping, red hand-writing.

'*Casablanca*.'

'Ah. What kind of films do you like?'

Kate stops to think about the question. It used to be so

straightforward. She liked the kind of films that she and Vi went to see. Films with explosions and gunfights. The kind of films she enjoyed were like theme-park rides – they had thrills and sudden drops. But she can't say that she likes that sort of film any more. Violence seems very violent, these days.

'I don't know what films I like. Maybe we can find some in here that I like.'

'You've not seen any of these before?'

'Um . . . this one.' She picks up *The Sound of Music*. 'I watched this when I was a kid.'

'What about this?'

She holds up a plain case – just a picture of the ocean and the words *The Big Blue*. Kate takes it from her and reads the description on the back.

'It's about the rivalry between two deep-sea divers,' she explains.

'Does it sound like the kind of film you might like?'

'I don't know. Let's find out.' Kate opens the case. Inside is a handwritten note, in large, careful writing. 'I think this is from your doctor.'

'Could you read it to me?'

'Dear Nova, about your embarrassing rash . . .'

Nova snorts. 'You're *funny!*'

'I'm really not,' she says, laughing. Anyway, it says, "Nova, thought you might enjoy the pictures of the sea, of fish and dolphins, and people moving in a totally different world, weightless." That's nice of him.'

'He's a nice guy. But I think he saw me as his project. Like, if he could teach me to see, it would be a big achievement.'

'Oh, you were his Eliza Doolittle!'

'His what?'

'*My Fair Lady*? We should watch that too. Are there not many people like you, then?'

Nova screws up her lips for a moment. 'Some. Not many. People who've been blind from birth . . .' She trails off, as though deciding how to phrase something. 'Well, we don't always cope well with learning to see. I think he was hoping that, with the right treatment, I might be different.'

'Oh . . . Do you want some more coffee?' Kate feels stupid, changing the subject, but doesn't know what to say.

'I made you uncomfortable.' Nova smiles.

'No . . . I just know what it's like, wondering if things are going to get any better.'

'Things aren't so bad, are they?' Nova puts her arm around Kate's waist.

'Not right now.'

Nova grins, thinks for a second, then, '*Pop!*'

'What?' Kate asks.

'To drink – if I'm going to watch a movie, I think I should have pop. And pop*corn*.'

Kate laughs again. She can't remember the last time she laughed this much, every day. Maybe never. Maybe not in her whole life. Sometimes she still feels like shit. But there is so much laughter as well.

'Well, I can do you the popcorn, but I'll have to go down to the shop for the fizz.'

'If it's not too much trouble.'

'No, I'll go now.'

Nova smiles and goes back to reading the cases. Kate walks to the door with a sudden, hollow feeling in her stomach. This is part of the deal they made on that first night. Kate had scrawled it on the back of a paper wrapper from an 80% cocoa chocolate bar.

```
WE (NOVA AND KATE) HEREBY DECLARE THAT
NOVA WILL LEARN TO SEE
IF!
KATE LEAVES THE HOUSE SOMETIMES
IF!
NOVA WILL LEARN TO SEE
IF!
KATE LEAVES THE HOUSE SOMETIMES
IF! . . .
```

It continues down the wrapper, the writing getting smaller and more cramped, as Nova dictated it to her. It had made her laugh at the time, but now she wishes more than anything that she didn't have to keep up her side of the bargain to stop Nova sinking back into blindness.

There is an envelope on the mat, addressed to her in hand-written capital letters. Kate tears it open with her thumb, but there is nothing inside. Frowning, she scrutinizes the envelope for anything to identify the sender. The postmark is London, but that's all. Maybe it's from her mum. It would be typical of her to forget to put the letter in before sending.

She slips her shoes on, takes her keys from the bowl by the door, and hovers, hand raised to the lock. She thinks of the soft covers on her bed, and wants to crawl back in there. Ridiculous – she pushes the key into the lock and leaves the flat.

While Kate is gone, Nova tidies the bedroom, shaking

crumbs off the sheets. When that's done, she sits on the bed and closes her eyes, enjoying the perfect quiet. She's relieved that Kate seems to want her to stay, even if only for the time being. More than any other thing she wants to stay in this place where time is soft.

Kate returns with the rustle of plastic bags, peering into the bedroom. To Nova, she looks pale, her expression unreadable. Nova can read her face better than anyone else she knows, but right now her face isn't saying much.

'You tidied the bed.'

'Thought I'd be helpful. You okay?'

'Yeah, of course.' She doesn't sound convinced. 'I forgot to ask what you like, so I got a few.'

They go to the kitchen. From a plastic bag, Kate produces three bottles – one bright red, one bright green, one brown (though it's so close to black that Nova can't tell the difference).

'Cherryade, limeade and cola.'

'The colours are so different!'

'I guess so.'

'That's something I never realized when I was blind. How ketchup is red and mustard is yellow and barbeque sauce is brown . . . and those ice-cream parlours with twenty flavours, all a different colour.'

'I guess I never thought about it.'

'You probably did, when you were a kid. At some point, you had to learn all that. But then you forget that there was a time when you didn't know.'

Kate smiles – a shape Nova takes pleasure in recognizing.

'So what colour would you like to try first?'

'The green? Is that green?'

'Yeah.'

'That one, then. Is that cherryade?'

'No, cherryade is red. Like cherries. This is limeade, like green limes.'

'Ah, of course.'

Kate goes to the kitchen and puts the corn kernels in a saucepan, then melts some butter. She shuts the curtains over the window and turns the lights off. When everything is ready they sit on the floor with their backs to the sofa, the TV table pulled close, glasses of fizz and a bowl of warm popcorn between them. Kate presses the right button on the remote control, a task that is still difficult for Nova, and the movie starts.

The Big Blue starts in black-and-white – something Nova has never seen on screen before. Early on, after the operation, she often saw things in black-and-white, as though her mind was a faulty television, colour flickering in and out of her transmission. They pause while Kate explains this to her.

Now the scene is in colour, but there is so little colour in the landscape Nova can hardly tell the difference – Kate explains that it is an ice lake, and that it's the white snow, blanketing everything. Nova can only see a field of pure white, with bands of shade, which must be hills and valleys. She can make out the buildings easily though, clear and rectangular, picked out against the surrounding nothingness.

The film passes in a kind of trance. Nova sees through the camera underwater, looking up at air bubbles moving over the layer of ice. Their shapes, like the light and shade of the snowfield, seem abstract. Waves, seen from above and below, change constantly. She's never sure what she is seeing, but after a while she stops trying. She enjoys the glittering light, the shifting shades of blue.

When there are fish, or dolphins, Nova tries to watch them in motion, to understand what they look like in real life. She saw fish at the zoo, but they didn't move like this. The first time she saw a dog walking down the street she thought it was another animal altogether. Though she had carefully memorized the shape of the animal from the flashcards in the rehabilitation ward, the motion of the dog, trotting down the street, each leg in motion and each leg doing something different, baffled her.

'Are those fish?' she asks.

'Uh-huh.'

She watches as a group of fish circle and flash in the light. Fish are even stranger than dogs, she decides – they glide from one place to another without moving themselves at all.

Nova finds it hard to focus on the story of the film – a series of conversations interspersed between visions of the ocean – but she enjoys watching the characters diving deep under the water. They dive without oxygen, only goggles and flippers, holding their breath for minutes on end. She has always perceived the world on one level, and even if she went to a different floor in a building, it seemed that the building had moved, not her. But the pictures of their bodies descending, until light is leached from the water, show her a world of great depth and height. She can see their bodies clearly against the field of blue.

Slowly, she moves her body closer to Kate, feeling the

warmth between them. Kate doesn't respond until, with a gentle sigh, she rests her head gently on Nova's shoulder.

Nova can't focus much on the film after that.

✴

Later, when night has fallen, they lie facing each other in Kate's bed again. Nova looks into Kate's eyes, but can't read her expression.

'You okay, bean queen?'

Kate smiles sleepily and nods. 'Yeah. Thanks for a nice day.'

They look into each other's eyes for a long time. Usually, Kate will tear her gaze away after a couple of seconds. Nova knows that this is because making eye contact is weird for people. Looking at a thing that is looking at you, looking at it . . . an endless feedback loop. That's what must be so compelling, Nova thinks, why people can fall in love at first sight. When you make eye contact, when you hold someone's gaze, it's the closest thing to knowing that you're not alone in the world.

Tonight, Kate doesn't look away. In the morning, neither will remember who fell asleep first.

Nova sleeps and dreams that she is sitting on the corduroy-lined armchair in her paternal grandmother's living room, eating a plate of potato dumplings with sour cream, listening to her grandfather (dead before she was born) telling her that he is going away to war – a war that has been going on forever and from which he will never return – and Nova wants to tell him not to go, except her mouth is full of potato and she's worried that she will get sour cream on her grandmother's armchair, so that by the time she has swallowed, her grandfather has fallen silent and Nova reaches out but he isn't there any more . . .

Kate sleeps and dreams that she is standing in the supply cupboard of her primary school, looking around at the shelves piled with pastel coloured sugar paper and bottles of acrylic paint, while Nova sits on a plastic chair in front of her, peeling and eating clementines and wiping her sticky hands on the sugar paper. When Kate tells her not to, she says that it's sugar paper and sugar paper is supposed to be sticky, and won't listen when she argues against, until there is a pile of sticky, crumpled paper at their feet, and Kate can hear footsteps – heavy, police-issue boots – approaching the cupboard . . .

Twenty-Three

'YOU'VE BEEN HERE BEFORE?' Kate looks up at the sign – ZEPHIRELLI'S – over the door to the café.

'Once or twice.'

Nova was in New Scotland Yard for the morning, and Kate met her afterwards to wander up through London. The city was bustling. They trudged up the wind-tunnel of Lower Regent Street, through Piccadilly Circus, with its shimmering adverts for luxury watches and hamburgers, until they reached Soho. Nova finds the city a little overwhelming, but she has Kate here to help her if she needs to close her eyes.

RULE OF SEEING NO.250
Cities, like forests, grow <u>upwards</u>. Tower
blocks, multi-storey car parks and lampposts,
all perpendicular. But, unlike the forest,
which is seeking sunlight, cities reach for
another resource – free space.

Kate hasn't told the police about the empty envelopes. They've been arriving every couple of days for the last fortnight. She hasn't told Nova either. It would only make her worry.

There is gold and silver tinsel lining every free edge in the café, which Nova likes. She finds decorations funny – the idea of changing the way things look to celebrate an occasion. And, you know, it is very *twinkly*. She likes the fibre-optic plastic tree that Kate has put up in the flat as a concession to Christmas. Over the counter, a red sign flickers –

HAP Y

X-MAS

They agreed not to get each other presents, but ate a roast dinner a week before Christmas Day, pulled crackers and told each other jokes. They watched one Christmas movie, then put the radio on. Nova had gone home on the train the next day, for her first sighted Christmas, and Kate had wished more than anything she was going with her, to see her unwrapping presents and lighting the pudding. She could imagine Nova's glee at seeing blue flames dancing on top of something she was about to eat.

It's been a month and two weeks since the first night Nova slept over at Kate's flat. Other than Christmas, she has barely left her side. She was there when the removal company went to Kate's old apartment to move her stuff. She was more of a hindrance than a help, always in someone's way as they were carrying a table or an armchair.

But Kate was always holding onto her hand, always close

to her. Nova could tell how difficult it was for her to go back to that place, the place she had shared with Tony, trying to pick it apart like the most complicated knot imaginable. She'd already given notice on the flat, now she just had to wait for everything to be wrapped up. If it helped for Nova to be there, she was happy to help.

Kate cooked for them, because Nova didn't cook much for herself. She taught her how to fry an egg and how to chop onions. Nova noticed that Kate never left her alone while she was doing these things. Her protectiveness was both sweet and frustrating at the same time.

Kate hadn't woken up screaming again, though she often had bad dreams and would be up in the night. If she was awake, Nova would get up as well and they would sit and listen to the radio, or sometimes they would put their coats on and go for a walk, the cold air playing around their ankles, feeling like they must have broken out of an institution.

Nova has only been back to her own apartment a couple of times to fetch clothes. Alex has been in touch, but he's used to her avoiding his questions. Nova isn't sure what she's up to, if she's honest. It just feels like she needs to be here for Kate.

And, though she tries not to think about it much, Nova wants to be here for herself.

'Are you listening?'

'Huh? What's up?' Nova jolts back into the present moment.

'Why is there a sandwich called *The Safinova Surprise*?'

A smile spreads over Nova's face – with everything going on, she had forgotten her favourite thing about Zephirelli's.

Nova finds a table while Kate orders. A minute later, Kate returns with a couple of coffees.

Nova is slouched in a corner booth, apparently at ease, but Kate senses she's nervous. She feels the tension in Nova's shoulders, the way her jaw is pulled into her neck. Her own body mirrors these tensions.

'Are you okay?' she asks.

'I'm fine. I'm just worried about you.'

Nova's sight has been getting slowly better, but the hardest things to read are expressions. She knows Kate's face best, but there is such a spectrum between happy and sad. Sometimes she will ask Kate to stop, to freeze just as she is, so she can memorize what her face is doing. Often, by the time Kate has frozen, the expression is gone, breaking into a smile. Actually, it's a good way to make Kate smile, and Nova likes making Kate smile.

The café is noisy, but they don't mind. It's nice not to feel overheard. The air is as humid as a shower cubicle; the cold windows sweat. Nova wonders why the table behind her cup of coffee is changing colour, patches of it flashing like the skin of a dappled deep-sea creature. She's not hallucinating – the low sun, slanting through the window, is hitting the wisps of steam rising from her coffee, turning them briefly into thin clouds. Another aspect of the intangible world has revealed itself.

Kate sips her coffee and thinks out loud. 'It's good . . . it's good that I found out what was going on.' Her voice breaks a little. 'It's good . . . isn't it?'

'Of course it is! What do you mean?'

'I don't know, I just feel so bad. I just keep thinking of his parents. They're nice people, you know? His mum knits cardigans for rescue animals for fuck's sake. They're not like him.

And his sister . . . she has children. His little niece calls me Auntie Kit Kat.'

'That's adorable.'

'I just keep thinking about our wedding, all the people there, everybody who expected us to be . . .' She trails off.

'Expected you to be what?' Nova leans in, resting her elbows on the table.

'Expected us to be *perfect*, I guess.' Kate shrugs. 'I never felt perfect, you know? I always felt too big, too loud, too . . . *too*. You know? But a couple can be perfect. It's stupid, but I always believed that – you fit together, and suddenly there are no jagged edges. I thought maybe we could be like that.'

She pulls a napkin out of the chrome dispenser and dabs her eyes.

'And now I feel like I've ruined it.'

Nova reaches over the table and takes Kate's hands. They're trembling. She wishes she had noticed earlier.

'You didn't ruin anything. None of this is your fault. You haven't spoiled anything for them. This is your life, not theirs.'

'I know.'

'Do you? What do you think would have happened if you hadn't confronted him?'

Kate shrugs. Her voice is tiny now, but Nova can hear it perfectly.

'I don't know what I would have done. I feel like I didn't have a choice.'

'Well, for what it's worth, I'm happy he's out of your life.'

Kate starts to say something, inaudible over the coffee machine being topped up, the sparkling sound of bacon frying in the pan, the builders holding a conversation two tables down. She's about to start again, but it never comes out. She breaks down, still holding Nova's hands. It only lasts a few seconds before she pulls herself together, wipes her eyes and clears her throat.

Suddenly, a waitress is next to them with their order.

'Two sandwiches?'

'That's us.' Kate smiles.

The plates are set down – one *Safinova Surprise* for Nova, and . . . Nova pauses, looking from plate to plate, trying to be sure.

'Is that . . . did you order *my* sandwich?'

Kate nods. 'Yeah, of course. I can't come to a place where you have a sandwich named after you and not order it, right?'

'Uh, yeah . . . of course,' Nova mumbles, trying not to show how momentous this moment is.

Kate picks up the sandwich.

Nova holds her breath.

Kate closes her eyes.

Takes a bite.

Chews . . .

''S'not bad!'

When she opens her eyes, a look of pure joy has broken across Nova's face. She's gazing into Kate's eyes as though she just proposed. Slowly, making sure to signal her enjoyment, Kate takes another, even bigger bite of the sandwich. With her mouth full, she says, 'Thuh peach slices reary work!'

Nova says nothing. She's not sure she could if she tried.

✴

The Rules of Seeing

It's getting dark by the time they get back to the flat. They don't say anything, comfortable in silence, watching the world together. Their breath steams. Birds are singing in the leafless trees. Everything is peaceful.

'What do you want to do?' Nova asks her, stepping through the door.

Kate looks down to the doormat, where there is a letter for her. She doesn't react to it. She will clear it away later, when Nova isn't watching.

'I don't know . . . I think I want to go to bed.'

'Oh, okay, sure. I'm not really sleepy though, it's kinda early. But I'll get my jammies on.'

It's half true – she's exhausted from everything that's happened, but also from a full day of seeing. But she's worried that if Kate goes to bed so soon, her nightmares won't be far behind.

'Okay.' Kate nods.

Nova decides to be brave. 'You want someone to sing you a lullaby?'

Kate's eyes widen, just for a second, but Nova catches it.

'Um, yeah?'

'Okay.' Nova seems to be studying her feet. 'I'll come find you.'

Nova goes and gets changed into her pyjamas, brushes her teeth, and goes to Kate's room. She's already in bed, curled up, as close to one edge of the bed as she can be. Her expression is unreadable; her eyes are pooled in shadow.

'I'm sorry, you don't have to do this for me.'

'Don't be silly.'

Nova sits on the edge of the bed. She wants to say something more, but this isn't the moment. Kate rolls over to face her as Nova climbs under the duvet. She shivers as her legs slide between the cold sheets, but Nova can feel the warmth coming from the other side of the bed. They look at each other, heads on their pillows.

'Come here often?' Nova tries to break the ice, but Kate just smiles. 'How are you feeling?'

'Generally?'

'Generally.'

'I'm . . . still freaked out. That he's just out there, somewhere. But I'm okay.'

Nova nods. She can tell when Kate is telling the truth. It's one of the things she likes about her.

'And, uh, how are you feeling about this? Me staying here, I mean. I haven't been mentioning it. But, if it's weird for you . . .'

Kate shrugs sideways, trying to act casual, though her heart is in her throat. 'It's not really weird, is it?'

'No, doesn't feel weird at all. It's nice to have company. I just don't want to presume.'

'Bit late for that, no?'

'I guess so.'

Kate turns the light off and waits. Nova pauses for a moment, then shuffles closer, slips her arm under Kate's neck and pulls her head onto her chest. She can feel Kate's heart beating. Beating fast.

Warm shivers run through Kate. Her body becomes hot, becomes molten, changes state, cools and reforms into a shape that is similar – but not identical – to the one it had a few seconds ago.

Nova starts to sing.

Her voice is very low and soft. Kate doesn't know the song and after a few moments she realizes Nova isn't singing in English. Perhaps this is a song her parents sang to her when she was a child. She can't decide what the language is. The melody doesn't sound like any lullaby Kate knows. It sounds old, like a song the trees or hills would sing.

Kate's heartbeat slows, followed by her breathing, until Nova is sure that she's asleep. She makes a snuffling noise like an animal, and Nova wants to reach out and brush her cheek, but she doesn't.

Kate sleeps, and there are no nightmares.

Twenty-Four

KATE IS WOKEN BY the sound of her phone buzzing. Today is New Year's Eve, she remembers. A new year and a new start. The phone keeps buzzing. It's still early, so she ignores it. She rolls over, becoming aware of the body in the bed next to her. Nova is sleeping. The covers have been thrown back, tangled up with her legs, one arm over her face. Her lips are parted slightly and her cheeks are flushed. Her breaths rise and fall so softly; a strand of hair quivers over her mouth.

Kate watches her for a minute, while her phone buzzes again, then stops. When it starts for a third time, Kate feels a sudden rush of fear – something is wrong. She rolls over, rummages for the phone in the pile of clothes on her side of the bed, retrieves it and looks at the caller.

Number withheld.

She answers the phone.

'Hello?'

There is nothing for a long moment but the hiss of the line.

Then she hears it, almost indistinguishable from the background noise – a tearing, sizzling sound. It's so familiar, but Kate doesn't remember where she has heard it before until the line has gone dead.

The sound of a rabbit being skinned.

Kate can tell that Nova has woken up next to her, but cannot make herself react. She's hyperventilating. Nova sits up a little in bed. 'Kate?'

'Mm?'

'What's up?'

'Nothing . . . I'm sure it's nothing.'

Nova sits up and looks at her properly, trying to read her expression.

'Okay, and I'm sure you're right. But could you tell me what it is that we're not worrying about?'

Kate manages to smile a bit at that, and explains what has just happened. Even in retelling the story, she calms down. Of course it's ridiculous. Of course she just heard the hiss on the line, and her imagination played a trick on her. Even the story of the rabbit that Tony brought home seems less significant, now she's said it out loud.

'Okay,' Nova says slowly, 'if you're sure it's nothing to worry about?'

'Yeah, it's fine. I'm just being silly. But . . .' she trails off.

'But?'

'But could I have a pass on leaving the house today? I don't feel like going out.'

'It's adorable that you think you need my permission to stay in, but sure. I've got nothing to do today, if you don't mind me hanging around.'

'That would be nice.' Kate nods, and feels the tension drain out of her. 'I'll go make some coffee, yeah?'

'Maybe you should have a herbal tea.' Nova teases.

'Maybe you're right. No caffeine for me!' Kate leaves as if for the kitchen, but goes first to the front door and checks all the locks. When she turns, Nova ambushes her with a crushing hug.

'Oof! Jesus, you're a ninja.' Nova doesn't reply or let go. 'You okay?' Kate asks, trying to breathe.

'Me? I'm fine,' Nova mumbles into her chest.

'O-kay. That's good.'

They break out of the hug, but some residual magnetism remains, making the separation uncomfortable for both. They walk through to the living room and Nova flops down on the sofa. Kate sits next to her.

'I'm so sorry – keeping you locked up here like a prisoner!'

'Don't sweat it, cinnamon roll, it's not so bad. I don't think the company would be this good in prison.' She takes Kate's hand and squeezes it.

'So, what do you want to do with your day of house arrest?'

Nova thinks for a second. 'Ah! I know.'

'What?'

Lopsided grin. 'We should make a fort!'

'Really?'

'Come on, Miss Architect – I bet you can make a really good sofa fort.'

Kate grins for a moment, thinking, then jumps up. She brings the duvet and pillows from the beds, then spare sheets from a cupboard. She grabs standard lamps from around the room and bag ties from the kitchen. She takes the sofa cushions, replaces them with the duvet and cushions. She takes the standard lamps and uses them to hang sheets, until she has made a canopy, like a tent in the desert.

'Happy?' she asks, peering into the fort, where Nova is already sinking back into the soft, sky-blue duvet.

'Very.'

Inside the tent they listen to music, talk and drink tea. Occasionally, Kate will disappear to put on a new record. The music – Bach and Vivaldi and others Nova can't name – surrounds them. If Nova stops to listen, they are surrounded by cellos, double basses, violins, flutes, clarinets, oboes, timpani . . . a harpist plucks in the doorway to the kitchen, a piccolo player sits in the alcove by the window. Kate said she had built speakers into the walls, but Nova can't shake the illusion of the ghostly musicians.

They sit and talk about nothing much for a while, then Kate grows quiet, and looks at Nova for a long time. When she was blind, Nova was aware of the different kinds of silence. Silences could be meaningful, each with its own flavour. But when she was blind, she was never conscious of being *watched*. It was something she knew must be happening, in the same way that she knew that radio waves and micro-waves were fizzing around her head. Maybe she was being watched, maybe she wasn't – Nova was like a particle in Heisenberg's thought experiment. Now the certainty of Kate's gaze is disconcerting, a beam of attention that pins her to the spot.

'What are you thinking?' Nova asks.

'That I want to protect you.'

'Protect me? I think I should be offended.'

'I know, I know. I don't mean that you *need* protecting. But that's what I'm thinking.'

Nova feels that this moment is significant, but isn't sure why. Invisible doors seem to be opening and shutting around her, letting in strange atmospheres, the air of alternate realities. She makes a noncommittal noise. 'What about you? Who's going to protect *you*?'

Kate sighs. 'I don't need protecting – I've got a fort, remember?'

Nova looks at her, trying to read her face, but her looking is not equal to Kate's looking – she cannot pin her down. She turns away.

'What do you want to do?'

Nova shrugs. 'Maybe it's getting up early, but I'm quite sleepy.'

'Me too. We should take a nap.' Kate looks at her lap.

'But you used all the pillows – I'd feel bad about dismantling your fort.'

'We don't have to. The sofa pulls out into a bed, remember?'

Nova stands outside while Kate huffs around, rearranging the insides of the tent like a cocoon.

'Come in, see what you think.'

Nova ducks inside the tent. As promised, the sofa has become a bed, filling the space. Kate stands at the foot of it, as though waiting. Nova searches through a list of translations for her expression and settles on 'worried'.

She steps closer to her.

She feels a little breathless.

The invisible doors keep opening and closing, and Nova knows that if she makes a wrong move she will step through the wrong one.

Kate has frozen. Nova reaches out and brushes her cheek. The touch seems to release her, and Kate closes the distance between them, hands coming to rest on Nova's hips.

Nova reaches up, brushing the hair back from Kate's temples, careful as can be. Kate leans forward into her touch.

They kiss.

All the invisible doors slam shut. A choice has been made. The inside of Kate's skull fizzes with secret energy. She breaks away, suddenly uncertain.

'I'm sorry, I—'

'Ssh.' Nova puts a finger to her mouth.

Kate's hands are shaking so much, she finds it hard to undo the five buttons on Nova's high-waisted jeans. The interpreter smiles at her huff of frustration, pulls her close and kisses her neck. Kate exhales.

Nova feels for Kate's shirt, moving methodically down the row of faux mother-of-pearl buttons. She lifts the shirt off very carefully, like a cape, then shrugs out of her T-shirt and jeans in milliseconds. They hug – just hug – for a moment, pressing skin to skin.

Together they fall back into the softness of the bed, further undressing each other. Kate looks at the cotton chrysalis she has made around them and thinks, briefly, of caterpillars changing into butterflies.

Everything is bright. Kate's hands hover for a moment, no more undressing to do, unsure of their purpose. They are naked. Nova places one hand on her back, moves in to kiss Kate again, and the moment passes. There is no more uncertainty in Kate. She's like water running downhill, pure motion. Eyes closed, the room hums with light, stained soft colours by the cotton sheets. Nova leads Kate in this new dance, but Kate follows close behind.

After a few minutes have passed, Nova opens her eyes and sees, rather than closeness, a vertiginous depth. Before, she has only guessed at depth – she knows that the desk is against the wall, and the chair is against the desk, and that these things are separate, next to one another. But for her everything is on one plane, two-dimensional. Shapes and shadows and colours are the only clues as to how one object is separate from another. Looking through one eye is the same as looking through two.

Until now.

Her eyes have joined together. Instead of being individuals, they move in unison, different angles of the same vision. As suddenly as that, in addition to height and width, she sees depth.

RULE OF SEEING NO.269
Before, if you thought about seeing depth, you thought about the Grand Canyon, or looking out to sea. But depth can be intimate – the contours of a body, the wrinkles of a world in miniature.

Their bodies are two landscapes, stretching in front of Nova, one brown and one pink. The distance to their toes seems so great that it would take a day's walk to reach them. There is no sky above either landscape, only a mirror-image of the first. There is no up or down, only above and below, changing places again and again. When she can take no more, she closes her eyes, returning to the comforting closeness, the smell of Kate's shampoo, her soft hands.

Finally, they rest, with no space between them.

They lie there for a long time, still except for their breath, rising and falling in unison. Kate isn't sure if she can even breathe out of step – their lungs have merged into one. No words come to her. Not even the stuff before words, the shapes of ideas. If she were able to form the thought, she might say she has stepped out of her own life.

With each embrace there was a mirror embrace, with every pleasure a mirror pleasure, until eventually she was no longer sure which side of the mirror she was standing on. Kate ceased to be Kate, and Nova ceased to be Nova, and they were two mirror images, spinning around each other.

Her reflection kisses her on the cheek, and asks something she doesn't hear.

'Sorry?'

'I said, are you okay?' asks the reflection.

'Yes.'

'I can't read your face.' The mirror girl seems worried. Kate puts her arms around her, draws her close, and presses her lips to her temple. She feels Nova's skin crinkle into a smile.

(Yes, Nova – not Kate, but Nova.)

'Okay, then. Good.' Nova kisses back for a moment, then slumps back onto the pillow.

Kate is quiet. She knows what Nova was asking, but doesn't know how to answer – she doesn't know whether it had been good or bad. It was beyond good or bad. For a second, everything felt infinite – the world stretching out around them like deep space. Part of her wants to return to that feeling.

Another part of her is scared. Scared to be a tiny drop in an endless ocean.

✳

Later, they order Chinese take-away. Only when the food takes an hour and a half to arrive do they remember it's New Year's Eve.

Inside the tent they eat vegetable dumplings with cherry sauce, strips of chilli-fried pork and piles of fried rice. Nova still hasn't got the hang of looking at the food she's eating. There is a gap between the pleasant smells she knows and the grotesque blobs and slicks in front of her. But the colours of this food are excitingly vivid, even if she still closes her eyes at the moment of consumption.

For the time being she's optimistic – of course she will learn to see. Why not? Miraculous things have happened in this room. In one evening she has learned to see in 3D. When she emerged from the fort, she thought for a moment that the new sense had deserted her as quickly as it had arrived. That stereo vision could be dissipated by an orgasm. But she's just getting used to it – it's becoming subtler. As she looks from the tent to the television, every object has its place on a plane that she never knew existed before.

While the things she sees are often mysterious, they have gained a useful separation. Separation is the mark of progress – the more separate things become, the more she understands. She has come from a single blur of light to a panorama of shapes, with their own outlines, and colours, and positions in space. Like the early victory of being able to grasp the red ball, this improvement opens a sense of hope – a sense that maybe she can keep getting better, and needn't lose her mind in the process.

She can do it, with Kate by her side.

Afterwards, they perform the bedtime rituals, taking turns to use the bathroom. Nova takes one of Kate's T-shirts to wear. There is a muffled noise from the window like popcorn popping in the pan, and they go to see – New Year's fireworks smatter the clear sky. Nova holds tight around Kate's waist.

'What do you think?' Kate asks.

'They're like tinsel for the sky!' Nova grins. 'That's just . . . *mental.*'

'Yeah.' Kate smiles, kissing the top of her head. 'It really is.'

They crawl back inside the ridiculous fort, which Kate is ridiculously proud of, close the distance between their bodies once more, and sleep.

3

Objects

Twenty-Five

January

KATE WAKES UP. THE light in the room is gentle, and she squints out at her surroundings, disoriented. What bed is this? What room? What are these sheets hanging over her head? Slowly, she remembers the fort, then the day before.

She looks to the other side of the bed.

Nova is sleeping still, tangled in sheets, her hair a mess, her limbs spreading out in every direction. Kate realizes that she has retreated to the far edge of her side of the bed. She watches Nova sleeping for a few minutes and this time doesn't feel guilty. Slowly, her eyes close again, and she dreams.

When Kate wakes again, someone is kissing her. For a moment, she thinks it must be Tony – her brain has been time-travelling while she slept, and she has woken up to a year in her past. But when did Tony ever kiss her awake? Kate opens her eyes and sees Nova, propped up on one elbow, looking down on her. Her hair is like a dark halo, her eyes crinkled in a smile. Kate still has the unnerving sensation that she's looking into a mirror.

'Happy New Year, string bean.'

'You too. So . . . last night really happened?'

By way of reply, Nova kisses her on the nose, on the forehead, on both cheeks. Kate laughs and pushes her off so that they are lying side by side.

'It wasn't a dream,' Kate says.

'Nope. Is that okay?' Nova asks, brushing her cheek.

'You're asking me that *after* you kissed me?'

Nova does a sideways shrug. 'Just answer the question.'

Kate pulls her closer and kisses her temple.

'Yes,' she murmurs, 'it's very okay.'

'Mmph. All right, I believe you,' Nova moans. 'Do you wanna go on a date with me?'

'It's eight in the morning.'

'A breakfast date, then. The best kind!' Nova pulls away and smiles winningly.

'Okay . . . but we'll need to wrap up warm.'

'Mmm, you are so *sensible*.' Nova growls, pouncing on her.

✳

The waffle place is almost empty, and there's music on the stereo, which Kate finds reassuring. It's good to get away from the quiet of the flat. Most of the shops on the street are closed. It's the morning of a new year and everyone is asleep. But this place is open for the stay-outs and stragglers. A girl in Day-Glo face paint is nursing a coffee in one corner. Two men in superhero costumes are slumped in a booth, waiting for their fried breakfasts. Kate and Nova fit right in, wearing yesterday's clothes under big coats and woollens. They order coffee and waffles – a savoury plate for Kate, with scrambled eggs, and a giant, whipped-cream-and-banana-split confection for Nova.

'Does it come with sparklers, like the picture?'

'If you want, miss.'

'Indeed I do, my good man.'

Nova reaches up and knights the waiter on both shoulders with the laminated menu, and he slouches back to the kitchen. They sit in silence for a minute, sipping their coffee and unbuttoning layers. Kate looks, disbelievingly, at the woman across from her. She is wearing jeans and a tight, black T-shirt. It has a picture of a lightbulb and the slogan – WATT IS LOVE? BABY DON'T HERTZ ME!

'How do you always look so good?' Kate blurts.

Nova blows a raspberry. 'Flatterer!'

'No, I mean, how do you always know what to wear? Did someone help you pick them out when you were blind?'

Nova puts her coffee down and holds up two fingers. 'Two simple rules. Rule One – everything goes well with blue jeans. Rule Two – don't give a fuck what anyone else thinks.'

'That's it?'

Nova picks up her coffee and slurps noisily. 'Yup.'

Kate shakes her head, laughing. 'I wish I could be more like you.'

'Like how?'

'You're so . . . natural. It's like you feel at home in the entire world. It's like nothing bad has ever happened to you.'

Nova's smile falters. 'I grew up a mixed-race, blind gay girl, babe. Plenty of bad things happened to me.'

'Oh, I didn't mean . . .' Kate takes her hand, and is about to say something more when their waffles arrive. Nova doesn't look at Kate for a while, shovelling the pile of cream and waffles into her mouth. She doesn't even comment on the sparklers.

Kate can feel Nova's discomfort, like a knot in her shoulders, so she looks out of the window instead. When she looks back, Nova is looking right at her.

'What?'

'I'm just thinking about your face.'

'What *about* my face?' Kate's nose wrinkles with suspicion.

'Of all the faces I've seen, yours is the only one I understand.'

'I'm . . . honoured?'

'You should be. Have you heard of Plato's theory of forms?'

'Definitely not.'

'Well, it's pretty crazy – Plato had this idea that everything we see in the world is a reflection of some otherworldly, perfect form. So, if you see a horse in a field, it's not *the* horse, just *a* horse. Your chair is just a shadow of the perfect chair, these waffles are just a reflection of the perfect waffles . . .'

'That's really dumb.'

'Take it up with the dead Greek guy, babe. What I'm trying to say is – that's what your face is like, to me. Your face is *the* face. The perfect face. All the others are just shadows.'

Kate's eyebrows are arched high. For a moment, Nova thinks she's said something wrong. 'I'd kiss you, but we're being watched by the waiter.'

Nova looks again – Kate's face has changed colour.

'I am *never* going to get tired of making you blush.'

The Rules of Seeing

It is the afternoon, and they're back at the flat. Kate has showered and changed into washed-out denim dungarees and a long-sleeved peach top. She hasn't worn the dungarees in years – Tony used to say that they made her look gangly. She shuffles into the kitchen, where Nova is trying to decipher the hieroglyphs on the microwave.

RULE OF SEEING NO.275
Sighted people get so good at recognizing shapes that they use them instead of words. They put pictures on toilets, road signs, bottles of bleach, no smoking areas, food mixers and hospitals. They never seem to get confused.

Nova turns and considers Kate.

'Hey, there, string bean Jean.'

Kate tenses for a moment before Nova's arms wrap around her.

'You look cute. I like dungarees.'

'Oh yeah?'

'Yeah. They're fun. They're like trousers that don't know when to stop.'

'Thanks . . . I think.'

Nova sits at the kitchen table while Kate walks around. Her nerves are catching up with her again.

'Are you sure you want to do this?'

'Yes.'

'It's just, you seem quite . . . pacey.'

Kate sighs and puts her back against the worktop. 'Yeah, I

am. But I want to see Vi. She's my best friend. We just had a stupid argument. It's been almost a year since I spoke to her. I want to tell her everything that's happened. And I want to apologize.'

'Okay, fine. She sounds nice, and it doesn't sound like she was a big fan of Tony. Plus, I want to meet your friend. So why the nerves?'

'Well, she doesn't know . . .' Kate trails off.

'She doesn't know you like women?'

Kate nods.

'Well, first things first – you don't have to tell her anything if you don't want to.'

'Okay . . . but I *do* want to.'

'Well, is she a massive homophobe?'

'No! Definitely not. But what if she's angry that I didn't tell her? What if she thinks I got hit on the head and now I'm gay?'

Nova is tempted to laugh, but resists. She stands and puts her hands on Kate's hips.

'I don't think that's possible, sweetie. But if she thinks it is, I'll fight her myself.'

Kate smiles for a second before the doorbell goes, making her jump. 'Oh! That'll be her. I'd better go . . .'

'Deep breath!' Nova calls after Kate, as she rushes through to the hallway. She had sent Vi a couple of messages, asking her around to the new flat and asking for forgiveness. Vi had replied after an agonizing wait, and said she would be round within the hour, with the baby.

Kate opens the doors and sees her friend for the first time in months. Vi looks the same as ever, but panicked. There is a baby strapped to her chest, a changing bag slung over one shoulder and a canvas tote full of panettone and dessert wine over the other.

'Kate! What the fuck is going on?'

Kate hadn't intended to worry her, but Vi must have picked up on something in her messages. She stumbles, her words all coming out at once.

'It's . . . I've . . . There are some things . . .'

Then, suddenly, Nova is behind her. 'Hi, there!' She holds out her hand to Vi, who shakes it.

'Um . . . hi?'

'Come in – you and Kate have some catching up to do. Would you like tea, coffee, wine?' Her grin is bulletproof, and Kate just lets her take control.

'Uh, do you have a beer? I think I might need one, breast-feeding be damned.'

'Sure! Come in.'

Vi follows Nova, and Kate follows Vi. The fear has melted away. Maybe she couldn't have done this on her own, but with Nova here, everything is going to be all right.

✶

By the time Vi leaves, it has started to rain. It is gentle at first, barely more than a mist drifting down from the sky. The road, pavement and buildings outside are slick, leathery black.

'Thank you.'

'What for?' Nova shrugs from the sofa. 'You're the one who did all the talking.'

'But I couldn't have done it without you. And you were so good with the baby.'

'His name's Finn, bean queen. And no worries – I love babies.' She smiles. 'Do you feel better?'

Kate sighs shakily. There have been tears, and there has been laughter. Vi was, to Nova's mind, a good audience – passionately hating Tony, laughing with surprise when Kate came out, mock-interrogating Nova about her intentions.

'I feel better . . .' Kate says, uncertainly. 'But also, it makes it all a bit more real.'

Nova goes and hugs her. 'You should get some rest.'

'Yeah . . .' She looks around the room, searching for a thought, then reaches into her pocket. 'Here – I want you to have this.'

'What is it?' Nova tries to make out the object in Kate's hand. It is shiny, but that's all she can make out.

'Oh, sorry – here. Vi has the spare, but I thought you should have your own . . .'

Nova feels the object.

It's a key.

✳

By the time they're ready for bed, the rain is heavier. The gutters overspill and small lakes form around the drains. Kate thinks of Winnie the Pooh and his honey pots floating around. They go to bed, and after a while they sleep.

Kate has been asleep for half an hour – not enough time to start dreaming – when the thunder starts. She wakes without knowing why, only to be answered a minute later by a second crack. A shiver runs up her spine, and she no longer feels sleepy. She's not scared; Kate has always liked the thunder.

In the dark, she can just make out Nova next to her. She has pulled the sheet up and over her face. Careful not to wake her, Kate gets out of bed and goes to the front room. The flat came with a pair of French windows with a Juliet balcony, overlooking the road. Kate has never seen the point of them, but now she opens the doors and feels the cool air whip around her. The crackle of rain fills the room.

She stands there for a moment, hoping – a thunderclap answers her hope. Goosebumps rise on her arms and thighs. Kate looks around the room and decides to drag the big armchair over to the window. She grabs a blanket from the sofa and sits, wrapped up, watching the rain fall through the beams of the streetlamps. The window is sheltered enough that she isn't getting wet, though occasionally the wind will blow a few drops inside.

The thunder gets closer, then further away, then closer again, as though it's prowling up and down the streets of Acton. Kate counts the seconds between the lightning and the thunder, though sometimes there is no flash. Far off there is a long, grumbling peal like the sound of a landslide.

Her excitement fades, but the sound of the rain is soothing. She doesn't want it to stop – she wants to be washed away by the sound of it. The sound is so all-embracing that she doesn't hear Nova approaching until she is right by the chair.

'Hey, there,' she mumbles, running a hand through her hair. 'Room for two?'

'Just about. Come on – I need your warmth.'

Nova climbs into the chair and Kate wraps the blanket

around her. Kate puts one arm around her neck and draws her close.

'Did I wake you?'

'No – I just rolled over and you weren't there. Do you like the rain?'

'Mm,' Kate says, thinking. 'It's the closest you get to nature, living in the city.'

Nova doesn't say anything, just nuzzles closer. Her breath is warm on her neck. They listen to the rain for a long time. The air grows cold.

'Hey, Kate?' Nova is barely audible over the rain

'Yeah?'

'Will you be my girlfriend?'

Kate looks out into the darkness, and for a moment the street and all the houses are illuminated by a blue flash.

'Yes.'

'Good . . . that's good.'

They sit for a while longer, until Kate is sure that Nova is asleep. Her feet are poking out from under the blanket and she's getting cold. She gets up and closes the doors. Nova is snoring in the chair. Kate puts her arms under her and lifts, surprised by how light Nova is. How light her girlfriend is. She carries her back to bed and gets in beside her, feeling the warmth grow in the space between their bodies.

Twenty-Six

March

'I CAN'T BELIEVE I'M GOING to see the sea! See the sea!' Nova is bouncing on the bed in her stripy bumblebee socks.

'Ugh, take it down a notch, babe. It's early.'

'I'll get you a coffee, *ma petite amie.*'

They could get the Eurostar to Paris, but Nova begged to take the ferry. So they get a lunchtime train to Dover, eating homemade sandwiches and planning their long weekend. By the time they reach the coast, it's late afternoon. The rain has cleared and the sky is brightening. The landscape around them is a slick, dark green, like something that has recently emerged from underwater.

'What's that, over there?' Nova points forward.

'What? You'll have to be more specific.'

'That . . . field? It's very dark . . . and flat.'

'That's the sea! You spotted it first — that means you get five pence.'

'Oh. It's very flat, isn't it? I imagined it being more . . . lumpy. Big waves, that sort of thing.'

'Well, it is. But we're still quite far away – it just looks flat from where we are.'

'Riiiight . . .' Nova sounds unconvinced.

'Didn't you see it when you were in Venice?'

'It was too foggy. Besides, I was just starting to learn back then. Everything was blurry. I didn't have you to teach me.'

They walk on, wheeling their noisy luggage, closer and closer to the sea.

'We have a little extra time before the ferry, if you want to go and have a proper look,' Kate says.

'Can we?'

'Yeah, I think I can see a way down.'

'Okay – lay on, Macduff.'

They reach the front and Kate leads them down some concrete steps, carrying both bags so Nova can focus on not tripping. The sea isn't more than thirty metres of sandy beach away.

'Can I get closer?' Nova asks.

'Come on, follow me.' She takes Nova by the hand and leads her to the tide line.

'All this sand! I feel like I'm in a sandbox.'

Kate doesn't know what to say. She just wants to let Nova experience this on her own terms. She has seen the ocean on TV, but this is different.

'It's very noisy, isn't it?' Nova says after a while, looking out to sea.

She is sensing a new degree of depth. Her stereoscopy has developed since that first night in Kate's fort, and she has gone from seeing things across the room to the length of the street. But the length of the street is the greatest depth on offer in London. Oxford had more in the way of scenery, but Nova has never seen as far as she is seeing now, the sea stretching

out –

    out –

        oooooout to a flat horizon.

She's used to water being transparent, or silvery in a puddle, or dull green, stained with pondweed. She doesn't understand how the water in front of her is related to those kinds of water. This water is solid grey. It doesn't look like the colour of a liquid at all. It looks like a hard, grey-blue mineral that is somehow sloshing around. The sea looks nothing like she imagined it. But what *had* she imagined? Already her old ideas are fading away, like a dream on waking.

'What do you think?' Kate asks. Nova thinks about this for a second.

'I think it's kind of scary. It makes me feel small.'

Kate nods. 'Can't disagree with you there. Come on, we better get going.'

They spend a long time in the queue for the ferry, and the air smells of car exhaust. Both of them are sleepy, but Nova is still excited. On the train she had read all their tourist guides for Paris. Her reading is still slow, but there are lots of pictures to enjoy.

'We can go up the Eiffel Tower! Or go to the Pompidou Centre. We could see the *Mona Lisa*!' She dissolves into laughter, as though this is a particularly good joke. 'Can you imagine that? I could actually *see* the *Mona Lisa*.'

Kate smiles, feeling her girlfriend's excitement bubbling through her veins like a drug.

'I can't believe we're going on holiday . . . I can't believe we're going on a ship! A ship on the ocean . . . *crazy*.' Nova smiles to herself, then yawns.

Finally, they are on the lower deck, walking past the ranks of parked cars. The air is thick with fumes. Kate leads Nova to the stairs.

'It keeps moving!' Nova says.

'Just watch where you're going, okay? I don't want to have to take you to the doctor.'

'All right, aaaaall right . . .'

They emerge on the upper deck and start to explore, through the cloying whiff of the duty-free shop, an expanse of café, and a darkened arcade where racing games, shooting games and dancing games all flicker and flash and blare music.

'I can't believe there's so much on this boat! It's like a whole village.'

They buy paper parcels of chips, saturate them with ketchup and vinegar, and find a table. It's next to a window so they can look out. Nova does so from time to time, then looks back in again, focusing on her food or her hands. She doesn't know what to make of the sea yet. She's heard a lot about it, but she thinks it might be an acquired taste.

When they've eaten, they go outside. Nova looks out to sea for a while, watching the previously stable horizon rise and fall. She turns back to Kate, who is staring down at the ribbons of white foam that twist and curl away from the hull of the ship.

'Are you okay?'

'Yeah, I'm fine,' Kate nods.

'I mean . . . do you feel better, for being away?'

Kate blinks a few times, quickly. A vision of her bedside drawer appears to her. At the back are two wads of envelopes, tightly bound with rubber bands, like creatures that might snap or bite. Fifty-six empty letters. She doesn't know why she still hasn't mentioned them to anyone. At first it was because she didn't want to worry over nothing. But they just kept arriving, every other day. Now the letters feel like a cancer that she's waited too long to do anything about.

She clears her throat. 'Not yet. But I think I will, when we stop for the night.'

Nova stands on tiptoes and kisses her cheek.

✦

'Cheers!'

'*Santé*, I think you mean.'

The light in the room makes Nova's head swim. There are so many glass mirrors. And it isn't just the mirrors – all the glasses are cut-crystal, all the cutlery is polished, and the lights in the room blaze from chandeliers. Everything is bright, in a way that Nova doesn't find unpleasant, but which makes it difficult to concentrate on the meal.

She tries to concentrate on Kate instead. All the light makes her look luminous, as though she's glowing from inside. Her expression is far from angelic, though. Nova has learned how to recognize frustration. On Kate, this is a coming together of the eyebrows; three asymmetrical, vertical lines on her forehead; a thinning of the lips as she purses them together and – Nova's favourite – a slight wrinkling of the nose.

She is trying to get a snail out of its shell.

'Come . . . out . . . you little . . . bugger!' She fiddles around inside the shell with the provided utensil – a thin, barbed fork. Nova decides not to comment and picks up her own snail and her own fork. She carefully finds the opening and the snail comes out in one.

'How did you do that?'

'I don't know, I just did it.'

'Ugh. I think I have a faulty snail.' Kate goes back to scrabbling, this time inside another one of the snails on her plate. Nova inspects the thing on the end of her fork – dark grey, shrivelled like a raisin, and covered in something green that she can only assume is garlic sauce.

'Don't look at it like that, just eat it!' Kate sounds disgusted. The thing in front of Nova is no more disgusting to her than any other food. All food looks spectacularly yukky. The crisp flakes of her breakfast cereal have the rough, uneven texture of gravel. The internal layers of lasagne look exactly like human flesh, cut into strips. Still, it's important find out what food looks like, for future reference.

Nova pops the snail in her mouth and chews.

Kate watches her. 'How is it? I've finally got one.'

'It's not bad . . . It mostly tastes like garlic butter. And chicken.'

'Ha. All right, here goes nothing.'

She chews in silence for a minute, then reaches for a glass of water.

'Man, that's one funky tasting chicken. Why did I let you convince me to order this stuff?'

The Rules of Seeing

'We're in Paris! You have to do all the stupid, stereotypical things that people do when they come to Paris!'

'Fine, but I'm looking forward to the next bit a lot more.'

✵

The absinthe tasting is just a few blocks away. Kate has eaten four courses, including the snails, but still feels hungry. They go into the bar and Nova explains everything to the owner in perfect French. He ushers them both to the bar with a hand on their backs, seating them by a tall, clear-glass tower. It has little taps coming out either side. He says something complicated in French to Nova, seeming to think that Kate will also understand, then leaves them.

'I love seeing you do that.'

'Do what?'

'Talk to people in another language. You're just so . . . natural.'

'Flatterer.' Nova grins. A barmaid arrives with two tall, elaborate glasses, with a little clear liquid in the bottom. There is a strong smell of aniseed and fennel. The barmaid starts chatting amiably with Nova, who explains that this is their first time.

The barmaid narrates what she's doing, putting a flat, slotted spoon on each of their glasses, on top of which she places a sugar cube. Both glasses are positioned under the taps of the water tower, and now the taps are turned, so that liquid drip drip drips onto each of the sugar cubes, dissolving them and running down into the clear liquid. As the water hits it, the absinthe changes colour.

'See how it's changing?' Nova says, peering into the bottom

of her glass with childlike wonder. Kate watches as, drop by drop, it turns from clear green to milky white. Nova is excited by changes like this – the moment the toast turns golden, the moment Kate's cheeks turn pink. They sit, holding hands, watching the sugar disappear.

They listen to the bustle around them, the dozens of conversations being held in French and other languages. Nova is half following a couple of the conversations without being aware of it. Kate just lets herself drift into the sound, enjoying the rise and fall of people's voices and the sense that, at last, she is somewhere far from home.

By the time the sugar cubes have fully dissolved, each glass is about half full of cloudy liquid. The barmaid returns and turns off each of the taps. She says something in French, which Kate takes to be cheers, and they clink their glasses and sip.

'Wow.'

'Yeah . . . you feel that?'

'Like your eyeballs have gone prickly?'

'I was going to say that the back of my head has fallen off.'

'Drink slowly. Maybe just one of these, yeah?'

They do not have 'just one'. The barmaid tells them they can't leave until they've tried it bohemian style, which involves lighting the sugar cube before adding the water. They watch the dancing, blue flames and breathe in whiffs of burned caramel.

RULE OF SEEING NO.294
**Flames look like bright bugs which have
landed on the thing they are devouring,
fluttering incandescent wings.
Do not brush them off.**

By the time they leave the bar, they're running late to get to the Eiffel Tower.

'You never told me you were an ice skater!'

'Because I *wasn't*. I thought I was, at the time . . .'

'You were in competitions!' Nova grins, imagining this.

'I took it very seriously, but I was never going to be professional.'

'How come?'

'Well, look at me! I didn't know that I was going to end up as tall as this.'

'Aw, poor bean sprout . . . Did you get to wear a sparkly outfit?'

'Oh, *hundreds* of diamante bits!'

Nova pulls them to a stop. They stand for a long moment, Nova's face turned up to Kate's. She speaks in a conspiratorial whisper.

'I want to kiss you.'

'You want to . . . here?' Kate hesitates. They've never kissed in public before. It's not something Kate insisted on, just that Nova seemed to know it might be a big step for her.

'We don't have to, if you're not comfortable,' Nova says.

Kate's heart is a tectonic plate, the fault lines rubbing together, moments before an earthquake. She leans down and kisses Nova – and Paris shakes, but does not fall.

'You taste of caramel,' Nova mumbles into Kate's lips.

'Really? You taste like a distillery.'

Nova cackles and pulls them on through the night. They follow a map that Kate has drawn on, until they reach the square where the Eiffel Tower stands. Nova cranes her neck up, taking in the array of lights disappearing into the sky. It looks like nothing is connecting the lights – as though the lights are all that's there.

'Come on then!' Kate pulls her on, 'We don't want to miss it!'

✴

They look out over the city. Around them, the tower glows. A tower of light, not steel. Below them the streets glow, though not as brightly. Paris is full of low mist, creeping through the streets between its high tenements. They look like canals full of clouds.

'My head is spinning,' Kate says.

'That's the absinthe.'

Nova hugs Kate close, grabbing the lapel of her coat and pulling it into her, sheltering herself against the wind.

'This is nice.'

'It is.' As they speak, the lights of the tower start to flicker, shimmering over the structure like the lights on a deep-sea creature. They look up, into the darkness. When it's over, they look back down, into each other's eyes.

'Whoa, head rush,' says Nova.

'I love you,' says Kate, at the same moment.

Nova freezes, then bursts out laughing.

'Oh, my God!'

'Hey! What? What did I do?'

Nova buries herself in Kate's scarf, convulsed with giggles. 'You did not just tell me that you love me *on the Eiffel Tower?*'

Kate feels herself blushing intensely. 'Well, it just felt like the right moment.'

Nova stops laughing and looks at her. She's still grinning and pulls Kate close again.

'I love you too.'

✳

They wake up late the next morning, in the small hotel bed. They are on the fourth floor, but can still feel Ligne of the Paris Metro rumbling under them. Nova gets up while Kate is in the shower and gets her boots on to go out. They haven't paid for a breakfast, and she's hungry.

Before she leaves, she spots the open sketchpad on Kate's side of the bed. A drawing done in biro. Kate had bought the pad on the ferry and done the drawing when they arrived, without prompting – the view from their window. It was a scatter of angled roofs, air-conditioning units and wonky aerials, all done quickly and seemingly without much thought. Nova had watched her work, feeling that it was a magic trick, turning 3D into 2D. She had never seen Kate draw before, only colour in other people's drawings. Today she will scan the giftshops of the museums they visit for some watercolour paints.

Nova descends through the hotel and steps out onto the street, feeling nervous at the number of people, the hustle and bustle. Even if she understands the language of this foreign country, she isn't fluent in the universal language of bodies moving around her, of cars and scooters and cyclists coming and going.

She successfully crosses the road and finds the spot that she remembers – a kiosk, set into the wall, where a man is selling loaves of bread, pastries and cheap coffee. She buys two coffees and a bag of croissants, while the man chats to her about the weather. She crosses the road, back to the hotel entrance.

There is a man standing at the end of the street, holding something rectangular and white that might be a newspaper. There is something about this man. Something familiar. He moves on. Nova walks back into the hotel, telling herself not to be stupid. If Kate can get over her paranoia, she can too.

The problem with not being able to see fully, to not understand everything that she sees, is that there are many interpretations for everything. Instead of one man looking like Tony, many men do. For Nova, there are too many details to pin down. And so, if she's inclined to think that Tony is in Paris, trailing them, that's exactly what she sees.

She pauses for a moment in the lobby, breathing, making herself calm down. She can't upset Kate. They have to keep moving forward. She doesn't know what their end destination is, but they will get there someday.

Someday they will be free.

Twenty-Seven

April

'THERE'S A BIT THAT you haven't got, bottom right . . .'

Kate shifts her weight, keeping balanced on the step-ladder. She takes a piece of tape from the window frame and presses it over the spot Nova pointed to. A chink of light disappears.

'Better?'

'Yes.'

The flat isn't dark, but the light seems evenly spread, without dark or light spots. The tinfoil on the windows has blocked out the winter sun – the kind of light that pinballs down from the sky, twanging off clouds, someone's windshield, ringing the windowpane like a bell on its way in. Now there is light, but it doesn't move in lines. It doesn't move at all. It's like a hanging mist. Kate sits down on the steps, and looks at Nova.

'So?'

Nova closes her eyes. The light is soft, the warm glow she knew from birth. She moves around a little. There are no flashes of light to tempt her into looking. That's the thing she had found about seeing – it was difficult, but it became addictive. Over time, closing her eyes felt more alien.

'It's perfect.'

'Good . . .'

Kate puts her arms around her. Nova is a little startled – before, she would have heard Kate coming, but after so long learning to see, her hearing has dulled. No, not dulled exactly. It has become less prominent in the mix, now that there is a new instrument playing along. With her eyes closed, she feels more blind than she was before, but she will get used to it. She's looking forward to getting used to it. She just needs a break, a rest from studying.

She has come to see Kate's flat as an essential part of her learning, a place where she doesn't need to be learning all the time. It has come to seem like a necessity. It still feels like an extended sleepover. They still sleep in the fort that Kate made in the front room.

Time has passed, and nothing has happened. Or rather, everything has happened – Kate feels like so many things never happened before in the rest of her life. It's been two years since she fell and hit her head, and she feels like she's finally starting to live again.

Her days with Nova are strange yet natural. Flashes of their first time keep repeating, echoes of the moment where she lost her sense of Kate and Nova and was only aware of one person. She's scared that, if she lets Nova leave now, she will be taking a part of Kate that she can't get back. The second time, she closed her eyes as Nova often does, focussing on everything else – the touch and taste of the woman next to her.

She draws all the time, and stains her own drawings with

colours that Nova buys for her – cheap poster paints from the corner shop, lurid acrylics from a Soho art supplier, hazy pastels that settle in the cracks of her hands like silted riverbeds. And the watercolour set from Paris, of course. The white plastic box is almost identical to the one her dad first bought her, and Kate will open it sometimes, just to inhale the powdery smell of the paints.

Her drawings are mostly of things in the flat – the toaster, the pillow fort, Nova's boots with their tangle of laces – because it is the transposition of these everyday objects onto paper that delights her girlfriend so much. But sometimes they go out and she will sketch the scenery. Sometimes she will sketch her reflection in a mirror. Sometimes, when she is sure her girlfriend is asleep on the sofa, Kate will sketch Nova in repose, then hide the result away. She draws and, in doing so, feels as though she is learning to see the thing she is drawing, for the very first time.

There is no sign of Tony. He seems to have disappeared. Kate still works from home, only now she sometimes has Nova to keep her company in the days, and that helps.

'Are you okay?' Nova pulls back from the hug to look into her eyes.

'Mm-hm. Just thinking.'

'Oh yeah?'

'I wonder if I'll ever get used to this . . .'

'You will.'

✦

Nova comes wordlessly into the kitchen, stands before Kate and places her hands on her shoulders, as though to kiss her.

But instead, she hops up into Kate's arms, wrapping her own arms around her neck.

'Oof, a little warning would have been good!'

'Are you saying I'm heavy?'

'No, Supernova – you're annoyingly light for someone who eats pepperoni-and-peach sandwiches.'

'Good . . .' Her voice is muffled, pressed into Kate's neck. 'Then there's no hurry to get down.' She kisses Kate's clavicle, making her squirm. Instead of trying to shake Nova off, she walks them both through the flat until she gets to the bedroom, then collapses sideways onto the bed. Nova screams.

'Woo! I wanna go again!'

'Shut up.' Kate kisses her.

'Why' (kiss) 'should I' (kiss) 'shut up' (kiss) '. . . oh, okay.'

✳

Kate returns from the corner shop to find Nova sprawled out on the living-room rug, surrounded by sweet wrappers. But she isn't eating – all the unwrapped chocolates are carefully laid on a plate next to her. She's playing with the wrappers, each of which is transparent and a different colour. She has smoothed them flat.

'What are you doing?'

Nova starts. 'Oh, hey, come here – look what I can do!' She holds up a blue wrapper in her left hand and a yellow one in her right, then slides them in front of each other. She looks at Kate, mouth open, as though she's just performed a magic trick.

'See? I made green!'

Kate laughs and pulls Nova close, kissing the top of her head.

'You're so clever.'

Nova smiles innocently. 'Oh, and here – you should have these.' She hands Kate the plate of chocolates.

'Feeder.'

Nova winks – a new skill – and goes back to playing with the wrappers, while Kate takes the shopping through to the kitchen. Nova is working on a new rule, sliding one coloured gel in front of another until she gets it clear in her head.

RULE OF SEEING NO.311

The rule of occlusion (see Rule No.1) can be confused by transparency. An <u>opaque</u> blue square overlapping an opaque red square is easy to see as closer. But a transparent blue square overlapping a transparent red square will look like three shapes – a red one, a blue one, and a purple one in the middle. It will be difficult to tell which of these shapes is in front, or even how they are separate.

'Come get your dinner.'

Nova sweeps all the wrappers into a pile and goes to join Kate in the kitchen.

✳

'Dammit, Nova!'

'What . . . what have I done now?'

'Can't you put your clothes in the laundry bin?'

She looks around – the flat is colourfully littered with Nova's socks where she has kicked them off, jumpers where she was too warm and pants where she had decided simply to strip off. Nova sighs extravagantly.

'Yes, mothership.'

'How did you even manage as a blind person? How did you find anything?'

Nova shrugs. 'It's like squirrels burying nuts – sometimes I remember where I left them, sometimes I don't.'

'But how do you know if things are clean?'

'The ol' sniff test.' She grins proudly, like a child showing off a bogey.

'Ugh, gross.'

✳

It is afternoon, and they're sitting listening to the radio, when Kate remembers something she bought from the newsagent's.

'Here – a present for you.'

She hands Nova a small, cold object, and her fingers try to make sense of what her eyes can't understand.

'It's a toy car,' Kate explains.

'Oh . . .' Nova is puzzled. 'I know I act a bit childish at times, but toys?'

'No, that's not it. I was thinking about what you said, ages ago, when we went to the zoo. Do you remember you said that you could understand what the tiger looked like, because you knew what a cat felt like, and a cat is like a miniature tiger?'

'Yeah, I remember.'

'And I was thinking – it's not easy, trying to feel a whole car. You can feel the bumper, or the wing mirror, but not the whole thing. But if you had a *miniature* one . . .'

As Kate talks, a smile is spreading over Nova's face. She can feel the four wheels, the slope of the windshield and the blunt end at the back. A shape starts to form in her head, becoming clearer with each pass her hands make over the car. She runs it up and down her palm on its four tiny wheels.

'Come on!' She grabs Kate's hand, dragging her from her chair. 'I want to go down to the street.'

'What, right now?'

'Yes, now come on!'

Nova stumbles her way to the door, too excited to wait. With Kate just behind her, she races down the staircase and through the door to the street. In front of them, the traffic speeds in both directions. Kate stands next to her, puffing a bit. They stand in silence for a second.

'Well?'

Nova doesn't want to say anything for a moment. Some shift is taking place in her head. She still has the toy car in her right hand and keeps running her thumb over its contours. Before, cars were bright blurs when in motion. Cars were like fish – they seemed to just float around. Even when they were parked, they looked like coloured blocks sitting by the side of the road. She throws her arms around Kate.

'You're a genius!'

'Can you see them?'

'Yes – I get them now. I get how they move. I can see all the details at once, all in one object. Do you think we can get more toys like this?'

'Sure. They do toy trains and planes, toy animals, all sorts of stuff. I'll get you a toy chest.'

Nova is hopping with excitement. She pulls Kate close and whispers in her ear.

'I'm going to make you my wife, some day.'

Kate feels herself blushing and clears her throat. 'How about a more immediate reward?'

'Name it.'

'Well, you could take me out for dinner.'

Nova grabs her arm. Quickly, they go back inside, grab their stuff and together they walk down the street, watching the cars go by.

La Cucina is on the High Street and, although Kate doesn't fancy talking to anyone but Nova, she knows Benny will get them a good table. All the time, Nova is telling her about the cars she can see, and how even the ones that don't look exactly like the toy car are becoming clearer.

'It all makes sense now!'

Kate can't pretend to understand what has changed – how Nova saw the cars before, or how she sees them now. But she is happy. It bubbles up like champagne, an uncorking of joy. They reach the restaurant and Benny emerges from the shadows as quickly as if he'd been expecting Kate.

'Katerina Tomassi! I thought you were dead!'

'Hey, Benny, how's it going? Nova, this is Benny, my cousin.'

'Nice to meet you.' Benny shakes Nova's hand, uncertainly outstretched, and raises his eyebrows at Kate. She's eaten at La Cucina plenty of times, but always with Tony. Her family has barely talked to her since she left him. Kate can't deal with

Benny reporting back to his mother, who will report back to her mother. She tries not to think about it.

Benny leads them through the busy restaurant, weaving through tables faster than Nova can follow, so Kate guides her with a hand on her arm. Physical contact is still novel, and still starts the strange feedback loop. They are shown to one of the red leatherette booths. It has a reserved sign on it, which Benny removes.

'Can I get you two anything to drink?'

'Bottle of red?'

'Right away, signora.'

He swoops off. Food and drinks arrive at regular intervals. They share grilled artichokes with aioli, deep-fried rice balls and a beetroot risotto. They drink the house red. They talk about each other. Kate is surprised by how much she still doesn't know.

She'd not known that Nova's mother was second-generation Pakistani, her father third-generation Ukrainian, and that they'd met at teacher-training college. She'd not known that her favourite food growing up had been pasta and tinned meatballs. She still knows so little, and she's hungry to know more. It feels strangely like she's discovering secrets about herself.

She'd fallen out with Vi for saying it, but it was true – Kate didn't do friendships. Her relationships were interludes between work and sleep. Before Tony, she told herself that when she found the right person, she would settle down. But she always suspected that the right person wasn't out there. It wasn't that she was lacking the right person, but that she was categorically the wrong person. When Tony asked her to marry him, she'd surprised herself by saying yes.

'My turn to interrogate you,' Nova says. 'So . . . what would your perfect day be?'

'That's a tough one.' The question from anyone else would have irritated Kate. It would have seemed contrived. But from Nova it feels genuine. It's an attempt to understand – in the same way she has come to understand the shape of a car – the particular shape of Kate's life.

'I don't know,' she says finally. 'To be honest, I used to love working . . .'

Nova laughs. 'Your perfect day is going to *work*? Oh, babe.'

'But it's true – I could lose myself in work. I looked forward to going in. I loved drawing up plans . . .'

'Making something people would enjoy living in?'

'Maybe . . .' Kate says, knowing that's not right. She'd always regarded the people as an inconvenience, something that had to be accommodated for in the plans, like air-conditioning vents or sewage pipes. Buildings were not like machines for living in, or whatever people said, but like giant, asymmetrical crystals. They had white spurs of steel, vectors of plate glass, planes of level concrete. They grew in her head when she closed her eyes at night. Buildings were simple. It was the people who were complicated.

She still enjoys working, but she doesn't feel the same about buildings any more.

'I enjoyed putting shapes together in ways that I'd never thought of before.'

'That sounds like what I do now, in reverse.' Nova leans closer, picking at a bowl of olives. 'I'm always pulling shapes apart, trying to see how this triangle and those circles and that curve add up to make a face . . . I'm sick of shapes.'

Kate doesn't know what to say to that. Nova sounds tired, in spite of her energy, but Kate is desperate to keep her spirits up. She can't stop now.

✳

On the walk home, Nova seems more positive, talking about how she is getting used to seeing intangible things like clouds and rainbows that meant nothing to her when she was blind. They reach the flat, go in through the downstairs door, and Kate holds Nova's hand as they walk up the stairs.

'So, how about a movie? I know we've been doing a lot of that recently, but we could try something from that box set . . .'

They have reached the top of the flight of stairs that lead to the front door. Nova stops talking because Kate's hand has tightened around hers.

'Kate?' Nova looks ahead, towards the door, and there is something hanging there, in front of them, but she can't understand what it is. The shape is new, novel, with elements of something familiar.

'Kate?'

She doesn't reply, but makes a guttural, choking noise, as though she's being strangled. She turns away from the door, and it's only then that she starts screaming. Even the screams sound choked. Nova can't see much, but can see well enough to know that there's nobody else there.

She's heard Kate wake from nightmares screaming, but this is worse. This isn't the stifled fear of night terrors – this is waking, broad daylight.

'Kate, please calm down. Please. What is it?'

Nova can't get her to talk, and her hand has slipped out of hers. Nova walks forward and Kate doesn't stop her. She puts her hand out to the thing that's hanging in front of the door. She feels rope leading down, which must be strung from the light fixture over the door. The thing on the end of the rope is quite small, furry, and slightly warm. She runs her hands over it.

'Please, come away.' It's the first thing Kate has managed to say. 'Please, don't look at it.'

Now Nova realizes what's in front of her – it's a rabbit. The rabbit that belongs to the downstairs neighbour, and lives in a hutch in their garden. She can see the black-and-white patches of fur. She can make out its face, tilted upwards as though it wants to be tickled under the chin. Somebody has killed it.

She goes to Kate, takes the phone out of her pocket and carefully dials 999.

✼

The police arrive. They take pictures, take the rabbit down and talk to the downstairs neighbour, who weeps and shouts and curses. She comes storming up the stairs to talk to Kate.

'You! Do you know who did this? One of your friends?'

'No, I'm so sorry, I . . .'

'If this is your fault, I'll see you suffer for it.' She jabs her finger in Kate's face.

'Hey, calm down.' Nova steps between them. 'She's had a shock too.'

The woman takes a breath as though to answer back, then starts crying again and stamps back down the stairs.

'Sandra, can you go talk to her?' It's the detective inspector, Paul Sandler. Kate likes him. He's about forty-five, his pale blond hair flecked with white, and he rubs the back of his head when he's thinking.

Kate keeps touching her neck. She can still feel the rope. The skin feels raw. It's like her whole body was hung up. They go and sit around the kitchen table.

Paul writes a few more things down, reads over what he has written, then looks into her eyes. 'Kate, maybe this is going to seem like a stupid question, but who do you think did this?'

She doesn't say anything.

'Kate? I might be wrong, but I feel like there's a story here that I'm not getting.'

The other officer, Sandra, returns from comforting their neighbour, and sits next to him. Kate looks at Nova, who is leaning on the work surface. Her expression wills her on.

'I don't know. I never thought he could do something like this. But . . .' She trails off, hopelessly. She can't understand her own life any more. Everything seems like a bad dream, in the way that dreams have no logic. Anything can happen in a dream.

'Kate?'

'My husband, Tony. We had a fight a few months ago, and he left. I, uh . . . I've been getting blank letters since then. I think they might have been from him.'

Kate tries to ignore Nova's face, turning upwards in shock.

'Okay, Kate. Can you give me Tony's full name?'

Kate swallows. 'Anthony John O'Neill. He – he's a DI in the Met . . .'

Later, she will wonder if she imagined it – the slight incline of each officer's head towards the other, as she says Tony's full name. It isn't that they look at each other. But it seems to her that a sign has passed between them. She tells the rest of her story, and they take down the details, but they do not smile as they leave and offer few words of sympathy.

Kate cannot not ask what they think they know, but it seems clear to her in the moment. She is the wife of DI Tony O'Neill, and she is not to be trusted.

Nova doesn't know what to say to Kate, doesn't know what to do. There doesn't seem to be anything. She doesn't want to confront her about the letters. Not now. She goes and makes cups of tea in the kitchen. Finally, the police are gone, and they are left alone. Kate fastens all the locks then stands there, frozen.

The cups of tea that they left a couple of hours before are sitting on the table, and Kate stands there with her coat still on, staring at them. Nova takes her hand.

'Come on, love. Come to bed.'

'Don't.' Kate pulls her hand away.

'Don't what?'

Kate takes a shaky breath. 'Just don't, okay? I can't do this right now.'

'Can't do what?' Nova feels like the air is being squeezed out of her.

Kate holds her hands out in frustration.

'*This*. Whatever this is. I . . . I can't.'

She grabs a single duvet and a pillow from the fort, which still stands in the front room, takes them back to her empty bedroom, and shuts the door. Nova stands there, eyes closed, listening to the blood rushing in her ears. Then she goes to the fort. She could try to dismantle it, take the double duvet to the pull-out bed in the study. But she doesn't want to accidentally knock everything over.

She crawls onto the bed with her clothes still on, pulls the covers over her and cries into a pillow that smells of Kate.

Twenty-Eight

May

NOVA BREATHES IN AND out a couple of times, readying herself for the return leg of the tightrope walk. She grips tight to the bag of dry-cleaning and starts to walk home.

Today the light is being especially difficult, coming at her from funny angles, bright one moment and dark the next. She supposes it's something to do with the clouds, but it's like listening to a song while someone keeps turning the volume up and down. Her eyes ache, and Nova wonders if she might go blind again from the strain.

When she gets home, Kate is at the kitchen table, quiet and still. She has put the radio on, not loud, but enough to cover her own silence. Nova stands in the doorway with the dry-cleaning, trying to find the courage to ask the only important question.

It has been a month since they came back from the restaurant. A month since Kate left the house. A month since they slept together. The police have no news for them. They are on their own.

Nova walks to the table and puts the dry-cleaning down. 'There you go.'

Kate doesn't reply, just grunts in recognition, and Nova's irritation finally allows her to ask the question she's been wanting to ask for the last week.

'Do you want me to go?'

Kate's head jerks up. She stares at Nova. There are dark circles under her eyes. Nova wonders whether she's sleeping at all, or just lies there in the dark in her bedroom. The thought makes her jaw ache. There's an agonising gap before she says,

'You mean leave? For good?'

Nova sighs.

'Yeah, that's what I mean, Kate. It doesn't seem like you want me here.'

'No . . . of course not. No, no, no.' Kate takes a deep breath, but when she speaks again, her voice is cracked. 'But I . . . I understand if you want to go.'

She looks away.

'I don't want to go anywhere.' Nova says, carefully.

'Oh.' Kate exhales shakily. 'Well, if you change your mind . . .' she trails off, and is silent again for a long time.

✳

Days pass without natural light, bleeding together.

Nova tries to bring Kate back to how she was before. Slowly, she talks more and seems more like herself, but in that time she never leaves the flat. Nova goes to work when she has to, and often returns to find Kate where she left her, on the sofa or in bed. She wonders if Kate has told work that she's sick, or if she's just falling further and further behind on her assignments.

They dismantle the fort and Nova continues sleeping on the sofa. Whenever she reaches out to touch Kate on the arm or brush her cheek, her touch isn't returned.

Nova is scared. She was ready for their relationship to be difficult. She knew that Kate was going through a bad time. But this doesn't feel like something she can fix, and Kate refuses to get help. Suddenly, Kate's problems seem bigger than ever, and Nova wonders, not for the first time, if she doesn't have enough problems of her own.

Their supplies of loo roll and toothpaste dwindle, and Kate forgets to do an online shop. Nova mentions this, and Kate goes quiet for a moment.

'Would you mind . . .?'

Nova understands what is being asked of her. She puts her shoes on and goes to the shop on the corner. She buys loo roll, milk and not-very-fresh bread. Even on such a small scale, shopping is one of the most challenging things she can attempt. It's difficult enough to distinguish one object from another, similar object – say a pack of loo roll from a pack of kitchen roll. But then, even in the corner shop, there are several types of loo roll, all boasting different qualities. With that, the gamble is small, but with other things she ends up buying something quite wrong – the clove toothpaste they both find disgusting. Or there's the butter that turned out to be cream cheese.

RULE OF SEEING NO.324
Some plastic bottles are transparent, so you can see what's inside. For example, it is easy

to tell the difference between lemonade and cola. But some plastic bottles are opaque, and their colour is misleading. For example, when looking for a pint of milk, avoid detergent in white bottles.

Nova can decipher words slowly, but the packaging is crammed with so many words, in so many colours, fonts, shapes and sizes, integrated into images or swirling around smiling faces, that she can often only get fragments of information. A few items have Braille on them, but not many. She asks the boy on the checkout a few times if she has bought the right thing, but he's sullen, and Nova gives up asking.

She gets back to the flat, exhausted, and hands over her haul to Kate. She's sitting at the kitchen table, and just mutters 'Thanks' when Nova sets the bag down in front of her. Nova takes a deep breath, and makes a spur of the moment decision.

She goes and puts her few things in a rucksack. She doesn't pack her toothbrush for fear of being too obvious. If she feels guilt, she packs it away to deal with later. When she is ready, Kate is still sitting in the kitchen.

'I think I'm going to go back to my flat, to check everything's okay.' She watches Kate's face for clues.

'Sure, sounds good.' Kate doesn't even look up. 'See you later.'

✳

Getting to the station is easy. She remembers what it used to be like – the negotiations with other travellers, the search for

Braille signs, the long moments standing on crowded platforms or echoing concourses. It impresses her, this ease, but saddens her too – is this what she made her compromise for? She had expected something deeper, an appreciation of reality – her hopes had verged on the mystical. All that she has gained is convenience, and vision just seems like another gizmo for getting her from place to place.

She phones work from the train, and tells them she won't be coming back. The call takes longer than she hoped, with her being passed from one person to another, none of whom seems to know what to do in the absence of a letter of resignation. But the job has always been a flexible one. She's on shifts that can be covered until a replacement is found. In twenty minutes or so, Nova no longer has a job in London.

RULE OF SEEING NO.349
If you look out of a train window, facing backwards, it looks like the world is shrinking down to a point, as though everything is being sucked into the event horizon of a black hole, and the train is the only thing escaping destruction.

She thinks of phoning ahead to Oxford. She could phone John, or Rebecca. But she would rather wait. She doesn't have much to be excited about at the moment, and the thought of surprising them gives her something to focus on.

She feels like she's suffocating.

The person she should call, of course, is Kate. She has brought the number up on her phone several times now, and hovered her finger (so precisely) over the call button. But every time she held back and put the phone away.

Kate hadn't called her at first, when she didn't return to the flat. Nova started to think she never would – that her disappearance was welcome.

By the evening, the messages started, and the calls. Nova ignored them to begin with, because she didn't know what she was doing. She sat in a café, not drinking the tea in front of her. She didn't want to talk to Kate until she had made her decision. But with each call she ignored, her decision hardened.

It's been an hour since Kate last called her, and she doesn't feel as if she could pick up if she tried. With effort, she takes out her phone and writes a message.

Kate – I'm going away.

She stops, stares at the message for a long time, but she can't make it seem true. She deletes 'away' then continues.

Kate – I'm going to Oxford, to stay with a friend. I'm sorry. You should get some help.

She thinks about writing more, but can't stand thinking about her words any more. She presses Send, turns her phone off and looks out of the train window as it starts to pull out of the station.

Twenty-Nine

July

'Y OU SHOULD EAT YOUR cake; I made it specially.'
Kate stares down at the piece of syrupy lemon cake
on her plate and feels sick. There is another half of this cake
in her bag already, to eat later. She knows her mum just wanted
to do something to make her feel better. Something tangible,
because she's not good at talking. It's always been like this –
cakes baked, presents bought, sentimental objects pulled out
of the attic for her to take home. But Kate doesn't want cake
– she wants her mother.

'Please, Mum; I'm trying to talk to you.'

Mrs Tomassi shifts as though trying to get comfortable,
though her armchair is fatly upholstered.

'I don't see what there is to talk about, Katerina.' She sounds
genuinely baffled.

'We can just talk, Mum. Talk about what's on our minds.
It's not . . .' Her hands form shapes in the air for a moment.
'Not everything has to be essential information.'

'You're talking in riddles again.' Her mother stiffens, sips her tea. China cups and saucers – Mrs Tomassi has an idea of Britishness that is firmly rooted in the 1950s.

'Not riddles, Mum. I'm your daughter, who has recently escaped an abusive relationship after discovering her husband was selling drugs that he had stolen from—'

Her mother winces. 'Do we have to talk about that, Katie? You're only making yourself worse by raking over it.'

'I'm not raking over it. I've not spoken to anyone else! Just you, and you won't listen.'

She slams the plate of cake down on the coffee table. Her mother's lips purse into a thin line.

'I'm listening, aren't I? I just think you should try to forget.'

'Well, I can't forget. That's what I'm trying to tell you. And I'm also trying to tell you . . .'

Kate doesn't mean to keep talking, but she's angry now, and can't seem to stop.

'I'm trying to tell you that I was in a relationship. The first relationship that had made me really happy in . . . in forever.'

Her face heats up. Why does she feel like a child every time she comes here?

'You met another man? You're not *divorced* yet, Katerina.'

'No, Mum. I didn't meet another man.'

Circling around the drain now, she can see the drop that she's about to make.

'What are you talking about? If you didn't meet another man . . .'

Kate sticks her jaw out, to keep the tears from coming. She can't say the words for a long moment, but her mother hasn't understood.

'I met a woman. I met another woman . . .' She looks down at the cake, bleeding sweetness onto the plate. Anything but look into her mother's eyes. 'I met a woman, and she was wonderful. And now she's gone and—'

She's about to say, 'I was in love', but her mother cuts her off.

'Get out.'

Kate looks up, in shock.

'What?'

'Get out of my house.'

She stands, and Kate finds herself mirroring her mother. She feels like she's standing in front of a mirror, now. She sees her mother's wrinkles, her sad, defeated face, and Kate feels old. When did she get so old? It just happened.

Wordlessly, her mother walks out of the room, into the hall, and Kate follows her. Kate hadn't known how her mother would react to this news – like so many other aspects of her inner life, her mother had artfully concealed anything that might be *distasteful.* But she did not think of her mother as a bigot. She did not know what she expected, but she did not expect this.

Her mother hands Kate her bag, and she takes it. She's too shocked to say anything else.

'Mum—'

Mrs Tomassi opens the front door, and stands out of her way. Kate walks through the open door, then turns.

'Mum—'

'Goodbye.' Her mother looks right at her. 'Don't come back.'

The door does not slam, which feels wrong, somehow. It closes gently, and Kate listens to the lock turning. It's like a dream, she thinks. She hasn't had a key to the house for years now. She looks up and down the street to see if anyone is watching, but she is alone.

Slowly, Kate walks away.

✳

Nova expected the funeral to be a small one, but half of Oxford seems to be here. It has rained while they were in church, and the earth is sweating in the heat with a musk-like body odour. The air is hard to breathe. She had imagined standing by the grave as the coffin was lowered, but she is at the back of a crowd. Faintly, she can hear the Methodist minister (another surprise to Nova) incanting the words.

She is wearing black. Before, she would have needed someone else to pick the outfit for her, but today she did it herself. Okay, the T-shirt has JURASSIC PARK on the front, but it's the best she could do. She doesn't have many clothes with her.

John Katzner didn't have much family, but it seems that Nova wasn't the only student he had befriended. The service, organized by the faculty, featured readings and remembrances. Words in translation and words in their original language. Nova hadn't been asked to say anything, but she doesn't mind. Nobody from the faculty knows her now, and she's not sure what she would have said.

Trying not to seem distracted, Nova scans the assembled faces for Rebecca. Not that she really expects her to be here, but she did promise. Perhaps, after turning up late, she's got lost somewhere in the crowd. But there is no sign. She can hear people are crying, though cannot see the tears on their faces unless their makeup has run.

The minister makes some closing remarks, as though drawing a debate to a close, rather than a life. The crowd starts to thin as, one by one, they make their way to the grave, get whatever they were looking for there, and move away.

Nova waits, for a long time, until most of them are gone and a small queue has formed of the remaining mourners. She is getting the hang of queues, slowly, though working out where they start and end still gives her trouble. People don't always line up properly, standing in all directions. She joins what she takes to be the back of the queue and shuffles forward every minute or so. A girl in front of her is sobbing heartily.

Finally, Nova reaches the graveside. A small wooden cross has been staked into the earth, with a brass plaque bearing an inscription she can't read. The smell of earth is thick here, and she feels sick. She seems to be the last person here, though she is aware of someone lurking a way off, presumably the gravedigger waiting to fill in the hole. Nova reaches into her pocket and pulls out a couple of Earl Grey tea bags, which she tosses down onto the pale coffin, already half obscured by earth and flowers.

RULE OF SEEING NO.355
There are no objects (see Rule No.92), but there are boundaries – contrast boundaries, colour boundaries, texture boundaries. Like the border between land and sea, these are not absolute, but they are helpful in

distinguishing the animate and the inanimate, the living and the dead.

'I'm sorry, John . . .' she begins, but can't finish. After all, he's the one who should be apologizing for leaving her high and dry when she needs him most. *Some tutor, you, John Katzner, for leaving a student hanging before her big assignment.*

She feels guilty for even thinking this, but it's true – without John, there is no job in Oxford for her (and none waiting for her back in London, because she's such a fucking idiot). Maybe Nova could not have predicted that he would die so suddenly, but she feels that she has made too many assumptions in the last couple of years. She has taken too many things for granted. Anyway, guilt is a familiar emotion these days. A little more guilt is no big deal. She's used to it.

She brings her hand up to her eyes.

'Hey!'

Hands grip her sides, making her jump.

'Jesus!'

'Whoa, language, Miss Safinova – you're on sacred ground.'

'Fuck off, Rebecca. This isn't funny.'

Nova turns to look at her. She could still be blind and know that Rebecca is drunk, but the evidence is there – the flushed cheeks, the skewed angle of her shirt collar, the way her head is cocked to one side, as though compensating for the tilt of the ground.

'Want to grab a drink?'

'No, I don't. Where the fuck were you? You said you'd be here.'

'I was here! In the crowd. Didn't you see me? I just had to pop to the loo.'

Nova lets it slide.

'Come on, the reception will be starting.'

Rebecca, reassured by the promise of a bar to prop up, hooks her arm around Nova's.

'Come on, babe, I'll take care of you.'

✳

The flat is quiet when she gets back. Of course it's quiet – it's always quiet now, and Kate wishes she hadn't gone to such lengths to block out the sound from the street and the flats around her. She wouldn't mind some of that noise now.

She goes and opens the doors to the Juliet balcony, and the sound of cars calms her down for a moment. She realizes she's shaking – a low, constant tremor. Just another fault that she's developed.

A failing machine.

She pulls an armchair over to the balcony, but doesn't sit down. She goes to the kitchen, gets a large glass of water, and takes it through to the bedroom. There, in the drawer of her bedside table, are all the sleeping pills her doctor gave her. She had complained about the nightmares that kept waking her up, or stopping her from ever getting fully to sleep, and he had eagerly written her a prescription for the pills. But they hadn't worked. Or, at least, though they kept her asleep, they didn't stop the nightmares. Which was worse – to be trapped in a nightmare and not wake up. So she had stopped taking the pills, but had not stopped picking them up from the pharmacy.

She takes the pills from the drawer, uncovering a note written on a scrap of paper. The writing is hers, but the words belong to someone else.

Nova's To-Do List

1) Go up a _really_ tall building.

2) Ride a _really_ big rollercoaster.

3) Look at family pictures, (see myself as a baby and the grandparents I never knew).

4) Watch the freaking _moon landing!!!_

Kate places the note back in the drawer and closes it. Her lungs are squeezing shut. She stares at the pills for a moment. Was she going to do this all along? But she doesn't like to pause – if she's still, she notices the tremor. Kate pushes the pills out of their plastic coffins, all of them, one by one, until she has a pile on the bed next to her.

The tremor has faded. Something about this makes her feel calm. It's as though she can see a door, right in front of her, that she can step through at any moment. As long as she stays by the door, she's calm. She can wait.

She picks up her phone and dials Nova's number. She has no intention of speaking to her – that's not the point. It's more like a last wish. She wants to hear her voice one last time. The phone connects, rings seven times, then goes to voicemail.

Hey, this is Nova! This isn't a voicemail – this is a telepathic thought-recording device. After the tone, think about your name, your reason for calling and a number where I can reach you.

There is a burst of cut-off laughter, and a beep. Kate says nothing, but thinks about what she would say, if Nova were here. She ends the call, switches her phone off, and puts it down on the bed.

She pauses for another second, but not out of hesitation – only to see if she's scared. But she only feels this deep calm, and so she picks up the glass of water and starts to swallow the pills, one by one.

✳

The reception is in one of the college lounges, a dark room, clad to head-height in wainscot oak panelling, with institutional beige walls leading up to polystyrene ceiling tiles and strip lights. Things are already underway by the time Nova and Rebecca arrive. There are a couple of trestle tables at the far end of the room, arrayed with glasses of red and white wine, with a smaller contingent of orange juice.

'I'll get you a drink, yeah?' Rebecca asks.

'Yeah, sure.' Nova shrugs. For a while she resisted the drinks that Rebecca plied her with, partly in the hope that the example would curb her worst excesses. But this hadn't worked, and Nova doesn't have much incentive to stay sober.

Rebecca disappears into the crowd and doesn't return for several minutes.

'Nova! God, I haven't seen you in forever!'

A girl hugs her without warning. Nova can see her face,

but remembers her from her voice. Monique. Ah, yes, Beginner's Spanish with Mike Wilkinson: she had scented pens and trouble remembering gender pronouns. She sighs internally that she didn't wear her dark glasses to the occasion – it's so much easier to pretend to be blind that way. She decides to get to the point straightaway, telling Monique the story of her miracle cure.

'Oh, my God, that's incredible! Congratulations!'

Rebecca returns by the time Nova finishes her explanation, hands her one glass of red and one of white, both of which seem to be for her, and vanishes again with a muttered excuse that might have something to do with talking to a friend. It's unlikely that Rebecca, physics PhD and natural hermit, has many friends in the Modern Languages department of a college that isn't hers, but Nova barely listens to her excuses any more.

She drinks down the red and makes a start on the white while Monique expounds on her Masters in Italian literary translation, which has inexplicably been ongoing for the last six years. Nova has just finished the white when her phone starts to buzz in her pocket.

More as an excuse to escape than to take the call, Nova holds the phone up like a talisman and moves towards the door. By the time she's standing in the corridor, the caller has hung up. She puts the phone away, breathes a sigh of relief and stands, back against the cold wall, listening to the muffled chatter in the lounge. The building smells of damp and seems echoingly empty other than the reception. Nova has an image of being inside a huge, dead body. A dead building, lying in state, where their party is the last fizzling bit of cellular activity before decomposition sets in.

The Rules of Seeing

She walks down the corridor until she finds an exit, and steps out into the cool of evening. Somewhere in front of her is the River Cherwell, and beyond that, a light is shining . . .

It takes Nova
a long moment to remember what
it was John Katzner told her about the sunset
and apply his words to the arc that is cut from the
grey fabric of the horizon to let the shimmering light

d a   n

                   c e

           o v e

   r

                  t h

                    e

         r i   v e

            r.

There is another buzz from her pocket.

Nova takes her phone out and blinks the tears away. The caller has left a voicemail. She looks at the missed calls log.

Kate Tomassi.

She dials her voicemail. Listens as the automated woman tells her she has a new message, followed by a beep.

There is no sound. Almost none – there is the soft fuzz of thermal noise, a faint digital flicker at about three seconds, and beyond that . . . can she hear breathing? Nova isn't sure.

The message ends. She presses the button to replay the message, closing her eyes and listening at a granular level to the drizzle of sound.

Nothing.

Nothing means something. Something is wrong, she thinks, then doesn't know why she thought it. It has been weeks since Kate tried to call her. Why now? And why leave a creepy, empty voicemail? That's not her style.

She thinks about what to do. Before she can overthink things, she calls Kate back, pressing the phone to her ear. The line rings once before going to voicemail. Nova hangs up.

She thinks for a second, the wine hazing her decisions.

Of course it's nothing.

But it's good to make sure.

She'd make herself look stupid.

But Kate rang first . . .

She pulls up another number in her phone book – Kate's friend, Vi – and hovers her finger over the call button.

'Um, Nova?'

A face has popped around the door. It's Monique.

'Yeah? What's up?'

'It's just, uh, your girlfriend . . . Becky?'

'Rebecca. She's not my girlfriend.'

'Yeah, well, it's just, she's a bit unwell . . .' Monique shifts uncomfortably. 'Maybe you could come help us?'

Nova sighs, puts her phone back in her pocket, and goes to bail out her drunk ex-girlfriend.

✴

The Rules of Seeing

Kate is sitting in the armchair by the window, trying to decide whether it's the light that's fading or her brain. On the table next to her is a slice of her mother's cake, oozing lemon syrup like a sickly, disembowelled organ. She'd had the idea it would be the last thing she would eat. It's sentimental, she knows, but isn't she allowed to be sentimental, when she's dying? Now she feels full and queasy from the pills, so the cake sits there, uneaten.

She feels heavy – heavy enough to go through the floorboards and bring down the building with her. She's amazed that the armchair can hold her.

Her breaths come less frequently, as though time is slowing.

She doesn't feel regret, and her life certainly doesn't flash in front of her eyes. She is stuck, like a fly trapped in syrup, in this present moment. This present moment that will be her last. She's a little annoyed that this moment – looking out at the rain – is the last one she'll see. It's interesting to find out, at last, how she dies, but mostly disappointing.

Searching for a better final image, Kate reaches out to the table next to the armchair. Her arm is clumsy, and she knocks the lemon cake to the floor. The plate shatters, but the impact sounds far away. Kate grabs the collection of papers that the plate was resting on – a sheaf of her own drawings. She looks through them for one that she likes, but they all seem so childish to her now. A picture of coats hanging in the hall. A picture of coffee cups. A picture of flowers in a vase. She throws them to the floor, one by one.

The last picture, hidden under the rest, makes her pause. It is a view of the sofa, taken from across the room. Nestled into the cushions, one arm thrown over her face, is Nova.

This picture is not so bad, Kate thinks. She has never been much good at drawing people, but she got the posture right here. She can almost see Nova's chest rise and fall in her sleep.

Kate closes her eyes, because her eyelids are also heavy.

The light fades.

I am an object, she thinks, *like a pair of scissors. They can do whatever they want with me, because I am just an object now.*

I'm just an object.

Kate stops thinking.

✱

Kate bobs up to the surface, unsure how long she has been under. Too long? She looks at the picture in her hands, an imperfect window onto an earlier moment. Something automatic kicks in. She does not want to die. Some part of her, unlocked as the rest of her brain switched off, does not want to die.

Slowly, with the difficulty of someone whose hands have been frozen by swimming in the sea, she gets her phone out of her pocket and presses the power button. As she waits for it to turn on, Kate dips under again, darkness washing around her . . .

9-9-9

She presses the button three times but cannot raise the phone to her face.

It's too heavy.

But there is a voice talking, a tiny voice from the receiver. Kate tries to form words, to say her address. The words come out as a slurred whisper, but she keeps repeating them, over and over, until she feels the darkness rising over her again, her mouth still working as the inky ocean washes in and silences her.

Thirty

August

IT'S BEEN ALMOST TWO months since Nova has been to her flat. It's good that she's going back, she reasons, if only to check that it hasn't burned down. She's going to visit her parents in a couple of days and wants to get some nice clothes to wear for them.

She rides the Bakerloo Line to Oxford Circus and changes for the Victoria Line down to Brixton. Two years after her operation, her vision is still improving. The Underground is less intimidating, but it still feels like being put through the spin wash at the launderette and spat out at the other end. By the time she reaches her flat, Nova is tired and ready to sit down and close her eyes. Shapes are swimming in and out of focus, familiar objects like cars and trees keep breaking down into their constituent colours and contours.

She's hungry, and buys a cheese sandwich from the corner shop she always used to go into. Brixton is as lively as ever, people drifting up and down the street, pushing carts of vegetables and fish on ice, wheeling refrigerators and stacks of fabric. Everybody seems to be arguing, enticing, catcalling. Nova has grown used to the library-hush of Oxford, and Brixton feels like an onslaught.

Finally, she pushes through the street door that leads up to her flat and walks upstairs. She puts the key in the lock to her front door, which seems sticky, as though stiff with underuse. She steps into the flat, remembering its familiar, musty smell. The air is stale. There is another smell, which she doesn't recognize – did she leave some food out, or has a mouse come here to die?

She walks down the passage. She slumps into an armchair, looking around at the cluttered contents of her living room, remembering the confusion of patterns, colours and textures. It amazes her that anybody let her live in this ridiculous, overcrowded space.

There is so much in the room, it takes her a good thirty seconds to see the man sitting in the chair opposite her.

RULE OF SEEING NO.382
There are two kinds of seeing – the 'where' and the 'what'. The 'where' tracks objects as they move through space. The 'what' decides what those objects are. These work together – if something is not moving, it may be hard to decide what the object is.

Nova has stopped breathing. Her body is tensed. She thinks of a caveman, seeing the shape of an unmoving jaguar through a confusion of jungle foliage. Fight-or-flight.

Is he sleeping? Maybe if she gets up and walks out very

slowly, he will never know she was there. Then she can call the police . . .

'Finally spotted me?'

It's not the voice of a jaguar. The voice is so familiar, it doesn't matter that she can't see his face clearly in the half-light.

It is Tony.

'What are you doing here?' The words don't want to come out, but Nova isn't going to let him see that he's scared her.

'Oh, I've been here ages. I expected you to be back much, much sooner. But then, I suppose you and Kate have been having fun.'

Nova almost corrects him, but thinks better of it. She's scared, angry, doesn't know what to do. She knows she can't escape him. Even if she's quicker on her feet it won't matter. She can't move around objects as quickly as he can, can't react as fast to what's going on. She realizes that her hands are still in her jacket pockets, and her hand closes around Kate's penknife. Several times she has considered throwing the knife in a bin, or down a drain, or – once – into the River Cherwell from Magdalen Bridge. Each time she put it back in her jacket pocket, where Kate first placed it.

'Good job I checked your address while I was working at the Met.'

'You got my address from work? That's so . . .'

'Illegal?' He's smiling, but she knows enough about smiles by now to know that this is not a nice smile. Nova once read that chimpanzees smile to show aggression, and it's that kind of smile. A fuck-you smile.

She has her thumbnail in the groove on the knife, and starts to coax it out. It's difficult to flick the blade out with one hand, but not impossible – she's done it before.

'Anyway, it's not like I'll be going back there any more.'

'You're a fucking psycho.'

He shrugs. 'Probably. It's not like I'm going to ask a shrink for a test. But I'm not stupid – pathological lying, tendency to get bored, manipulative . . . I fit the bill.'

'You sound pretty relaxed about it,' Nova says, feeling as though she's in a shark tank. There is a hollow space behind Tony's words – how did she not notice that before?

'You're forgetting another psycho trait – lack of remorse.' He bares his teeth again in a not-smile.

Nova plays for time.

'So you've been living here? All this time?'

He shrugs. 'Some of it. Couldn't risk it too soon, when my old friends at the Met were still doing their job.'

Nova doesn't want to make him angry, she just wants to get out. She wants to warn Kate. He stands, and she tries not to flinch, but it's hard. He walks over to her, reaches out and grabs her by the neck. Nova makes a guttural sound, feeling his fingers squeeze the soft flesh under her jaw.

'Don't worry, dyke. I'm not going to kill you. Not yet. This is just a warning. No, not a warning . . .' he corrects himself. 'A taste of what's to come.'

He leans down, still holding her neck, putting his other hand on the arm of the chair. She thinks about kicking him, but what would she do next? He's easily twice her size. She can feel her jugular throbbing under his grip. She's trapped. Nova can feel his breath on her face, can taste its staleness, the taste of whisky and not much else. She forces herself not to panic – to stay still.

She's not sure what he's going to do to her, but when she stops struggling he takes his hand from her neck and moves it down to his jeans zipper.

His other hand is still resting on the arm of the chair.

Nova brings the knife out of her pocket, raises it above her head, and brings the blade down on Tony's hand as hard as she can. She thinks she will miss, but Kate's knife finds its target, sinking through the soft flesh between the metacarpals, right into the wooden frame of the armchair underneath.

Tony bellows. He grips Nova even harder by the neck, lifting her clean out of the seat and throwing her across the room. She lands, choking and gasping. The blade is embedded in the armchair. While he works on pulling it out, Nova jumps up and runs from the flat.

✳

Nova doesn't want to tell Kate about what has happened. She doesn't want to tell her that she has seen Tony. But she needs to tell the police, and she needs to warn Kate. There's no way of getting around it. She quickly walks away from her flat, then ducks into a corner shop.

She calls Kate, tells her to call the police and keep the door locked. Kate sounds quiet on the end of the phone – she doesn't shout or cry. She doesn't react when Nova tells her he grabbed her by the neck. She sounds like she's taking an order for pizza.

Nova hangs up and realizes that she's bleeding – a thin

stream of blood from her neck has stained her top. Tony's nails must have dug in. She buys tissues and holds one to her neck while she calls the police and reports the break-in. They come quickly and pick her up from the shop. Another team is checking her flat. She explains the situation, and they take her in a car to Kate's. As she steps through the door, Nova realizes she never thought she would return to this flat.

Kate is standing by the window.

She is thinner, perhaps, than last time she saw her, but Nova knows the shape of her better than any other.

Kate rushes over, ignoring the police, and puts her arms around Nova, squeezing the air out of her. Then she pulls back and kisses her on the lips, as though nothing has changed between them. Nova freezes, too surprised to react.

'I'm sorry, I'm so sorry . . .'

Nova isn't sure what has happened to Kate between her making the call and her getting to the flat. She seems to have been shocked back into life, but Nova can't react.

'Are you okay? Your neck . . .'

'Just a cut, nothing bad. They patched me up.' She shrugs out of Kate's grip, forcing a smile.

The police talk to them for a while. A forensics team is being sent to look over Nova's flat, another team is searching Brixton for Tony, though he's probably moved on already. They're searching CCTV. Eventually they leave.

When the door is finally closed, Kate turns to Nova.

'Listen – I want to go away.'

'Away?'

'I don't want to be here any more. I don't want to be in this flat, I don't want to be in London.'

'O-kay . . .' Nova says slowly.

'I don't want to be here, Nova. And I don't want . . . I can't let him hurt you again. I don't want to feel like a sitting duck in my own home. But I don't know where to go.' She starts to pace up and down the room, so full of nervous energy that Nova can't keep calm around her. Nova could tell her about the trip she's taking to see her parents, but holds back.

'And . . . you want me to come with you?'

'Yes.'

'Because I'm your good friend?'

Kate looks at the floor, her energy deflating for a second.

'No . . . not my friend . . .'

She steps closer and kisses Nova again, but Nova breaks free.

'Look, Kate, we're not going out any more. I know I ran out on you and I feel shitty about that—'

'I'm better, Nova! I'm better now – just look at me.' She grins, not recognising the irony of the words 'just look'.

Nova chooses her words carefully. 'You seem better, sure, but I've got problems of my own.'

'And I can help you with them! I was just . . . I was just in a really, really bad place, when you left me. And I don't blame you for leaving – I was being a shitty girlfriend. A shitty person.'

Kate doesn't mention what she did, with the pills. She can't let Nova know. She can't even bear to think of the word, 'suicide'. Since that night, she has been living in a sort of limbo. She remembers Nova talking about this – how she was neither blind nor sighted. Kate is neither fully committed to living or dying. An in-between person. All she sees is a chance to make things better. For now, she will lie. She will make-believe as much as she has to in order to grab this chance.

Maybe it's not too late.

Nova feels tears coming and tries to hold them back. If she starts now, she's not sure when she'll stop. Things are over with Rebecca – Nova is not ready to be tangled in someone else's life again so soon. She tries to change the subject.

'Look, the police are doing their best, I'm sure they don't want you to up and leave—'

'But the police can't find him! He was one of them – he knows how to hide. They're not going to find him just like that. And what if he finds us first?'

'You are safe, so long as you stay *here.* '

It seems crazy to leave, when everybody is doing their best to protect them. Kate seems to know what Nova is thinking.

'We'll make it fun! We can make it a holiday. We can go wherever. Scotland, the Isle of Man, some cottage in Cornwall.'

'And how are you going to travel?'

'I can drive us. We'll stop at different places. How does that sound?'

Nova searches for something, anything, to deflate this plan. 'Whose car?'

Kate hasn't thought about this, and paces around for another second, kneading her hands.

'Ah! Vi has a car. A nice one she hardly uses. I'm sure she'll lend it to me if I ask nicely.'

'Kate, I understand if you want to get away but I'm not—'

'Nova, he could have killed you.' Kate's voice cracks. 'I can't let that happen again. I just can't.'

Nova shakes her head, trying to clear her thoughts.

'I have plans . . . I'm going to see my parents.'

Kate has gone very still. 'Your parents?'

'They're going on holiday in a couple of days.' Nova can't seem to stop talking now. 'They'll be away for a fortnight, and I'm sure they would be happy for us to use the house. We could explore Yorkshire, go walking on the moors . . .'

'Your parents?' Kate echoes.

'Is that a problem?'

Nova isn't sure if she's trying to stop Kate's plan, or whether she really wants this to happen. She's not sure what she's trying to achieve any more. Kate wrings her hands, and Nova doesn't have a translation for her expression.

'Okay. We can do that. We can go tomorrow, yeah?'

Nova closes her eyes. 'I think so. Let me talk to them.'

Kate closes the distance between them and wraps Nova in her arms. The smaller woman doesn't try to break away. Her heart is pounding.

'I'm sorry.' Kate breathes into her hair. 'I'm sorry for everything. Please take me back. Please?'

'Kate . . .'

'Please, I'll be better. I've never regretted anything more than letting you leave. For *making* you leave.'

The tears start to fall, and Nova can't talk. She tries several times, while Kate watches her face for any clue, but the sobs well up and stop her. Finally, when it becomes clear that no words can escape, she resorts to a gesture – something she has learned since the operation.

She nods.

Thirty-One

THE PLAN COMES TOGETHER fast. Vi is hard to win around for about five seconds, her excitement overcoming any suspicion. Kate doesn't bother to fill her in on everything that has happened.

She doesn't mention that Nova is back.

Vi is just happy that she's calling. If Kate had much time to think about that, it might break her heart. Kate misses her. If life ever becomes normal again, Kate wants Vi to be part of it. She explains the road trip, tells Vi she will pay rental prices for the car. She agrees, but tells Kate to keep her money. After some haggling, they agree a token sum, and that she will return it with a full tank of petrol. Kate asks her to drive it over to the flat.

They meet on the street outside, Kate not wanting Vi to come into the flat and find out what's going on. She hugs her, something that Vi rarely does.

'How's it hanging?'

'Not bad,' Kate replies, trying to look normal.

'So, you ready for your trip?'

Kate forces a smile. 'Yeah, yeah. Should be good.'

'How have you been? You seem better,' Vi prompts.

'Yeah, I am.' Kate nods. 'So much better.'

'Okay. Well, uh, here are the keys.' Vi tosses them over. 'Be good, yeah?'

Kate isn't sure if she's talking about the car or something else. She takes a good look at the car. It's very red, with a low profile, sleek lines, a convertible. She knows that the car rarely gets taken out of the garage. Vi's everyday car is old, beaten-up, with the bonnet and back doors different colours.

Vi watches her for a moment more, moving slightly from one leg to the other. Her energy makes Kate feel restless.

'Well, look, take care, okay? It's good to see you. Enjoy the car. I've left some mix CDs in there for you.'

'Oh, God.' Kate grins.

'You'll love them!' She shouts, retreating down the street.

Kate watches her go.

✳

The next day is hazy. It feels more like October than August. It doesn't rain, but a cool, unending mist falls. This suits Kate – she doesn't want to drive with the top of the convertible down. She doesn't want to be seen driving this flashy car. Today feels like the perfect moment to slip away.

She prods Nova out of her sleep on the sofa. She brings her a cup of tea to the bathroom, which Nova insists on drinking in the shower. She makes them sandwiches in the kitchen and carries them down with their pillows from the bed. The convertible is about as full as it can be and still have space for two people. When they're both in the car, they turn to each other.

'You ready?' Kate asks. Nova nods once.

'Hit it.'

She guns the ignition, feeling the car come to life around her. The engine roars. It's louder than she would like, but there's something reassuring about that raw power. She looks in the mirrors, too many times, before pulling out. She drives quickly down the street, trying not to check every car for watching faces.

Kate wonders if the police are watching and whether they will notice them going. It takes a long time to get out of London, the traffic slow and syrupy in the bad weather. She concentrates on the driving, always checking behind to watch the cars, taking a mental note of each of them.

A silver SUV has been following them through two round-abouts and a junction. She's getting ready to do something, to try to lose it, when the SUV turns off down a side street. The knot in her belly loosens momentarily, but she soon goes back to checking the other cars.

Nova seems happy enough in the passenger seat, pushing buttons on the car's old-school pre-set radio. Kate leaves her be; she doesn't want to jinx anything. She just wants to get onto the motorway, to get out of London. She wants to be far, far away from her address, her work, her supermarket, her bank, her dentist, her hairdresser, her electrician, her doctor, therapist and police contact, her mother and extended family, her entangled life. She feels the details of her existence shrinking with every mile she puts on the clock.

Eventually, Nova notices the road in front of them, and stares, entranced, a wide grin plastered over her face. Kate doesn't ask what she's seeing – she's not sure she would understand the answer anyway.

RULE OF SEEING NO.385
**Sitting in the front seat of a car is like diving
deeper and deeper into a painting, watching
as the trees and buildings grow and disappear,
only for more to spring up on the horizon,
endlessly starting again.**

By the time they're on the motorway it's raining properly, a hard rain that hammers the windscreen. The wipers slap back and forth, giving flashes of clarity.

'Can you really see the road through that?' Nova asks.

'Yeah, it's okay.'

'To me, it looks like . . . like nothing at all. It looks like everything is melting!' She pauses for a second. 'You're *sure* that you can see what you're doing? We're not going to crash?'

'Yes!' Kate laughs, for the first time. 'Yes, I can see where I'm going. Relax, okay?'

'Okay, but if you want to pull over, that's okay too.'

Kate reaches her hand over the gear stick to take Nova's hand, to comfort her.

'Both hands on the wheel! Both hands on the wheel! I'm *fine*.'

Kate smiles and does as she says.

✳

'Okay, slowly ease your foot up.'

'Like this?' The car jerks forward, then comes to a halt. The engine dies.

'I said ease it up, not jerk.' Kate sounds more amused than angry, but Nova wants to get this right.

'Can I try again?'

'Of course.'

They are in the car park of an A-road service station, somewhere near Nottingham. The lot is practically deserted. Nova has decided that Kate should teach her to drive, even if she isn't allowed a licence.

'Okay, here we go. Slowly bring the pedal up, until you feel it . . .'

'Yes!' Nova yelps, as the car starts to move forward.

'Yes, okay, good. Now, we're starting to come up to this wall, so I want you to start turning . . .'

Nova turns the steering wheel, and the car smoothly curves around to the right.

'This is fun!'

'Okay, just take it slow. I don't want to do anything to Vi's car.'

They crawl around the car park, roughly following the boundary wall. Finally, Nova puts on the handbreak and turns to her driving companion.

'I think I'm ready. Let's hit the road.' She grins in a way that Kate can't be sure that she's joking.

'Definitely not.'

✳

The sun is setting as they approach Bradford, the sky white-grey and orange near the horizon. Nova's dad used to call the sunset 'ash and embers', though she couldn't understand how the sky could be like a burned-down fire. They drive in silence, too tired to make conversation. They've meandered their way up the country, taking in a stately manor and a teashop along the way. They come off the motorway, idle in traffic, watch billboards and warehouses inch by.

In the fading light, Kate looks at the town where Nova grew up. Thousands of sodium-yellow streetlamps are flickering into life, and the city seems to slope up into the darkening sky, purple-black streets mingling with purple-black thunderclouds, so she's not sure where the city ends and the night begins.

'Home sweet home,' Nova says, without enthusiasm.

'Glad to be back?'

Nova peers through the windshield, clears her throat, and proclaims, 'The thing about learning to see is that everywhere becomes a place you've never visited before. Even home.'

Kate drives in silence for a moment, absorbing this. Then she starts to giggle.

'What?'

'That was pretty good – you should write it down.'

'Hey, don't mock me. I'm a very deep person. There's a lot of inner turmoil. Turbulent, emotions.'

'I know, Heathcliff, I know. You want a sherbet lemon?'

Nova crosses her arms and huffs.

'Yes.'

Kate reaches over and pops the sweet into her mouth, then asks,

'Do I look presentable?'

'You look beautiful.'

'Yeah,' she jokes, 'but you used to be blind.'

Kate smooths down her hair, looks over her outfit in the rear-view mirror, decides that she will have to do. The car is parked in front of a sandstone terrace house. The light has faded from the sky.

Kate is more than nervous. She never imagined this situation. When they get out of the car, Mr and Mrs Safinova are already waiting in the doorway of the house, light and warmth spilling onto the street.

Nova is nervous too, but tries not to let this show. She's not sure why she invited Kate. They are not in a relationship. She thinks maybe she expected her to say no. But why take the risk?

She walks up the path to the home she grew up in, towards the rectangle of light that must be the front door. She can see the outlines of objects standing between her and the light. She realizes that these must be her parents.

'Mum, Dad!' She hurries down the path, not afraid of tripping, and throws her arms around them both. She breathes in, inhaling their smell. She has seen her parents several times since the operation, but for her, this is how she knows her parents best – in the world of scent. Her dad's old-fashioned cologne, the smell of his ironed flannel shirts. The smell of rose hand cream from her mum. Surrounded by their smells, closing her eyes, Nova feels that these are the ingredients that made her, and could remake her.

Kate stands behind, watching as Nova disappears into this triangle. She watches the embrace of both parents and feels as though she herself is being embraced. Accepted. And, with that, she no longer feels nervous. Nova breaks away from her parents and steps to one side.

'Kate, this is my dad, Peter, and my mum, Uzma.'

Mr Safinova does a little bow.

'Parents, this is Kate.' She smiles, something of her mischievous grin coming back.

'Nice to meet you, Kate.'

Peter extends his hand to shake. He's tall, about Kate's height, with the same dazzling blue eyes as Nova. Uzma is small, and has the same smile, the same upturned nose.

'Lovely to meet you, Kate.' Uzma steps forward, hugging Kate. To Kate, it feels as though she is hugging Nova – the older woman is the same height, the same build, fits into her arms in the same way.

'It's really good to meet you.' Kate breaks away, smiling. She feels safe with these people. For the time being, she forgets to be afraid.

'Come on then, let's eat!' Peter ushers them into the light. Kate notices that Nova has closed her eyes, walking through her childhood home blind. She knows the space of the house so well, she doesn't need to think about getting around it. Then, seeming to remember her, Nova opens her eyes and takes Kate by the hand.

'Come on, this way to food!'

They walk into the dining room, which is small and mostly filled by a wide table, laid with a red-and-white gingham cloth. It is laden with food. Kate can't believe the number of dishes. There are candles lit, flickering on the table and on the shelves around the room. It's very warm in there. In fact, Kate thinks, it's very *everything* in there – there is a superabundance of warmth, steam, smells, colour, flickering light.

Sitting on the other side of the table is a young man, perhaps Nova's age. He stands up, extending a hand.

'Surprise!'

'What!' Nova steps back in surprise. 'What are you doing here?'

'Mum told me you were coming. Thought I'd make the effort so we can have a family reunion. Just for tonight.'

'Short notice . . .' Nova seems puzzled, though Kate doesn't know why.

'Well, it's been a while since I've seen you . . .' he trails off, then turns to Kate. 'I'm Alex, Jillian's brother.' He shakes her hand a little stiffly.

'Nice to meet you.'

'So, kid brother, killed any patients recently?' Nova throws her arms around him and ruffles his hair.

'It's really not nice to ask that, you know?'

'You'll get over it.'

Alex grabs a spoon and starts dividing the spoils. Nova's family chats contentedly, catching up on the gossip of each other's lives. Kate is glad that they seem so talkative, unconcerned with quizzing her for the time being. She forgets to call Nova 'Jillian', but they just find this amusing. She eats and listens, daydreaming about what her life might have been like if she had grown up in this house.

There is no real end to the meal, they just stop eating, or pick at the leftovers, leaning back in their chairs. This room is so warm, Kate feels as though the heat is sinking down into her bones. She feels as though she has had a chill for the longest time, and she's only now sweating it out. It's a start, nothing more, but the shadows are seeping out of her pores.

Peter clears away plates and covers some of the dishes, while Uzma makes mint tea.

❋

When everyone is ready to go to bed, they spend a while in the hallway, where the family photographs are all hung in little frames. Kate feels her breath catching, as she sees, for the first time, the Nova that existed before she knew her. Here she is, in a pink party dress, aged maybe four or five, with cake frosting on her grinning face. Here she is, a teenager, wearing dark glasses, with a great, golden guide dog draped over her lap on the sofa. The dog is bigger than she is.

'You had a guide dog?'

'Jilly never liked having the dog,' Uzma says.

'I liked the dog, Mum, I just didn't like picking up after him.'

Here she is at graduation in a dark gown, surrounded by friends. All of them are holding rubber ducks, for some reason. Here she is on a family holiday, aged maybe ten, skinny, battered legs on display, holding a white stick that glows in the foreign sun.

Kate understands for the first time that Nova grew up blind, had existed as a blind person for thirty-one years, had known no other life until just before they met. Kate has been so tightly wrapped in her own problems, she wonders how the other woman stayed sane, with all that has changed in her life. She feels bad, not for the first time, for complicating Nova's already complicated life.

'It's been lovely to meet you, Kate.' Peter says, shaking her hand again.

'Oh, Dad, always so formal!' Nova nudges him in the ribs.

'Should we hug, Jillian? Is this a hugging thing?' Peter asks his daughter.

'Yes, Dad, I think it should be.'

Peter hugs Kate, and while they are close, whispers in her ear, 'Look after her.'

Kate isn't sure if Nova has heard, but when they break apart she nods at him quickly.

Uzma and Peter go up to bed. Alex hangs around for a while, looking at pictures with them and trading insults with Nova, but he's yawning every other sentence.

'I should hit the hay. See you in the morning, ladies.'

Nova hugs him. 'Nighty night, Stinky.'

Kate watches Alex go upstairs, and when she turns, Nova is watching her.

'What's up?'

Nova doesn't answer, just reaches over and grabs her by her shirt, pulling her into a kiss. The hallway is silent for a long minute. Nova bites Kate's bottom lip; Kate runs her hands through Nova's hair. They break apart.

'Good to have you back.'

Kate nods. 'I'm sorry I was gone so long.'

Thirty-Two

THEY ARE SITTING IN Jade Dragon, the Chinese restaurant down the road from Nova's family home. This morning they waved goodbye to Nova's parents, then her brother. They caught the bus up to the moors and spent the day singing 'Wuthering Heights' at each other. Kate had brought some colouring pencils and a pad, and used them to sketch Nova sitting on a rock, looking out over the muted landscape. Now they're sated by the meal, their drinks, the optimistic fortune cookies, their conversation. They sit in satisfied silence. Nova plays with a chopstick, Kate looks at her girlfriend's hands as she twirls it like a tiny baton. Finally, she asks,

'Where did you get your tattoo?'

'This?' She points to the soft skin between thumb and index finger, the tiny, blue-inked heart. 'I got it in Oxford.'

'Does it mean anything?'

Kate has always been drawn to the tattoo. She worries it might be the start of a story she doesn't want to hear. Nova smiles, looking at the heart.

'Not really.' She shrugs.

'Not really?' It's not like Nova to be cryptic.

'Well, I got it with my ex, Rebecca.'

'Oh . . .' Kate feels a knot tightening in her belly. 'Sorry, I shouldn't have asked.'

'It wasn't like that. I mean . . . I didn't get it for her. I got it because I wanted to. I liked the idea of showing . . . ugh, this is corny.'

'Go on – be corny.'

'I liked the idea of showing love to the world, even if I couldn't see it myself. That I was sending a message in a foreign language . . .'

She trails off, shrugging her embarrassment again.

'So why did you get it with your ex?'

Nova laughs. 'She just came along to make sure the tattooist didn't draw a cock and balls on me.'

Kate snorts. 'Oh, my God.'

'What? You can't trust everybody, babe – being blind is a full-time gig.'

Kate grins and – seeing the waiter approaching – motions for the bill. He doesn't seem to notice.

'What is that?' Nova asks.

'What's what?'

'That thing you just did with your hands? Like you were writing on your hand?'

'Oh, I was asking for the bill, but he didn't see me. Didn't you know people do that?'

'Nope. You'll have to teach me.'

They are quiet for a moment more, while Nova pushes grains of rice around on the tablecloth.

'Did it hurt?' Kate asks.

'Did what hurt?'

'The tattoo?'

'Yes, very much. Here – kiss it better.'

She thrusts her hand out, and Kate kisses it quickly, aware of the other diners around them.

'You're really interested, aren't you? I think I should give you a tattoo.'

'What? No!' Kate shifts back defensively.

'Don't worry – this tattoo is totally invisible.'

Kate is wearing a short-sleeved T-shirt. Nova takes one of her plastic chopsticks and starts to draw on the skin of Kate's forearm. Kate closes her eyes and a shiver runs up her spine. She feels the shapes as Nova draws a spiral, waves, lots of small circles, all down her arm. She feels as though, if she opened her eyes, she would see Nova's shapes blossoming on her skin like inky bruises. Electric shivers pass over her. She moans quietly.

'You like that?' Nova is grinning.

'Yes. Maybe not, um, in the restaurant . . .'

Nova grins wider and doesn't stop, working her way up her arm now, tracing loops and arrows, triangles and squares, houses and fish and trees – all the shapes she knows. She traces a heart, tricky with its peculiar, mirrored curves.

Kate's breath shivers out of her.

'That's . . . enough.'

Nova puts the chopstick down. 'How do you do that bill thing? I think we need to get you home.'

✯

They don't make it home. At the junction there is a tattoo parlour, its neon sign bright in the darkness.

'Hang on – stop. Stopstopstop!'

'What? What is it?' Nova peers through the glass, but can't understand what sort of thing this shop sells. 'Are you hungry? I said you should get dessert.'

'No – it's a tattoo place. I want to get a tattoo.'

Nova laughs. 'What? I can't let you do that. You're drunk.'

'I've had two small glasses of wine.'

'Well, you're crazy then. What tattoo do you want to get, anyway?'

Kate pulls her close by her hand. 'Guess.'

'I don't know . . . something about architecture? A nice bridge, maybe?'

'You're the dumbest genius I ever met.' Kate takes Nova's left hand and kisses her between thumb and index finger. Recognition dawns on Nova's face.

'You want *my* tattoo?'

'Is that okay?'

Nova's lips twist, and Kate is sure she's going to say no. She's sure she has overstepped a boundary, made things weird again.

'Okay, you can get it.' She nods quickly. 'Come on. I hope you have ID, young lady.'

Kate's resolve wavers when she steps into the shop. The air is thick with disinfectant and the stereo is playing sludgy rock. One wall is covered by mounted frames of designs, which can be flipped through like a book, running from blue anchors and hearts to Technicolor Japanese carp and leering demons, three-dimensional faces and flowers to geometric patterns and MC Escher tessellations, which Nova stares at in puzzlement.

RULE OF SEEING NO.389
Sighted people are so good at seeing that they get bored of it, and make things called optical illusions. Endless staircases and impossible cubes can exist on paper, but not in the real world.

'How can I help you, ladies?'

The tattooist emerges from the back room summoned by the sound of the bell over the door. He's in his forties, head shaven, with a roll of fat forming at the top of his neck. His arms are covered in bruise-colour tattoos of blue and green and yellow.

'Can I . . . can I just get a tattoo, um, now?'

The man laughs, not unkindly.

'Sure, if it's not too big. Or we can do a consultation, and I can book you in for later. Whatever.'

'Now is good. It's only a small thing.'

Kate sits in the leatherette chair, feeling the butterflies in her stomach. Nova shows him the tiny blue heart, and the man grins.

'I reckon I can manage that, yeah.'

He goes and prepares a gun. He fetches antiseptic and swabs Kate's hand. Then he grabs her by the wrist. Kate feels her breath catch at the sudden contact.

'You okay?'

'Yeah, sure – you just startled me is all.'

'All right. Now just keep your thumb and index finger stretched out nice and wide, so the skin is taut . . . good.'

Kate holds her breath as the needle buzzes, as he dips it in an ink well, and as it comes down on her hand. Nova holds her free hand, and Kate feels like a child going to the doctor for an inoculation. What she's inoculating herself from, she doesn't know.

The pain begins, and Kate lets out her breath. This isn't so bad. It's not sharp, like she thought it might be, but more like burning. Like being branded.

Blue ink pools on her skin, and the tattooist wipes it away with a cloth. Blood bubbles through the grate in her skin, mixing with the ink. One more round of buzzing, feeling the rattle in her bones, and it's done. The tattooist puts a plaster on and gives Kate some advice on keeping it clean.

They pay the man and stumble into the night. They laugh and laugh at a world where things are quick and easy. A world where people find each other and stay found. Halfway home, Nova stops Kate with a hand on her arm.

'What is it?'

'Look up.' Nova is craning her head up to the sky.

'What? The stars?' Kate looks down at the other woman's face. Her mouth is open.

'Yeah, I've never seen them like this.'

Kate looks up again. It is an unusually clear night, and away from the light pollution of London the stars are crisp and bright. She recognizes Orion and the Plough. She thinks that, if their roles were reversed, Nova would know a lot more constellations than that.

'Those are the most distant objects I've ever seen.' Nova

says. 'The most distant objects I ever *will* see. Not that long ago, I couldn't see the walls of the room I was sitting in. Now I'm looking at objects that are so far away, their light has been travelling for millions of years . . .'

She turns slowly on the spot, looking up.

'Every atom that we're made of came from one of those things. They're the first shapes. When enough stars had burned out, planets could form, and oceans, and fish, and streetlamps and, and . . . ice-cream cones! All the other shapes . . .'

She trails off, staring at the heavenly furnaces. Kate doesn't know what to say. She holds Nova's hand while she watches the distant light.

They stumble through the door, laughing and shrugging out of their coats and shoes. The house is dark and silent, but still warm. In the heat, Kate feels the ache from her hand, but it feels like a love bite.

'I'll get the kettle on, shall I? Hot chocolate?'

Nova doesn't reply, bending down to pick something off the mat.

'What's this?' she asks, holding it up to Kate.

'It's a letter. Wasn't it there earlier?'

Nova frowns and opens the envelope, which has nothing written on it. She takes out a piece of paper and reads.

'Note from your neighbour?' Kate asks, unwrapping her scarf.

Nova hands the paper to her wordlessly. There are just four words written on it, in familiar handwriting.

I'm watching you both.

Thirty-Three

NOVA HAS HER EYES closed.

She's sitting on a chair by the window, her arms resting on the sill, forehead pressed to the cold glass. Opening her eyes, she turns to look at Kate, who is lying on the bed. She has been here before – is life repeating? Nova examines her for a long moment, trying to read clues in her body language, to tell if she is waking or sleeping, but gleaning no useful information. This is what Kate is like all the time now.

'Are you awake?'

'Mm.'

Nova thinks she is about to say something else, but nothing comes.

'Do you want to . . . do something?'

There is a long pause.

'Like what?'

Nova sighs, pressing her fingers to her eyes. Since they came to the hotel, in the centre of Bradford, they have left the room only to get meals in the hotel restaurant, before hurrying back.

It has been a week.

They have watched the television a lot, although Kate doesn't seem to be aware of what is on, and Nova has given up trying to interest her. She knows that Kate only puts the TV on to keep her quiet.

They had both phoned the police after finding the note from Tony. Nova explained the situation to the local force, while Kate spoke to Paul Sandler in London. It took Nova a long time to convince them that this wasn't some sort of prank. When the local police finally arrived, and agreed to search the car, they found a small black box attached to the underside with cable ties. Both the car and the tracker had been taken into police custody, while arrangements were made for them to stay at this hotel.

'We should go out,' Nova says.

'No, we shouldn't.' Kate opens her eyes and looks at her, sat by the window. She pushes herself up on her elbows, then sits on the edge of the bed. It's the most that she's moved in hours.

Nova looks to the window, then to the bed. She feels impatient to move, to do something, to be anywhere but this room. They are like magnets repelling. She's no longer scared. She can't live like this.

'Well, I'm going out.'

Kate looks at her, sharply. 'I don't feel like going out, Nova.' She sounds angry at the suggestion.

'That's not what I said. I said *I'm* going out. I'm going out now.'

Kate is shaking her head. 'No, you can't . . . It's not safe.'

Nova feels her pent-up anger like a magma chamber, ready to erupt. She has endured so much because Kate has endured so much. She feels bad for wanting more, but she can't be a prisoner in this stale little room any longer.

'I don't care! We left the car with the police. We're in a huge city . . . He's not going to find us!'

Kate doesn't say anything for a long time, doesn't even move. Nova thinks that she's going to argue, that she is going to plead for Nova to stay, or offer to take her out. But she does neither.

'Fine then. Fuck off if you're going to be like that. Do you know how difficult—' she breaks off, silenced by her own rage.

'How difficult it's been? How can you even ask me that?' Nova is shouting. 'I've been through it all, Kate. *I'm* the one he grabbed by the throat. *I'm* the one you dragged all this way, to sit in a crappy hotel for a week while the police stake out my parents' house.'

She isn't crying – not quite – but if she blinks the tears will fall. She doesn't want Kate to see that. She turns, grabs her jacket from the chair by the bed, and leaves.

✳

On the street, the air is cool. Nova stands for a long time, gulping down cool air like it's water and she's been thirsty for the longest time. Her blood is still humming, but being out of the room quickly calms her. She is okay. Kate will be okay too, when Nova comes back to her. They just need some time apart.

She listens to the sound of cars passing by. As she watches, a small van drives past, lit up from inside. It's playing an electronic tune from speakers on the roof. 'Greensleeves'. Suddenly she is full of a crazy joy – she is here in this city that she grew up in, and an ice-cream van just drove past, playing 'Greensleeves', and it's wonderful.

Slowly, carefully, she starts to walk down the path, staying close to the buildings. She has gotten so much better at seeing, she realizes – she could never have done this when she started out. Perhaps she will never be fluent in this language, but right now that doesn't seem important. She has all that she needs to get by.

Before she could see, Nova's mental maps were huge and detailed. She knew large parts of London by heart. When she started to learn to see, those mental maps degraded, like paper charts sodden with watery light.

She is heading in the direction of Centenary Square, with its Gothic City Hall and the mirror pool fountain – things she has heard of but never seen. Nova can't believe she has been here for a week and hasn't been to the square. She walks down cobbled streets and paved streets, through alleyways where men sit and smoke in doorways, down broad avenues with high buildings.

The buildings are beautiful and strange to Nova – all sandstone, weathered and stained different shades, like gingerbreads that have burned at the edges.

Nova realizes that for the first time in her life, she is thinking in visual metaphors. She has used them before in conversation, like calling her maths teacher *dull as ditchwater*, but for the first time they make sense. Nova can see, in her mind's eye, burned gingerbread men, and can see the buildings, and can see how they are alike. She sees how the comparison is pleasing.

She pauses at a café that sells iced buns and looks through the glass at the colourful confections on display. She thinks about buying a macaroon – cloudy with dried coconut and jewelled with a single glacé cherry – but decides to hurry on. She crosses streets, her sight an easy thing, her limbs light and full of energy. She feels she could run all the way to the square.

It's cool, but Nova wants to sit outside. She finds a café overlooking the square, where she drinks an overpriced espresso and watches the pigeons. There must be thirty or forty of them, competing for crumbs, trying to seduce one another or run away. She watches the complex dance. With her heightened vision, she sees not only individual objects but systems of objects – she sees not only the individual pigeons, but the whole group of pigeons as they circle and swarm, a constantly changing weather-system of creatures that separates and reforms.

Nova's brain flares.

A sense of health and well-being surges up in her, like a spring. She feels love – a love of the world, a love of objects and people, a love of shapes and colours. Love like a super-power. She breathes in and out. Her body blazes with golden light as the pigeons weave their dance. Then a little boy runs toward them, and the pigeons take off, and Nova forgets to breathe for a long moment.

RULE OF SEEING NO.399
**Learning to see is often a thankless task.
Then, sometimes, the world opens up, and you**

**understand something you could never have
understood before, like the way a bird takes
off from the ground and flies through the air.
The world will never look the same again.**

Nova thinks of Kate, back in the hotel room, and feels a tug
of sadness that she isn't here to see what she is seeing. But it
doesn't matter – Nova knows, somehow, that everything is
going to be all right. She is going to make it all right. A little
time apart is no bad thing for them, but when she sees Kate
again, she will be able to make her understand.

She can make things work.

Finished, she gets up and makes her way across the square,
weaving through the crowds. The movement is not effortless,
but rather it is a satisfying challenge – not so difficult as to
be frustrating, but difficult enough that Nova can make a game
of it.

She feels like a saint returning from the wilderness. The
vision of the dancing pigeons has tired her, and she will take
her time getting back to the hotel. But the memory glows
behind her eyes. She sets out from the square, following the
path she came by. The city is a whirl of winding paths, dark
doorways and crumbling sandstone. Nova is intoxicated, but
feels no need to stop.

Not far now – she can't wait to see Kate and make things
better. She's walking down a small avenue. There is nobody
ahead of her. This part of the city seems deserted. She passes
a doorway where there might be the outline of a man, but she
is tired and can't be sure.

She hears footsteps behind her, but thinks nothing of it.

The Rules of Seeing

The footsteps are fast, and Nova is about to step closer to the wall to let the person pass when an arm goes around her waist, and the other hand goes to her mouth. She cries out, from surprise rather than fear. It's too soon for fear. That will come, but for now it is just the shock of being grabbed that makes the air burst from her lungs.

She breathes in, realising only now that a rag is clamped over her mouth and nose. She smells something like spilled petrol but sweeter. Now the fear is rising, only something else is stifling it. Her head and legs feel heavy. She struggles, elbowing her assailant a couple of times, hard, in the ribs. She hears him grunt in pain.

Nova knows without seeing his face.

She struggles for another half-minute, as her body becomes a wet rag. She stamps on his feet and throws her head back, slamming it into his face. She feels something crack – his nose, perhaps.

'Fuck! Little bitch,' she hears him say, but quietly. She is slipping silently into the shadows of this shadowy city. The last light bleeds out of Nova, and she is gone.

Thirty-Four

KATE HAS BEEN LYING on the bed, staring at the ceiling, for the last three hours. Seen as a sped-up, time-lapse film, she would have looked almost statue-like, like the carving on a tomb. Only her breathing would have given her away, flickering up and down like the wing beats of a hummingbird. If Kate had watched such a film, she would have reflected that appearances can be deceiving.

From the moment Nova left, to the moment her phone buzzed with a new message, Kate's thoughts have been changing like a tropical storm, a supercharged system that swings from rain and thunder to sunshine and back again. She loves Nova. She hates her. This is all her fault. None of this is her fault.

She hasn't been sleeping well for so long now, she doesn't know what the truth is any more. All these feelings are just points of view, and the more she changes parts, the less she can see her own story.

There is one thing that she is certain of, and she holds on

to it like it's her last possession in the world. It is the only idea that, regarded from the many points of view, still seems true. This lends it the air of something cosmic. The fact is like a force of nature. Like gravity, or light.

The fact is – things are over with Nova.

Of course, Nova does not know this yet. She will not like it, though Kate suspects it will not be a total surprise. Whether Kate loves or hates her is unimportant, because either way, she wants Nova to leave. Either Nova doesn't deserve Kate or Kate doesn't deserve Nova.

Their relationship could never have worked, not even in one of the alternative universes Nova is so fond of talking about. Nova has a term for this kind of thing – bounded infinity. It means that, even if you have an infinite universe, there are still some things that will never happen. Kate remembers the way she explained it.

'So, you can have a world where the Nazis won the war, because that nearly did happen. You can have a world where Kennedy was never assassinated, right? Like, Lee Harvey Oswald ate some bad chow mein and couldn't get to the book depository. But you can't have a planet Earth made entirely of meringue.'

'A world made of meringue would be pretty good though,' Kate had replied. 'Imagine the meringue Grand Canyon, or the meringue Notre-Dame.'

'I'm sorry,' Nova had said, shaking her head mock-seriously, 'it was just never meant to be.'

That is how Kate feels now – their relationship was a beautiful, ridiculous impossibility. It went against the natural order of things. A planet made of meringue. Kate wants to live on that other planet, but it's always been a fantasy. She will tell Nova when she gets back. She will arrange for her to return to London. She will put her on a train and forget about her.

What happens to Kate after that doesn't matter.

When her phone buzzes on the bedside table, she doesn't look at it straightaway. It is so long since she has moved, moving no longer feels natural. But she needs to pee, so she gets up and goes to the tiny bathroom. When she comes back to the bed, she picks up the phone. There are three messages now, from an unknown number.

I have her. If you come get her, I won't hurt her. I don't want her – I want you.

Do not get the police involved. Come alone. If you fuck up, she'll be dead before you get near.

The third message is the address of another hotel, but Kate can't take it in. She feels a rushing energy overtake her body. It's like she's taken a drug and the trip is starting. The feeling is all-consuming. Her breath speeds up, her muscles clench and unclench, over and over. Before she knows what she's doing, Kate is crouched by the edge of the bed in the foetal position. She's shaking so hard the phone drops out of her hand.

The room has become distant. All that Kate understands is her own fear, her own body failing. She realizes, too late, that she is having a panic attack. She remembers what Nova told her, the first time she'd been there for one of her panic attacks.

Notice something you can see.

Kate looks at the pattern on the carpet.

Notice something you can feel.

Kate notices the plastic bed frame, pressed into the small of her back.

Breathe slowly, counting back from one hundred.

Kate follows the instructions, counting back, forcing herself to take deeper breaths. By sixty, she feels herself taking control again. She stands, too impatient to finish. The room spins, and she rushes to the toilet to be sick. It clears her head – she knows what she has to do. It won't be easy, but she has to do it. She has to do it for Nova.

Suddenly, all the other points of view have fallen away. Kate knows what her story is, and she knows how it ends.

Thirty-Five

KATE HURRIES THROUGH THE streets, trying to look calm. If she looks too distressed, someone might try to stop her to make sure she's all right. Kate can't let anyone stop her now.

The fear is starting to fall away. Maybe she has gone beyond the fear, beyond the upper limit of what a person can feel. Maybe she is in shock. Or maybe it is the certainty she feels now – so certain that it doesn't seem like anything can derail her.

Kate has never believed in fate. Her mother read her horoscope every day, but Kate thought it was all hokum. There was no such thing as fate, just as there were no such things as soulmates. But now she feels something is guiding her actions. Not fate perhaps, but something like physics. The end of a long, complex reaction that started the moment she met Nova. This is where it ends. A kind of entropy. Kate is ready for it – a final blaze of energy as her atoms rearrange themselves into something more stable.

The hotel is right ahead.

✳

Kate stands in front of the door – this is the room. Her breath is ragged. There is no noise, though Kate can barely hear over the rush of blood in her ears. She reaches out to try the handle, then hesitates. She reaches out to knock, then stops again.

She imagines Nova in the room. She imagines Nova in pain. She reaches out, grabs the handle, and turns it. The lock clicks and the door opens. Kate steps through, into the dimly lit room.

'Hello? Who's in here?'

Kate can't see the room yet – in front of her is a short passage, with a built-in wardrobe on the right. At the end of the passage she can see the room branching off to the right. She can see the edge of a window, with a gauzy curtain drawn, and a chair in the corner. She can't hear or see anyone.

'Hello? Anyone here?'

Kate thinks maybe this was all a ruse, and she has been led to an empty hotel room. She is tempted to leave without looking inside. Then she hears it – a muffled cry.

'Nova!'

Kate rushes forward, not thinking of anything but the noise she just heard – small, stifled, but unmistakably Nova. She has reached the end of the passage and looks into the room. There is a single bed. Tied to the bed, blindfolded and gagged, is Nova. She's about to step forward when she hears a noise behind her.

The door has already swung closed on its automatic hinge, but now there is a click as someone locks it. Kate turns. The wardrobe is open, and Tony is standing in the passageway.

He's smiling.

'I thought you weren't coming.'

On the way to the hotel, Kate had felt a strange resolution. She had felt as though nothing could scare her any more, because she was resigned to her end. But now she's not so sure.

Tony looks different, though she would never have mistaken him. His hair is not long, but it is unkempt in a way it never was when he worked for the police. He has grown a beard. Both hair and beard are greasy and matted. There are dark circles under his eyes, and his face is thinner. Kate feels her cheeks hollowing out as though she's sucking them in. Under different circumstances, Kate might have felt sorry for this man. A man so clearly down on his luck. A man in need of kindness.

'Hello.'

Kate feels her mouth forming the word, though she's starting to feel distant from her own body. She is somewhere between the victim and the victor. She feels the bonds on Nova's wrists and ankles as though they're tightening around her own. But she also feels her chest rise and fall to the breaths that expand and contract Tony's ribcage. She feels weak and strong, powerless and powerful, trapped and totally, terrifyingly, free.

He advances a couple of steps. Only now does Kate see the knife in his hand, long and serrated.

'You took your time. I thought you might have grown tired of your toy.'

'Let her go.'

It's a long time since Kate has seen Tony. She can't believe she hasn't spoken to him in so long. She had forgotten the sound of his voice, and the way he stoops his head forward when he talks to her, as though talking to a child.

'I'll let her go. But, first, I need to know that I have you. This is a trade, remember?'

Behind her, on the bed, Nova suddenly yells through her gag. Kate isn't sure whether it's a warning or just a cry of fear, but she tries to ignore it. She tries to focus on Tony in front of her. While her focus is on him, she feels strong. While she looks at his arms, his wide shoulders, she feels strong. White bombs are exploding in her muscles and brain. She feels something like anger, but simpler.

'I'm here, aren't I? You already locked the door.'

Tony takes another step forward. His hand is so tight on the knife handle, she can see the lightning-branched veins in his arm.

'Get back. Into the chair.'

She starts to step back slowly. She is fully in the room now, and the bed is in her peripheral vision, but Kate tries not to focus on it. Tony is still advancing in front of her – she keeps her eyes locked on him. Without turning, she feels the chair behind her and sits down.

'Good, now stay there.'

Tony walks into the room, not looking away from her, and feels for a pile of ropes on the bed. Kate knows she must act now or never. His eyes flick away from her for the briefest moment, to the ropes in his hand. She launches forward, out of the chair, as though she's going to tackle him to the floor.

Kate is not small – she's been reminded of that too many times. She is tall. That, and the power singing in her blood, makes for a powerful impact. She hits Tony hard, and he stumbles back.

But she has made a mistake. She wanted to grab his arm, to try to dislodge the knife from his grip. But his arm is still free. He falls backwards, near the foot of the bed, cracking his head on the wall. Kate falls with him, landing on his chest. At the moment they hit the floor, she feels a searing pain in her shoulder blade.

She does not scream. As the pain hits her, she gasps for air. She can feel the knife moving through the layers of her muscle.

Kate pushes herself up. Tony is struggling, but he's not moving quickly enough. The blow to the head has made him sluggish. Kate gets up so that she is kneeling over him. She's vaguely aware of Nova's muffled screaming, but the sound is distant.

She starts to hit him. He has lost his grip on the knife, which is still deep in her shoulder. It flashes pain every time she throws a punch, but she doesn't stop. She doesn't think about blood loss, or severed arteries, or the damage that she is doing just by moving. She balls her fists and pounds at Tony's face and chest.

She feels his nose crack under her blow, and sees blood spurt from one nostril. She punches his jaw and temples, and he can't seem to bring his arms up to fight her off. For a moment, Kate thinks she has won.

His arm grabs her shirt and wrenches her back, and Kate falls to the carpet. She doesn't quite land on the protruding knife, but it's jarred enough to tear the flesh, then come free. Kate starts to get up on all fours, feeling the blood pouring down her back. She can see the knife, covered in her gore, on the floor next to her. She reaches out to take it.

A heavy blow lands on the back of her skull. Kate feels the floor crashing into her face. Then nothing.

✳

She is awake. She is upright. Sitting.

She is in a chair.

Her hands are held together in her lap, almost casually. Has she nodded off on the train? But there is a strange feeling in her wrists. Kate opens her eyes with some difficulty and looks down.

Her wrists are bound.

The room. She remembers. Kate resumes life after her brief, painless interlude, like a nightmare she can't stop dreaming. She moves her ankles experimentally. They are free. Only her wrists are bound. She looks up and sees Tony. His back is to her, but he is turning. She quickly closes her eyes.

He is talking, and for a moment Kate thinks he is talking to her.

'I wanted to do this while she was awake. So she could watch it happening. But I think maybe this is better . . . She'll wake up, and know that she couldn't stop it happening.'

Kate doesn't know what he's doing, but she hopes Tony doesn't notice her breath speeding up. With each breath, the wound in her shoulder parts again, like a second mouth gasping air. Her back is cold with blood. How much blood has she lost? How much more can she lose?

She pretends to be asleep while he rummages in a bag next to her. She hears him straighten up and go back to the bed. Nova isn't making any sound. Why isn't she making any sound?

The Rules of Seeing

'Don't worry; it'll be over soon.'

Kate takes a chance and opens her eyes. Tony has his back to her again. She can see Nova on the bed. She's still tied up, still gagged, but the blindfold is off. For the moment, her eyes are fixed on Tony, and Kate doesn't want her to look over and see that she's awake.

It's only now that she sees the bottle on the bedside table. The bottle is white plastic and has a safety cap. She can't see the words printed on the label, but she can see the hazard labels – a red diamond, a yellow triangle, a blue circle. Like shapes from one of Nova's lessons. Whatever's in the bottle, it's dangerous. Kate thinks she already knows what it is, but she hopes she's wrong. Tony keeps talking in fits, more to himself, it seems, than Nova.

'It'll be over soon. And she'll wake up. And she'll see you again. Of course, *you* won't see *her* . . .'

He makes a sound like a laugh, but it's more of a retching, coughing sound. Nova still hasn't made a sound. She's forcing herself not to. But Kate can see clearly that she's shaking – every inch of her trembling.

Tony is unscrewing the cap of the bottle. As though a malevolent spirit has been released, the room is immediately full of the smell of whatever liquid it contains. It is a strange smell, like nothing Kate knows. It sticks in her throat; she wants to gag. She realizes what is in the bottle, without seeing. It's acid. He's going to blind Nova for a second time.

Tony turns away from Nova for a moment. Kate clamps her eyes shut, praying he didn't see her. He grabs something else from the bag at her side and returns to the bed. When Kate looks again, he's placing a cloth over Nova's eyes. Nova is struggling, and her head is relatively free to move. The cloth keeps coming off, and she goes back to glaring at him. He bends closer.

'This is happening, okay? You'd rather have the cloth than not. This stuff can eat right through your head.'

Only now does Nova cry out, as Tony places the cloth back over her eyes. Her breath is fast and shuddering. Her hands grip tight to the mattress.

'That's better.' Tony says. His voice is soft, as though he's talking to a child. 'Now just hold still.'

He brings the bottle down.

Kate leaps out of the chair, arms raised in front of her. Tony must hear her, because he starts to turn, but Kate is too quick. She can't get her wrists free of the ropes, so she puts the bonds around his neck and tugs him back from the bed.

Tony makes a sharp, strangled noise as the ropes cut into his neck. Kate kicks her knees forward, into the back of Tony's legs, and lets herself fall, dragging him back with her.

They fall together, hard. Their combined weight makes the impact a heavy one, and Kate is crushed by his body on top of her. The new mouth in her shoulder blade screams. For a moment, Kate loses awareness, all the breath knocked out of her. Her hands loosen their grip, and Tony tries to wrestle free.

She comes back to consciousness, though she can't draw more than the tiniest breath. Still, she pulls back on the rope, feeling it dig into Tony's neck. He's still holding the open bottle of acid, and Kate can hear a sloshing noise. There's a sharp pain on one of her wrists – a splash of acid, eating its way into her skin.

At the same moment, Tony cries out, still strangled by the rope. Kate doesn't know where the acid has landed, but she knows it is on Tony, and he's feeling the same pain as her, only worse.

There is a fizzing sound.

Kate realizes that if she stays under him the acid will trickle down and find her. Tony's strength has faltered with the pain, though his weight is enough to keep her down. With a last burst of strength, Kate forces their bodies to one side with her legs. For a second she thinks she can't do it, that Tony will hold her in place until the cascade of acid finds her. But he is too distracted to fight her.

She shoves him off, to her right-hand side. She holds onto the rope and continues to pull. Tony kicks back with his legs, catching Kate hard in the shins. Her strength is failing – she can't hold on much longer while he fights. The pain in her shoulder and wrist is just the start of it – her body feels like it's been in a car crash. She can't draw a deep enough breath, even with Tony off her.

She holds on, feeling her strength fade. Then, just as she thinks she must let go, and let Tony turn on her, he goes still. For a second, Kate thinks he must be bluffing. But Tony doesn't move again.

Kate takes her hands from around Tony's neck. He rolls over on to his back, and Kate can see the lurid red streak, diagonally across Tony's face and eyes. The acid is still eating into him. Kate feels her stomach lurch and for a moment she thinks he is dead, but she can hear him wheezing faintly.

Kate looks at Nova on the bed. Her eyes are wide and full of tears. Kate needs to get her free, but to do that she needs to untie the rope around her own wrists. She looks around and sees the knife lying on the floor, still covered in her blood. She crawls over and picks it up clumsily, then holds it between her knees and begins to saw the bonds on her wrists, back and forth. She keeps blinking the tears out of her eyes so she can see.

The rope gives after a minute, and Kate is free. She crawls back to the bed on hands and knees. She doesn't trust herself to stand. Nova is watching her, unable to help. Tony stirs on the floor, but Kate ignores him, instead pulling the gag out of Nova's mouth.

'Don't!' Nova gasps, her mouth dry. 'Tie him up first, then you can untie me.'

Kate knows she's right, though she just wants to get them both out of the room. She takes a spare length of rope from the bed and starts to tie it around Tony's wrists. She's halfway done when he wakes up and starts to struggle. His eyes are clenched tight shut, but his hands seem to know where she is. Kate wrestles with him, tying and retying the knots binding his wrists. Finally, it is done.

Kate stands unsteadily, watching him struggle. She kicks him hard in the stomach, watches as he doubles up and then falls silent. She turns back to the bed, taking up the knife again, and cuts through the ropes binding Nova to the bed. Nova sits up quickly and faces her.

'Are you all right? Are you hurt?' Kate says.

'I'm fine. I'm fine.' Nova puts her hands on Kate's face, to calm her down.

'I thought I'd lost you!'

'Me too. I thought you wouldn't find me.'

Kate looks down to Tony, lying on the floor. The carpet around him is stained with blood, and patches of it are pockmarked by the acid. There is a terrible smell in the air.

As she looks, he opens his eyes and looks back at her. Or rather, Kate realizes, he looks at nothing. Whether he has lost his sight for good, or whether it can be reversed, he is blind now. He casts about, trying to see anything. But all Tony can see is the inside of his own head. A private darkness.

Nova is saying something to her, which Kate can't hear.

'What's all this – this blood? Is this all you? We need to call someone, we need to . . .'

Kate turns to Nova and smiles. She leans in, until their foreheads are touching.

'I love you. I always . . .'

The pain fades, and all she can see now is Nova's face. Her blue eyes. She falls forward, resting in the crook of her neck.

Kate slips into her own darkness.

Thirty-Six

New Year's Eve

Nova sits by the window, watching the cars driving down the road. In her hand she's holding a toy car, and she runs her fingers over it, again and again, as though trying to discover something new. There are lots of cars outside, even on this last day of the year. She sighs, setting the car down and turning away from the window.

The flat is quiet. She goes to the kitchen and makes herself a cup of tea, then goes to sit on the sofa. The same sofa where Kate made the fort, all that time ago.

It seems like a lifetime.

There is a remote control for the stereo on the coffee table, and Nova could turn it on now, to be surrounded by the phantom musicians. But for now, at least, she wants the silence. She doesn't want anything going on in her head except her own thoughts.

She looks around the room and sees everything clearly. Perhaps she is still not fluent at seeing, and perhaps she never will be. Seeing will always be a second language. But her vision is rich and detailed, and it is easy. She still makes conversational mistakes, calling a cat a dog, calling the moon a streetlamp. But these are small things. Her vision is not just something to help her get from A to B. There is beauty in the things she sees.

Nova tries to remember the first time she came to this place. She sensed immediately that it was a good place to be. Back then, her vision was a patched-together thing, a jerry-rigged contraption. She saw parts of the room, like someone holding a candle to a cave painting, illuminating a tiny circle of detail, but not the whole.

But the vision hadn't been important – she knew that this was the place she wanted to be. The place she always wanted to stay.

It is raining. It has been raining all day, but now, as night falls, it seems to be getting heavier. When Nova hears the first peal of thunder, it's as though she has been electrified. She knows what she has to do.

The French windows are stiff with underuse, but she gets them open. The room fills with the sound of falling rain. It's as heavy as the time before. She pulls the armchair over to the window, grabs a blanket, and watches the rain. The light fades from the sky, but the rain goes on and on. The thunder comes closer and Nova hugs herself.

RULE OF SEEING NO.???
After seeing has become easy, there are moments when the thing you are looking at evokes a memory, like an old scent, or a piece of music you haven't listened to for years. You

**may feel nostalgic, homesick, or heartbroken.
Try not to be surprised.**

She closes her eyes, losing herself in the sound of the rain.
She could stay like this forever. She wants to be washed away.

The sound is so all-embracing, she doesn't hear the front
door opening. Her eyes are still closed when a warm body
slides into the chair next to her.

'Hey, sweetie.'

'Hey. I didn't hear you.'

'You okay? You're crying.'

Nova reaches up and feels the tears on her cheeks. 'I didn't
realize. But I'm fine. I was just enjoying the sound of the rain.'

'Good.'

Kate kisses her and wraps the blanket around them both,
and they watch the rain fall. Blue flashes light up the street.
They say nothing for a long time.

'Kate?'

'Uh huh?'

'Can I stay here?'

There is a long pause, broken by a peal of thunder, and
Nova gets ever so slightly smaller, curling in on herself.

'What, in this chair?'

'No, I mean, can I stay here . . . in your flat?'

Kate pulls back to look at her, frowning. 'Of course. You
have a key . . . You're paying half the mortgage!'

Nova doesn't say anything, unsatisfied with the answer. Kate
sighs, smiling.

'Yes. You can always stay here.'

Nova looks her in the eyes – really looks – and she can

understand what Kate's face is telling her. Other faces are still hard to read, but if she concentrates, she can understand Kate. Then she looks back at the rain, and the rain keeps falling. It seems to fall endlessly through the universe, in an unbroken line. The world fades away, and the rain is like static on a TV. It is formless, a not-shape.

'Okay, then,' she says at last. 'I'll stay.'

Acknowledgements

To my parents Sue and Tim, the teachers who taught me everything. I couldn't have done this without your love and support.

To my brother Jim, curator of obscure books and films, for a lifetime of inspiration.

To my grandparents, Joseph and Christina, John and Jean, for endless love and care.

To my agent, Laura Macdougall, whose support and encouragement seems (and possibly is) superhuman. She made this book possible. Plus, she makes a mean chilli jam.

To Charlotte Ledger, my brilliant editor, and the cool cats at HarperCollins for their belief in this story. I couldn't have wished for a lovelier, more talented bunch.

To the kids of 281 Donnelly, Stirling, for all the cups of tea and the recipe for sausages. Stay off the streets.

To Laura Friis-West, Corinna Booth, Andrew Freeland and Chris Wynne – great readers and better friends.

To the Tillins, young and old, for their support and many happy times.

Joe Heap

To Sophie Hignett, who kept me on the road.

To Charlotte Maddox, Sonny Marr and Mary Rodgers, for endless support and cups of tea.

To Alice, for showing me how it's done. We go together like peaches and pepperoni.

To Sam, our absolute beginner.

Thank you.